D0355455

BITTER HARVEST

(Harvest Trilogy, Book 2)

Michael R. Hicks

This is a work of fiction. All of the characters, organizations and events portrayed in this novel are products of the author's imagination or are used fictitiously.

ISBN: 978-0984673094
BITTER HARVEST (HARVEST TRILOGY, BOOK 2)

Published by Imperial Guard Publishing
http://AuthorMichaelHicks.com

ACKNOWLEDGMENTS

Writing a book is always a team effort, and this one is certainly no exception.

To start off, I'd like to thank Tom Swigart, a longtime friend and colleague who taught me how to add, and helped me figure out just how bad the harvester plague was going to be.

Then there's my primary editing team: Mindy Schwartz, Steph Hansen, Marianne Søiland, and Frode Hauge. They spent a lot of time going through my mishmash of prose, and through their efforts my writing skills (and your reading experience) continue to improve.

After the editors come the beta readers, who had the joyful task of reading through the edited draft and helping me refine it. I'd like to offer a big round of applause to Melody Rose, Kevin Boucher, Jay Lamborn, Rich Duncan, Patricia Egen, and Tera Montgomery for their time and patience in helping me make this book a better reading experience for my readers (like you).

Last, but certainly not least, I'd like to thank my wife, Jan, who is my alpha reader. Her support and faith in what I can do have helped lead us into a new life, and I love her all the more for it.

FOREWORD

This is the second book of the *Harvest* Trilogy, and picks up the tale a year after the events described in *Season Of The Harvest*. If you haven't read that first book yet, I highly recommend that you do, especially since it's free as an ebook on my web site at AuthorMichaelHicks.com.

But if you just want to dive into *Bitter Harvest*, that's okay, too, as there's enough backstory in this book that you won't be completely lost. I hope.

Now it's time to buckle up, dear reader, for the ride is about to begin...

CHAPTER ONE

"Are you worried?"

Bryce Moore glanced over at Angelina Matheson, who rode in the passenger seat as he drove the rented sedan east across the Arlington Memorial Bridge into Washington, D.C. It was late January, and the temperature was hovering in the mid-thirties. The landscape was still draped in a mantle of snow left by the worst storm of the winter, two days before. White sheets of ice clung to the banks of the Potomac River, a stark contrast to the dingy gray frozen muck that lined the roads. Directly ahead, the Lincoln Monument rose from the white landscape like a tremendous ice sculpture, framed by yet more threatening, gray clouds. The weather forecasts all predicted more snow.

Fortunately for those concerned about such things, the previous storm had hit after the inauguration ceremony. Bryce suppressed a cringe as he recalled the election campaign that had culminated in a crushing defeat for the incumbent party in November. To call it acrimonious would have been a ridiculous understatement. President Norman Curtis had made clear early on that he had no plans to run for reelection. This had saved him the embarrassment of not being offered the nomination. There would be no political redemption for a president who had authorized a nuclear strike on American soil during peacetime, no matter the reason. Most of his remaining time in office had been divided between helping people in central California where the bomb had detonated, and fending off impeachment proceedings by Congress. There had also been a lot of talk on the Hill about forming a war crimes commission.

The opposing party's candidate had carried the election in a landslide.

But the question of what to do about Curtis lingered. As far as the public knew, the bomb he had ordered dropped over Sutter Buttes in California had been to save the world from a biological super-weapon developed by the Earth Defense Society. The EDS, as it was more popularly known, had been described as a terrorist group, and was blamed for a series of worldwide attacks that had destroyed the world's largest repositories of seeds, killing thousands of people in the process. The public story was that the FBI had hunted down the Earth Defense Society and cornered its members in a Cold War-era missile base north of Sutter Buttes. That was when the government found out, or so the story went, that there was a biological weapon in the base that, were it ever released into the atmosphere, could potentially obliterate human life on the planet.

Faced with that nightmare possibility, Curtis had ordered a B-52 to destroy the base with a nuclear weapon.

In the aftermath, the administration had proclaimed that the Earth Defense Society had been destroyed, and that the FBI and the United States Air Force had saved the human species from extinction.

As Bryce, Angelina, and a handful of others knew, this story was a lie carefully bound by strands of truth. If a war crimes commission were formed to investigate the dropping of the bomb, it would inevitably lead to the exposure of that truth.

More than that, it would no doubt lead to the revelation that two of the Earth Defense Society's most prominent members, Jack Dawson and Naomi Perrault, who had both been at the top of the FBI's most wanted list, were alive. Not only that, President Curtis had created a highly secret agency to investigate the true origins of what insiders had come to call the "EDS affair," and had put Dawson and Perrault, with fabricated identities, in charge. If that secret ever leaked, though the EDS had been the "good guys," the political ramifications, at home and abroad, would be staggering.

The personal implications for Jack and Naomi, who had accepted Curtis's offer to start new lives as Bryce Moore and Angelina Matheson, could be fatal.

Jack grimaced as he recalled the last video teleconference he and Naomi had held with Curtis, who had always used their real names in the tightly controlled meetings and video sessions. The now-former president had held meetings, by video or face to face in the White House, every two weeks. For a long time, before the truth had been revealed, Jack and Naomi had thought he was a collaborator with the true enemy, what they called the harvesters. But like the other "collaborators" the harvesters had gathered around them, Curtis had been duped, and had spent the rest of his time in office trying to atone for the sin of ignorance. While Jack had never liked the man, he had come to respect him.

But the last words he spoke to Jack and Naomi as the President of the United States offered little comfort. "This is it," he had told them. Deep lines of worry were etched across his forehead. "I've spoken to the incoming administration and briefed President Elect Miller on your agency and mission. Unfortunately..." He bit his lip and looked away for a moment in a gesture that had profoundly disturbed Jack. It was the first time he had ever seen Curtis falter. "Unfortunately, he thought the entire thing was a bunch of hogwash."

"What?" Naomi had leaned forward, her face a mask of disbelief.

"I assume you had the Secret Service detail verify his status?" Jack asked.

Curtis nodded. "Yes, it was done with our feline friends and thermal imagers." He looked down at the top of the conference room table for a moment. Then he said, "The transition between the administrations has been strained, to say the least. Daniel Miller doesn't want anything more to do with me than is necessary, and I can't really blame him. Who would believe any of this? The only reason I do is that one of the bloody things tried to kill me. And the rest of it..." He waved a hand dismissively.

"Where does that leave our agency?" Beyond their own safety, Jack and Naomi had been worried about the vital work they had been doing at the Soil Erosion Analysis Laboratory, or SEAL, the boring-sounding name given as a cover to their agency. "There's still an enormous threat out there."

"I just don't know," Curtis told him. "I just don't know."

The summons to come to Washington and meet with the new administration officials had finally come after Curtis was out of the White House and Miller had been sworn in as president. Jack and Naomi, using their aliases, of course, had flown from their small agency's headquarters in San Antonio, Texas to Reagan National Airport. It had been the first communication from the administration, despite repeated calls and emails. They had simply been stonewalled.

Upon their arrival in Washington, instead of being met by a limousine and driven to the White House as they had been in the past, they'd had to rent a car for the drive to the vice president's residence on the grounds of the U.S. Naval Observatory in northwest D.C.

It was not an auspicious beginning.

"Jack, did you hear me?" Naomi always called him Jack, because the middle name of his alias was John, just as her identity conveniently had Naomi as one of two middle names. It hadn't been intended for convenience, although they tended to use it as such, but for security. In case they slipped in public, there was a plausible explanation. She reached over and gently gripped his arm.

"I'm sorry." He blew out a breath. "Yeah, I'm worried. I understand Miller wanting to keep Curtis at the end of a ten foot pole. But giving us the cold shoulder all this time..."

"I know. I think what worries me more is that we haven't heard from Richards."

Carl Richards had been a senior Federal Bureau of Investigation special agent who, through a series of tragedies in the EDS affair and his status of hero at its explosive conclusion, had wound up as the acting Director of the FBI. He had worked closely with Jack and Naomi, but a week ago had stopped returning their calls. Jack had been worried that something had happened to the irascible man, but Dr. Renee Vintner, another survivor of the Earth Defense Society who worked as a consultant for the FBI, had assured him that Richards was fine, at least physically.

"But something's up," Renee had said. "He won't tell me anything about it, but I know he's really upset."

Jack took the exit for the Rock Creek and Potomac Parkway and headed north past the Kennedy Center and the Watergate Hotel. "I can't believe Carl would hang us out to dry."

"I know he wouldn't if we were in danger," Naomi answered. "But he's also a creature of duty, Jack. If Miller's tightened his leash, Carl isn't going to fight it. That's just the way he is."

Jack couldn't think of anyone he'd want covering his back more than Richards, but Naomi was right. So long as Richards wasn't asked to do anything illegal or downright underhanded, he would do what his boss said.

They drove in silence the rest of the way, both too preoccupied with whatever awaited them to enjoy the winter beauty of snow-covered Montrose Park. Jack got off on Waterside Drive, then took a left onto Massachusetts Avenue. He drove around to the north entrance of the Naval Observatory compound, where he and Naomi presented their identification to the guards. After checking the computer in the guard post, the anti-vehicle gates were lowered, and they headed in.

The vice president's residence at Number One Observatory Circle was originally built to house the superintendent of the U.S. Naval Observatory, and was located in the northeast quadrant of the circular compound. Jack parked where the guard had indicated.

Naomi had read that the house boasted more than nine thousand square feet of living space, but Jack wasn't sure how they had shoehorned that much into the compact-looking structure that had been built in the Queen Anne style, with a prominent turret and large veranda gracing the front.

As they got out of the car, they were met by four Secret Service agents, who again checked their identification cards and drivers licenses before escorting them up a set of stairs and into the house through the rear entrance.

Jack had to restrain himself from shaking his head as they were led through the kitchen. Leaning close to Naomi, he whispered, "Are we such an embarrassment that we can't just come through the front door like everyone else?"

"Looks like it." She spoke the words through gritted teeth, and Jack could see the color rising in her cheeks. She was furious.

The Secret Service agents led them from the kitchen past the staircase that rose from the reception hall, then ushered them into the sitting room.

There, waiting for them, was Vice President Andrew Lynch.

Two other men were also in the room. Carl Richards, whose expression was carefully neutral, and another man that Jack didn't recognize.

"Mr. Dawson. Dr. Perrault." The vice president stood and extended his hand to shake theirs, even as they stood there, gaping at his use of their real names. "You know acting Director Carl Richards, of course. And this is his replacement, Kyle Harmon. He'll be taking over the FBI shortly, as the Senate has already confirmed his nomination, although that isn't public knowledge yet."

After Jack and Naomi shook hands, trying to recover from the double shock of having their identities exposed and discovering that Richards had been ousted as the FBI's Director, Lynch said, "Please, sit down."

Jack and Naomi sat on the white sofa that backed onto the north-facing windows, while Lynch, Harmon, and Richards sat in matching armchairs facing them.

"Sir..." Jack began, but closed his mouth as the vice president held up his hand.

"Let me do the talking for now." Lynch made it quite clear he was in control of this meeting. "You'll have a chance to ask questions when I'm through."

"Yes, sir." Jack sat back in the sofa, forcing down his temper as he crossed his legs, trying to look relaxed. He flicked a glance at Richards, who was examining his shoes with rapt attention.

"Unlike the president, I'm not one to mince words," the vice president continued, "so I'll come right to the point. The Soil Erosion Analysis Laboratory, the cover for the agency that former President Curtis created to investigate the so-called harvesters, is disbanded as of today. All the government assets will be turned to the Department of Homeland Security. All the personnel who had been assigned to the agency will be given two weeks severance." He looked Jack, then Naomi, in the eye. "That includes the two of you."

"Do you have any idea what you're doing?" Naomi interrupted Lynch's monologue. "There's still a terrible threat hanging over the country, and probably the world. We're the only thing that stands against it!"

Lynch shook his head. "Dr. Perrault, with all due respect, please tell me one thing, just one, of significance that you and Mr. Dawson have unearthed since your agency was formed?"

"If our work is going to be judged simply on a metric of reports produced, or..."

"*Just one*, Dr. Perrault." Lynch held up a hand with his index finger raised. "Just one thing that could either substantiate the threat or prove that you could do something against it with the millions of tax dollars the government has given you, other than rewriting or refining data that you already had."

"We've made huge strides in understanding the harvester genetic code, and we've also learned a great deal about how they manipulated people like President Curtis and FBI Director Ridley."

At the mention of Ridley's name, Richards looked up from the floor, a haunted expression on his face.

"We've also mapped their social network," Jack added. "That allowed us to identify the industrial areas they were targeting, and..."

Lynch cut him off. "What about the bag?"

Jack and Naomi exchanged glances. Richards looked up again at that one.

The Bag, as it had come to be known, was their boogeyman. The harvesters had used humanity's technological base to create strains of genetically engineered crops, starting with corn, that served as a means of artificial procreation. Any earthly creature, including human beings, that consumed the seeds or the fruits of the resulting plants would literally be transformed into one of the monsters. They had seen the results during the terrifying last hours in the old Cold War missile base in California that had served as the secret headquarters of the Earth Defense Society. The harvesters, through their proxy corporation New Horizons, had created thousands of tons of the lethal corn seed, and with great fanfare had shipped them from a central processing facility. It would have been a global disaster, except that Renee Vintner had pulled off a brilliant infiltration of the routing information for the tractor trailers hauling the seed, directing them to secure disposal facilities instead of distribution centers.

Everything had gone well, except for one thing: a solitary bag of seed, perhaps a hundred pounds, was missing. That could be anywhere from one hundred and twenty-thousand to more than three hundred thousand individual seeds. Each could produce a corn stalk, and every kernel on every ear of corn was a biological weapon. The bag had been on the manifests, but had not been on the truck. And there was no record of what had happened to it.

Over time, most had simply assumed it had been a mistake. But Naomi, in particular, knew how thorough the harvesters were. She was convinced the bag wasn't a clerical error. She, Jack, Richards, and the others who knew the truth remained terrified that the bag existed.

But they hadn't found it.

"The Bag, doctor," Lynch said. "You've made no progress at all in finding it, have you?"

"No, sir." Naomi shook her head, but kept her eyes fixed on Lynch.

"It's not for lack of trying, Mr. Vice President," Jack told him. "But the records were destroyed when we blew up the processing facility, and it's been like trying to find a particular grain of sand on a beach that's miles long."

"The FBI has come up empty-handed, as well, despite focusing tremendous resources on the problem." The new FBI Director shot a less-than-kind glance at his predecessor.

"The bottom line," Lynch said, " is that it's impossible for the president to justify the funding for an agency that's not producing anything. Going over the same samples and regurgitating the same information in different ways isn't going to cut it. As I understand it, finding The Bag was the number one priority, but that's gotten absolutely nowhere. And no one is really even sure if it existed in the first place. As I'm sure you're aware, one of the president's big planks, along with undoing the ecological disaster in central California, is cutting government waste. And we're starting with your agency."

After a brief pause while Jack and Naomi digested that news, Lynch continued. "As for your false identities, DHS and FBI will issue a low profile joint press release explaining that both of you had been working undercover and had infiltrated the Earth Defense Society. We'll say that putting you on the most wanted list was to assist your efforts at infiltration. That can then be tied into Special Agent Richards' heroic deeds at Sutter Buttes, as the Curtis administration previously reported to the media." He gave them a sympathetic look. "The president and I understand what Curtis was trying to do by giving you false identities. But the fact is that President Miller is determined to distance his administration from everything Curtis did with the EDS affair. In the inquiries that Congress is planning, your identities and roles in what happened are bound to come to light, and President Miller isn't about to get caught holding the bag, if you'll pardon the expression. Better we return you to the mainstream now, with a positive spin, than have you discovered later during an inquiry."

Jack could understand the president's reasoning up to a point. But he also had no doubt that he and Naomi would likely be the focus of unwanted police attention for the rest of their lives. And some people would never believe that he hadn't been involved in the crimes of which he had been accused, which included killing FBI agents.

He glanced at Naomi, but she was staring fixedly at Lynch. The skin of her neck and cheeks were a bright red. Richards looked like he'd been whipped. Jack closed his eyes for a moment, trying to control the sickly sensation of free fall that had threatened to overcome him.

Opening his eyes, Jack caught the vice president's gaze. "Is anyone going to continue to pursue the possibility that The Bag exists, or is everything just going to be dropped and swept under the rug?"

"That's no longer your concern, Mr. Dawson."

CHAPTER TWO

Howard Morgan stood at the window that ran along one side of the conference room, looking over the Los Angeles skyline. It was late afternoon, and for a change the sky was clear of haze after last night's heavy rain. His eyes, dark as his skin, took in the light of the setting sun reflected from the glass and steel structures much like the one in which he stood.

The conference room was on the top floor of the head corporate office of Morgan Pharmaceuticals. Morgan had built the company from the ground up over the course of fifteen years, taking it from a very small pharmaceutical test lab to an industry powerhouse netting three billion dollars in annual profit. The company had capitalized on its lab experience, of course, but had also branched out into vaccine development and other areas. But he didn't want to just produce more of the existing vaccines or even develop better ones. He wanted to create something revolutionary, something that would rival Jonas Salk's success with his polio vaccine, or Edward Jenner's victory over smallpox.

Or something even greater.

While profit and the prestige of his company were certainly part of Morgan's motivation, he had far more personal reasons for wanting a monumental breakthrough. His oldest son had died of AIDS, and his wife had died two years later, a victim of breast cancer. His two younger children, Alissa and Charles, were both in college.

The research arm of the company had two entire divisions focused on breast cancer and AIDS, with three more divisions working against various other communicable diseases.

Despite several major advances made by his company in disease research, the singular victory he sought, a breakthrough that would leave his mark upon mankind, continued to elude him.

And that was the reason for this meeting.

He turned away from the expansive view outside to face the twelve members of the board. His apostles, as he sometimes referred to them, sat around the gleaming mahogany table, their attention fixed on him.

Dr. Adrian Kelso, the company's scientific advisor, sat at the table opposite where Morgan was standing, and had a decidedly unhappy look on his face.

"Adrian," Morgan said, "do you mean to tell me that after nearly a year and an investment of thirty million dollars in research, we essentially have nothing."

Kelso's bushy eyebrows shot up at that. "No, sir, that's not at all true! We've learned a great deal from the Beta-Three samples, and in time we'll learn much more. It's a treasure trove!" He held out his hands, as if in supplication, to Morgan. "But the simple fact is that the technology represented by Beta-Three is so advanced that we have no hope of replicating it any time soon. We might have our arms around the system that's used to deliver the payload in the next two to three years. Just that will be a revolution for distributing vaccines and administering inoculations. But the Beta-Three payload itself?" He threw up his hands in another of his many gestures. "It'll be at least that long before we can even map the gene sequence, let alone fully understand or reproduce it. Whatever it is, it's far more complex than the human genome."

Morgan folded his arms and paced around the room, the slow, measured click of his heels on the floor the only sound in the uncomfortable silence.

Beta-Three, as it was known, was the company's crown jewel. But, as only a very few beyond this room knew, it wasn't a product of his company. While Morgan considered himself an honorable man, he was also honest enough to recognize the opportunist within him. In the high stakes world in which he lived and breathed, honor and opportunity often collided. He sided with honor as much as he could, but was unafraid to set aside his scruples when necessary.

The samples to which Kelso referred were the result of such an opportunity that had arisen from a disgruntled employee within the now-defunct New Horizons Corporation, whose assets Morgan Pharmaceuticals had purchased. The deal had been consummated through an intermediary, and the seller had been paid handsomely for a sample of the latest line of genetically engineered corn, then known as *Revolutions*. Much to Morgan's surprise, the source had provided not just a few sample seeds, as had been expected, but two thousand four hundred and thirty-eight of the tiny, precious objects. A full pound of them, in a sterile nitrogen-filled container that the employee had somehow smuggled out of the New Horizons plant that had subsequently been destroyed by the Earth Defense Society terrorists.

Only two people other than himself knew how Beta-Three had been acquired. Everyone else was bright and loyal enough not to ask questions.

The seeds had been placed in secure storage in one of the company's research sample vaults. Access to them was highly restricted, although successively more researchers had been brought in on the project because it had exceeded all of Morgan's initial expectations for the value of the technology it contained. If Dr. Kelso had been given his way, an army of thousands would be working on it, with Kelso leading the way.

Morgan would have liked to oblige him, but the situation with Beta-Three had become troublesome. After the New Horizons disaster, the Curtis administration had clamped down, brutally hard, on every application of genetic engineering applied to commercial seed. The *Revolutions* seed from New Horizons had been identified as a biological weapon of mass destruction that the Earth Defense Society had somehow engineered and infiltrated into the New Horizons plant.

Why the EDS had then destroyed the plant was a bit of a mystery that was still being batted around.

Morgan didn't particularly care about what the spin doctors in Washington said. But the possibility that the seeds could be a bioweapon had given him pause, just as he was considering both planting some seeds in a test field and feeding some to test animals to analyze the results.

With federal investigators rampaging through the genetic engineering community, he had set those ideas aside, judging them too risky. But by then Kelso and his people had learned enough about the seeds to have an inkling of the massive potential of the technology they contained, and Morgan had judged that pursuing this golden goose was worth the risk of incurring the government's wrath.

And so, instead of destroying Beta-Three, he had ordered research to be continued under the auspices of one of the vaccine research divisions, thereby getting it out from under the direct scrutiny of federal investigators keeping watch on the genetics research divisions. They would only conduct analysis of the existing samples under very secure conditions, but analyze it they would.

The good news had been that newly elected President Miller had made no bones about reversing Curtis's policies on genetic engineering. "Full speed ahead!" Those were the words Miller had used in a meeting with corporate executives, including Morgan, from across the industry. It was music to everyone's ears, although they understood the reality that Miller was beholden to them, considering the millions that the men and women in that room had contributed to his campaign. Even now, so early in the new administration, nearly all of Curtis's restrictions and regulations on the genetic engineering community had been rescinded.

Morgan stopped pacing and turned to face Kelso. "That's not acceptable, Dr. Kelso." Kelso flinched. Unlike most of his peers, he actually hated being called *doctor*, and Morgan only called him that when he was displeased with him. "We have in our hands what is probably the most advanced genetic technology in the world." Despite his discomfort, Kelso nodded emphatically. "And I am not about to sit here and wait for years before we even know what it can do!"

A woman at the far end of the table cleared her throat.

"Yes, Karina?" Morgan's eyes bored into her. It was a clear sign that she had better have something truly earth-shattering to say.

The woman was not intimidated. A tall, athletic blond, Karina Petrovsky was Morgan's chief of security, and the one who had arranged the deal to acquire Beta-Three. She was as intelligent as she was attractive, and the combination of those traits had served her extremely well in her job. "Sir, this morning I happened to see a press release that may bear on the situation."

Morgan nodded for her to continue.

Holding his gaze with her own ice blue eyes, she continued. "The FBI and Homeland Security reported that two individuals who had been in the Earth Defense Society and had been killed in California were working undercover for the government and are very much alive. Their names are Jack Dawson and Naomi Perrault."

"Perrault?" He'd only heard Dawson's name on the news when the manhunt for him was on last year. Dr. Naomi Perrault, however, was another matter entirely. He had tried to recruit her, but New Horizons snatched her away. It was a loss he had always deeply regretted.

Petrovsky smiled. "Yes, sir. As you know, Dr. Perrault was a senior researcher at New Horizons. She worked on the *Revolutions* project until a year before that product was to be released. While she is apparently in good standing with the government, my sources say that she just lost her job with a think tank that President Curtis had established, but that President Miller has now shut down." Tilting her head to one side, she asked, "Perhaps Dr. Perrault would be interested in continuing her work?"

* * *

Jack, Naomi, Carl Richards, and Dr. Renee Vintner sat around the small dining room table in Richards' apartment. Even while he was working as acting Director of the FBI, Richards had refused to move out of the one-bedroom bachelor pad where he had lived for the last twelve years.

Of course, it was no longer a bachelor pad. He now shared it with Renee. Their relationship had been highly discreet, which meant that the entire Bureau knew about it. But that was because the people he and Renee worked with were extremely perceptive, and no one had cause to raise a stink about it. Richards had been an extremely popular director during his brief tenure, despite his longtime proclamation that he was the FBI's "number one asshole." Renee had been popular because she was one of those people you simply couldn't help but like. Assigned to work as a liaison at the FBI with the agency headed by Jack and Naomi, Renee had worked closely on a daily basis with Richards. They had also shared the horrors of what had happened at Sutter Buttes. Impossible as it seemed, a romance had blossomed between the two.

Jack and Naomi had heartily approved.

The mood around the table now, however, was somber. It was the day after the meeting with the vice president. They had wanted to get together right away, but Richards couldn't get away from work the previous evening until nearly midnight.

Pouring another round of wine as they continued to dig into the spaghetti Richards had prepared, Jack said, "You look like you need a vacation, Carl."

"At least I've still got a damn job." Looking as if he was going to be sick, Richards set down his fork and rubbed a hand across his face. He had said very little since Jack and Naomi had arrived. Renee had tried to lighten the mood with some good-natured ribbing, but Richards hadn't risen to the bait as he normally did. Even the antics of their three Abyssinian cats, whom he had christened Huey, Dewey, and Louie, chasing a tightly wadded ball of aluminum foil across the floor failed to elicit a smile. Richards looked across the table at Jack and Naomi, an expression of misery on his face. "You two have to know that I wanted to tell you what was coming. While I didn't know the specifics, I knew over a week ago that you were going to get shit-canned, but I couldn't say a damn thing. Harmon, our new boss, put a gag on me."

"He's a jackass." Renee shook her head, glancing at Richards. "They should've just left well enough alone and kept you on as director."

Richards waved away her assertion with a look of irritation. "I don't care about that. I never wanted the damn job, and only did it because President Curtis asked me. And because I owed it to Director Ridley." The others nodded, recalling that former Director Ridley, deceived by the harvesters, had died a particularly agonizing hero's death that had struck Richards hard. "It's a political appointment and that's that. I'm relieved, to be honest. I thought I had a bunch of bullshit paperwork to deal with before. How anyone stays sane in the boss's chair is beyond me."

"Oh, you're so full of crap!" Renee poked him in the shoulder. "You enjoyed it and don't say otherwise." She looked over at Jack and Naomi, rolling her eyes. "God, Carl, you're such a contrary old fart."

Richards picked up his wine glass and muttered something into it, but the others could see he was trying hard to suppress a grin.

"So what are you two going to do now?" Renee's voice turned serious.

Jack and Naomi exchanged glances.

"We've got enough saved away to tide us over for a bit while we figure something out," Jack said. He looked at Richards. "I think it's probably safe to say that I won't be returning to the Bureau or working in any law enforcement job. Even with our names officially being cleared, there are still going to be a lot of people who won't believe it, and plenty of hard feelings after the deaths of the agents at Sutter Buttes." Richards nodded, clearly unhappy. Jack shrugged. "Hell. I don't know. I'll figure out something."

"It's too bad you both officially died," Renee said. "Otherwise, you'd be rich."

"I think that's called water under the bridge." Naomi tried to smile, but it didn't reach her eyes. She had made millions when she worked at New Horizons, but as part of the deal following of the Sutter Buttes disaster, she and Jack had "died" and been reborn with new identities. Unfortunately, in an unavoidable step in maintaining the fiction of her death, her unwitting attorney had executed her will and distributed her estate. Her money, her home, and even her beloved car, a Tesla Roadster, were gone.

Jack, too, had lost his home, his old battered Land Rover Defender, and the comparatively small amount he had socked away in his retirement and bank accounts from his time in the Army and working for the Bureau.

All the money they had now was what they'd saved while working at SEAL. Even being paid on the government's senior executive scale, the relatively brief time they'd been working there had left them only enough to make it for a few months. They needed to find work, and soon.

"To be honest, I'm a lot more worried about The Bag," Naomi went on. "Jack and I can find work and keep ourselves afloat. I have no doubt of that. But I just can't believe that President Miller is going to pretend like the harvesters never happened, and that there's still not a horrible threat out there!"

"The search is going to continue at the Bureau," Richards told her, "but it's being bumped to the back burner. Part of me can't blame Miller much, because we haven't found a damn thing! Not a single lead's turned up, the records from the production facility were destroyed, and the workers who knew anything were all killed. We interviewed every employee at New Horizons before the company closed its doors, but outside the very small circle that you used to be in, nobody knows squat about the *Revolutions* research or The Bag, not to mention the harvesters themselves. Kempf and her cockroach friends kept things awfully tight."

Naomi had been an insider at New Horizons, and had been chosen by the creature posing as Dr. Rachel Kempf, the director of the *Revolutions* seed project, to work on the final phases of the project's development. But Naomi hadn't been fooled, and after pretending to agree to Kempf's bizarre proposal, she had been kidnapped to safety by the Earth Defense Society. But every time Kempf's name had been mentioned since then, Naomi couldn't help but shiver involuntarily.

"And as far as we know," Richards went on, his nasal voice dropping lower, "all the harvesters are dead, and dead bugs tell no tales." He held up a hand as Jack made to protest. "I'm not saying more of the bastards might not be running around, but I don't have anything, not a shred of evidence to the contrary that I can give the boss or the President. Until we have something, they're not going to change their minds."

"But how can they ignore the evidence we *do* have?" Jack twirled some spaghetti onto his fork. As he spoke the words, he looked at the food on his plate, knowing that everything they were eating was organic. None of them had touched anything that wasn't organic since learning the truth of what New Horizons had been doing. And none of them had touched a single bit of corn, organic or otherwise. He looked up at Richards. "We might not be able to parade a harvester in front of Miller, but there *is* evidence they existed. Christ, just the security camera footage of the harvester impersonating Clement that was killed at the White House should have been enough."

"Honey," Renee answered, "if you show some of these guys something like that, something that clearly is beyond our everyday experience, the first thing they do is say it's a scam. Look how many people still don't believe the Holocaust was real."

"I hate to say it," Jack said quietly, "but I wish we had some real physical evidence."

Richards snorted. "We would have, if Curtis hadn't ordered the harvester impersonating Clement to be destroyed. That was pretty damn stupid."

The others nodded unhappily. There had been several harvester corpses at the EDS base at Sutter Buttes, but they had all been burned when the main part of the base was destroyed. The remains of the five harvesters that had taken part in the attack on the Svalbard seed vault had been flung into the blazing pyre of the vault after Naomi and Jack had destroyed it, having discovered that some of the seeds within had been contaminated.

Other than that, no biological samples remained, either of the harvesters or the seed that contained their genetic code. There was nothing left to prove the harvesters had existed other than the data the EDS had maintained in its other facilities. Those installations had been closed by order of President Curtis, and the data transferred to Jack and Naomi's agency.

But it was "just" data. As far as they could truly prove, it had all been just a bad dream, a brilliant hoax. A nightmare that had culminated in the dropping of a nuclear weapon on central California.

"Even if the government is going to shelve it, we're not," Jack said. "We're going to keep an eye on the web and dig around, and keep digging." At the pained look Richards gave him, he added, "We'll be discreet. Besides, it's really all we've got now."

Naomi's phone rang. "Excuse me," she said as she pulled it from her purse. She was about to hit the ignore button when she saw who it was from.

Howard Morgan.

She recognized the name, as Morgan Pharmaceuticals was one of the companies that had tried to recruit her before she accepted the position with New Horizons. Morgan himself had interviewed her, and she had been extremely impressed with him. But New Horizons had offered her nearly twice as much money. In that phase of her life, money had meant far more than anything else, and she had taken the job with New Horizons, working for Rachel Kempf. Or what had masqueraded as Kempf.

With a tingle of excitement, she touched the answer button. "Dr. Perrault."

"Dr. Perrault, this is Howard Morgan. Let me first say that I was extremely relieved to learn you were alive. I was also wondering if I might be able to entice you to work for me."

CHAPTER THREE

Kapitan Sergei Mikhailov stared out the window of the Mi-17 helicopter as it swept low over the endless hectares of fallow farmland of southern Russia. He tried to ignore the knot in his stomach that seemed to tighten with every kilometer that passed on the way to their objective, an agricultural research facility outside the town of Elista in the Republic of Kalmykia.

He glanced up at *Starshiy Serzhant* Pavel Rudenko, who sat in the seat across from him. Rudenko bobbed his head and attempted a smile, but it came out as a grimace. Even Rudenko, a veteran of the savage fighting in Chechnya years before and one of the toughest men Mikhailov had ever known, was worried.

Mikhailov keyed his microphone to talk to the pilots. "How long until we reach the target?"

"Ten minutes."

Holding up both hands for Rudenko, Mikhailov extended all ten fingers. With a quick nod, the big NCO released his harness and began a final check of the other twenty-three men, a platoon of Mikhailov's company, in the helicopter. The rest of the company had been left on standby back at Novorossiysk.

While Rudenko checked that the men were ready, Mikhailov pulled a battered canvas map case from one of his uniform's cargo pockets and took a final look at the operations map, reviewing the situation in his head.

His company was part of the 23rd Airborne Regiment of the 76th Airborne Division at Pskov, in northern Russia. Under normal circumstances, the 7th Airborne Division, headquartered at Novorossiysk, would have handled any operations this far south.

But, as Mikhailov had learned the previous afternoon when his unit had been deployed, the circumstances were far from normal.

Three days ago, all the researchers at an agricultural research facility about thirty kilometers east of Elista had disappeared. Fifty-three men and women had simply vanished into thin air overnight. After a round of frantic calls from their families to the authorities, police units were dispatched to the remote facility. They, too, disappeared. The senior police officer had reported arriving at the facility, but that was all. There had been no calls for help from anyone.

Family members had then gone to the facility. They had seen many cars, including those of the police, parked at the facility, but there had been no sign of anyone. Those who had gone through the gates, which were normally guarded day and night, and entered the building had disappeared. Others, fearful of entering, had returned home and contacted the police.

The surviving family members finally raised enough of an uproar that the local authorities were able to get the Army involved. A squad from the 247th Airborne Regiment of the 7th Airborne Division had been sent in to investigate. The helicopter carrying them had landed outside the facility gates. Once the paratroopers were on the ground, the helo took off and circled the facility, the pilots watching as the men below entered the complex of buildings.

The paratroopers never came out. The pilots circled as long as they could, trying to regain contact with the ground team, but they were gone. Vanished. Shaken and deeply disturbed, the helicopter crew returned to Novorossiysk, where they reported what had happened.

That had taken place yesterday morning. Before noon, Mikhailov was in front of his division and regimental commanders, receiving his deployment orders. He was disturbed not so much by the nature of the deployment, but by the revelation from the division commander that the former President of the Republic of Kalmykia had very publicly claimed to have been contacted by aliens in 1997. The general had not mentioned it as a joke. While most had dismissed the claim as the raving of a rich and eccentric man, others had expressed more concern over the possibility that the republic's former president had revealed state secrets to the alleged aliens. The general had thought the detail was relevant, considering the strange nature of the situation for which the airborne troops had been called in. And Mikhailov had been the clear choice to lead the mission in light of his experience on the island of Spitsbergen the year before.

If Mikhailov's suspicions were correct and Kalmykia's eccentric former president had been contacted by harvesters as far back as 1997, there seemed only one likely scenario for what was now happening at the research facility outside Elista. The researchers had likely been trying to duplicate the work there that Jack Dawson and Naomi Perrault had told him had happened in the United States. The major difference was that Jack and Naomi could combat the harvesters there. Here in Russia, where the Earth Defense Society had no resources, the harvesters could have gotten away with anything.

This facility was a case in point. It was not a government operation. It was privately owned, but it was not clear by whom. It had no name. To those who worked there, their families, and people from the nearest villages, it was simply known as "The Facility." It was an enigma, and a very dangerous one.

Staring at the operations map on the wall of the briefing room as the general had given him his instructions while his regimental commander sat in silence, Mikhailov had felt a cold stab of fear lance through his chest.

By afternoon, he and his men were on an Il-76 transport aircraft, flying south to Stavropol, the headquarters of the 247th Airborne Regiment. And at the crack of dawn this morning, he and his men were on an Mi-17 helicopter, flying the two hundred and fifty kilometers from there to the research facility. The pilots who had delivered the ground team yesterday were flying Mikhailov in. He prayed that he and his men would have better luck than their previous passengers.

Rudenko returned to his seat, giving Mikhailov a thumbs-up. He did not have a headset, and there was no point in trying to talk above the roar of the engines and rotors. Rudenko made his own last minute check, pulling a massive pistol from a holster under his left arm. It was a Desert Eagle chambered for .50 Action Express rounds, and was a twin to the one Mikhailov carried. Three months after the atomic bomb had been dropped on California, killing Jack, Naomi, and the others of the Earth Defense Society, an unmarked box had mysteriously appeared in Mikhailov's apartment, sitting on the kitchen table. The box contained the two handguns, two spare magazines each, and two hundred rounds of ammunition.

When he saw the two handguns, the same as Jack carried when they had all met on Spitsbergen during the battle for the Svalbard seed vault, Mikhailov knew that Jack and Naomi must still be alive. The guns were a message, and a gift for him and Rudenko. The older NCO, upon receiving one of the weapons, had been mightily impressed. No stranger to the workings of the black market and smuggling in general, Rudenko could only shake his head in admiration, both at the weapon itself and what it must have taken to get them to Mikhailov.

Checking back through the small box in which he kept those things most important to him, Mikhailov found the small slip of paper Naomi had given him on Spitsbergen. On it was a phone number and a nondescript email address. With a tingle of excitement, he sent an email to the address with only his name, as Naomi had instructed. Fifteen minutes later, he had his answer: they were alive, as were most others from the EDS, although that was to be kept secret. Mikhailov had breathed a huge sigh of relief: he had been greatly saddened at the news that Jack and Naomi had been killed.

After that, he had received a great deal of information from his "dead" American friends on the harvesters. He had not been able to share it with anyone but Rudenko, who did not profess to understand much of it, but it had helped Mikhailov to better come to grips with what had happened on Spitsbergen, and proved that he hadn't imagined it all as some claimed he had.

Since then, except for some training on the firing range when it was deserted, he and Rudenko had kept the Desert Eagles out of sight, for he didn't want his superiors to ask inconvenient questions.

Mikhailov had hoped to never have occasion to use the huge handgun, but was now comforted by the weapon's bulk. Rudenko dropped out the magazine and checked that it was fully loaded before slamming it back into the big pistol's grip. Then he pulled the slide partway back to make sure there was a round in the chamber. Satisfied, he slid it back into the holster.

The two men also carried KS-K semi-automatic shotguns, as did half the men in the company. The rest carried the standard assault rifles used by the airborne troops. It was an unusual mix of weapons, but his division commander had authorized it without argument. He had read Mikhailov's report of the action on Spitsbergen, and was a firm believer that more firepower was always better. Mikhailov would have liked to get flamethrowers such as those used during the Great Patriotic War, but they were no longer in service. Instead, two men in each squad were carrying RPO-M thermobaric rockets. They were extremely powerful weapons that could level a small building, but couldn't be used in tight quarters. They would be his last resort.

His reverie was interrupted by a call from the pilot. "There it is."

Mikhailov looked out the window. Two hundred feet below them was the facility, which had four buildings. One, the lab building, was roughly thirty meters by sixty. Behind it were three much larger rectangular buildings, identical in appearance and more than a hundred meters long. Two of the larger ones were where test crops were grown under controlled conditions. While they technically weren't greenhouses, that's how Mikhailov thought of them. The third large building was for livestock, and next to it was a feed silo and a large water tank. All of the buildings were joined by enclosed connectors so the researchers could move between them regardless of the weather.

Around the facility were several fallow fields. The facility specialized in developing hybrid strains of corn, but the growing season was months away yet.

Except in the greenhouse buildings. There, under artificial light and heat, corn and other plants could be grown year round.

"Take us around the facility," Mikhailov ordered. He looked up as Rudenko leaned against the side of the fuselage next to him, looking out the window. The older man's face bore a stony expression.

"Understood." The Mi-17 began a slow circle of the facility.

The parking lot in front of the two lab buildings was full of cars. Nearly two dozen more, including the police vehicles, were parked along the entrance road. Another half dozen were parked outside the gate.

There was no one moving about, or visible in the small windows of the lab building. There were no bodies or signs of violence. It was as if the buildings of the complex had simply consumed everyone.

The thought sent a shiver down his spine.

As the Mi-17 continued its circuit, the rear of the animal husbandry building came into view.

"*Chto za huy*!"

Even above the clamor of the engines, Mikhailov heard Rudenko's curse.

The rear wall of the animal husbandry building where cows, horses, goats, and other livestock were kept as guinea pigs for the crops the facility developed looked like it had been beaten from within by a giant hammer. The metal siding bulged outward at irregular intervals and in odd shapes. Mikhailov could swear that one of the bulges formed the near perfect outline of a cow. Seen on a television show it would have been comical. Here, it was terrifying.

Several sections had also been knocked out, the metal and insulation of the walls bent outward as if something had burst from within the building.

Whatever had been inside had clearly gotten out.

Mikhailov momentarily considered changing his plan. He had intended to land his platoon at the front of the complex and sweep through the buildings with what he hoped would be overwhelming force if they met any resistance. Now, he wondered if he should not drop a squad at the rear of the complex as a blocking force in case whatever was inside, if anyone or anything indeed remained, tried to escape.

"Let the helicopter be our eyes to watch the rear," Rudenko suggested, reading his mind. "It has teeth in case anything tries to escape."

Outside the window, Mikhailov could see the rocket pod hanging from the helicopter's weapons pylon. A matching one hung on the other side.

The burly NCO leaned closer. "Best we keep the men together when we go inside. I do not like the looks of this, *kapitan*."

Accepting Rudenko's suggestion as the hard-earned wisdom that it was, Mikhailov nodded his agreement and keyed his microphone. "Pilot, let's finish circling the complex, then set down outside the main gate."

The Mi-17 began to move forward again. The other parts of the facility appeared to be undamaged, and in two minutes the helicopter had set down.

Mikhailov had moved to the rear and was the first on the ground as the cargo ramp extended.

"Let's go, you sons of whores!" Rudenko's bellow sounded above the cacophony of the whirling rotors as the soldiers rushed past Mikhailov to spread out in a protective perimeter around the helicopter. Their weapons held at the ready, safeties off, they watched for any signs of movement.

Mikhailov had debated on what to tell them. Aside from two men, survivors of Spitsbergen who still remained in the Army and whom Mikhailov had left back at Stavropol, none of the soldiers in his company had any idea of what had happened a year ago. They knew nothing of the harvesters, and he did not need their imaginations running wild. There was also the possibility that Mikhailov's fears were groundless and that whatever had happened here had nothing to do with the abominable creatures.

In the end, he had settled on a terrorist scenario. That was something the men could understand, even if they did not understand why the mission had not been left to the *Spetsnaz*.

Behind them, the helicopter lifted off and flew to a position behind the complex where it could cover the rear.

"Take first squad and check the vehicles," Mikhailov ordered, his breath steaming in the cold air as he raised his binoculars to scan the small windows of the buildings. There was nothing.

"Sir." With hand signals and a few spoken words, Rudenko had the men form a skirmish line, with the soldiers of the first squad inspecting the vehicles outside the gate. They checked everything: inside, underneath, in the trunks, and under the hood. All the vehicles were unoccupied. All were unlocked.

"There's nothing, sir," Rudenko reported. "No bodies, no blood. The drivers must have just parked and gone into the complex."

"And never returned." Mikhailov pursed his lips. "Very well. Let's go."

Rudenko passed the order, and the men of the platoon formed into two columns. They quickly moved through the main gate in the four meter-high fence before spreading out in a line facing the lab building.

Rudenko had the first squad continue to check the vehicles parked along the hundred meter entrance drive that led from the gate to the main parking lot. On either side of the drive were fallow fields, through which the rest of the platoon kept pace. Their weapons were trained on the windows and main entry door to the lab.

As they neared the parking lot itself, Mikhailov glanced at Rudenko, who shook his head. There was nothing, and no one, in the vehicles along the drive.

One of his men, standing next to one of the police cars, held up his hand, and something in his fingers glittered. The keys. The soldier shrugged, tossing the keys back into the car before moving forward.

When they reached the cars in the parking lot, they were confronted with a mystery.

"*Bozhe moi*," Mikhailov whispered as he gingerly opened the door of a green hatchback. The dashboard of the car was missing. It hadn't been torn out or removed, for the metal fasteners were still in place. It was just that the plastic had disappeared. The entire interior, other than glass, metal components and wires, all of which looked as if it had been highly polished, was gone.

The tires of the cars were also missing. But not the metal rims or even the metal parts of the valve stems. Only the rubber parts of the tires.

Kneeling down next to one of the car's front wheels, Mikhailov picked up two mesh ribbons draped over the rim. They were the steel belts that had been molded into the tire when it was made.

"*Kapitan*. This one is locked. And look inside."

Dropping the shiny steel belts as if they were burning his fingers, Mikhailov moved to where Rudenko stood, two cars away. The interior of the car was much the same as the others, except for something on the metal liner of the dashboard. Mikhailov saw two shiny metal rods, about twenty centimeters long, and a dozen gleaming metal screws. They looked vaguely familiar, but he couldn't place them.

"I took a bullet in my leg in Chechnya," Rudenko said quietly. "It shattered one of my shin bones. The doctors fixed it with a metal rod and screws that look almost exactly like that."

That is when Mikhailov made the connection. He had seen such things in x-rays before. "But that is impossible!"

Rudenko shrugged. "*Moi kapitan*, it clearly is possible. We simply do not know how. And I am not so sure I wish to find out." He paused. "Curious. I wonder why they are on the dashboard?"

"I do not care to guess." Mikhailov looked toward the door leading into the lab building. "Let us..." He paused, considering. He could simply go in behind a barrage of grenades and all guns blazing, but that might needlessly destroy evidence of what had happened here. There was also the chance that there were survivors or hostages, although in his gut he did not believe it. "Let us treat this as a reconnaissance, unless we meet resistance or find that there are truly 'terrorists' holding prisoners."

"And if we do meet resistance?"

"We are to defend ourselves, kill anyone or anything who opposes us, and do our best to save any civilians who may be alive."

"Sir!" Rudenko quickly got the platoon organized. When he was done, four men were positioned around the entrance door, while the rest of the platoon was lined up to quickly file inside.

He gave his captain a thumbs-up.

With butterflies filling his belly, Mikhailov clutched his shotgun. His men watched him intently. "Go!"

A soldier yanked the door open and the other three men of the entry team stormed inside.

CHAPTER FOUR

Dr. Vijay Chidambaram leaned back in his chair and rubbed his eyes. For nearly twelve hours a day for the last week in his cramped and stuffy office in the Andhra Pradesh Department of Agriculture's headquarters in Hyderabad, India, he had been sifting through a mountain of folders his assistant had piled onto his desk. In those folders were hundreds of reports detailing the state's crop production, and it was his job to prepare the quarterly summary briefing that would go to the state's Minister for Agriculture. Vijay wouldn't be giving the briefing himself, of course. His boss would have that particular honor as he was trying to further ingratiate himself to the minister. Vijay didn't mind. He hated giving briefings. If given a choice, he would much rather be rooting around in the soil, looking for worms.

No, his task was to gather and wade through the data so his boss could give the minister good news every quarter. It was a good job, a prestigious job in its way, and he knew that he was very lucky to have it.

That didn't change the fact that he hated it. The job had been a gift, in a way, from one of his uncles after Vijay had returned to India from the United States after what had happened the year before in California. He had been, and still was, in heart if not in name, a member of the Earth Defense Society, fighting its secret war against the harvesters. But after the American government had absorbed the EDS and wrapped it in secrecy, Vijay had been left out in the cold. He knew that Jack and Naomi had fought tenaciously for him to be included in their new agency, but the government had demanded that everyone working there had a top secret security clearance. Unfortunately, Vijay wasn't a U.S. Citizen, which was a non-negotiable requirement.

Disheartened, Vijay had decided to return home. He had been offered a field research position by the central government, but his uncles and aunts, who filled in for his long-dead mother and father, had protested vigorously. The job, they had claimed, was unworthy of his talents, and one of his uncles was close to a joint director at the Andhra Pradesh Ministry of Agriculture. After a few phone calls and a meeting with the joint director, Vijay had a new job that paid over twice as much, had an office and an assistant, and made the family look good. Enjoying the work wasn't part of the bargain.

With that checked off the list, his family was now working on finding him a suitable wife. Vijay was quite happy as a bachelor, but had given up trying to dissuade them. Better that he simply accepted his karma. The only saving grace had been that the family's astrologer had not offered any good news on the subject, despite unrelenting interrogation by (and not a little extra money from) Vijay's aunts.

Opening his eyes again, he leaned forward and carefully dropped the folder he had just finished reviewing onto the growing stack on the floor. But the stack on his desk was still far taller.

He checked his watch: it was nearly four in the afternoon, but he wouldn't be going home for quite a while yet.

With a sign of resignation, he took the next folder and flipped it open to the report inside, cringing as he saw that it was handwritten, and in a particularly atrocious scrawl. Far more used to typing on the computer than writing by hand, he could barely understand his own handwriting these days, let alone anyone else's.

Aligning a wooden ruler, a treasured keepsake from his childhood, under the first line of squiggled figures in the report, he was just typing the first set of numbers into the spreadsheet on his computer when his cell phone rang.

Thankful for the interruption, he picked up the phone and flipped it open. He saw on the display that it was one of his colleagues and friends, Dr. Naresh Sharma, and pressed the answer button.

Before Vijay could even say hello, he heard Naresh shouting through the phone.

"Those bastards! They did it again!"

"Naresh, what is it? What are you talking about?"

"AnGrow," Naresh spat. "I just inspected one of their fields and found they'd planted again without authorization. More GMO maize that hasn't received proper approval. Damn them!"

"Just a moment, Naresh." Grimacing, Vijay stood up and closed the door to his office, ignoring the questioning glance from his assistant who sat at a small desk outside. This was a conversation he didn't want anyone else to hear.

AnGrow was an agricultural company in India that had worked closely with New Horizons and other biotechnology companies to help them gain a foothold in the Indian market. But with as much money as those companies could throw at government officials, the foothold had become an invasion beachhead. Genetically engineered strains of nearly every food plant on which India's population depended had been created or were being developed, and companies like AnGrow fought to bring them through the byzantine government regulations to commercial production. Whether the means employed to do that were entirely legitimate or not, as Vijay was painfully aware, depended entirely on one's point of view.

While New Horizons itself had gone bankrupt and had its assets bought up by other companies, AnGrow had continued to prosper. Most of its revenues came from acting as an intermediary for foreign agriculture firms wanting to do business in India, but it also conducted its own lab and field research.

Part of that research, of course, involved planting genetically engineered plants in test plots in various parts of India. Such tests were supposed to be coordinated and approved by the central and state agriculture ministries, and eventually approved by the Genetic Engineering Approval Committee, or GEAC, for production of the crops being tested.

But in several instances (those that had been discovered, Vijay reminded himself), the biotechnology companies had planted test strains of genetically engineered crops without approval or authorization. Organizations concerned about biotechnology applications in the country, particularly after the disastrous experience with genetically engineered cotton, had raised a protest, but their cries had largely fallen upon deaf ears in the government. Far too much money was at stake, and far too much was changing hands. No one could prove it, but Vijay knew it was happening. His boss, for example, met frequently with executives from AnGrow on the side, and boasted a posh residence well beyond his government pay. Vijay was torn: he wanted to have the man investigated for taking bribes, but such a thing would have backlashed against his family. For that reason, and that alone, did he hold his tongue.

AnGrow had been on his watch list for a long time, of course, ever since he had entered the fold of the EDS and had discovered their connection with New Horizons as the EDS tried to map out the enterprises in which the harvesters might be involved. But try as he might, he could never discover any sinister connections to AnGrow. They appeared to be motivated by nothing more unusual than greed.

Taking his seat again, Vijay lowered his voice. "Okay, tell me what happened."

"I recently took twelve samples from an AnGrow maize test plot outside of Koratikal. When I tested them, three matched the approved test strains. But the other nine did not. I have submitted them for more testing, but I have never seen anything like this, Vijay. Whatever they have planted here, it's totally new."

"It is not a Bt variant?" Bt was short for *Bacillus thuringiensis*, a bacterium that produced toxins with insecticidal properties, and whose genes were commonly inserted into various commercial plant species to provide them with built-in protection from insect pests. Or so the theory went.

"No, no. Not at all," Naresh said. "While the outward structure of the maize is typical, it shows significant differences at the cellular level. The cells you would expect to see are present, but there are also other elements that I haven't been able to classify. They appear to be protein shells, perhaps, containing what might be some sort of nucleic material. RNA, perhaps? I do not know. All I do know is that it is very, very strange, and should not have been there." He paused, awaiting a reply. "Vijay? Vijay, are you there?"

Vijay sat in his chair, immobilized by an icy band of fear that had tightened around his heart. Naresh's words came back to him, echoing in his mind: *They appear to be protein shells, perhaps, containing what might be some sort of nucleic material.*

While it was conceivable there was another explanation, Naresh's description was far too close to the RNA delivery system that the harvesters had conceived for the *Revolutions* line of genetically engineered seed produced by New Horizons. But the RNA it would deliver to anyone or anything that consumed the corn would not cure disease as had been promised. Instead, it would transform the unwitting human or animal into a harvester, as had happened to a hapless rhesus monkey at the EDS base in California. If crops that contained harvester genetic material ever got loose in India, or anywhere else on Earth, mankind could easily face extinction.

He moved his lips, but no sound came out. After clearing his throat, he said in a shaking voice, "Naresh, has that plot been harvested?"

"I don't know. I took the samples last week, but didn't have time to analyze them until now. But if it hasn't, it will be soon. It is early in the year, so it is the Rabi harvest, of course. AnGrow claims the plot was planted in mid-October, if one can trust anything they tell us, and the plants were clearly nearing harvest time when I took the samples. And the bastards will probably sell the harvest to the locals to make a few more rupees."

"Where are you now?" Vijay logged out of his computer and headed out the door. "I will be gone for the rest of the day," he barked at his assistant, startling the boy, as he strode quickly out of the office. While the fear was still with him, he knew he had to act. He had to *know*.

"I am at the lab, of course." Naresh worked at one of the state agriculture ministry's two seed testing laboratories in Hyderabad. "Did you want to come by and we can get dinner?"

"Forget dinner. I'll pick you up in twenty minutes."

* * *

The two hours it took them to drive from Hyderabad to Koratikal were the longest in Vijay's life. When he arrived at the lab to pick up Naresh, he had taken a look at the suspect maize kernels and the slides Naresh had made. Vijay's specialty was the study of creatures such as worms, bees, and butterflies that assisted plant growth and reproduction. But he knew enough from his experience with the EDS to recognize the encapsulated delivery system that New Horizons had created, largely with the unwitting help of Naomi Perrault. He also knew that the technology involved in creating that system wasn't something another company could have easily reproduced, especially since all the records of how it had been created had been destroyed.

Over Naresh's protestations, they had skipped dinner, and Vijay had driven like a madman, speeding east on National Highway 202 in his Maruti Swift as if he were in the last few kilometers of the Monaco Grand Prix. Just past the village of Raigiri, he left the highway and headed toward Mothkur Road, and turned north when he reached the town of Atmakur, about four kilometers south of Koratikal.

Following Naresh's directions, he made his way along a series of back roads to where the AnGrow plot was located. The sun had set, and they had to backtrack twice to find the right plot in the growing darkness.

"Damn." Bringing the car to a stop next to the small AnGrow sign marking the plot, he stared at the empty field. The corn had been harvested, and even the stalks were gone, no doubt to be used as food for livestock or to burn for cooking. "We're too late."

"We should file a complaint with the GEAC. What AnGrow is doing is outrageous."

"More than you know, my friend," Vijay told him, sick to his stomach. "More than you know. Let's see if we can find someone who might know about this."

"The workers are from a village right down the road." Naresh pointed in the direction the car was facing. "I spoke to them when I took the samples."

* * *

As they drove toward the village, they caught up with a group of men trudging along in the same direction.

Vijay pulled just ahead of them and stopped the car. He and Naresh got out and faced the approaching villagers. "Excuse me," he said.

The men came to a stop, looking at him, then at the car, then back at him.

"We're from the State Ministry of Agriculture," he went on. "Can you tell me when the AnGrow field back there," Vijay pointed in the direction of the plot, "was harvested?"

"Just today," one of the men said quietly, wiping sweat from his brow with his arm. "We harvested that plot this morning."

"Do you know what happened to the maize?"

All of the men smiled. "Some was taken by the AnGrow people," the same man said. "The rest they let us take in exchange for harvesting it for them. They are very kind."

Vijay leaned forward, a flare of hope in his chest that he wasn't too late. "You haven't eaten any of it yet, have you?"

In the dim light, the men exchanged uneasy glances, and he could tell what they were thinking. That corn was food on their table, and without it there very well might not be any. They were afraid he would try to take it away from them, and if he had the power and authority, he would.

Unfortunately, he had neither. In the uncomfortable silence that followed, the hope that had blossomed a moment earlier faded and died.

Vijay reached into his pocket and pulled out a business card, handing it to the closest man. "The maize AnGrow gave you was not given a safety approval by the government," Vijay told the men. "It was experimental, and might make you and your families very, very sick. It might even kill you. If someone falls ill any time in the next day or two, please call me immediately."

The man looked at the card, and Vijay wondered if he could read what it said. Even if he could, these men were terribly poor, and making a telephone call was not simply a matter of reaching into a pocket for a cell phone. They would have to walk to the nearest village where they could use a communal telephone. "This is very important," Vijay told them, his voice laced with urgency. "You *must* destroy any of the maize you took from this plot. Do not eat any, and do not give it or the stalks to your livestock. Think of it as being poisonous. You must burn it. All of it. Do you understand?"

"Yes, sir," the man said, bobbing his head. The others did, too.

Vijay's heart sank as he saw their expressions in the dim light. He could see the facade of obedience overlaying the duplicity born of desperation. They had no intention of destroying the corn based merely on his say-so. He would have offered to buy the corn back from them and any other families that had taken it, but they probably would only have given him some in exchange for the money, and kept the rest to eat. After all, he had no way of knowing exactly how much the AnGrow people had left behind. And who was he in the eyes of these poor people? It was not that they were determined to be dishonest, but that they were stricken with poverty.

And soon, he felt sure, they might be stricken with something far, far worse.

"Please," Vijay begged. "Call me right away if anyone falls ill."

Then he turned and walked slowly back to the car, a confused Naresh beside him.

* * *

"So," Naresh said when they reached the car. "Do you want to tell me what that was all about? I know I get irate over the abuses of AnGrow and their ilk, but wasn't that a bit extreme, trying to frighten those men like that?"

"They should be frightened. If that maize is what I think it is, they should be terrified and burn every kernel and stalk." He started up the car and began the long drive back to Hyderabad.

"Just what is it, Vijay? It might help if you would tell me what's going on." He gave his friend and colleague a speculative look. "You've never been quite the same since you came back from America, you know. You even brought back a cat." He shook his head in disbelief.

"Yes, I did. And I'll never be without one again." Unlike in America and some other countries, cats were hardly popular in India. They were often shunned as bad omens. Vijay himself had been raised to believe that, but his time with the EDS had changed his views. He was not sure he could ever accept a cat as a loving pet, but he could certainly welcome one as a living alarm system. He only wished he could have it with him at the office, but that was out of the question. "Naresh, you remember the *Revolutions* product line New Horizons was bringing out right before their production facility was blown up by terrorists, yes?"

"Of course! The terrorists that the American President nuked?"

Vijay nodded, cringing inwardly. No one outside of the EDS and a few American government officials knew that he had been a member of the EDS and had been in the facility when it was bombed. "Yes. Well, the *Revolutions* maize, the corn, was designed to deliver an encapsulated RNA payload to the host that consumed it. It was ingenious, really: even if you cooked the maize, so long as the temperatures were not too extreme, the delivery system and payload would remain intact."

Naresh whistled. "That's amazing! And that's what AnGrow planted here?"

"I believe so, based on what you told me." He glanced over at Naresh. "But the payload was not a miracle cure, as New Horizons claimed. It was a delivery system for what I can only characterize as a transgenic weapon that would infect the host."

"And do what?" Naresh was staring at him.

"It would transform the host's DNA, and the host itself, into another form."

"Vijay, that's impossible."

"No, it is not, my friend." Vijay shook his head slowly. "I know that I must sound to you like a lunatic, but I witnessed this myself. If the maize those poor fools took into their homes is what I believe it must be, our country, perhaps the world, is in terrible danger."

"And just what are we supposed to do? Call in the Army?" Naresh laughed as Vijay turned onto Mothkur Road, heading west toward Hyderabad. "Vijay, you have just been working too hard. You need to get some sleep, my friend."

"I think it may be a long time before I sleep again. And we can't call in the Army, but I know who is the next best thing.

Someone who understands." He pulled his cell phone from his pocket and hit the button to fast-dial Naomi's number. He hadn't spoken to her in quite some time, but he made sure that her and Jack's numbers were programmed into his phone.

"Hello," he heard her voice answer after the first ring. "Vijay?"

He was about to answer when he saw the glare of lights in his peripheral vision. Turning his head, he looked up in time to see the grill of a big Mazda cargo truck that had just pulled out from a side road, looking like a freight train as it loomed over his car.

The boom and burning stench and smoke as the airbags deployed.

Shattered glass, the horizon tumbling as the car rolled.

The roar of crushed metal and plastic.

Tires screeching.

Screams.

Darkness.

CHAPTER FIVE

"Hello? Vijay?" Naomi hadn't spoken to Vijay since he'd returned to India. She had felt terrible about how the government had treated him, but both she and Jack had been powerless to help him through the flaming hoop of his security clearance. While the two of them had the support of President Curtis on almost everything, he had been resolute on the issue of security clearances for the employees of SEAL. And after learning how many officials in the government with clearances had been subverted by the harvesters, he had ordered even more stringent checks made for anyone remotely affiliated with SEAL's research. Even though all the harvesters were believed to be dead, Curtis wasn't willing to take any chances.

Dr. Vijay Chidambaram, along with eight others from the survivors of the EDS who had wanted to join SEAL, had been respectfully but firmly turned away.

From the rental car's speakerphone, she heard a tremendous crash and what sounded like the start of a scream.

"Vijay? Vijay!"

There was no answer. The line was dead.

"Damn." She hit the button on the car's steering wheel to bring up her phone's address book. "Call Vijay."

After a moment, she was rewarded with the ringing tone, followed by Vijay's voice. "Hello, this is Vijay. Please leave a message." Then he said something in Hindi before the beep signaling the start of the recording.

"Vijay, this is Naomi, returning your call. Please give me a call back." She paused. "I hope everything's all right."

She pressed the button to end the call as a chill of foreboding, tinged with guilt, swept through her. She had intended to call Vijay to see how he was doing, but had never gotten around to it.

Her attention was momentarily diverted by the car's navigation system, which told her to turn left at the next light off West Olympic Boulevard. As she did, the headquarters of Morgan Pharmaceuticals, a slab-sided monolith of shimmering glass and steel, came into view.

Pulling into the parking lot and lowering her window, she stopped at the guard post, which was occupied by two armed men in black uniforms.

"I'm Dr. Perrault," she told the guard who moved to the side of the car and leaned down toward her. "I have an appointment to see Dr. Morgan."

The guard studied her face carefully before his mouth offered a warm smile. "Of course, Dr. Perrault. Dr. Morgan's expecting you." He produced a badge bearing the company's logo and handed it to her. "Please make sure you wear this at all times while in the building." He pointed toward the entrance. "Just park in the reserved spot right there, the one closest to the door. Dr. Morgan will be out to meet you."

Naomi looked where the guard was pointing and caught sight of a familiar figure who had just emerged from the ten foot tall glass doors leading to the lobby. Howard Morgan stood in the morning sun reflected from the buildings around them, hands in his pockets and a smile on his face. He nodded to her, and she smiled back.

"Thank you," she told the guard, who nodded and stepped back.

She pulled forward and parked.

Howard Morgan somehow covered the distance to the car without her seeing him do it, and he opened the door for her.

"Dr. Perrault! What a pleasure to see you again."

"Thank you, Dr. Morgan." She took his hand and shook it. His grip was firm, hinting at restrained strength, and his gaze remained fixed on hers. He had a deep, resonant voice that she could have listened to all day. "I really appreciate this. Your call couldn't have come at a better time."

With a final shake, he released her hand and gestured toward the entrance. "Believe me, Dr. Perrault — may I call you Naomi?

— I'm the one who should be appreciative. One of the very few times in my career that I kicked the garbage can clear across my office was the day you accepted the position with New Horizons. My only regret was that you hadn't tried to squeeze more money out of me." He held the door open for her. "I would have been more than happy to beat their offer."

"I'm the one who made a mistake." Her heels clicked over the polished marble floor of the lobby, and she glanced up at the enormous atrium that rose seven stories above. Two glass elevators moved rapidly up and down, taking people between floors. A third was at the ground floor, with a young woman standing by.

"Nonsense!" Morgan flashed his badge at the guards who manned the inside checkpoint. They called his name in greeting as he led the way through the security scanner. "For double the pay and the opportunity to work with Rachel Kempf, hard-nosed as she might have been, you would have been a fool not to take the job."

The scanner went off as Naomi passed through. She stopped, turning to the guards by reflex. "It must be my phone."

"You're with me, Naomi. And I doubt you're carrying anything more dangerous than that genius mind of yours. You're a hero now, not a terrorist. Remember?"

He said it with a smile and winked, but his comment made her feel stark naked. After a year of living the life of someone else, of having her true name leading the list of hated terrorists, even ahead of Osama Bin Laden, it was unnerving to hear someone call her by her given name.

She felt her pulse quicken, and sweat broke out on her palms. The same thing had happened when she'd gone to the airport to return to San Antonio from Washington. She and Jack had been provided with new documents reflecting their true names, along with letters from the head of Homeland Security and the Transportation Security Administration to help them through the security screens at the airport. Even though everything had gone smoothly, it had been a surreal experience, as if she were falling down the rabbit hole.

"I'm sorry, Naomi." Morgan touched her arm. "That was thoughtless of me. I can't imagine what a time you've had. I hope you'll let me make it up to you."

Shaking her head, she forced a smile in return. "Don't apologize, Dr. Morgan. I'm just not used to being me again, I suppose."

"Please," he said as the two of them joined the young woman in the executive express elevator, "call me Howard."

When the door opened and they stepped out of the elevator into Morgan's penthouse office, he waved his assistant away, and the young woman disappeared when the elevator doors closed.

Naomi stood and stared at what lay before her. "Wow."

The walls were entirely of glass, with stainless steel columns spread evenly around the circumference to provide structural support. Aside from three nearby buildings which were taller, the office offered an unobstructed view of the entire Los Angeles metro area. Off in the distance, she could make out the famous Hollywood sign. She also saw that there was a large patio with high end deck furniture, and that a number of the glass panels that formed the wall could be opened to let in fresh air.

Well, as fresh as any air could be in downtown LA, she reminded herself.

A treadmill occupied one corner, a wet bar with a wine cooler was next to the elevator, and several comfortable looking chairs and two sofas were arrayed around a central fireplace. A desk with a glass frame and topped with what looked like black granite was set off in one corner, almost as an afterthought. There were no paintings or photos.

With a view like this, she thought, *anything else would be superfluous*. She couldn't imagine what it must be like at night.

"Come on in and make yourself comfortable, Naomi. Something to drink? Are you hungry at all?"

She sat down on one of the sofas."I wouldn't mind a glass of wine, but it's a bit early for that." She could have used something to soothe her worry over the strange call from Vijay.

Morgan cocked an eyebrow at her. "Well, it's past noon somewhere in the world, you know. What would you like?"

"White Zinfandel if you've got it."

He smiled. It was a warm smile, genuine, and Naomi decided that she couldn't help but like this man. "My dear doctor, there is very little in this world that I either don't have or can't get. Especially for you." He took a bottle from the wine cooler and poured her a glass. Then he went to the liquor cabinet poured himself a scotch. With a conspiratorial grin, he said, "I'll confess that this isn't the first time I've imbibed a little earlier than is customary."

Handing her the wine glass, he settled himself on the opposite end of the sofa before holding up his glass. "Cheers."

"Cheers." Naomi took a sip, savoring the flavor of the chilled wine..

After a moment of comfortable silence as they both enjoyed the drinks and the view, Morgan said, "Naomi, I have a vision of changing the world. Of leaving a true legacy, something I can be proud of." He gestured toward the panorama of Los Angeles. "I've made my fortune. And I could just keep making that mountain of money bigger. But I want something more than that. I know this must sound like a lot of hogwash coming from a rich corporate suit like me, but I want to do something *good*."

"Making vaccines and the other work your company has done in developing pharmaceuticals certainly qualifies as good, Dr. Morgan...Howard."

He shook his head. "That's not what I mean, Naomi. Those are the profit engines for the company. Yes, they go toward serving the public health, as it were, but we're not doing anything that someone else isn't already doing. In many cases we do it better, but it's all old hat, and it's all simply for profit. I'm tired of taking incremental steps. I want to make a quantum leap forward in the human condition, something for the history books."

He set down his drink and leaned forward. "I know something about what you were working on before you left New Horizons." At the change in her expression, a mixture of disbelief, horror, and outrage, he added, "Please, let me finish."

Setting the wine glass down on a side table before her shaking hands could spill it, Naomi said, "Go on." She felt as if the fabric of her dress had suddenly turned into shards of glass, gouging into her skin.

"I don't know all the details, of course. But I know enough. I know that you perfected a food-based delivery system for RNA payloads that could be used to combat disease, or even correct genetic defects." He leaned closer. "That's my dream, Naomi. To take the revolutionary work you began and bring it to fruition for the good of the world."

He picked up his drink and sat back, taking a sip. "I also know that something went very badly, terribly wrong at New Horizons, and I'm not interested in the whole business with the Earth Defense Society. I don't much care about the past, except for whatever lessons we can learn from it. I'm interested in the future, and I want — I *need* — you to be part of it."

It took Naomi a moment to gather her thoughts. She had never actually considered carrying on the work she'd done at New Horizons. Upon reflection, the role she had played, what she had created in her time there, had been groundbreaking by any standard. And it could have, should have, been used for good. Even though she had been driven by greed at the time, she believed that what she was doing would help people, and potentially end the suffering of millions.

And it would have. She knew that in her heart. While her main work had been focused on developing the delivery system, she had also learned a great deal from Rachel Kempf about the payload. Kempf had been a harvester, but the knowledge she had shared, and that Naomi had built upon, had opened Naomi's eyes to unguessed vistas of genetic possibilities. She had the knowledge to recreate not only the delivery system itself, but to guide specialist researchers in designing payloads that could be tailored to destroy specific diseases. While Kempf had lied about the true contents of the payload New Horizons had designed, the truth was that the system worked. In the right hands, the delivery system could have saved untold lives. Naomi had spent more than one sleepless night wondering at how things might have been, had her work not been corrupted and twisted by the harvesters.

Looking up at Morgan, she told him, "I need some time to think about it."

"No, you don't."

She felt a flare of anger, but Morgan spoke before she could react.

"Naomi, this is the best place for you right now. I'm well informed, and I know that the government has let you go. That's fine, because you don't belong there." He waved his hand, a dismissive gesture. "Sure, you could find a job somewhere else, and you'd do well. But you won't find any other place, no company or institution, that has resources and technology on a par with ours, and the very personal and direct interest of the CEO backing your efforts. Were you to take any other path, you would not only be shortchanging yourself, but would inflict a tragic loss on humanity. We might eventually be able to recreate what you did at New Horizons, but it'll take us years. I have some very smart people working for me, and that's what they're telling me. But you could get us there in months."

Morgan stood up and walked to his desk. Opening one of the slim drawers, he removed a piece of paper. He sat on the couch next to Naomi and handed the paper to her. "Here."

She recognized what it was: a check, written out to her. She gasped when she saw the amount.

"That's right," Morgan told her. "Five million dollars. Consider that your base pay for the first year you're with us, plus the usual laundry list of benefits and stock options that'll easily double the value of that check."

"Howard," she said, "I still don't know..."

"Listen to me, doctor. I can't hold you down and torture you into taking the job." He smiled. "I've tried brazen flattery and have now enticed you with gold. If those won't work, maybe trust will do the trick. So here's the deal. Don't give me your answer now. But I want you to take that check to the bank as soon as you leave here and deposit it. If you decide to come work for me, show up for work tomorrow at your convenience. If you decide that you're not interested, I want you to keep the money, no questions asked, on the chance that you may change your mind later."

"That's very generous, but I couldn't do that, Howard." She didn't want to make the commitment without talking to Jack first, but she knew in her heart that she was going to take the job. She would be a fool not to, for any number of reasons.

Morgan crossed his arms, a knowing grin on his face. "I'll be free at two o'clock tomorrow afternoon to walk you through the orientation."

* * *

"Jack, he offered me the job, and I want to take it." Back in her hotel room after having gone for a three mile run and taking a hot bath, Naomi had made a video call to Jack over the web. He had stayed in San Antonio to manage the shutdown of SEAL, which mostly meant doing what he could to alleviate the shock of the people who worked there, all of whom were being systematically kicked out on the street. The two week severance was a sop that would have brought cries of protest and outrage in any other federal agency. But SEAL was different. There were no civil service protections for its employees; they served, and could be dismissed, at the pleasure of the government. Jack did what he could to ease their pain, but they were all well and truly screwed.

It was nearly midnight in Texas, and Jack looked exhausted. But he visibly brightened at her words. "It's nice to hear some good news for a change. We could use a lucky break after this cluster." He ran a hand through his hair, a nervous habit. "When does he want you to start?"

Naomi saw movement in the corner of Jack's video pickup, and Alexander's big head appeared, his nose suddenly filling the view from the webcam. With a single meow, he jumped off the desk. She could hear him tearing off down the hallway, no doubt chasing after Koshka, her cat.

"He wants me to start tomorrow." She was a little nervous about how Jack might react. He respected her freedom and her individuality, but they were also a couple very much in love, even if not married. Yet. She hated to leave him holding the bag in San Antonio, but she had to admit to her own streak of selfishness. She couldn't wait to get started on the work Morgan had promised her.

"Tomorrow?" He sat back and pursed his lips. After a moment's consideration, he said, "Hell, why not? I'll have the mess at SEAL wrapped up by the end of the week. With that done, there's no reason to stay here, and I sure don't have anything cooking on the job front. We'll have to sort out what we want to do with finding a place out there and selling the place here, but I can handle this end while..."

"Jack," she interrupted him, "just finish up at work, grab the cats, get your tight little ass in that SUV, and head out here. Forget about the house and all the other stuff for now. We can deal with that later." She touched his face in the monitor with her fingers. "I want you here with me. Right now."

"There's nowhere in the world I'd rather be, baby. Believe me. But we don't have a lot of money in the bank to pay a mortgage on a house here and rent a place there until we find a house to buy. And a place out there is going to be a fortune compared to what we paid here."

Naomi grinned. "Honey, cash right now is *not* a problem. Howard Morgan wrote me a check for five million dollars, and I deposited it in our account this afternoon."

Jack's jaw dropped. "Holy shit."

Naomi nodded. "That's what I thought!"

"Okay." Jack blinked and shook his head. "Five mil? Seriously?"

"Yep. And his people are going to take care of finding us a place to live here and selling the house there. It's all set. So get your buns out here as soon as you can."

Naomi watched as a huge weight seemed to fall from Jack's shoulders. Then a sly grin crept onto his face. "You know," he told her slowly, "I could probably get used to being a kept man. Being a gigolo to a genius millionaire sure as hell beats working as a government manager or FBI agent."

"I'll still make you earn your keep, you know."

"I'm counting on it."

Naomi's expression suddenly became more thoughtful. Troubled. "Jack, there's one thing that I need you to look into. I got a call from Vijay Chidambaram this morning."

"The bee and worm guy? What did he say?"

"That's the problem. He didn't say anything. When I answered the call, I heard, I don't know, like a big boom and maybe a scream on his end. It was really distorted and I'm not really sure. What bothers me is that I've tried to call him back several times, and I've only gotten an out of service recording. I haven't been able to track down his family on the web, and I want you to check on him for me, if you could. I want to make sure he's all right."

While SEAL was being shut down, Jack still had all his security clearances and access to nearly every system in the intelligence community. He likely wouldn't have to dig very deep to find Vijay, but he still had the resources to dig as far as he needed, at least for the next few days.

"You've got it. Anything else for your pleasure, ma'am?"

"You'll find out when you get here," she purred. "That, I can promise."

CHAPTER SIX

"Lights." Mikhailov's quiet order echoed through the eerie darkness that filled the lobby of the lab building. Aside from the glass door, there were no windows, and the lights were off. He stood behind the men of the first squad, who had spread out across the lobby, covering the reception desk and the three closed doors behind it.

One of the men reached for the bank of light switches near the entry door and switched them on.

Nothing.

"Tactical lights."

His men turned on the small but intense flashlights attached to their weapons.

"*Bozhe moi,*" someone whispered.

In the harsh beams, Mikhailov could see that this part of the building had been reduced to a shambles. The reception area was also likely the lab's administration office, for he saw desks, file cabinets, and computers. Or what was left of them.

The place looked like a tornado had whipped through it. Or a battle had been fought.

Moving forward slowly until he could see behind the counter that ran from one side of the room to the other, Mikhailov could see that the big metal filing cabinets had been upended, and one of them had been crushed in the middle and was covered with dried blood and flecks of gore. Papers were spread everywhere, crumpled and torn, many of them stained with spatters of crimson. The white tile of the floor was splashed with stains of dark brown. Blood.

Of the computers, one looked as if it were half melted. Of the others, all that was left was metal and silicon. Everything that had been made of plastic or rubber was gone. Mikhailov saw a pile of electronic components that he suddenly realized had once been a telephone, now without its plastic skeleton.

Rudenko pointed to the door on the right, and Mikhailov nodded. While one soldier yanked the door open, two more moved through and cleared the room beyond. The pair of desks inside were upended, their blood-splashed white laminate tops facing the doorway. The tops had also been slashed and scored, and the end of one had been lopped off. There were also a half dozen holes in each desk in various places, about as big around as his little finger. At first he thought they were bullet holes, but they didn't have the paint splintering around the edge that he would have expected to see. These looked more like sharp spikes had been driven into them. A dark viscous substance, still glistening, oozed from them.

One of his men leaned forward, extending a finger to touch the liquid.

"Touch nothing," Mikhailov ordered. He had not only seen harvesters himself, he had also read the reports Naomi and Jack had sent him by encrypted email, and he knew they had stingers that could produce this sort of damage. "It is deadly poison."

The man recoiled and took two steps back. The others looked nervously at the desks, then at Mikhailov.

Mikhailov knew then that if they found anything alive in this place, it would not be human. He turned to Rudenko.

"*Da, kapitan?*"

"I have reconsidered my earlier orders. I believe that anyone we may find in here will be like our *Spetsnaz* friends on Spitsbergen." During the ill-fated mission to Spitsbergen the year before to secure the Svalbard "Doomsday" seed vault from terrorists, four *Spetsnaz* — special forces — soldiers had been attached to Mikhailov's company. They had all been harvesters, and had managed to kill most of Mikhailov's men. "The men are to consider anyone they encounter to be hostile, even if they appear to be a civilian."

"Understood, sir."

"And warn them not to touch anything like that liquid. They must take great care."

"Sir." Rudenko moved out of the office and repeated Mikhailov's orders to the men outside, his voice calm and just loud enough to carry so that all could hear. Each soldier nodded his understanding.

Mikhailov looked again at the remains of the computers. "Pull the hard drives and whatever remains of any thumb drives or disks." Even if the plastic had vanished, the data on the drives would still be intact, and might be able to tell the story of what had happened here.

Under Rudenko's watchful eye, a pair of men quickly gutted the remains of the computers and handed the hard drives to Mikhailov. Another man produced a handful of USB drives, which now looked like the innards of electronic beetles bereft of their plastic exoskeletons. Mikhailov placed them in his cargo pockets.

Catching Rudenko's eye, Mikhailov gave him the hand signal to proceed.

There were two other doors in the reception area. One was a bathroom. Empty, except for more bloodstains on the floor and mirror.

The final door opened onto the main hallway that ran the length of the building. Like the office and reception area, it was pitch black except for the soldiers' flashlights.

As they slowly moved down the hall, they passed another set of bathrooms — empty — and several storage and utility closets, also empty. There were more signs of struggle, but only a few traces of blood could be seen. The same was true of the cafeteria. The tables and chairs had been knocked over, and there were more spatters of blood, but not many.

Then they found the labs. There were two, in large rooms on either side of the central hallway that occupied the bulk of the building's first floor.

"You lead third and fourth squads to check the left side," Mikhailov said to Rudenko. "I will take the first and second into the right."

"Sir."

"Slow and quiet," Mikhailov ordered the men behind him as he led them into the right-side lab. His whispered voice sounded like a shout in the unnerving silence that surrounded them. Even the buzz of the helicopter was barely discernible through the building's thick walls. "Spread out and check *everywhere.*"

The men moved a pace at a time as if they were walking on explosive eggshells, holding the stocks of their weapons tucked tight into their shoulders, fingers on the triggers as they swept the labs with the beams of their flashlights.

Much like the administrative area, the labs were a scene of utter devastation. What Mikhailov guessed must have been millions of rubles of delicate equipment had been toppled over, thrown, or smashed. Freezers the size of small cars had been knocked to the floor, their thick stainless steel dented, punctured, and even torn. One bore gouges all the way through the metal. The gouges looked like claw marks.

The men who saw that glanced nervously at one another, but they maintained their silence.

Mikhailov was suddenly aware of the vast darkness above them. "Check the ceiling."

Instantly, half a dozen lights pointed upward. Most of the tiles in the drop-down ceiling had been knocked out. Beyond that, there was nothing but the concrete forming the floor of the second level, along with pipes, and conduits.

"*Kapitan.*"

Mikhailov moved forward to where a pair of soldiers were crouched near one of the big freezers.

"Sir, look at this."

Kneeling down, Mikhailov shone his light over a pool of viscous, foul-smelling amber liquid at least two meters across. As disgusting as it was, it clearly was not the same as the poison residue they had seen on the desks in the administrative office. There was a stain across the floor suggesting the pool of liquid here had originally been considerably larger, but had evaporated. Bits and pieces of things glinted under the glare of the lights. Some looked like electronic components. Others he couldn't identify.

"What is that?" He pointed to a pair of shiny nuggets near the edge of the reeking mass. One of the soldiers drew his combat knife and dragged the things out of the ooze so they could get a better look.

It took Mikhailov a moment of staring at them to realize what they were: gold crowns that had once been on someone's teeth. Glancing at the two men, Mikhailov suspected that neither recognized what they were looking at. It was too macabre a thought.

The soldier was about to wipe the blade of his knife on his pants to clean it off before returning it to its scabbard.

"No," Mikhailov told him. "Don't contaminate your clothing. Leave the knife here." The man reluctantly set the knife down on the floor. Mikhailov drew his own and handed it to him. "Here. Take mine." It was a mental placebo, Mikhailov knew, for whatever ghastly abomination had caused the destruction here would certainly not be killed by a simple knife.

"*Spasibo, kapitan*." The soldier gratefully slid his captain's knife into the scabbard before standing up and backing away. The other soldier joined him, clearly relieved to distance himself from the foul-smelling pool.

Getting to his feet, Mikhailov eyed the refrigerators. There were three of them. Two lay on their sides, the doors open and the contents, hundreds of vials and dishes, spread across the floor. The third had fallen front side down, with the door still shut. "Turn it over. Check inside."

Four men, grunting with effort, managed to heave the heavy unit on its side with a loud boom that echoed through the building.

Mikhailov's radio suddenly came to life. Rudenko. "*Kapitan?* We heard something."

"It was just us. We had to move something heavy. How goes your search?"

"We have cleared most of the lab area here. No contacts. Everything in here has been torn apart, as if by a pack of enraged bears. And it is much the same as with the cars: anything made of plastic or rubber is gone. Only metal and things like stone or ceramic remain. But there is hardly any blood. No bodies, no parts of bodies, either."

"It is much the same here, although there are things made of plastic that yet remain. Proceed with your search. We will link up with you near the rear doors."

"Understood, sir. Rudenko, out."

Three soldiers now held their weapons pointed at the freezer door, which had remained firmly closed.

"Open it."

A fourth man clambered onto the side of the freezer that now faced the ceiling and reached down to grasp the heavy duty handle.

Mikhailov aimed his own shotgun at the freezer door. "Now!"

The soldier on the freezer yanked on the handle, then leaped back out of the way to get clear of the line of fire.

As if in slow motion, fixed in the beams of half a dozen flashlights, the door fell open, banging heavily onto the floor.

Something leaped out, screeching.

Mikhailov and the others opened fire.

The results were spectacular. Mikhailov and the three soldiers who had been covering the freezer door were armed with shotguns, but the rounds with which they were loaded did not contain slugs or buckshot. Instead, they were loaded with a special military version of zirconium-based shotgun shells often known as Dragon's Breath. After studying the reports Jack and Naomi had sent him, he thought these might be an excellent weapon to combat any harvesters, which were extremely vulnerable to flame. Like the big Desert Eagle pistol, he had never expected to have to use them. The ordinary Dragon's Breath shells could not be fired from semi-automatic shotguns such as the KS-K, but Rudenko had managed to have a batch modified so they would. The Dragon's Breath spewed a torrent of incendiary particles, burning at roughly three thousand degrees Celsius, to a range of fifteen or more meters, and were the next best thing to an old-style flamethrower. They could not take down targets at any significant range, but Mikhailov had never expected them to.

Three massive gouts of flame erupted from the muzzles of the shotguns as the soldiers fired, engulfing the freezer and the lab area behind it in a blinding pyrotechnic display. The fireworks were punctuated with the bark of assault rifles firing on full automatic.

The rat that had somehow been trapped inside the freezer, and had dashed out when the door had been opened, was incinerated by the Dragon's Breath and chopped to pieces by the assault rifles.

"*Cease fire!*" Mikhailov lowered his weapon, his ears ringing from the shots. He blinked his eyes, trying to clear the blinding after-images left by the Dragon's Breath shells.

Every flashlight and weapon was focused on the smoldering remains of the rat. Stepping forward, Mikhailov prodded it with the end of his weapon. Satisfied that it was nothing other than what it appeared to be, he breathed a sigh of relief, coughing in the swirling smoke of the gunpowder and zirconium that now enveloped the lab.

He turned as Rudenko burst into the room, half a dozen men behind him, weapons at the ready.

"*Kapitan?*" The NCO stopped beside his company commander and looked at the rat. He grinned. "A shame that we could not have interrogated it."

"It is cooked and ready to eat if you are hungry, my friend." Mikhailov clapped the older man on the shoulder. He didn't show it, but his insides were quivering like jelly.

"You know that I prefer them raw, sir." He trained his weapon around the lab, taking in the destruction that appeared in the beam of his light. "Aside from this rat, sir, this place is empty. The other side is clear."

Mikhailov nodded. "I agree. Let us move on to the greenhouse buildings." He paused, looking at the rat again. "If anything is in there, it certainly knows now that we are here."

* * *

The connector to the first of the huge greenhouses, like the hallway back in the lab building, was pitch black. None of the lights worked. The power was obviously out, but that was not all: some ceiling fixtures had been smashed, the shattered remains of the long fluorescent tubes crunching under the men's boots.

The platoon moved through the connector with half the men hugging the left wall, the other half the right. When the first pair of soldiers reached the double doors leading to the first greenhouse, they stopped and looked back at Mikhailov.

He signaled for them to proceed. The first two men pulled the doors open, while the rest of the platoon rushed forward into the darkness.

As he stepped beyond the doorway into the greenhouse, Mikhailov sucked in his breath through his clenched teeth. He had known the buildings were big, but his view from the helicopter could not have prepared him for how cavernous they truly were, especially in darkness. For a moment, he felt as if he'd stepped into outer space. The flashlight beams seemed tiny and utterly inadequate to the task at hand.

"Spread out." Rudenko's hissed command was followed by the sound of quickly moving feet as the men of the platoon moved out along a walkway. A strip of concrete about two meters wide, the walkway appeared to extend the length of this side of the building.

Mikhailov was not sure what he expected, but this was not it. As he adjusted to the eerie vastness of the building, taking in what was illuminated by the beams of the flashlights as his men spread out, he saw...nothing.

He saw a raised frame, about knee high, that ran beside the walkway. Kneeling down to take a closer look, he saw that it contained nothing more threatening than soil.

"This greenhouse is empty," Rudenko said quietly.

Da." Mikhailov reached out and scooped some of the dirt into his hand. Instead of the nutrient-rich loam he expected, the soil felt gritty as he rubbed it between his fingers. Bringing his hand to his nose, he could find no trace of the earthy smell that was typical of good growing soil. He may as well have been holding sterilized sand.

With a sudden shiver, he tossed it away and dusted off his hand on his pant leg.

"Look at this." Rudenko shone his flashlight along the surface of the soil. There were regularly spaced holes, about as big around as his open palm, stretching off into the distance. And the soil looked very smooth, as if it had been tamped down. Leaning forward, he shone the light into one of the holes. It wasn't smooth, like the hole had been dug or drilled. It looked like the mold into which one might pour plaster to make a cast of a plant's roots.

Mikhailov grunted. “Odd. You wouldn’t plant anything in holes like that. And if the plants had been harvested...”

“The soil would be greatly disturbed. And there wouldn’t be perfect holes like that, as if the roots had been dissolved away.” Leaning closer and whispering so the men could not hear, Rudenko asked, “*Kapitan*, what has happened here?”

Mikhailov looked at him. “From the information that Jack and Naomi sent me, I know the harvester larval form consumes great quantities of carbon, among other things. This would explain the plastic and rubber that disappeared from the cars and devices like the computers. Even the plants and bodies, which contain much carbon and other elements the harvesters must need. I do not relish the thought, but that could easily account for what we are seeing.”

Rudenko just stared at him, and Mikhailov knew what he must be thinking. Including the plastic and rubber from the cars, plus the corn stalks here, the amount of carbon compounds and other materials that had disappeared from the facility must amount to some number of tons.

“I now wish we had the rest of the company,” Rudenko whispered. Mikhailov had wanted to bring his entire unit, but had been turned down by the division commander in Novorossiysk. The general had not thought the additional manpower and expense of sending three helicopters instead of one was justified.

“I wish we had a full regiment.” Mikhailov stood up, and Rudenko joined him. “We may need more than that if we have to chase these things down in the countryside.” He looked at the line of men that spread the full length of the building. “Have the men sweep forward across the field. I do not want to miss anything, especially if it might be something that can surprise us from behind. And have them beware of the holes. We don’t need any twisted or broken ankles.”

“Sir.” Rudenko quickly passed the orders.

With Mikhailov leading the way along the walkway that extended straight from the door to the lab building across to what he assumed would be the next connector, the platoon carefully advanced across the field.

Much to everyone's relief, they found nothing. There was only the strangely smooth earth and odd holes. Unlike in the lab building, there were no signs of struggle.

"Maybe all the buildings will be empty," Rudenko observed hopefully as the platoon moved through the connector to the second greenhouse.

As before, two men opened the double doors and the platoon rushed into the darkened expanse.

"Then again, maybe not."

The beams of their flashlights revealed the frightening visage of stalks of corn, twice the height of a man, stretching away into the darkness.

CHAPTER SEVEN

Jack fell more than sat into his chair. The days since the vice president had told them they had to shut down SEAL had been a nightmare. It wasn't the same, of course, as the fighting he had done in Afghanistan or against the harvesters. But with every employee he called in to his office to thank for their service and then dismiss, with every computer and piece of furniture he signed over to people from Homeland Security, he felt as if another nail was being hammered into the coffin of humanity's future.

While there was evidence that all the harvesters had been killed, no one could answer the question of where they'd come from. Were they an extraterrestrial species as many believed? If so, were there more of the things out there, lurking among the stars, that would eventually come to finish what they'd started? Humanity would have no consolidated defense if they did. Beyond a fairly small group of people who had direct knowledge of them, the world had been kept in ignorance about their existence. And even if the truth were divulged publicly, how many would believe it? Most would simply think it was another tabloid hoax. Alien invaders from Mars. Right. The power of denial was too powerful to overcome by simply trying to inform people.

And the opposite extreme, if the evidence was overwhelming and undeniably credible, would be uncontrolled panic and chaos. Unlike little green men, who would stand out in the crowd, the harvesters were perfect mimics. Your husband or wife, your best friend, could be one. Or maybe an annoying neighbor, or your ex-wife or -husband. Who could you trust? And how many innocent people would wind up dead because someone thought they might be a harvester, or were merely using that as an excuse to get rid of someone?

Jack's people had been working on those issues as a sideline, trying to come up with scenarios to help other agencies like Homeland Security and FEMA formulate response plans. But there had never been any integration or cooperation, even under Curtis. He had kept the lid on too tight, not even allowing anyone in other agencies to be cleared on SEAL's true mission. And President Miller, of course, had pulled the plug on the entire thing.

But Jack's biggest worry was The Bag. He was sure in his gut that it was out there somewhere, that it hadn't been just an administrative mistake in New Horizons' shipping inventory. Everyone who had been working at the New Horizons plant where the seeds were genetically modified and then prepared for shipment had been killed when the EDS had destroyed the place, and no records had been kept anywhere else. The FBI had seized every computer, thumb drive, paper file, and anything else that might have contained information on the manufacture and shipment of the horrid seed the harvesters had created. An army of special agents led by Carl Richards had gone over all of it, but had come up with nothing on the harvesters' operations. They had found other interesting tidbits, various violations of U.S. law that had put most of New Horizons' executives behind bars and effectively destroyed the company, but that was all.

But there wasn't a shred of information, and no one left alive, who could tell them the fate of The Bag. It hung over Jack like the Sword of Damocles, even as his own power and ability to do anything about it was literally being pulled out from under him.

"Shit." Jack rubbed his eyes, then leaned forward, putting his elbows on his desk and cupping his chin in his hands. He'd been at work for almost thirteen hours straight, trying to tie up as many loose ends as he could as the lights were figuratively and literally switched off around him.

The secure phone rang. He looked at the caller ID and saw that it was Renee. He smiled, the first time since he'd spoken to Naomi and heard the news about her new job.

He picked up the phone. "If you're through with that Richards guy, I'm ready to elope to Vegas."

Renee cackled. "Oh, don't you wish. I wouldn't mind going to Vegas, though. I just need to convince my tightwad boyfriend that it might actually be fun."

Jack had to laugh at the thought of Richards in Vegas, casino hopping with Renee. "You'd wear him out in no time."

"I do, anyway. What a pathetic old goat." Her voice turned serious. "How are you holding up, kid?"

"I'm fine, just tired of this bullshit. Everybody's gotten a pink slip. Now it's just me, a few die-hards helping me to clear out, and the Homeland Security guys taking all the gear. I'll be glad when it's over."

"Yeah." Renee sounded dispirited. "I've still got my contract with the FBI, but they have me working on other stuff now. But I, uh, I'm still poking around, if you know what I mean."

"It's a good thing. You'll be the only one left with any sort of classified access."

"That's actually what I wanted to talk to you about, Jack, aside from your romantic obsession with me. I've got a couple of things for you. For starters, I tracked down Vijay C." She had thought the world of Vijay, but for the life of her could never pronounce his last name. Jack had taken a cursory look into his whereabouts, but in the bureaucratic quagmire he was in, he just didn't have the time. So he had asked Renee, who was far better at tracking down information, if she could take up the hunt. "He's in a hospital in Hyderabad, India, in critical condition. He was in a bad car accident, apparently a hit and run by some sort of tractor trailer rig. There was a passenger in the car, another employee of the Andhra Pradesh Department of Agriculture, but he didn't make it. I'm emailing you and Naomi the contact information for the hospital."

"Do they know if he's going to pull through?"

"It's hard to tell from what I was able to find out. I ran his list of injuries by one of the medical experts here, an M.D., and she wasn't very optimistic about his chances. Frankly, she was surprised he'd managed to survive at all."

"Damn." Jack sat back in his chair and stared up at the ceiling for a moment. "He hasn't been in touch with anybody for how long, since he left the States? I wonder what he was calling Naomi about?"

"I don't know. But Vijay wasn't given to much in the way of social calls. If he were calling, it was most likely about business."

And *business*, to the survivors of the EDS, could mean only one thing.

"Was there any information on who did this? If it was a hit and run, it might not have been an accident."

"I checked, but couldn't find anything. Carl even gave me the green light to call the Andhra Pradesh State Police. They were very helpful, but weren't able to tell me much more than I already knew. There weren't any witnesses, and the vehicle that hit Vijay's car hasn't turned up. The police were sure it was a large truck based on the damage." She paused. "His car was smashed flat as a pancake. They had to cut him out of the wreckage."

"Christ. Okay, keep tabs on him, will you? I'll talk to Naomi and see what she wants to do."

"Will do. The next thing is sort of weird that I picked up on my news search." Renee had created a set of automatic queries that constantly sifted national and international news services, blogs, and social media sites for anything she could think of that might point them toward The Bag. Almost everything the searches picked up was garbage, although a lot of it made entertaining lunchtime reading. "One of the Russian news services reported some sort of mysterious goings-on at an agricultural facility in the southern part of the country. It's like one of those crazy things you'd see on one of those hokey paranormal reality shows. I would have skipped past it, except for one thing: the Army sent some airborne troops out to investigate."

"Not just police?"

"Police had been sent, apparently, but they just went poof. So they brought the army in. The odd thing is that they deployed from Pskov, which is up in northern Russia."

"Pskov." Jack suddenly felt queasy. "Mikhailov and Rudenko are stationed there."

"Yeah. The news didn't say which unit, but it's odd because there's an airborne division and a bunch of regular army units in the South, not far from this place called Elista."

"Did you try to reach Mikhailov?"

"Sure did. I sent him an email to the account we set up for him, but there hasn't been an answer yet."

"Great. Any more good news?"

"Actually, there is one more thing. Bad shit comes in threes, right? After taking a look at the shenanigans in southern Russia, I got a wild hair and did a few more searches for weird stuff. I came up with a couple more episodes for the paranormal freaks, one in southern China, and the other in southeastern Brazil. Both were within the last three weeks, and were eventually written off by the authorities as hoaxes."

"I have the feeling you're telling me this because you don't think it's coincidental."

"Would I ever do that?" Renee snorted. "I was trying to figure out what common denominator these whacko places that I can't pronounce might have. It took me a while, but get this: the places in China and Brazil were right in the middle of prime corn growing regions, and those two countries are the second and third largest producers of corn in the world behind the U.S. of A. That place in Russia is right smack in the middle of their corn belt, too." She paused. "So was where Vijay's car got creamed over in India. Only Brazil and India have harvest seasons this early in the year, but I'm sure the other countries have greenhouses for playing around with stuff off-season. Call me a skeptic, but I'm having a hard time swallowing this particular cornbread."

Jack snapped forward in his seat. "Holy shit. But you said that the events in China and Brazil were hoaxes?"

"That's what the local governments trotted out after a few hysterical news reports about mass disappearances. But both China and Brazil sent in police or army units to check things out, and found everybody where they were supposed to be. Mostly."

"What do you mean by *mostly?*"

"They found the adults and older teens. The younger kids all seemed to be off at grandma's house in the next village. There also weren't any dogs or other smaller animals around, and the same with big animals like horses and cows. They must all have been off visiting grandma, too."

The queasy feeling in Jack's stomach had congealed into a cold metal ball. "The harvesters can't mimic things that are much smaller or larger than their natural form," he recalled aloud. "So they couldn't mimic anything that wasn't roughly adult human in size."

"That's what I was thinking. No specific mention was made about cats, but I'm sure there weren't any of those around, either."

"Did you tell Carl?"

"What do you take me for, a dumb-ass? Of course I did. And the poor dear went straight to the new director. The stupid asshole tossed Carl out and swore he'd take Carl's badge and gun if he ever came to him with such 'patent nonsense' again."

"Crap." Jack paused a moment, thinking. "Okay, let me ask you something. Are we just jumping to conclusions here, reading too much into all this?"

"Sure we are, Jack. This stuff I'm seeing could be pure crapola and might have nothing more malignant behind it than my Aunt Bernice." Her voice lowered. "But we've both seen the boogeyman, and we know he's real. And I think where we're going to find him, if he's still really out there somewhere, is in junk like this that otherwise we'd just laugh at in the grocery store checkout line. These news tidbits are potential indicators, but if someone who didn't know about the harvesters checks them out..."

"They'd just think it was a hoax," Jack finished for her.

"Bingo. If this pans out, Jack, we could have an epidemic on our hands."

"I know." Jack had a hard time imagining the implications. Two dozen harvesters had nearly had the world in their chitinous claws. Granted, they had been here who knows how long and had time to infiltrate key areas of the government, military, and industrial infrastructure in various countries around the world. But if humanity ever faced hundreds or thousands of the things, there was no telling what hell might be unleashed. "If these incidents represent harvester infestations, they could only have originated with The Bag, right?"

"As far as we know, yes, but that's still an assumption. We don't have any way to know what else the harvesters might have been up to."

"Okay, I'll grant that. But let's start with The Bag, and for the moment let's say that some of these incidents are what we think they are. How could we have multiple outbreaks so far apart, and in a window of only a few weeks? What's the link, besides them being located in corn-producing regions?"

"I don't know, Jack. If we look at it as an epidemic, there has to be a vector, right? A delivery agent, like fleas carrying the plague. I guess we should think of the New Horizons plant as the index case, since that's really ground zero for The Bag. Assuming, of course, that we're not just making this up out of paranoia."

Jack stared at the wall across the room, his eyes unfocused and mind spinning through possibilities. "It's the timing. If there's a vector, let's assume it's someone from the facility, someone we missed somehow. He or she must have stayed out of sight for a while after the New Horizons facility was destroyed."

"Maybe they weren't lying low, Jack," Renee mused. "If I remember correctly, Naomi said that this corn variant was fast growing, taking about sixty days from planting to harvest. So if the corn's ready for harvest now in late January, it must have been planted sometime in late November or early December, right?"

"The presidential election," Jack mused. "Curtis's policies on exporting or smuggling any genetic material or technology out of the country without authorization were as tough as the terrorism laws, but Miller had made a campaign promise to open up the floodgates again. So maybe our vector was waiting for a better time. Curtis was a lame duck, Congress hated those policies because they put a huge stick up corporate America's ass, and the incoming President made it clear he was going to tear down that particular wall."

"So if our little thief holding The Bag," Renee snorted at her own pun, "had been busy lining up buyers, he — or she — would have been ready to do a little kettle corn carpetbagging."

"And any of those countries, and more, would have paid a small fortune for the technology in the New Horizons seed."

"It's ridiculous, Jack. Wild speculation."

"I know. Totally preposterous."

"Shit." Renee blew out a breath, and it sounded like a tiny hurricane on Jack's end. "What do you want me to do?"

Jack thought a moment, trying to get past the feeling of being caged. Right when he most needed the authority and resources he'd had at SEAL, he was losing them, becoming Joe Civilian again. "I doubt there's any way we'd be able to pin down buyers coming to meet our hypothetical grain salesman here in the U.S. There are just too many variables. So let's assume for the sake of argument that he did most or all of the traveling, at least to deliver the seeds." Jack had a hard time imagining that getting the seeds out of the country would be difficult. The vector could have sewn a few in the liner of his jacket, or just dropped some in a plastic bag and stuffed it in his pocket. That was the biggest weakness in his little election day trigger theory: getting the seeds through customs wouldn't have been hard, so whoever it was must have been sufficiently worried about the steep penalties of the GMO tech transfer policies that they hadn't dared to take anything out before Miller opened the floodgates again. "Let's run with that. Make a list of anyone who traveled between the last week of October and mid-December, for starters, to all the countries with potential events. Then see if you can cross-index any matches with phone records or any other personal data for people affiliated with bio-tech companies or government organizations. If we don't find anything juicy, we can expand the date range of the search."

"I like how you said *we*, Jack, considering that you're going to have your ass on the beach in LA in a few days, watching girls in skimpy bikinis while I do all your dirty work. Which, I might add, I can't legally tell you about after Friday."

"Yeah," Jack replied, a trace of bitterness in his voice, "there's always that."

"Don't worry. I'll figure out some way to let you know what I find without getting our asses thrown in jail. What about potential buyers for that technology here at home?"

"I don't even want to think about that Renee." But her logic was irrefutable. The most logical market the buyer would sell to first was right here in the States. "And there's something you're wrong about."

"Oh, do tell."

"I won't be laying on a beach in LA working on my tan. After I get this mess cleaned up and hook up with Naomi, I'll be on the first flight out to India. If Vijay discovered something, I want to find out what it was. Assuming that he lives long enough to tell about it."

CHAPTER EIGHT

As Mikhailov stood there, staring at the stalks of corn that were clearly ripe for harvest, he was struck with indecision. The last thing he wanted to do was to send his men through it, as their visibility would be reduced to arm's length, even with the flashlights. If anything was hiding in this forest of malevolent-looking stalks, his men wouldn't stand a chance. If he had thought there was the slightest chance that anyone was left alive in this place, anyone human, he would have ordered his men in without a second thought. Going in harm's way was what soldiers did. But he had no intention of mindlessly sending them into a potential slaughter for nothing.

There was something else that puzzled him. "Why is this even here?" He turned to Rudenko. "Why is this corn not all gone like whatever had been planted in the other building?"

"Perhaps it — they? — were sated?"

"I do not believe so. The lab building was devastated. The greenhouse behind us was cleared out. While we have not yet seen inside, we know the animal husbandry building that lies before us suffered damage." He looked around. "But in here, in between, all appears normal. None of these plants have been touched. Why?"

Rudenko shook his head. "Perhaps they had no taste for this kind?"

"Or perhaps they do not care to eat their children." Mikhailov moved closer to the nearest stalk, looking carefully behind it with the aid of the light attached to his shotgun. The eerie shadows cast by the plant sent a shiver up his spine. He turned to Rudenko, whose eyes shone like curved glass in the glare of reflected light. "Move the men along the central walkway here to the other side of the building. Then burn everything to ashes."

With obvious relief, Rudenko turned and quickly relayed Mikhailov's orders. The men of the platoon began to move quickly along the central walkway, keeping their eyes and weapons trained on the corn stalks and whatever might be lurking behind them.

* * *

Ryadavoy Pavel Ivanovich Sleptsev heaved a sigh of relief as he heard the whispered orders for the platoon to move forward into the next building and get out of this accursed place. The corn stalks, standing twice his own height, their shadows dancing in the moving beams of the flashlights, made his skin crawl. A native of Saint Petersburg, a city boy, this was as close as he had ever come to being on a farm. He did not consider himself a coward and would never admit it to anyone but his closest friends, but his stomach was bound in a tight knot of fear. While he had no better explanation, it was clear to his young eyes that whatever happened here had not been a terrorist act.

"Come on." The man next to him, Kamensky, headed toward the central walkway.

Sleptsev turned to follow him.

"*Help me.*"

He stopped at the whispered words, his head whipping around. The voice had come from behind him. From somewhere in the corn.

"Help me, please! I'm hurt." It was a young woman's voice, now barely above a whisper. She was obviously in pain. "I can't move."

"Kamensky!" The other soldier didn't hear, and Sleptsev dared not raise his voice any more or Rudenko would cut his balls off for violating tactical discipline.

Kamensky's silhouette disappeared into the darkness.

Sleptsev was alone.

Turning in the direction of the woman's voice, he pointed the light of his weapon into the corn, careful to keep his finger off the trigger so he didn't accidentally shoot her.

"Listen," he said urgently. "I'm going to get you some help. I'll be right back."

"No, please!" She sobbed. "Don't leave me! Everyone else left me. I've been here all alone. If you leave me, you'll never come back!"

"Yes, I will! I promise. It'll just take a moment."

"Please, just take me with you. I can't stand it here."

He tensed as he heard a rustle of movement. A hand emerged from the corn. An arm, then a face as the woman, barely more than a girl, dragged herself toward him, panting with exertion. Her face was dirty and caked with blood, her blond hair matted. She looked at him, a desperate expression on her face, with one bright blue eye; the other was swollen shut by an ugly blue-black bruise that ran from her forehead to her cheek.

That clinched it. He couldn't just leave her here in the dark. "Okay," he told her, slinging his weapon over his back. "You're going to be fine. Give me your hand, I'll carry you."

A stinger as long as his hand whipped out of the corn and plunged into his upper neck, just above the collar of his uniform.

Eyes wide with shock and surprise, Sleptsev tried to raise his arms to pull the thing out, but couldn't. His arms were useless, paralyzed, as a wave of burning agony swept through him. He collapsed to his knees, then slumped forward, his last breath gurgling out of his ruptured trachea as the scrotum-like base of the stinger continued to pump poison into his body.

The stinger pulled away, and he heard a sickly, wet sucking sound in the darkness above. Someone knelt beside him, and for a moment he dared to hope it was Kamensky. Then he felt his rifle and the RPO-M rocket being unslung from his back, and his clothes quickly being stripped off. The flashlight was again flicked on, and in its reflected glow the last thing he saw was the image of his own face as his body was dragged into the rows of corn.

* * *

"Sleptsev," Rudenko called as the young soldier passed by, the last one of the platoon to file by, "what the devil took you so long?"

"I am sorry, *starshiy serzhant*. I thought I heard something in the corn, but I was imagining things." He paused. More quietly, almost embarrassed, he added, "I do not like this place."

Rudenko grunted agreement. “Come on. Cover me. I have a little job to do.”

Sleptsev nodded, then followed Rudenko into the connector that led to the lab building.

“Watch the corn,” Rudenko ordered. “If anything moves, don’t hesitate. Shoot.”

“Understood.”

Propping his shotgun against the wall so the light reflected from the ceiling, Rudenko pulled out a white phosphorous grenade and some fishing line. He tied the grenade in place against the lowest hinge of one of the double doors. Then he tied the filament to the hinge of the opposite door, and then to the pin of the grenade.

“A little surprise for any of those *svolochi* who might try to run this way,” he muttered to himself. He knew that Mikhailov could have put a squad on this side of the complex to block anything that might come out of the corn fields when they burned, but he didn’t want to split up his men. A squad, not truly knowing what they were up against, might be quickly overwhelmed.

Grabbing his shotgun, he tapped Sleptsev on the shoulder. “Come on, let’s go.”

The two crossed the walkway, making their way toward where Mikhailov had gathered the rest of the platoon.

“Ready, *kapitan*.” Rudenko was secretly happy to be back with the rest of the men. He had felt uncomfortably exposed while he and Sleptsev had been on the far side of the field. Rudenko could swear that there were eyes in the corn, watching them. Waiting. Before Spitsbergen, he would have told himself that he was just being an old woman. Now he told himself that he was just being prudent.

Three men stood on either side of Mikhailov and Rudenko. The rest of the men were in the connector, some guarding the doors to the last building of this nightmare complex, the rest watching for the fireworks about to erupt here and ready to act as a reserve in case of the unexpected.

“White phosphorous grenades.” Mikhailov’s order was followed by the rustling of web gear as the men extracted the special grenades. They normally did not carry so many, but it had been another modification Mikhailov had made to their weapons loadout before the deployment. "Now."

There were seven *pings* as the pins were pulled and the safety handles flew from seven grenades, six from the soldiers and one from Rudenko, as they sailed into the darkness of the greenhouse building.

A few seconds later, Rudenko and the others were rewarded with muffled *whumps* followed by a spectacular fireworks display as the grenades exploded, sending burning fragments of white phosphorous soaring in graceful arcs over the dark corn stalks.

The response was instantaneous. A series of piercing, unearthly shrieks echoed through the building as the fragments of white phosphorous, burning at nearly three thousand degrees Celsius, transformed the corn field into a raging inferno. While the harvesters were extremely tough, with a skeletal structure formed of a natural carbon composite, their Achilles heel was fire. The parts of their bodies that they could morph to make them look human caught fire as easily as kerosene.

"Steady!" Rudenko bellowed to be heard above the din, sensing the fear of the soldiers around him. He tightened his grip on his KS-K shotgun, his right eye glued to the sight.

There was a sudden bloom of light on the far side of the walkway at the entrance to the connector to the lab building as the booby trap Rudenko had set went off. There were more shrieks, and he could see three apparitions, wreathed in the glare of the white phosphorous that covered them, performing a dance of death. He saw two other shadows dart toward the connector, then retreat: the grenade had covered the walls, floor, and ceiling with white hot flame, an impenetrable barrier to creatures whose bodies were inherently flammable.

The shadows disappeared behind the corn on the far side, no doubt trying to make their way to this side through the few patches of stalks not yet ablaze.

"*Contact right!*" Mikhailov's warning was followed by a volley of Dragon's Breath shells from the soldiers on that side who were armed with shotguns, punctuated with the staccato firing of an assault rifle. Someone screamed.

One of the soldiers on Rudenko's side turned to look.

"Watch your sector, you idiot!"

As the man's head snapped back to watch the left side, something leaped at him from the corn.

Rudenko had seen a harvester in its original form once before, on Spitsbergen, but its appearance was still a bone-chilling shock. While he knew that they were totally alien in appearance, his mind was actually expecting them to look human, just as they had on Spitsbergen when they had assumed the form of the *Spetsnaz* soldiers who had murdered most of his company.

The dark shape that lunged at them now wasn't remotely human. It was insectile, the dark skeleton exposed and glistening in the light. Multi-jointed arms with rapier claws at the end reached out for the soldier in the middle, the one whom Rudenko had warned. Parts of the thing were covered in doughy tissue, and there was some sort of pod attached to its thorax, from which a whiplike stinger had emerged to stab the soldier in the eye.

The soldier went down, screaming, as the thing snatched at him.

Rudenko had the impression that it wasn't trying to attack the man so much as get him out of the way so it could escape.

That, however, it would never do. Two shotguns and an assault rifle fired simultaneously at point blank range. Both the beast and the writhing soldier disappeared in a flare of Dragon's Breath and a hail of bullets.

"What was that?" One of the men turned a fearful face toward Rudenko.

"Terrorists!" Rudenko would have laughed at his own lie had the situation been any less serious.

"They have advanced body armor!" Mikhailov added to the lie. It was far more palatable than the truth.

That seemed to calm the men somewhat as the inferno grew in front of them. The heat was becoming too much to bear, but Mikhailov had them hold fast.

Two more shapes burst from the corn down the walkway on Rudenko's side. One of them was a spinning pyre, its form masked by the flames.

The other was that of a young woman. Naked, with claw marks on her flesh, she stumbled toward Rudenko and his men, holding an arm up to her face to ward off the heat and flames.

"Fire!"

For once, the men hesitated.

"Fire, damn you to hell!" Rudenko pulled the trigger on his shotgun, sending a torrent of Dragon's Breath that enveloped the girl.

Her nude body exploded into flame. The flesh oozed and melted, falling in burning gobbets to the walkway. An insectoid head emerged as the face dissolved, the chitinous jaws opening to let loose a shriek.

The two soldiers with Rudenko fired. The girl-thing disappeared behind a wall of fireworks from the Dragon's Breath shells. The screeching stopped, and the twitching corpse fell to the hot concrete, the soft flesh still burning, popping and spattering like grease in a pan.

"Pull back!"

Rudenko felt a hand on his shoulder. Mikhailov.

"Pull back now!"

Grabbing the two soldiers with him, Rudenko pushed them back toward the connector, covering them as they withdrew. His hands and face were blistering from the heat now, and he would not be surprised if he suffered second degree burns.

Before him, the flames from the corn rose all the way to the ceiling of the building, and the place was rapidly filling with thick smoke.

The screeching, at least, had stopped. Any of the things that had been in here were now dead.

Now all that remained was to clear the animal husbandry building and then manage to leave the facility alive.

* * *

Mikhailov led the platoon down the connector to the entrance to the last of the large buildings, where the livestock had been kept.

The connector was filled with smoke, and most of the men, including himself, were coughing.

Taking up position right behind the four soldiers who stood at the doors, Mikhailov ordered, "Go!"

Just as they had before, the men flung the doors open and charged inside, the rest of the platoon moving in right behind them. A pair of men pulled the connector door closed behind them, both to shut out as much of the smoke as they could, and to protect the platoon from being surprised by anything that might have survived the inferno in the building behind them.

Unlike the other buildings, there was some light in this one, shining through the smashed wall panels at the rear. Mikhailov could see animal pens, food and water bins, tools, and a variety of other things as he quickly took in his surroundings.

As the damage on the exterior suggested, this building, too, was a shambles. Everything firmly attached to the walls or sunk into the concrete floor had been dislodged, mangled, or otherwise destroyed. Some of the animal pens, where he assumed cows had been kept, had been knocked over, the metal rails bent outward. He could hardly imagine the panic such placid animals must have experienced to cause them to do such damage.

"Rudenko!"

"Sir!"

"Once we are finished, we will level this place." Mikhailov prodded a crushed metal bucket that, in the beam of his weapon's flashlight, sparkled in the light, as if it had been newly made. "I don't want anything bigger than my thumb to remain intact. Take the men with RPOs and have them stand guard outside until we are finished. I'll contact the helicopter and let them know we're almost ready for extraction."

"Understood, sir." Turning, he bellowed, "Ryzhik! Alexandrov! Lesokhin! Sleptsev! Take up positions outside and cover our asses until we blow this place to hell!"

* * *

Mladshiy Serzhant Isaak Moseevich Ryzhik had never been so relieved as when he stepped out into the sunlight through the hole in the back of the animal husbandry building. He had never seen combat, but had been in enough serious fights in sleazy bars in Moscow to not be easily frightened. But in that accursed building full of corn, he had been terrified. Whatever those things were that had come out of the flames at them, they had not been terrorists. Ryzhik did not consider himself a genius, but he knew that much.

He waved at the Mi-17, which was in the process of setting down about a hundred meters away. The crew chief, who was standing in the open side door, tossed him a salute.

"Over here." He led the three other men to a position about forty meters from the building. "This should be a good spot for the fireworks." He unslung the RPO-M rocket from his back, and the other men followed suit. It was a camouflaged tube about a meter long with a rounded black front cap, a removable trigger grip near the front, and a stepladder sight. Ryzhik flipped up the sight, then set the tube on his right shoulder, holding the trigger grip with his right hand and the foregrip with his left.

Sleptsev imitated what Ryzhik had done, pointing the weapon in the same direction, at the facility.

"Right." Ryzhik set down his rocket. "Now keep your eyes on the building and wait for the captain's orders. Sleptsev! *Sleptsev!*"

Beside him, Sleptsev had smoothly pivoted, pointing the RPO-M behind them before squeezing the trigger.

With a boom and a cloud of smoke, the rocket shot from the tube, the back-blast knocking Ryzhik to the ground. The projectile didn't stream flame or smoke as it flew toward its target, but it was clearly visible as it sailed right through the side passenger door of the Mi-17 and into the rear of the helicopter.

The crew chief had seen it coming and had leaped clear, but that didn't save him. The helicopter vanished in a huge fireball, sending chunks of the still-spinning rotor blades, metal from the fuselage, and other bits and pieces flying to a radius of more than a hundred meters.

Ryzhik had recovered his wits enough to grab his assault rifle. A curse on his lips, he aimed at Sleptsev, who was turning back toward him, and fired.

The bullets slammed into Sleptsev, but they had no effect. Ryzhik's eyes widened as he saw some flying out the other soldier's back.

But there was no blood, no sign of pain on Sleptsev's face as he raised his own weapon and fired a dozen rounds into Ryzhik before turning on the other two men, who were still standing there, staring in shock.

After gunning them down, he tossed his rifle to the ground and retrieved Ryzhik's RPO. Taking a knee, he flipped up the sight and took aim at the hole in the wall of the animal husbandry building through which he had escaped to freedom.

* * *

"*Chyort voz'mi!*" Mikhailov's curse at the sound of gunfire outside was drowned out by the roar of an explosion. The comforting *whump-whump-whump* of the Mi-17's spinning rotors had disappeared. "The helicopter's down!"

There was more gunfire outside.

"*Kapitan!*" Rudenko took him by the shoulder. "If whoever's out there gets the RPOs, we're in trouble."

Mikhailov had a sudden sensation of *déjà vu*, recalling the airport terminal on Spitsbergen as it exploded, destroyed by the harvesters masquerading as *Spetsnaz*, killing most of his men. Behind them was the inferno of the greenhouse building containing the corn. The walls to either side were intact, with no doors to the outside. The ceiling was too high to reach. And beyond the rear wall lay an unknown threat that had destroyed their helicopter, and probably killed the men he had sent out there.

Rudenko reacted first. Pulling Mikhailov along, he shouted at the top of his lungs, "Follow me!"

Dashing toward the right side of the building, which happened to be the closest to where they'd been standing, Rudenko yanked two high explosive grenades from his combat harness. "Grenades to the wall!"

Snapping back to reality, Mikhailov snatched a pair of grenades from his own vest and pulled the pins. Two other men did the same. "Now!" Mikhailov rolled them toward the base of the wall, and the other men followed suit.

They dropped to the ground, and a few seconds later eight grenades went off, blowing a gaping hole to the outside.

"Go, go, go!" Mikhailov was on his feet, shoving the other men toward the breach. He had no idea how much time they had, if they had any at all. "Come on! *Move!*"

He heard a familiar bang outside, and his gaze locked with Rudenko's. Both men had heard it often enough to recognize it as the sound of an RPO being fired.

Mikhailov turned toward the rear wall, his mouth open, screaming for his men to take cover. Then he felt himself being lifted off his feet, Rudenko's bulk propelling him backward. His back slammed into the bottom of a big freestanding livestock watering trough. Flipping it on its side, Rudenko dived in beside him. The sergeant just had time to flip it upside down over the top of them before the building was torn by fire and thunder.

CHAPTER NINE

"I hate the thought of you leaving so soon."

Jack kissed Naomi's hair and ran his fingers along her spine. They'd spent most of the time in bed since he'd arrived from San Antonio. While their original plan had been for him to hop into his SUV and drive out to LA with the two cats, Vijay's untimely accident and the troubling news Renee had uncovered had put him on a much tighter schedule. He had arrived at work that morning, the essentials already packed up in the car, and rushed through the final signing off process that was the end of the short-lived SEAL project. He had brought Alexander and Koshka along, and they waited impatiently in their crates in his office while he performed his final duties as a servant of the people of the United States.

Then he was off to the airport, where he caught a flight to LAX. Naomi had bought two tickets for him in first class, and Jack had talked the flight attendants into letting him board the plane with both cats. Koshka had accepted everything with quiet dignity, staring up at Jack from her spot on the seat beside him, while Alexander had voiced his indignation loudly and repeatedly from his spot on the floor. Jack had felt like the parent of a howling baby until one of the flight attendants had bribed the big cat to silence with a full serving of salmon.

Once in LA, Naomi had met him in a chauffeured car, courtesy of Howard Morgan, and the two of them quickly caught up on recent events as they headed to their new condo. Jack had the brief impression of the walls being made out of money before he turned the cats loose.

Then Naomi led him to the bedroom so they could get caught up on other things, because they didn't have much time. While Jack was in flight from San Antonio, Naomi had booked a flight that evening that would take him from LA to Hyderabad.

"Yeah," he told her, "I don't exactly want to go, either. But we've got to get to the bottom of this, and Vijay may be our only solid lead."

"I still think I should go with you." Naomi brushed a hand across his face, her fingers lingering on the scars left by shrapnel when Jack had been wounded in Afghanistan.

Jack smiled. "We've been over that already, and you lost, fair and square. Listen, your place is here, doing the genius things that only you can do. I know you want to be there for Vijay, but this is a job for a hired gun, as Renee likes to say. Hired guns can be replaced. Brilliant geneticists can't."

She propped herself up on an elbow, fixing him with her blue and brown eyes. "You may be a hired gun, but you're not replaceable, Jack. Not to me." She kissed him softly. "Don't you ever forget that."

"Yes, ma'am."

As he leaned forward to kiss her, the bed suddenly bounced as Alexander's twenty pounds landed near their feet. Like a chaperone who had caught his charges about to do something naughty, he wriggled his way between them and flopped over on his side. Wrapping his forepaws, half the size of Jack's palms, around Naomi's arm, he began to purr.

"You turd." Jack rubbed the big cat's head while Naomi giggled. "I see he missed you, too."

There was another bounce, and Koshka, still bearing the scar of where a harvester had nearly killed her, joined them. Unlike Alexander, she was content to sit near their feet, watching her feline companion's display with obvious disdain.

"I hate to say this, but I wish I could take you with me, you big lug." Jack shifted his scratching to under Alexander's chin, and the big cat's purr grew even deeper. While the scars weren't as obvious as the one Koshka bore, Alexander, too, had been savaged by a harvester. Alexander had saved Jack's life twice, and Jack felt acutely vulnerable any time the big cat wasn't with him. Even though all the harvesters had supposedly been accounted for, there were still only three ways to tell if the person next to you might be one: look at them with a thermal imager, try to set them on fire, or have a cat.

Of the three, Jack trusted feline instinct the most. "But you need to stay here and help Koshka watch over Naomi." He frowned. "Speaking of which, did you happen to ask Morgan about feline security services?"

"Yes, but he wasn't exactly wild about the idea." Naomi sat up so she could reach Koshka, who deigned to accept her human's attention. "Cat hair and clean rooms don't exactly mix, and he just stared at me when I suggested they keep cats at the security checkpoints. But I did get him to agree to let me take them to my office." She shrugged. "He just has no idea of what we've been through. None of them do." She was silent for a moment. "Maybe we're just being paranoid."

"Paranoid's a good thing in my book, at least until we've sorted out what's going on. If it's nothing, fine. I just need to know you're safe."

She leaned over and kissed him. "I can take care of myself, you know."

"I know. That's one of the many things I love about you." He happened to catch sight of the clock. "Crap. I'm going to have to get going."

"Not quite yet." Naomi gently shooed Koshka from the bed, then did the same to Alexander, who gave her a hurt look. "We've still got a little time left."

Then she pulled Jack back into her arms.

* * *

In the thatched hut that was the home of his family near Koratikal, Naveen Reddy shivered with fever. And yet, strangely, he did not feel ill. Not exactly. He felt more like he had smoked *ganja* after a very hard day in the fields. He was placid, lethargic. Tired.

His wife chittered at him, berating him as she always did for being a lazy scoundrel. He looked at her, and smiled to himself. He saw her mouth still moving, but the sound of her voice, an angry buzz that followed him everywhere but to the fields, had faded away to blissful silence. There was no one else in the hut, for their three children had already left for school. Their education was the one thing that he had insisted on, despite his wife's endless objections.

Naveen also noticed, as if he were a separate being within himself, that the aches and pains that never left him were gone. Like his wife's voice, they had faded away into the pleasant numbness that had crept over his body with the onset of the fever.

A glint of white caught his eye. It was the business card the government man had given him, there on the floor next to the mat on which he lay. When the fever had come, he had been tempted to call the man.

But going to Koratikal where there was a phone was a long walk, and he was sure it would be for nothing. Naveen had been sick before, and he would no doubt be sick again. It happened sometimes. It was simply the way of things, and this would be no different. His body would recover, and he would again have to listen to the incessant nattering of his wife.

No, there was no need to call the government man, not that Naveen could have done so now. He was too tired.

Still marveling at the miracle of seeing his wife jabbering but not having to hear her, he closed his eyes and fell into a sleep filled with strange dreams.

* * *

Jack looked out the window of the car, feeling a keen sense of disorientation at the British convention of the driver being on the right and the passenger on the left. Behind the wheel was Surya Chidambaram, another of Vijay's cousins who had insisted on picking Jack up from Rajiv Gandhi International Airport and taking care of him while he was in India. Surya's black Mahindra Scorpio SUV sped down Pathergatti Road toward the hospital where Vijay remained in critical condition.

"Are you sure you don't want to get some rest first?" Surya was a handsome man, about five years younger than Jack. He had studied engineering at Caltech, and had been extremely successful at one of the many high technology companies that called Hyderabad home.

Jack had taken a liking to him instantly.

"I'd love to, but I've got to talk to Vijay as soon as possible. I just hope I can get something intelligible out of him." Jack felt like he'd been run over by a bus in forward and reverse after the grueling trip halfway across the world, but he knew the clock was ticking. As exhausted as he was, he couldn't delay talking to Vijay.

Surya glanced at him. "I hope you won't be disappointed. I saw him yesterday, but he wasn't very lucid. He's still in terrible shape."

"Yeah." Jack felt a sense of grim foreboding settle over him as they drove on in silence.

At the hospital, they were taken to the intensive care unit. Unable to help himself, Jack stopped in his tracks as he entered Vijay's room. The only part of the man's body not wrapped in bandages or a cast was his face, which bore several sets of stitches and was horribly bruised. His bed was surrounded by equipment that beeped, hissed, and whirred in a mechanical rhythm.

"Just a few minutes." Vijay's attending physician had been reluctant to admit Jack at first, but Surya had managed to persuade him.

"We won't be long," Jack promised, wondering if Vijay would even be able to respond to any questions.

With a curt nod, the doctor left the room and closed the door.

Approaching the bed, Jack looked down at "the worm guy's" battered face. "Vijay, can you hear me?"

Surprisingly, Vijay's eyelids fluttered open instantly. It took his eyes a moment to focus. "Jack." He paused, his eyes shifting in small jerks to Surya, who nodded gravely. Then he looked back at Jack and whispered, "I was hoping Naomi would come. She's much better looking than you."

"She would have, big guy, but I drew the short straw to come check on your sorry ass." Jack grinned. Then, the grin fading, he asked, "Can you tell us who did this to you?"

Vijay twitched his head from side to side. "Not important now. Jack, I think seed from The Bag may have been planted by AnGrow near Koratikal." Speaking in halting phrases, Vijay told them exactly where the plot was located.

"I know of that place, cousin."

Looking back to Jack, Vijay whispered, "Some maize was given to the locals. They may be infected."

"Good God." At Surya's confused look, Jack said, "I'll tell you later."

"That is not all," Vijay whispered urgently. "More of the maize was taken by AnGrow. I don't know where. It was planted without authorization, but someone there must have record of it."

"We'll find it," Jack reassured him, knowing that it was an empty promise. Tracking it down at home in the States would have been difficult enough. Here, as a stranger in a foreign land, it would be almost impossible. The only shot they might have at finding anything would be Renee, assuming she could hack into AnGrow's network, and assuming anyone handling the deadly seed from The Bag had left an electronic trail behind.

Vijay suddenly grimaced, and the beeping from his pulse monitor became more rapid.

"You've got to rest," Jack said. "We'll take care of this."

"Wait," Vijay gasped. "Surya, call your brother. You and Jack must not go to Koratikal alone, unarmed."

Surya wagged his head from side to side. "I'll call him, but what do I tell him?"

Vijay did not answer. His eyes glazed over just before his eyes closed.

Jack darted a glance at his vital signs, fearing that the stress might have killed him. But his heart continued to beat, its pace slowing now as Vijay faded into unconsciousness.

"Christ." Turning to Surya, Jack said, "Come on. We've got to get out to this Koratikal place." As they left the room, he added, "Why did Vijay want you to call your brother? Who is he?"

"He's a captain in the National Security Guard, the Black Cats."

"Black Cats?" Jack asked, never having heard of them before.

"They're our equivalent of your Delta Force, I think. His unit specializes in counter-terrorist operations."

Jack whistled. "That's a bit of good luck." He glanced over at Surya, who had a troubled expression on his face. "Why so glum?"

"My brother hates me."

* * *

"Naveen. *Naveen!*" Preethi Reddy hissed like a cobra as she stomped into the hut, the only home her miserable good for nothing husband could provide. Unlike many, who were content to accept their karma, Preethi cursed it every day as she asked the gods why she had been saddled with such a lazy fool.

While it was clear that he had caught some sort of fever, she was sure he was only using it as an excuse to get out of a day's work, casting them another handful of rupees further into the depths of poverty. She deserved better.

There he was, still asleep. But if he thought he was going to have an undisturbed rest, he was badly mistaken.

"Naveen, stop faking and get to work. Did you hear me? I will not have you set such a poor example for the boys when they come home from that silly school."

Her mouth snapped shut as she saw his hands. His fingers were deformed, as if they had melted together.

And his chest wasn't moving. He had stopped breathing.

"Naveen?" She knelt next to him, suddenly terrified. As much of a lazy charlatan as he might be, she did not relish the thought of becoming a widow, living as an outcast to her family and village. "Husband?"

She reached out to touch a large spot on his chest that resembled a vicious bruise. The tips of her fingers slipped into his flesh. Except that it was no longer flesh, but something else.

With a scream of horror, she pulled her hand back. Her scream grew louder as she saw that Naveen's flesh was still connected to her fingers, stretching out like soft putty between them before it parted.

Then she felt the pain, a fierce burning sensation that began in her fingertips where globs of Naveen still clung to her. Even as she watched, her mouth still open in a shriek of terror, the mottled, bruised tissue of her husband began to quickly cover her fingers, then her hand.

She ran outside, shaking her hand in desperation, trying in vain to cast away the final evil that her husband had visited upon her.

Hearing the screams, the others who lived in the village emerged to see what was the matter. Preethi grabbed a man who came forward to help her, and some of her husband's flesh stuck to his skin. In a matter of seconds, he, too, began to scream as the fiery pain took hold.

As the village erupted in panic outside the hut, what had once been Naveen Reddy began to move.

* * *

Despite his misgivings, Surya had called his brother as soon as he and Jack had left the ICU. While Jack had stepped away to give him some privacy, he couldn't help but notice that the conversation had been a heated one. Surya had quietly but passionately argued with his brother for more than five minutes.

With a deep sigh, he hung up and pocketed his phone. "He's on his way," Surya told him, as if he had just received a death sentence, "but he won't be able to get here until this afternoon. He has to take a plane here from Delhi."

"Are we going to pick him up?"

Surya laughed. It was a bitter sound. "No. The only way my brother would ride in my car would be if he were dead. He'll be picking us up here."

"Damn." Jack followed Surya into one of the waiting rooms and took a seat beside him. He hated the idea of waiting, but there was no sense in just he and Surya going to the village. They had neither weapons, nor authority. Surya's brother, however, would at least be able to report back to his superiors if the village had been compromised. Assuming the three of them survived the encounter.

But if they were going to do this, they had to do it as a team, and it didn't sound like Surya and his brother were exactly on the same side.

"So what happened between you two?"

Surya was silent for a moment, staring at the floor. He said, "It's because of our younger sister, Pravalika. Both Kiran and I loved her very much, but he was closer to her than I was. They were born only a year apart, five years after me. They treated me more like an uncle than a brother." His lips curled into a wistful smile that rapidly faded. "Eight years ago, I was driving her to visit a friend and I made a mistake. A terrible mistake. There was an accident, and Pravalika was killed." He looked at Jack, his eyes filled with pain. "My parents eventually found it in their hearts to forgive me, but Kiran never could. Not that I deserve it. And since that day he has hated me with every fiber of his being."

"God, I'm sorry." Jack was no stranger to death in its many terrible forms, but that would have been a terrible burden of guilt to bear. "But Surya, if he hates you so much, why did he agree to come?"

"Because I told him that Vijay said he had to." He looked at Jack with wounded eyes. "He would have never come if I had asked him. But Vijay, even though we are his cousins, he has been more like a favorite uncle to us. To both of us. He helped me get into university and find the job I now hold, and helped convince our father to give his blessing for Kiran to join the Army." He managed a wan smile. "Vijay was the only one in our family who believed that Kiran could do it, and stood up for him against my parents. That, let me tell you, is no easy thing to do. And he was right. Kiran was born to be a soldier."

"It'll be good to have someone like that, but I wish he would've brought a company of his Black Cats with him."

Surya looked him in the eye. "Jack, you still have not explained why you and Vijay want him here. Why have we called in a counter-terrorist expert, rather than someone from the Ministry of Health?"

"If the people in that village have been infected as I suspect, your health ministry won't be able to help them."

* * *

"They've been infected by genetically engineered maize? That's preposterous." Despite the warm afternoon, the emotional temperature in the Indian Army Mahindra Jeep driven by Surya's brother, Captain Kiran Chidambaram, had fallen well below freezing as they headed east out of Hyderabad toward Koratikal. "And even if it's true, why would Vijay have wanted me to come? He must have been out of his mind."

Like his brother, Surya, Kiran was a handsome young man, in excellent physical condition. He also had the look in his eye of a warrior who had braved the crucible of combat. Jack knew the type. He was one himself.

"He wasn't crazy," Jack said from where he sat in the passenger seat. Surya sat in the back, not having spoken a word since Kiran picked them up at the hospital. "Trust me."

"Trust you?" Kiran stared at Jack, his dark eyes blazing. "Why should I?"

"Because I worked with Vijay before he came home to India, and I've seen the effects of the infection he's talking about with my own eyes. You don't want to let this particular genie out of the bottle. It doesn't just make people ill. It can make them..." Jack struggled to find an appropriate word. "It makes them very violent. Let's leave it at that."

Behind them, the sun was beginning to set, and the land around him was cast in a golden glow that would soon turn to darkness. Jack began to question the wisdom of coming out here this late. Facing harvesters under any conditions was dangerous. Doing it at night and unarmed, and possibly facing more than one, was suicidal. But he hadn't felt there was any other choice. He had to know, and if there truly was a harvester infestation here, the authorities had to be alerted in time to contain it. If that was even possible.

Kiran returned his attention to the road. "Fools. And I am a bigger fool."

They drove on in silence, following the route Vijay had given them to the field where he and Naresh had gone. Surya guided Kiran, who didn't bother responding, but simply drove like an angry automaton.

"Here," Surya suddenly said. "I think this is it."

Jamming on the brakes, Kiran brought the jeep to a skidding halt, the tires sending up a flare of dry dust around them. He switched off the ignition and sat there, staring straight ahead.

Ignoring him, Jack got out, with Surya right behind him. The sun had faded below the horizon in the west, leaving the world in twilight.

Looking down near his feet, Jack saw a small placard that had been kicked over. Leaning down, he turned it over to see the AnGrow logo on the other side. "It looks like this is the place."

There was a slight breeze, just enough to rustle the stalks of maize in the unharvested fields nearby.

Then he heard something else that made his blood freeze. It was the faint but unmistakable sound of someone screaming.

He turned to Surya. "Do you hear that?"

"Yes." He pointed. "I think it's coming from over that way. There's a small village there."

"Damn."

Kiran got out and came to stand next to him. "I hear it, too. What the devil is going on?"

"Let's go find out." Jack gestured for Surya to get back in the jeep, and he piled in behind him while Kiran hopped back into the driver's seat. Starting the engine, he put the vehicle in gear and headed down the road toward where the screaming was coming from. His face bore a grim, worried expression.

"What are we getting into?" The anger had leeched out of Kiran's voice. He spoke those words with the tense calm of an experienced soldier.

Shaking his head, Jack told him the truth. "I'm not sure, Kiran. And believe me, I hope to God that I'm wrong about all this. But..."

The rest of his words were stolen by the sight of a child, a girl maybe twelve or thirteen years old, who suddenly appeared in the beam of the headlights, stumbling toward them. Her eyes were wide, glazed over, as if she were in a trance.

Kiran stomped on the brakes, bringing the jeep to a skidding halt. He leaped out and ran toward the girl.

"*Stop!*"

Jack's bellowed warning gave Kiran pause.

"She could be infected. Let me take a look first. Stand back."

The girl had stopped, but she didn't look up at them. She stared at the constellation of dust motes reflected in the jeep's headlights, and Jack could hear her moaning softly. Somewhere behind her, farther down the dark road, he could hear more screams.

Reaching into his pocket, Jack withdrew a disposable plastic cigarette lighter. Trying to ignore the terrified screams, he approached the girl with slow, measured steps as the other two men watched in shocked silence.

Holding up the lighter toward the girl, he flicked the igniter. An inch-tall tongue of flame appeared, flickering slightly as Jack continued to move toward the girl.

Her eyes, moving in a jerky, spasmodic fashion, turned toward the flame.

Only a pace away now, Jack leaned forward, extending the lighter toward the girl's shoulder closest to him.

"Jack, what are you doing?" Kiran stepped forward.

"Don't move!"

Kiran stopped, and Jack could sense the outrage in him as the flame of the lighter brushed the girl's skin.

She flinched, and her eyes blinked. Other than that, she made no reaction.

With an enormous sense of relief, Jack let the lighter's flame die. Naomi had told him that the harvesters had an instinctive reaction to open flame. Even the intact malleable tissue, the parts of their bodies that allowed them to take the shape of other creatures, of harvester corpses reacted. Without a cat or thermal imager, it was the only other way to test someone to make sure they were really human without taking a tissue sample or trying to draw blood that they didn't have.

"Surya, get her in the jeep. See if you can get her to tell you what happened." Jack doubted the girl would talk, as she was clearly in deep shock. But they had to try.

Without a word, Surya gently guided the girl to the jeep, helping her into the back seat.

To their left, they heard someone or something moving quickly through the maize toward them. Jack was about to shout for Kiran to get back into the jeep when an ear-piercing shriek of agony, unmistakably human, came from whomever it was.

The agonized scream suddenly stopped. Or was cut off.

Kiran was standing right beside him now, staring into the darkness beyond the reach of the jeep's headlights. "What the devil is happening? Bloody hell, I wish I had my sidearm."

"It wouldn't do you any good." Jack was momentarily stymied by indecision. The smart thing would have been to turn and run. Right now. He knew what must be happening here. But Kiran and Surya had to witness the terror for themselves, or they would never believe it. Right now, they could write off what they'd heard as being a lunatic or terrorists, and no one would ever believe what the girl might say, assuming she ever recovered. "Can you call in your unit?"

"As much as I would like to, what would I tell my commander? All I know for certain is that people are screaming, but I don't know why. I haven't even heard any gunshots." He shook his head. "He would tell me this is a matter for the local police, not the NSG, and he would be right. But you don't want to call the police, do you?"

Jack shook his head. "No. They wouldn't be any better off than the civilians. We need military grade hardware and men who know how to use it."

"And you still refuse to tell me exactly what we're facing?"

"Kiran, this isn't something I can tell you in words beyond what I've already said, because you won't believe it. You can't. You'd think it was a cruel joke or that I was simply insane. Please trust me on this. I learned that lesson the hard way. You can only believe if you see it. And even then...even then you'll want to deny what you've seen."

Another piercing cry erupted from the maize, closer now. Both men flinched, their eyes reflexively darting in the direction of the sound.

"Shit," Jack cursed. "Come on. We've got to get closer to the village."

He turned and trotted back to the jeep.

With a last look into the scream-filled darkness that lay before them, Kiran, his mouth set in a grim line, followed.

Starting up the jeep again, he drove them forward into the unknown.

"Yes, Naomi." Harmony smiled. "As I'm sure you read in the documentation, we'd been working on developing a similar system to what you'd done at New Horizons, creating a mechanism to deliver genetic payloads through food. Our first host plant was a commercial wheat strain, rather than corn, but the underlying principle was the same." Her smile turned to a frown, which seemed to drag down her entire, thin frame. "We could engineer the payload delivery shell in the mature plant and its seed, but the system wasn't stable. The shells consistently collapsed, compromising the payloads."

"We beat our heads against the wall on that one for a long time," Randall Wyckoff, Lab One's second in command, for lack of a better term, growled. "We couldn't maintain the shell integrity, no matter what we tried, until Dr. Kelso showed us..." He stopped, and shot an uncomfortable glance at Harmony.

"Tell her everything."

They turned to see Morgan standing at the rear of the lab, as if he'd appeared out of thin air. No one had heard the vault door open.

Harmony bent forward and whispered to Naomi, "I have yet to figure out how he does that!"

"It's magic, my dear. Merely magic." Morgan smiled as he strode toward where the others had gathered in a semicircle around Naomi. Taking a seat, he gestured for Harmony to continue. "Naomi's fully cleared for this project. If she's going to help us, she has to know everything." His eyes swept the room before settling on Naomi. "Hold nothing back."

"Yes, sir." Harmony bobbed her head, then took up where Wyckoff had left off. "A year ago, Dr. Kelso brought us samples of what we call Beta-Three." She flicked a quick look at Morgan, who nodded. "From what we know from the press and the articles that you and Dr. Kempf published on the topic, we believe they're samples of the *Revolutions* seed you were working on at New Horizons. Which generation, of course, we have no way of knowing. But that's how we made our breakthrough last year. Naomi?"

Naomi was staring at Harmony. Naomi's hands were gripping the arms of the chair so hard her knuckles were bled pure white, and her heart was hammering in her chest. She knew that it would have been impossible for them to have obtained a sample of the corn from the New Horizons lab at Lincoln Research University. While that lab's outward appearance was less imposing than Lab One, the security had been nearly impenetrable.

That left only one real possibility for the source of the Beta-Three samples. The Bag.

Morgan stood up and stepped toward her. "Naomi, are you all right?"

Suppressing her sense of horror, she focused a frigid gaze on Morgan. "Let me get this straight. You have samples of the New Horizons corn seed, the *Revolutions* variant?" She glanced at Harmony. "Don't tell me it was a pre-production sample, because that would be pure and utter horse shit."

Everyone else in the room shrank back, giving the clear appearance that they wished they were anywhere but trapped in the vault for what was shaping up to be a battle of the Titans.

Morgan made no attempt to dodge her question or throw up a smokescreen. "Yes, we do have samples of *Revolutions*." He returned to his seat and held her eyes. "Naomi, while I have some lofty humanitarian ambitions at this point in my life, I'm also an opportunist. In this industry, with such high stakes, anyone who doesn't take advantage of every possible opportunity is left behind and eventually crushed or absorbed. Part of my staff is devoted to keeping tabs on what our competitors are doing and, if the opportunity arises, finding ways to leverage their gains for our own purposes."

"Industrial espionage, you mean."

Morgan shrugged, but the gesture was unapologetic. "Call it what you like. But in this case it wasn't so Machiavellian." He looked over at Harmony. "Why don't you all take a coffee break for a bit?"

Harmony nodded, then quickly led the others, all of whom had unmistakable looks of relief on their faces, out of the room.

Waiting until the vault door cycled shut behind them, Morgan continued. "What I'm about to tell you must be held in strict confidence, Naomi. Only three people in my company, including myself, know this. I'm telling you because you need to know everything, but I'd appreciate it if you would keep this to yourself."

"All right." In truth, the only thing preventing Naomi from running from the vault and leaving Morgan's employ was the burning desire to find out what had happened to The Bag. She, Jack, and the others who had worked at SEAL had been fruitlessly searching for a year for any sign of what had happened to it. And now she had finally found at least one piece to the puzzle. Regardless of her other feelings, she had to find out the story behind it. What she did afterward largely depended on Morgan's next words. "Go on."

"About a month before the New Horizons facility where the *Revolutions* seed was produced was destroyed, we were approached by a New Horizons employee who claimed to have access to it. He didn't have access to the technical data, but could provide specimens of the final product. In exchange for a king's ransom, he did."

"How many samples did he provide?"

Morgan tilted his head to one side. "Precisely two thousand four hundred and thirty-eight *Revolutions* seeds."

Naomi blanched. "Is that all? Only a pound's worth?" The Bag had held a hundred pounds of seed, every one of which was a potential weapon of mass destruction. If Morgan only had one pound, that meant that ninety-nine more pounds of seed were out there in the world, being handed out by a dealer to totally unsuspecting buyers. The strange incidents Renee had reported in Brazil, China, and Russia snapped into horrible focus. On top of that was Vijay's mysterious call.

A wave of cold foreboding swept over her, and she wanted nothing more than to snatch up her phone and call Jack to make sure he was all right. *I'll call him*, she promised herself, *as soon as we're finished here.*

Misinterpreting Naomi's reaction, Morgan smiled. "Only a pound? My dear, I paid more for that pound of grain than I would have for the same weight in fine diamonds. Our contact drove a very hard bargain, and is probably on the beaches of Tahiti right now, sipping a tropical drink."

"Please, Howard," she whispered. "Please tell me that you haven't planted any, and that none has been fed to anyone or anything."

"No, I assure you that we've kept it under very strict control. While I'm not aware of the specific nature of the dangers they may pose, I took the government's gloom and doom story about them being weapons of mass destruction quite seriously. Most of the specimens have been kept in cold nitrogen storage. We've actually used only fifteen for research, and Dr. Kelso is the only individual who has direct access to the specimens." He paused and looked at her significantly. "Aside from you, that is."

Looking into Morgan's eyes, Naomi decided he was probably telling the truth. He certainly hadn't responded to her concerns with smoke and mirrors. For that, she felt a profound sense of relief. She needed to be able to trust him.

"Howard, I know you're not going to like this, but I've got to know who your contact was and get the FBI on his trail. I have reason to believe that he's been selling samples to buyers in other countries, and we've got to find out who has them and stop him from selling any more."

At that, Morgan slowly shook his head. "Naomi, what I've told you about the Beta-Three samples was in confidence and must never leave this room. If you ever mention a word of this to anyone, I'll deny it, along with firing you, of course, and probably filing charges of slander. While you might think I deserve it, I don't really fancy finding myself in federal prison."

"That's not what I think at all. But you don't understand what could — what will — happen if this seed gets out of a strictly controlled lab environment. The government wasn't exaggerating when they said the *Revolutions* seed was a weapon of mass destruction." Her brown and blue eyes bore into him. "Please, Howard. If you want to do humanity a true service, help us find the rest of this seed. Before it's too late."

Morgan sat back and crossed his arms, a speculative expression on his face. "I'll consider it. But that consideration will only be given on two conditions. First, that you tell me exactly what this seed really does. And second, that you give me your word that you'll help me do what I hired you to do, and take this abomination, whatever it is, and try to create something good out of it."

Considering his offer only for a moment, Naomi said, "Agreed, but you won't believe what I'm about to tell you."

Morgan's mouth curled up into a smile. "Try me."

With worried thoughts of Jack circling in her mind, Naomi began to tell him about the harvesters.

* * *

"Son of a bitch." Renee glared in turn at each of the three computer screens arrayed in front of her in her cubicle at the J. Edgar Hoover Building, the headquarters of the FBI, in Washington, D.C. Each displayed half a dozen web browsers, specialized analysis applications, and FIDS, the FBI Intelligence Information Report Dissemination System. None of the information shown in any of the windows pertained to what she was supposed to be doing. She knew she could get in hot water for it and, worse, get Carl in trouble. But once she was on the trail of something, she couldn't let go.

She'd been working on the angle that Jack had suggested, trying to ferret out individuals who had traveled to Brazil, China, India, and Russia within a few weeks of the election the previous November. That search, which had involved cross-indexing records from half a dozen intelligence agency databases and passport lists from the State Department, had yielded one thousand, three hundred and fifteen names.

Then she began the hard work, ferreting out information on who these people were and their employment background, looking for any potential ties to New Horizons. For some people on her list, that information was easy to find. For others, it took hours of digging.

Now, with red-rimmed eyes, she stared at the final result: zero matches, even after expanding the date search to a full sixty days around the election.

Quietly muttering a string of obscenities, she retraced her steps to make sure she didn't miss anything. She knew that whoever was selling seeds from The Bag could have stayed in the U.S., with buyers coming to him or her. But somehow she doubted it. If someone was peddling something that had been designated by the government as a weapon of mass destruction, he (Renee always thought of bad people as "he" until proven otherwise) wasn't just going to invite people he didn't know into his living room to chat about the deal. He was going to feel more comfortable meeting somewhere overseas, most likely in the country that was home to the potential buyer where he'd be safe (or so he hoped) from any prying U.S. Government eyes.

That supported the initial hypothesis that Jack had come up with, but something was obviously missing.

She glanced at the State Department passport database again. Upon reflection, the peddler would have been an idiot to be traveling under their real identity. And he could certainly be using multiple passports, which would make even more sense for someone trying to fly under the radar, so to speak.

It wouldn't have been easy to pull off a stunt like that, but if her bad guy had managed to put together a portfolio of fake passports, using each one to travel to one or two countries with potential buyers, he wouldn't have shown up in her initial search at all, nor would any of his aliases have shown up in the relational search she'd run against people who'd worked for New Horizons.

Of course, if he were traveling under one or more aliases, there was nothing to say that he couldn't be using non-U.S. passports, as well.

Calling up the passport database again, she ran searches against all travelers to each of the countries from September through December of last year, saving off the results, including the passport photos.

Then she ran another search of foreign travelers to the U.S. during the same time period from those countries, and saved off the data.

Digging through her personal collection of programs and files, she hammered together a routine that would compare the images in the huge pile of results that she had saved off and present her with any likely matches. She knew it would likely generate a lot of junk results, and wouldn't find her bad guy if he had made any real effort to disguise himself for his passport photos. But it was the only way she stood a chance of finding him in the hundreds of thousands of records she'd saved.

"Well, this ought to bring the network to a crawl."

With a tired grin, she clicked the button and the program began to run.

CHAPTER ELEVEN

As the jeep rolled forward toward the darkened village, Jack had to use every ounce of willpower not to beg Kiran to turn them around and get the hell away. The headlights swept across the rutted dirt road, and twice Jack saw large pools of a dark, viscous liquid. He shuddered at the sight, knowing that he was seeing all that was left of one or more human beings.

In the seat behind him, the girl had begun to moan. Surya had his arm draped protectively around her shoulders, holding her shivering body close. Like the jeep's headlights, her eyes were fixed straight ahead, unwavering, unblinking.

On the right, barely illuminated by the edge of the beam cast by the headlights, the maize stalks shook as if something large had just passed by.

"What the devil was that?" Kiran glanced at Jack, then snapped his eyes back to where the maize had been disturbed, now only a few feet from his window.

The girl's moans grew louder.

As the outlines of the village huts emerged from the darkness, a figure stepped from the maize to stand in the middle of the road. It was a woman, one of the villagers. She stared at the jeep with an unblinking gaze.

Kiran brought the jeep to a stop a dozen meters from her. "Another survivor."

"Don't be so sure." Jack leaned forward, his body tense as a coiled spring. He had expected the harvester — *harvesters*, he corrected himself — to attack. He'd never believed they'd make it even this far.

"Wait, no!" Surya's cry from the back seat was punctuated by the sound of one of the jeep's rear doors being flung open.

Jack saw the girl dash past him, running for the woman who still stood in the road, staring at them. "Shit! Stop her!"

As he and Kiran got out, Surya was already running past them in pursuit of the girl. He managed to grab her just before she reached the woman. The girl began to scream and kick at him, her arms held out toward the woman, who was now watching them with an expression that was utterly, terrifyingly empty.

"Surya, get back!" Jack watched in slow motion, his gut churning with horror, as the woman's chest *changed*. Her right breast seemed to bulge outward, distending the fabric of her sari. In a blur of motion, a stinger the length of Jack's hand shot out. It struck Surya in the chest, just above his heart, and missed the girl's face by only a few centimeters.

"No!" Kiran screamed as he reached his brother. He took Surya's free hand, as Surya was still clinging to the girl with the other. Kiran tried to drag them back toward the jeep, but the stinger remained firmly stuck in Surya's chest, and the woman, the *thing*, refused to let go. Between them, the umbilical of the stinger, which looked like a snake that had been turned inside out, thrashed like the tentacle of a squid.

Jack knew they only had one chance of survival, and it was perilously thin. Grabbing up a handful of the dry maize husks from the edge of the road, he held his lighter beneath them and flicked the igniter. The flame immediately caught. Holding the tip of the flame to the husks, he watched in growing frustration as the husks blackened and tiny fragments glowed, but it refused to catch fire. "Come on, damn you. Come on!"

He looked up as he heard a wet ripping sound, and Surya shrieked in agony. Kiran had pulled the stinger, which Jack saw had barbs to which bits of Surya's flesh still clung, clear of his brother. The two men collapsed to the ground, the stinger dancing over them with obvious menace, venom dripping from its tip. The girl lay beside them, completely still, her eyes closed.

The woman, the harvester, began to move closer to its prey, and Jack now heard something moving in the maize on both sides of the road.

They were out of time. And still the damned-to-hell maize husks refused to catch fire. The lighter was so hot now it was burning Jack's thumb as he pressed down the button to keep the flame going.

"Kiran! Get up! Get them in the jeep!"

Galvanized by Jack's voice, Kiran, who had been staring at the abomination now advancing toward him, got to his feet and bent over to pick up his brother.

"No," Surya told him, his face twisted in agony. He pushed Kiran's hands away. "The girl. The girl!"

"Bloody hell," Kiran hissed as he obeyed his older brother. Reaching down, he swept the girl into his arms and dashed back to the jeep.

* * *

Surya faced the thing that was now nearly on top of him. The stinger had been pulled back into the creature's thorax, the wet umbilical disappearing into the flesh. Only the tip of the stinger protruded from the torn fabric of the sari where the right breast should be, glistening in the jeep's headlights like a serpent's tooth.

But something else was emerging from the thing's chest now, resembling a skinning knife as long as Surya's forearm. He whimpered in fright and pain and tried to push himself away from the thing with his feet. He could no longer move his arms, for they were completely paralyzed. And behind the wave of paralysis followed a burning agony as he had never before known.

He was vaguely aware of Kiran taking the girl to the jeep, and he hoped that they and Jack would reach safety.

As he watched his death approach, the thought of the girl comforted him. She reminded him so much of Pravalika, his young sister, and the moment of her death as their car slammed into an oncoming car flashed through his mind. To die now was his karma, he realized. And, perhaps, his sacrifice in trying to save this poor village girl would help ease his soul's rebirth into the next life.

Despite the agony burning in his flesh, a great sense of relief washed over him. He closed his eyes, an image of Pravalika, laughing and smiling, fixed in his mind as the blade stabbed into his abdomen.

* * *

Jack watched as Kiran shoved the unconscious girl into the back of the jeep. That's when the maize husks decided to explode into flame.

With a gasp of pain, Jack dropped the lighter and ran toward the harvester that now stood over Surya. Vijay's young cousin screamed as the creature's organic carving knife sawed into his guts.

The thing snapped its head up and it crouched to spring away from Jack, but didn't get the chance. Kiran swung the utility axe he had grabbed out of the jeep, lodging the blade into the thing's malformed chest

Jack threw the wildly burning handful of maize husks at the harvester, then turned and dove to the ground. Remembering that Kiran wouldn't know what would happen, he screamed, "*Get down!*"

Behind him, the first burning bits of maize husk touched the creature's malleable flesh. In the next instant the harvester was burning as if it were coated in rocket fuel. With an unholy shriek, it yanked the blade from Surya and staggered in circles as the fire quickly consumed it, the flames lighting up the area for dozens of meters in every direction.

Jack looked up. Near the huts in the village, he caught sight of several people on the ground, some still, others thrashing around. Two of them raised their arms toward him, screaming in desperation for him to help them. Their voices tore at his heart: there was absolutely nothing he could do to save them.

Over the crackle and screeching of the burning harvester, Jack heard yet more noises coming from the maize around them. Some sounded as if they were receding, perhaps other harvesters running away from the flames.

But some were coming closer.

Getting to his feet, he ran to help Kiran, whose uniform was scorched and smoking. Together, they lifted Surya from the ground before they began a stumbling run for the jeep, carrying Surya between them.

Jack thought they might just make it when Surya screamed and his body was yanked right out of their grip.

Whirling around, Jack and Kiran stared in uncomprehending horror. Surya was being dragged backward across the ground. He was in the grip of an amorphous mass, like a gigantic amoeba whose bruise-colored, mottled surface glistened in the headlights. Part of it, a pseudopod, was attached to Surya's lower back. As Jack watched, he could see the coloration of the thing change along the boundary where it held its victim, the blue-black-yellow flesh taking on a decidedly crimson color. Blood, Jack realized with sick certainty. He also caught glimpses of something yellow-white through the thing's translucent flesh, and it took him a moment to realize that he was seeing the bones of Surya's spine.

Stepping forward, Kiran reached for his brother, but Jack held him back. There were tears in Kiran's eyes.

"Surya! *Surya!*"

Surya's eyes were open, bulging, his gaze fixed on his younger brother. Surya took in a gulp of air and began to scream, but it died in his throat, replaced by a wet gurgle as the thing that held him in its grip ate into his lungs.

"I forgive you," Kiran whispered as Jack grabbed the back of his uniform and dragged him away toward the Jeep. "I forgive you."

There was a spark of understanding in Surya's eyes just before they glazed over as death took him.

Shoving Kiran into the passenger seat, Jack ran to the driver's side and got in. Starting up the jeep, he threw it in reverse and jammed his foot down on the accelerator. He turned around in his seat so he could see out the small rear window, guiding the jeep in an undulating path away from the village. The road was just barely visible in the glow cast by the reverse lights, not really enough to drive by, but he didn't care.

He caught a glimpse of something black and angular in the rear lights. There was a wet crunch and a violent bump as the wheels ran over something. Jack winced, but kept the accelerator pressed to the floor. He wasn't going to stop now for anything. Nor was he about to look back toward the village.

If he did, he might again see the other wet shapes that he had glimpsed oozing out of the maize to join the one that had killed Surya.

* * *

After nearly flipping over when he tried to negotiate a sharp turn in the road, Jack stopped the jeep. He guessed they had gone at least two kilometers from the village, maybe three, and thought they might be safe here for a few minutes, if anywhere could be called safe anymore. He kept his hands on the steering wheel, gripping it tightly as the shakes hit him. His stomach was a sour, twisted ball in his gut.

Beside him, Kiran had been completely silent, his eyes staring straight ahead, as if focused on an invisible point on the windshield. He held his fists clenched tightly in his lap. In the back seat, the girl remained unconscious.

"Kiran." Jack reached over and touched the younger man's shoulder.

Flinching away as if Jack had slapped him, Kiran slowly turned his eyes, the whites around the dark irises glowing in the light from the jeep's instrument panel, to stare at Jack. "Surya." Kiran licked his lips. "We must go back. I cannot leave him there."

"He's gone, Kiran. You can't help him now. I'm sorry."

Kiran's eyes misted over, and his face twisted into a snarl. "What were those things, Jack? What the *devil* were they?"

"We call them harvesters. We don't know where they came from originally, but as you saw, they're not human. But they can perfectly mimic humans. That's what makes them truly dangerous. They've been with us, with humans, for a long time, and infiltrated key industries, the military, and even some governments, including ours. We killed all of them last year, all the living ones we knew about, at least, and stopped their plan to infect humans on a mass scale with a genetic weapon, something that would literally transform us into them." He leaned his head back and closed his eyes for a moment. "The weapon was delivered through corn, although they were working on other crop delivery systems, too. But we were able to destroy it all. All except for one goddamn bag that someone made off with. We've been trying to track it down ever since." Opening his eyes, he turned to face Kiran. "That's why Vijay called us, called you, and wanted us to come here. This company, AnGrow, must have gotten some seeds and planted them. The villagers ate the corn, and then...well, you saw what happened to them."

"It's impossible."

Jack's eyes narrowed. "Tell that to Surya. You saw it. Accept what you saw. I know it's hard, but those things are real. And we've got to stop them from spreading." He reached in his pocket, ignoring how badly his hand was shaking, and pulled out his cell phone.

"Who are you calling?"

"Someone who might be able to help." Jack punched one of the fast-dial numbers. "And I suggest you do the same. You need to get your unit down here now, before these things get their act together. In a few more hours, you won't be able to tell them from humans without a thermal imager or exposing them to open flame." He suddenly thought of Alexander. "Or a cat."

Kiran looked at him as if he were insane, but then pulled out his own phone.

* * *

Carl Richards had just sat down in his chair after pouring his morning coffee when a jarring, buzzing ring tone sounded from his phone.

Pulling the phone out of his suit jacket pocket, he glanced at the display. It was Jack. He hit the answer button before the second ring sounded.

"Richards. What have you got, Dawson?"

"We've got a brushfire, Carl." Dawson sounded utterly exhausted. "A bad one."

A trickle of ice water ran down Richards' spine. His throat was suddenly dry. "What happened?"

"Vijay was right. AnGrow, which Renee said was one of the Indian companies New Horizons had worked with here in India, must have gotten seeds from The Bag. The fools planted the stuff in an unauthorized test plot near a little village a few klicks from this place, umm..." Richards heard someone in the background say something. "Yeah, Koratikal, east of Hyderabad. The village is near there. I'll get you the exact coordinates later. The AnGrow guys took some samples away with them and let the villagers have the rest to eat."

Richards felt as if he had just been pushed out of a plane at ten thousand feet without a parachute. "Casualties?"

"I don't know for sure. I don't have any idea how many people were in the village to begin with, how many ate the corn, and how many might have gotten away once the, uh, symptoms became evident." He paused for a moment. "We have one definite survivor with us, a girl in her early teens. She's in deep shock, catatonic. Two of Vijay Chidambaram's cousins went with me to the site. One of them didn't make it. The other is a captain in the Indian Army's counterterrorist outfit, their equivalent of Delta Force. He's on the phone now to his commander to try to get some troops in here to contain the outbreak."

"How are you holding up?"

"I'm alive. That's about all I'm sure of. It was bad, Carl. Those poor villagers. And Vijay's cousin Surya. He was killed by one of the larval forms. But there was more than one of those creeping horrors, Carl."

"Dawson? Dawson, are you there?"

"Yeah. I'm fine."

"You always were a lousy liar." Richards' voice was uncharacteristically soft. He hated to admit it, even to himself, but he thought a great deal of Dawson, and couldn't imagine what he must have seen that night. Richards had never seen one of the larval forms like the one that had killed the test animals in the EDS base before it had been destroyed. The larval stage was only a theory Naomi had come up with. Renee had been the only one to catch a glimpse of the thing, which had later transformed into the adult harvester form that they'd come to know and love. "I'll wake up the legal attachés at our Embassy in Delhi and get a fire under their butts, and make some calls to the Pentagon. I might not be able to do much, but a few people over there still owe me some favors. So tell your Indian Army buddy..."

"Kiran. Captain Kiran Chidambaram."

"Tell Kiran that I'll do whatever I can to help line up military assistance if they decide they want it." He sighed. "Then I have to try to sell this to the boss and try to get him to push it up to the President. Renee's told me about the other places where there might have been incidents, and who knows where else these damn things might show up now."

"Don't forget the AnGrow guys," Jack told him. "They took samples of the corn. If we don't seize it, we could be looking at a second generation in a few months."

"I will. But Dawson, if these things are as widespread as Renee thinks they might be, that may not matter." It was hard for Richards to conceive of the potential havoc large groups of harvesters in the world's most populated countries might be able to wreak. They had to be found and stopped. Fast.

"I know." Jack sounded uneasy. "Look, Carl, I've got to go. We're only a few klicks from the village and I don't want to sit here any longer. The larval forms can't move very fast, but the adults sure can, and it's so dark out here that we wouldn't see a freight train coming at us. Give Naomi a call for me, and let her know I'll call her as soon as we get back to Hyderabad."

"Okay, kid. Get moving and stay safe."

"Roger that."

Richards heard the click as Dawson ended the call.

Blowing out his breath, his mind spinning, Richards tried to catalog all the things that had to be done.

First things first. He pulled out his other phone to give Naomi a quick call. As he dialed her number, he tried to think of how he would convince his director, a man who held Carl in contempt, that a disaster of biblical proportions was unfolding across the globe.

CHAPTER TWELVE

"He's awake."

Mikhailov heard the words as if they had been spoken from far away, the sound of the person's voice muffled, indistinct.

His eyes flickered open. Around him was a world of white, filled with fuzzy shapes. Beside him, something beeped.

One of the shapes grew larger. It took him a moment to realize that it was someone's face, leaning down toward him. "Mikhailov, can you hear me?"

This was a different voice, one he recognized. It was that of his regimental commander.

Parting his lips to speak, Mikhailov noted how dry his mouth felt. "*Da, Polkovnik* Zaitsev." He licked his lips, which were like sandpaper to his parched tongue.

"Here. Sip this." The *polkovnik*, or colonel, placed a straw between Mikhailov's lips, and Mikhailov sucked on it greedily. "Not so fast, my young friend." After a few more sips, Zaitsev took the water away.

Mikhailov looked around, his eyes blinking rapidly as his eyes adjusted to the light. "Rudenko? He is alive?"

"Here, *kapitan*."

Mikhailov was rewarded with the sight of his senior noncom, who stood on the opposite side of the bed from Zaitsev. His face was horribly bruised and his bushy eyebrows had been seared off. Both hands were in bandages, but otherwise he seemed none the worse for wear. Rudenko offered a wide smile from his battered face and he threw Mikhailov a salute.

"This is the second time you have saved my life, Rudenko. If you keep this up, we may have to come up with a special award to give you. I'm not sure that any of our military orders quite do you justice."

For the only time since he had known the burly man, Rudenko was clearly embarrassed. But, as Mikhailov noted with a smile, he also puffed up with pride at such words being spoken about him in front of the regimental commander.

"Rudenko's action has been duly noted, *kapitan*," Zaitsev said with an approving nod to Rudenko. The colonel's voice lowered slightly, and Mikhailov could sense some of the good will draining out of it. "But now we have some things to discuss that cannot wait. The division commander sent me here — you're in the military hospital in Stavropol, by the way — to find out what the devil happened at the facility. I have already heard Rudenko's recounting of it, but want to hear your own." He frowned. "This is the second time a unit you were leading was virtually wiped out, *kapitan*. That is not a record we are fond of."

Mikhailov shifted his gaze from Zaitsev to Rudenko, who now stood stiffly beside him, his eyes carefully fixed on his captain and a blank expression on his face. Mikhailov had seen that look before, just before Rudenko had beaten four soldiers into bloody pulps for hazing new recruits against Mikhailov's express order. "Were there any other survivors?"

Rudenko shook his head. "No, *kapitan*." He glanced at Zaitsev. "None of our people, at least."

"That's what you told me earlier, Rudenko," Zaitsev snapped, "and it still makes no sense."

Mikhailov turned his attention back to Zaitsev, his heart a leaden weight in his chest. He had hoped that at least some of the men would have escaped the inferno at the facility when the harvester had fired the RPO into the animal husbandry building, but apparently not. If any had survived the blast, the harvester, or harvesters, must have hunted them down and killed them.

But what chilled him and sent his heart monitor racing was the thought that the horrid creatures were loose. Who knew how many of them were now wandering free?

"Sir, did you read my report from the Spitsbergen operation?" Zaitsev had taken over the regiment only six months before, and so hadn't been directly involved when Mikhailov's company had been deployed to Spitsbergen a year ago.

"Yes, the division commander insisted that I read it. I won't say that I believe it, but I read it. Creatures masquerading as *Spetsnaz*, and even as a Norwegian soldier? Mikhailov, if I had been in the commander's shoes, I would have relieved you and sent you to an asylum." His voice softened slightly. "And yet, the commander believes you. He also felt it would be inappropriate for your report on this operation to be seen by anyone else until he has had a chance to read it, so he sent me here to get the information personally." He leaned back on the stool on which he sat and took out a small notebook and a pen. He wore a pained look on his face, and Mikhailov could imagine that Zaitsev was less than pleased to be playing errand boy and note-taker for the general. "Any time you're ready to begin, Mikhailov."

"May I first ask how long I've been out?" He looked back at Rudenko.

"Two days, *kapitan*. It has been two days."

Mikhailov felt sick. "*Bozhe moi*. They could be anywhere by now!" He turned to Zaitsev. "Were any more troops sent in to secure the site?"

"Yes, the 7th Airborne Division sent in a full company from Novorossiysk after you failed to respond to their radio calls, but there was nothing to secure." He nodded toward Rudenko. "The fire you set in one of the green house buildings burned down everything that wasn't blown up by the RPOs. And then there's the destroyed helicopter and its dead crew. The Air Force wants you to answer for that, but they can have whatever is left of your carcass after I finish with you." He looked at Mikhailov with a speculative expression. "You do realize that you may be brought up on charges for this if you can't prove the existence of these creatures of yours?"

"They exist, *polkovnik*." He shared a quick glance with Rudenko. "Believe me, they exist. The only question now is whether we have a chance of stopping them."

* * *

The tension in the FBI Director's conference room had been growing by the minute, and showed no signs of stopping. The Director, Kyle Harmon, sat at the head of the table. To either side of him sat the Executive Assistant Directors responsible for the National Security Branch and the Criminal, Cyber, Response and Services Branch and all of their division heads.

At the far end of the table sat Carl Richards, who headed up the Criminal Investigative Division, although he wasn't sure if he would be in that position more than five minutes after this meeting ended. Everyone at the table, with the exception of his direct boss (the Executive Assistant Director for Criminal, Cyber, Response and Services Branch), who had discovered something intensely fascinating on a ceiling tile above the director's head, was staring at him.

The meeting hadn't gone well from the beginning. Richards had figuratively thrown down the Weapons of Mass Destruction flag, sending an email to everyone he could think of in hopes of getting the director to call a meeting. It had been totally inappropriate, but his entreaties to his own boss had fallen on deaf ears. No one wanted to hear any more stories of the harvesters or The Bag. It was like hearing about Iraq hiding weapons of mass destruction even after it had been conclusively proven that there hadn't been any. Except in this case, the weapons were very real, and in their own way were far deadlier than nuclear bombs or chemical agents.

Facing the men and women around the table, all of them colleagues and some of them friends, or as close to friends as Richards ever allowed himself to get, he met their eyes and refused to be cowed. He knew that this meeting would probably spell the end of his career and make him a pariah among his peers. Next to watching Director Ridley die in her hospital bed after the harvesters had taken away their "gift" of healing her Lou Gehrig's disease, this was the most difficult thing he had ever done. He had faced situations that required great physical courage, and would much rather have been in a cage with a dozen hungry lions than here. The Bureau had been his life, his reason for existence, and he was offering it up as a sacrifice in what he knew would be a vain attempt to get the men and women in this room, individuals who could help stop the coming storm, believe that a storm was indeed coming. He knew from the moment he walked in and saw the director's look of disgust that he didn't have a hope of convincing them, but Richards had to try. It was his duty. And after this was done, when all the dust had settled, he would probably be on the first plane to Nome, Alaska. He hoped Renee liked snow.

"Sir, if we don't get a lid on this thing now, we probably never will." Richards was looking Harmon straight in the eye as he brought his briefing to a close. None of those gathered here had said a single word, either commenting or asking questions. That in itself was a very ominous sign, but he didn't let it deter him. He couldn't afford to give up. "Dawson reported that an entire village in south-central India was infected. We have what looks like a similar incident in southern Russia, and..."

"*Goddammit!*" Director Harmon, while not normally given to profane outbursts, exploded, slamming a palm down on the table. "Richards, this has gone far enough. I don't even know where to start. Not leaving this whole harvester issue behind, abusing your authority by calling in the legats in New Delhi, cavorting with Jack Dawson, who's not exactly on my favorites list, or calling all of us in here with some ridiculous claim that we've got aliens running wild in India and Russia." He leaned forward. "In case you'd forgotten, this is the FBI, and while we certainly have concerns overseas, our primary job is here at home. Are there any aliens running rampant around here?"

"Not that we're aware of, sir. But they're perfect mimics, and..."

There were snickers and moans from around the table. And now, rather than staring at him, people were looking away. Glancing at their watches. Flipping open their schedulers and notepads. Doodling. Giving every non-verbal signal they could that he was wasting their time.

Richards felt a surge of anger rising to the surface, but clamped down on it, hard, before it made him say anything that would be even more damaging. At this point he looked like a fool and a freak. He didn't need to break out any flamethrowers to incinerate the bridges that had already collapsed into the river under their own ponderous weight. That wouldn't help. His anger giving way to bleak dismay, he realized that nothing would. Not until it was too late.

Director Harmon blew out his breath. "I don't ever want to hear another word about this foolishness. Is that unmistakably clear, Richards?"

"Yes, sir." He said the words, but wasn't about to give Harmon the satisfaction of beating him down. He held the director's gaze until Harmon turned away.

To the chief of the International Operations Division, Harmon said, "Since Richards already rousted our people in Delhi, let's make the most of a bad situation and follow through with the offer to provide any support the Indians might need. A little goodwill, even if it's unnecessary, can't hurt." Looking around the room, but pointedly avoiding Richards, he added, "I'd like the executive assistant directors to stay for a moment."

The meeting was over. Carl looked at his watch, noting with professional detachment that he had taken exactly nine minutes and forty-seven seconds to destroy his career. Richards gathered up his notes, shoved them in his folder, and made for the door. He forced himself to take a measured pace and not rush. He wouldn't be seen as running away.

As he strode down the hall toward the elevator, he heard his colleagues emerge from the conference room behind him.

Deciding that he and everyone else would probably be more comfortable if he took the stairs, he passed the elevators and palmed the bar on the door to the stairwell. He took the steps quickly, shedding his dignified facade now that he was out of sight.

He was surprised when he heard the door open, and even more surprised when he heard someone call his name.

"Carl!"

He stopped on the landing and looked up to see Mozhdeh Kashani, the chief of the Directorate of Intelligence.

"Wait up."

Wondering what this was all about, Richards did as she asked. Mozhdeh was an attractive woman of Iranian ancestry, about five years younger than he was and — he had no trouble admitting to himself — at least five times as smart. She was petite, the top of her head only reaching Richards' shoulder, but anyone who thought she was just another pretty face had another thing coming.

Richards had been in a meeting once where someone from another agency, here to coordinate on the community effort against a terrorist operation, made that mistake. The man must have felt as if he'd been trampled by a heavy cavalry charge after she had finished with him.

"What can I do for you, Mozhdeh?" As she caught up to him, they both continued down the stairs at a much more sedate pace.

"I think it might be more what I can do for you."

He snorted. "What? Salvage my career? Good luck with that. I'm just thinking of how to tell my girlfriend that we'll probably have lots of snow in our future up in Alaska."

"You're a survivor, Carl. You'll manage. No, I meant the harvesters."

Even at the mention of the word, Carl's jaw clenched. But he realized that she wasn't playing games. Mozhdeh had been instrumental in helping to set up SEAL, and she was one of the few people in the Bureau who'd ever really taken the harvester story seriously. None of them had ever actually seen a harvester, only photos and videos, so it was hard for anyone to buy off on something that could just as easily been cut from an alien autopsy movie.

"I had one of my analysts cross-check what you'd sent me about the suspected incidents. He couldn't verify if it had anything to do with the harvesters, of course, but there's definitely something going on. The Defense Intelligence Agency confirmed that there were some unusual movements of Russian airborne forces in the last few days. There's been a news blackout in two areas in China, one of which was in a region you'd flagged, and we've got imagery of three small towns in Brazil — again, in areas that you picked up on — that have been burned to the ground, but no official explanation of what's happening. As for India..." She shrugged. "Nothing we've got so far stands out, but if what Dawson says is credible, I believe it."

Richards stopped and turned to face her. "You believe Dawson?"

She looked at him with her dark eyes and nodded. "He worked for me on several cases after he left the academy. He was a little self-absorbed and carried a lot of emotional baggage, but he had a gift for seeing things others couldn't and a sense of honor almost as deeply embedded as yours."

"Flattery. From you, I'll take it."

"Don't let it go to your bald head." She started down the steps again. "I never believed any of the charges brought against him after the lab was destroyed. To do something like that simply wasn't in his nature. I wish he was still working for us. I'd love to have him in intel."

"Well, don't hold your breath on that."

"I know. Anyway, if Dawson says there's something going on, I believe it. If you *both* say that there's something going on, then it's time to start getting scared."

"Then why didn't you speak up in the meeting?"

She glanced at him, then shook her head. "That's your problem, Carl. When it comes to politics, you're an idiot."

"No argument there. I never claimed otherwise."

"Nor should you, but up here in the nosebleed section, it's a critical skill. Harmon's a political animal, much more than Ridley was, and he's not going to make any waves for President Miller. And everyone else in that room back there has a long knife out, waiting for the first instant that your back is turned. Remember, when President Curtis put you in as acting director, he bounced you ahead of all of them. They worked for you because they had to and because you rose to the challenge. While you were competent in the job, more than anyone had been willing to give you credit for, you didn't make any friends among the people in that room."

Carl suddenly saw flashbacks of some of the meetings he'd held and the orders he'd given while serving as acting director. Some hadn't been pretty, but to him at the time, that didn't matter. The only thing that he cared about was getting the job done. Even now, had he been given the opportunity to turn back the clock, he wouldn't have changed a thing. He might have reamed one or two people out even harder.

He gave her an unapologetic shrug as they reached her floor. He held the door open for her, but didn't step out of the stairwell. His own office was on the next floor down. "I suppose so. But that brings up an interesting question. Why do you care what happens to me?"

"I didn't say that I did. But if these incidents pan out and a real threat emerges, we're going to need you and people like you." She flashed a brilliant smile. "You're an asshole, Carl. It's in your nature." The smile disappeared as if a light switch had been thrown. "But I can't think of anyone I'd rather have watching my back if things go to hell. In the meantime, I'm going to request that Renee be reassigned to my office to work with my analyst on this. He's a young guy who needs someone to show him the ropes, and if Harmon gets word of it I can say she's using it as a training scenario. That'll keep both of you out of trouble, and I can take any heat from Harmon. Stay in touch with Dawson and let me know what you find out, but otherwise keep your head down and your mouth shut. If you don't, getting shipped off to Nome will be the least of your worries."

CHAPTER THIRTEEN

"Oh, my God, Jack." Naomi shuddered after Jack finished telling her what had happened after the villagers had eaten the corn planted by AnGrow. She couldn't imagine the nightmare it must have been for those poor unsuspecting people. And Jack, without any weapons, charging straight into the middle of it, could have ended up just like poor Vijay's cousin Surya. "Promise me that you'll never do anything that stupid again."

On the far end of the line, thousands of miles away, Jack laughed. It was a strained, awkward sound. "Let's just say I won't be putting that sort of thing at the top of my to-do list for a while."

"Promise me, Jack."

After a pause, he said in a small, tortured voice, "You know I can't."

Naomi closed her eyes. Part of her had so wanted Jack to say yes, even though she knew it would have been a lie. He'd told her once that he'd never made a promise that he knew he might not be able to keep, and she knew that his sense of honor simply wouldn't let him walk away from a situation where he thought he might be able to help, or where he felt he had to do something, even at the cost of his own life. She'd lost too much already, and didn't want to lose him, too.

"Well," she told him, wiping her eyes clear, "if you do something idiotic like that again I'm going to kick your ass."

Jack managed a chuckle. "Oh, no, not that!" Then, more seriously, he said, "Listen, I'll try to stay out of the crossfire. I pretty much have to now, anyway, as the Indians don't want me messing around in what's become official business. Kiran's got the ball now. I filled him in on the background. I don't think he really believes half of it, but there's no doubt he thinks the harvesters are real. The question is whether he can convince his commander and the other authorities here that there's a real threat, and that it's not just terrorists. But from what I heard, it's starting to get bogged down in bureaucracy and turf. Is it a military problem or a health and safety concern? Which ministry is going to take the lead?" He blew out his breath. "If these things get loose there at home, we'll have a tough time dealing with it. Here, Kiran seems to think that the bureaucracies are so stove-piped that the only chance for any decisive action is to bring in the military, but the civilians are reluctant to do that if it's not really a terrorist threat."

"Have they deployed anyone to the village?"

"I don't know. I haven't heard anything about that. He said he'd try to keep me in the loop, but I'm hoping that no news is good news, that Kiran's too busy to call. With any luck, he and a couple companies of troops are heading there in helicopters as we speak. I guess we won't know until later."

"Did you tell Vijay about what happened to Surya?"

"God, no. He's still in such bad shape, the last thing he needs is a shock like that, and the guilt trip to go along with it. He's going to blame himself for sending Surya along." Jack paused a moment. "Kiran said he wanted to tell him. I guess he and Surya were pretty tight with Vijay, and it's going to hit him hard. I also convinced Kiran to post a guard on Vijay, and had him bully the hospital staff into letting me bring over Vijay's cat to keep him company."

"Why do you think he needs to be guarded?" As soon as the words left her mouth, she knew why. Surya. While Naomi understood much of the biology of how the harvesters mimicked their victims, what she was far less sure of was how they took on behavioral traits. Some former EDS researchers were convinced that the harvesters somehow could absorb the memories or thought patterns of their victims, but Naomi had never subscribed to that opinion because there wasn't any real evidence to support it. All they knew for certain was that adult harvesters could rapidly and flawlessly step into the lives of their victims. How they did it remained a mystery that they'd never solve without more live harvesters to study. Unfortunately, it looked like there were now plenty of those available, assuming they could be captured.

Surya, however, represented a unique case, in that he was killed by a larval form. Naomi had no idea if his body was anything more than a source of nutrients for the creature, or if it retained other information that might allow it to mimic him as an adult. She just didn't know. On the chance that the larval form could put to use the knowledge of its victims, it would "know" that Vijay was a threat and try to eliminate him.

"Forget I asked that," she said. "What did you tell Vijay, or was he even conscious?"

"He woke up when the cat pounced on him. The hospital staff was really unhappy, especially since I guess they don't really like cats much over here. But Vijay seemed happy enough to see the furry beast. And that way he'll have some warning of any unpleasant visitors."

"Has there been any word on AnGrow and the other corn they took?"

"Not a peep." Jack's voice was laced with disgust. "I got a lot of platitudes and 'We'll get back to you on that' from the Ministry of Agriculture. AnGrow throws a lot of money around to the politicians here, according to what Vijay could tell me, so I don't think we're going to have any luck getting through to them."

"So what's the plan now?"

"As much as I hate to say it, I think I need to track down Mikhailov and see if he knows anything about the incident in Russia. Carl managed to pull some strings with their embassy here for a visa, so I'll be on a flight out tomorrow morning."

"But what about the incident there in India?"

"At this point, I think I've done all I can here without becoming terminally frustrated or being locked in jail. Kiran's in a much better position to influence things until Vijay is back on his feet, and I don't see any point in banging my head against a brick wall with the government. I'm just a civilian, anyway, and don't have any official status." He sighed. "Listen, not to change the subject, but how are you doing?"

"Aside from wanting to clobber you for being an idiot, I'm fine." It wasn't quite the truth, but wasn't exactly a lie, either. She wanted to tell him about what she'd discovered about Morgan's

Beta-Three, but decided not to. After the horrors he had suffered through that night, he didn't need any more. Beta-Three was a nightmare for Naomi to deal with. "But all my technical mumbo-jumbo can wait. It's got to be dreadfully late there, and you need to get some sleep."

"I'm not sure I'll ever sleep again, Naomi. Not after what I saw tonight."

She wanted to reach through the phone to touch him, to hold him. "Just get some rest. Stay safe and don't do anything stupid or I'll have to hurt you."

He laughed, and that made her smile. "I love you, too."

The line went dead.

Taking in a shuddering breath, Naomi put her phone in her purse. She was in her office, where she'd spent most of the night waiting for word from Jack after Carl had let her know he was all right after the incident at the village. She would have spent that time in the lab, but no personal electronics of any kind were allowed in the vault, and there was only one phone, which was a dedicated line to Howard Morgan.

She looked down as she heard a squeak, and found her cat, Koshka, staring up at her with bright blue eyes. Koshka rarely gave a traditional meow, but could growl like a dog when she was annoyed, usually at Alexander. Naomi leaned down to stroke Koshka's soft white fur, her fingertips brushing over the long scar in the cat's flank that had been left by a harvester. "I'm sorry, honey, but I've got to get back to work." She stood up and reached over to scratch Alexander, who was laying atop a filing cabinet, watching her with his deep green eyes, under the chin. "Stay out of trouble, and don't chew up any more network cables, okay?"

Alexander's inscrutable feline expression gave her no reassurance of any such thing.

Closing the door behind her and hoping that Alexander wouldn't necessitate a sixth call to IT support, she headed down the hall to the elevators, taking one of them to the basement where Lab One was located. The Beta-Three crew was already hard at work.

"You look like you haven't slept." As Naomi entered the vault, Harmony Bates handed her a cup of coffee, which Naomi gratefully accepted.

"I haven't. Jack almost got himself killed last night." She collapsed more than sat into her chair, the emotional strain and exhaustion suddenly catching up with her.

"Is he okay?" Harmony pulled up a chair and sat down, her blue eyes wide with concern.

"Yes, but it was close." She shook her head. "I respect what Howard's doing here, but I'm starting to wonder if any of it's going to matter."

"Is it really that bad?"

Naomi nodded. Morgan had insisted that he tell the others on the team about the harvesters. She didn't want to, because she feared that it would destroy her credibility in their eyes, but Morgan had insisted.

"Doctor," he had told her quietly after she'd finished her tale, "I'm not sure I can believe what you've just told me. But if it's true, the Beta-Three team needs to know just what they're dealing with. I don't want them working on something that potentially dangerous without all the information we can give them."

And so Naomi had told them. Some had at least been willing to consider what she'd said, while others had written off her story — and her, most likely, even though no one had said as much — as a joke. Harmony had been, and Naomi was sure remained, a skeptic, but hadn't dismissed the information out of hand. She was a scientist who realized that humanity's collective knowledge was only a tiny drop of water in the great ocean of the unknown, and that there were many mysteries, great and small, in the world around her. But, like any good scientist, she wanted to see empirical proof, processes that could be observed, data that could be recorded and analyzed, before she believed. "Yes, it's that bad. I know it's hard to believe in these things, but only a dozen of them, along with people they'd unwittingly suborned, nearly did us in." Reaching out to activate her computer, she added, "And I'm wondering if things aren't even worse."

"What do you mean?" Harmony scooted her chair closer and looked at the screen as Naomi brought up several files for display.

"Howard would probably be annoyed with me, but I jumped ahead a little bit, since you and the others have the work on the delivery system well in hand now."

Harmony smiled, and Naomi returned it. Naomi had helped the team leap over the obstacles in creating a stable shell to act as a delivery system for the genetic payload that had stymied them for months, and Harmony had been genuinely grateful.

It was an interesting contrast to Dr. Kelso, Naomi thought. He popped into the lab twice a day like clockwork to check the work logs and chat briefly with Harmony, but thus far he had refused to go out of his way to even say hello to Naomi. According to bits and pieces she'd heard from Harmony and the others on the Beta-Three crew, Howard Morgan had been less than overjoyed at the progress the team had made under Kelso, especially after exorbitant sums of money had been spent on the project. While Kelso had other responsibilities as the company's head scientist, Beta-Three had been his baby, and Naomi had unintentionally usurped the limelight. She was well aware of how bitter such enmity could become, and she hoped that she could somehow patch things up with Kelso. She didn't need any enemies here, and there was far too much important work to do to let petty ego-driven squabbles sap any of their momentum.

Pushing thoughts of Kelso aside, she tapped a few keys. The image of a DNA double helix appeared on the monitor, and with another click Naomi transferred it to the high definition wall screen, where the complex, twisting molecule leaped into clear definition.

Its structure, however, wasn't like the stereotypical twisting ladder that the public was used to seeing in science exhibits. This one had irregularly spaced extrusions along its length, and was much more tightly coiled than was typical for DNA molecules normally found in nature.

Harmony stared at the image. "What am I looking at, Naomi? I've never seen a strand that looked anything like this. And it's *huge*."

"This was taken from one of the original harvesters, what I'll call Group A. We managed to kill or capture several, from which we took samples for study. And you're right: it's enormous. Human DNA has nearly three billion base pairs. Harvester DNA has more than eight hundred billion." Harmony whistled. "Aside from its size, another thing we found from the samples we obtained is that there was no polymorphism in Group A. None. With humans, for example, there would be variations in the genes to account for the all the many differences in our bodies. But the Group A harvesters were like a group of identical twins or clones."

"But that's impossible! Even if there were no spontaneous mutations, there must have been at least some minor differentiation caused by natural radiation or exposure to mutagenic compounds in the environment."

Shaking her head, Naomi told her, "While we know the harvesters, through the admission of one in our base just before it was destroyed, are very sensitive to ionizing radiation, they're either amazingly resistant to DNA damage or have a phenomenal ability to repair it, or both. We ran a lot of tests, and all of them came out the same. Zero polymorphism on a macro level, and zero deviation in the DNA sequences across samples from a given individual and across the limited group to which we had access."

"That's incredible."

"You think so? Look at this." Naomi tapped a few more keys, and another DNA molecule appeared beside the first one. "This is a DNA sequence from a blood sample taken from the rhesus monkey in the EDS lab before it completely transitioned to what I believe may be a larval form of the creature. It had been infected by what we believe to be a sample of Beta-Three corn. Let's call this the first member of Group B." Naomi shivered involuntarily, remembering what had transpired in the lab after the ill-fated monkey had been completely overtaken.

"They're outwardly similar, if not identical." Harmony's eyes traced both the diagram and the details in the text next to each diagram. "Wait." She pointed to a long set of base pair sequences in the second map. "That's clearly different."

"Exactly." Naomi scrolled and zoomed the two maps so they were focused on the same region for easier comparison. The text changed to display only those molecular sequences that appeared in the diagrams. "I ran a comparison in the computer, and this is the only segment that's been altered. It hasn't just been modified, but has been expanded. There's a great deal more information in here than there was previously, especially considering how huge the Group A DNA structure is to begin with." She leaned back and folded her arms, staring at the screen. "The only problem is that I have absolutely no idea what genes are affected. We'd only been able to map a few genes to specific physical traits of the harvesters because they're monomorphic and we had so few specimens to work with, not to mention the sheer size of their DNA structure. We didn't understand them that well to begin with, and now we have this."

Harmony was staring at the two DNA sequences, a look of horrified wonder on her face. "They somehow engineered something this complex into a new generation, delivered by a viral RNA payload? That's incredible!"

"To say that the Group A harvesters were geniuses with genetics is a graphic understatement. We think they've been gently pushing us along in the biotechnology realm to the point where they could do this. The question is why? What does this sequence do?"

The two of them sat there for a moment, their eyes fixed on the display.

"Hmm."

Naomi turned to see Harmony's mouth moving as she silently read through some of the DNA sequences in the Group B strand.

"Oh, my God." Harmony turned to Naomi. "I think I recognize this! Hang on." She quickly scooted her chair to another computer and typed madly for a moment. With a click of the mouse, a third DNA segment, only a bit smaller than the massive harvester DNA strands, appeared on the wall display. Turning to look at it, Harmony zoomed into a particular area. The sequences displayed in the text weren't exactly the same as the Group B harvester DNA, but the similarities vastly outweighed the differences. "Let me run a comparison with this sequence."

After a moment, the computer displayed the results on the screen: ninety-four percent.

Naomi sat forward, her pulse quickening. "What is this?"

"It's a sequence from *Amoeba dubia*, which has a DNA sequence almost as long as the harvesters do: six hundred and seventy billion base pairs. I did my post-doc on *dubia*, and this was one of the sequences I examined." She smiled at Naomi's skeptical look. "I know what you're thinking: out of six hundred and seventy billion base pairs, why would I look at this particular set? It wasn't chosen at random, believe me. I was building on some previous work that had been done that had tentatively tagged the function of these genes. Part of my post-doc was to prove or disprove that hypothesis."

Unable to help herself, Naomi interrupted. "Harmony, what do these genes do?"

"Well, in *Amoeba dubia*, they played a key role in reproduction. This doesn't represent the entire scope of the reproductive genes, of course. But I was able to determine that they're definitely related to the process of cellular fission."

Barely able to breathe, Naomi stared at the image of an *Amoeba dubia* that Harmony had added to the wall display. Naomi had known that the original harvesters could not reproduce, either due to sterility or some other unknown factor. She had assumed that the deadly Beta-Three corn was intended simply to create harvesters through transgenic manipulation of unsuspecting hosts, just as had happened with the rhesus monkey back at the EDS base a year ago.

That was bad enough, but at least the number of harvesters would have been limited by the number of available hosts, if nothing else. While human losses potentially could have been horrendous, there had been numerous scenarios played out and contingency plans made for throwing up a sort of barrier or firebreak, isolating the human population from potentially infected food.

Kempf, one of the Group A harvesters and Naomi's one-time mentor, obviously took that into account when she created the RNA payload carried by the corn that New Horizons had intended to ship to the world. Inability to reproduce had been the only real weakness of the harvesters, and she had engineered a solution. If the new generation of harvesters could reproduce on their own, without the need for a host, there would be no stopping them.

"Oh, my God." Forcing down the bile that surged into the back of her throat, she got up and ran to the lab entrance, where she waited impatiently for the vault door to open. Once she was through, she kicked off her heels and sprinted down the hall, then up the stairs to her office so she could call Jack and the others to warn them.

CHAPTER FOURTEEN

While it was self-aware, the thing did not apply the concept of a name to itself. It simply *was*, and was driven by the imperatives basic to survival in what it instinctively knew was a hostile environment. By its own definition, any environment in which it did not have predatory dominance was hostile.

It had traveled a long way from its point of origin, the strange metal creche where it had grown from the mindless form, had molted, and finally *become*. It had killed all the humans that had destroyed its birth place, using the knowledge it had absorbed from its most recent victim, the soldier that had once been *Ryadavoy* Pavel Ivanovich Sleptsev. Its mimicry had initially been imperfect, as the thing was still young and inexperienced. But with every moment it had traveled from the flaming pyre it had left behind, it improved, matured.

The thing was aware that others of its kind had survived the deadly flames. Some had left the creche — the *facility*, it corrected itself — early, soon after becoming. A few had left right after they had molted, assuming their adult physical form, but before the higher cognitive processes had been awakened by latent genetic triggers. Those had crashed through the flimsy walls after the last of the animals had been consumed. Where they had gone and what fate had overtaken them, the thing did not know, nor did it care. They were nothing but beasts that would attack and kill even their own kind to establish dominance. And obtain food.

Food. The thing had dined on several creatures, human and otherwise, during its journey to feed its still-developing body. While it was an adult, it was not yet fully mature. Its digestive system was highly adaptable, and it could consume nearly any source of protein. It had, however, developed a taste for humans. Not because the taste or nutritional value was better than other food, for anything it consumed had to be broken down with extremely complex salivary acids first, but because through consumption came knowledge.

"This is as far as I can take you, my friend."

The thing turned to look at the human in the driver's seat of the small car. It was dark out, nearly midnight, with rain pouring down as the man pulled the car to a stop along highway A154 in Stavropol. The man had picked the thing up along the highway twenty kilometers back. Unlike the last human the thing had encountered, this one would live.

"Thank you." With a smile, the thing got out of the car and stepped into the rain. A nearby street lamp threw out a pale globe of light that turned into a kaleidoscope of glittering fragments, caught by the individual drops of rain. It had never seen the like, and took a moment to marvel.

"Close the door, would you?" The man's voice was irritated.

"Sorry," the thing that looked like Pavel Sleptsev told him amicably. "Have a safe trip." It slammed the door closed and threw the man, whose name it did not know, nor cared to, a jaunty salute.

The car pulled away from the curb and, its engine wheezing, accelerated down the road. The thing watched it until the red tail lights faded from view.

A few other cars passed by, throwing up great waves of water as they hit a deep puddle not far from where the thing stood. This, too, was a new experience. It held out a hand, watching as the rain pooled in its palm. Through the malleable flesh, it could feel the wetness and sense the temperature of the rain. Its true eyes, hidden behind the false eyes it presented to its prey, watched the ripples and splashes in a visual spectrum that ran from high infrared to low ultraviolet. Its sense of smell was acute, and it could discern the many chemical compounds in the air and in the water. While it had no names for the elements, it instinctively differentiated between them, just as it could see different colors. It found carbon, sulphur, and many others that it understood to be the by-product of human industrialization, what to them was contamination of the environment. The thing did not care about such things, for it instinctively understood that they would have no effect on it.

Finished with its momentary reverie, it began to make its way along the roadside deeper into town, letting Pavel Sleptsev's memories guide it like a transparent map in its brain.

* * *

Mayor Grigori Putin sat at the bar of the sleazy dive that just happened to be the favorite nightclub of many of the airborne troops garrisoned in Stavropol. Aside from a ridiculous-looking disco ball that pulsed over the tiny dance floor, casting glittering light over the dozen or so men and women who shimmied and ground their bodies together, the place was dimly lit and filled with a haze from tobacco smoke. Putin suspected the illumination was kept so low to keep anyone from noticing the cockroaches that probably ran rampant inside the scabrous establishment. The music, the latest trash from Britain, he thought, was so loud that the pounding bass was creating tiny waves that flitted across the top of the vodka in his glass.

Taken with a sudden sense of inspiration, he turned to the crowd behind him and held up the glass. "*Poshyol ty'!*" He grinned as half a dozen faces turned toward him. "Fuck you!"

The faces broke out in wide grins, and Putin was bombarded with exuberant epithets as he brought the glass to his lips and tossed down the vodka. Putin was one of the few officers who came here, and he'd been doing so for a long time. He was well known in this place, both for his outlandish behavior and for buying the house rounds of liquor.

With a howl, he slammed the glass down on the bar before grabbing the bottle to pour some more.

It was then that he caught sight of an unfamiliar face moving uncertainly through the crowd. Unlike the other military men here, aside from Putin himself, he was in uniform and stood out from the mix of fashionably dressed women and grungy-looking young men. "You there!" He waved the bottle in the young man's direction. "Hey, you stupid shit!" The soldier saw him. "Yes, you, you fucking retard! Come here and have a drink."

The man made his way through the crowd and hesitantly sat down on the stool next to Putin. Putin leaned forward on the bar and crawled on his elbows until he could reach down behind it to where the bartender kept the dirty glasses before they were washed. Snatching up the first one his groping hand closed upon, he squirmed back onto the stool and poured a drink and shoved it in front of the soldier. "Here, boy, you look like you could use this. It might put some hair on your ass."

"Thank you, sir." The soldier nodded and wrapped a hand around the glass, but didn't lift it to his lips.

Putin sucked down half the vodka in his glass before noticing that his companion hadn't taken a drink. "What's wrong? Drink up, boy."

The soldier fidgeted, an uncomfortable look on his face. "Sir, I can't. I'm on medication and can't drink."

Putin sputtered and slammed down his glass, sending a spray of vodka across the bar. He peered more closely at the soldier. "What's your name?"

"Sleptsev, sir. *Ryadavoy* Pavel Ivanovich Sleptsev."

"I know about every bastard in the entire regiment here, but I don't know you." His eyes narrowed. "You're not one of those pussies that came down from Pskov, are you?"

Sleptsev smiled. "I must confess that I am, sir."

"Then what the hell are you doing here? I heard they were massacred the other day."

"That is true, sir." Sleptsev's smile fell away, replaced by a look of terrible sorrow. "I came down with the company, but was violently ill when we arrived. That is what the medication is for, why I can't drink with you. The company commander ordered me to stay behind, and I haven't yet received orders to return to Pskov." He shook his head. "He was a good man."

"Who?"

"Our commander, *Kapitan* Mikhailov."

Putin gaped at Sleptsev for a moment, then burst out laughing. "They must not have let you out of the barracks before now, Sleptsev. Mikhailov, that lucky bastard, made it out of that fuck-up alive. I heard that his bulldozer of a NCO, Rudenko, hauled him out."

For just a moment, Sleptsev's face went completely slack, as if all the tension had gone out of the muscles of his face. He blinked, then said, "No one told me, sir! I thought all this time that everyone who went there was dead!"

"Those fucking imbeciles at regimental headquarters." Putin shook his head in disgust. "It's no wonder we lost the Cold War. For what it's worth, boy, I'm sorry. Our regiment sent out men to find out what happened to yours, but all they found was burned out debris, a blown up helicopter, and lots of bodies. A full company is still out there, dicking around for nothing." He frowned. "I'm not sure Rudenko did Mikhailov any favors by saving him, though. The good captain is probably going to wind up in front of a military court, what with losing all those men here, on top of the company he lost in Spitzbergen last year. It looks bad for the Army, you know. The brass doesn't like to be embarrassed. Stupid fuckers." He suddenly turned around, put his hands to his mouth to amplify his voice, and bellowed into the crowd. "*Poshyol ty'!*"

Another round of curses and catcalls, accompanied by a few poorly-aimed shot glasses, answered his latest challenge.

Satisfied, Putin stood up, swaying unsteadily. "God, I have to take a piss."

Sleptsev rose from his stool. "I think I'll join you, sir. It was a long walk from the barracks."

"Just don't pee on my boots, or you'll be licking them clean, boy."

Pushing his way through the crowd, Putin exchanged good-natured insults and curses with the men and more than a few of the women he passed. At last through the throng, he made his way down a narrow hallway that held several doors. Lively banter and laughter could be heard from some rooms, moans and cries from others. "Fucking cathouse."

At the very end were two doors, both unmarked. Putin kicked open the one on the right, surprising two men and a woman who were snorting a white powdery substance off a cut piece of glass over one of the two sinks.

His face clouding with a red rage, Putin roared, "*Get the fuck out of here!*" All signs of his inebriation gone, he lunged forward and slammed a fist into the nearest man's face, driving his head into the stained porcelain sink with a reverberating *clang*.

The woman shrieked and ran, dropping the glass holding the powder. It shattered on the tile floor.

The second man cocked his fist, ready to hit Putin from behind. Sleptsev delivered a savage kick to the man's groin, then drove a knee into the man's face as he bent over, his mouth open in a silent scream of pain.

Putin grabbed the first man by the collar and hurled him out the door, and Sleptsev followed suit with his own victim.

"If I ever see you in this place again," Putin screamed, the veins in his neck bulging, as the trio escaped down the hallway to the bar, "I'll fucking kill you!" He spat after them.

After slamming the door shut, he told Sleptsev, "Lucky for them they were just civilians. If they'd been some of our own, I'd have pounded them into paste. What's wrong with people like that, doing drugs? Isn't vodka good enough?"

Stepping up to the wall and the long metal gutter that served as a urinal, Putin undid his fly. "It shouldn't be so much work just to take a piss."

He cried out as he felt a white hot pain in his back, just above his kidneys. A veteran of many bar fights and half a dozen combat actions in Chechnya, Putin reacted instantly. He whirled around, bringing up his elbow to hit his attacker — it could only have been Sleptsev, he thought — in the face.

Except that it wasn't Sleptsev. Not entirely, at least. Putin saw that the younger soldier's face had softened like warm putty, and something, a tentacle, perhaps, protruded from his chest and disappeared behind Putin.

Sleptsev leaned back, impossibly far, as if his spine had elongated, to avoid Putin's attack. Putin let his own momentum continue to spin him around, and he slammed his right fist into Sleptsev's exposed side.

Instead of his hand rebounding after feeling the satisfying crunch of a broken rib or two, Putin's hand disappeared into Sleptsev's body, the younger man's flesh extruding outward to capture Putin's entire forearm.

Putin gaped in amazed horror. "What the fuck are you?"

The only response from the slack-faced soldier was an agonizing bolt of pain in Putin's back, as if someone had shoved a knife even deeper into his body.

With his free hand, Putin reached around to try to grab whatever it was and pull it free. He recoiled as his hand clamped around something slick and slimy, that pulsed like testicles during orgasm.

The creature that had masqueraded as Sleptsev wrapped its arms around him, pulling him into a tight embrace. Then the putty-like flesh of the young soldier's face parted to reveal what was truly underneath.

Putin's scream died on his lips as he was drawn into a dark abyss.

* * *

The human's struggles peaked as its head was drawn into the thing's mandibles. While they had teeth, the jaws were not intended primarily for tearing, but for gripping prey while the salivary acids did their work. Ignoring the muffled screams, the thing's saliva began to reduce the skin and muscle of the human's face, then the bone of its skull, to elements that could be digested.

But this was not merely an act of consumption, of feeding. Long strands of cilia, much like very fine hair, rode along with the salivary acids. Through these organs the thing sensed the chemical composition of what it consumed, and with that information, the thing could adjust the content of the salivary acids to break down nearly any organic material into food.

More than that, however, the cilia could identify electrochemical impulses associated with the cells of the nervous system. Like a forest of antennae, they collected the data produced by and contained within the prey's brain, and through a highly complex process evolved over countless millennia translated this information into memories and knowledge that the harvester could access within its own central nervous system.

Since this process took longer than simple feeding, the thing drew its latest victim into one of the three toilet stalls and closed the flimsy door. It knew that there was little chance of being disturbed for some time after the violent display that it and its prey had put on, expelling the three humans who had been here.

Once it was finished, it stripped the human of its clothing and slipped out of its own. Then it altered its shape, the flesh oozing along its exoskeleton to become an exact mimic of Putin. It donned his uniform, then buried Sleptsev's uniform in the overflowing trash can.

Opening the door a crack, it took a quick glance down the hall. It was empty.

The thing took one last look at Putin's headless, naked body, and a thought emerged from among the mass of memories it had taken.

Fingerprints. While it had already destroyed the face and teeth, which could be used to identify the human, the body could still be identified from the tips of the fingers.

Taking the prey's hands into its mouth, it dissolved the fingers up to the first knuckle. It knew the body would be discovered, but identifying it would be difficult.

The thing wanted to ingest more of its victim, but there was no way to tell when its feeding might be interrupted by one of the humans outside.

Extending an arm, the limb stretching beyond what a human could manage, it propped open the small window near the ceiling that looked out upon the dark alley outside. Then it shoved Putin's body through, ignoring the wet splat it made in the rain-drenched garbage.

Checking its appearance in the mirror, the thing pulled open the door and headed back into the club. The humans there turned to see it emerge, shuffling slightly, perfectly mimicking its drunken prey. It made what it knew the humans would consider a crude gesture and shouted. "*Poshyol ty'*, you whores and sons of whores!"

As if letting out a pent-up breath, the club-goers hooted and jeered, happy to see that Putin was in one piece after the earlier altercation with the druggies, who had been none too gently shown to the door.

While the thing had slipped into the role of its most recent victim, it had no intention of dallying here. It had come here based on Sleptsev's memories. He had been to this place before, a place frequented by army men, human predators that the thing might be able to manipulate to its own ends. Putin had simply been a convenient victim.

No, it could not stay here to reinforce its new persona. It had unfinished business to attend to at the military hospital.

* * *

After arriving in Moscow, Jack called Rudenko on his cell phone. None of the calls Jack, Naomi, and Renee had made from the States, or the calls Jack had made from India, had gone through. After arriving in-country, Jack had first tried to reach Mikhailov again, but had only gotten what he assumed must have been an out of service message spoken in Russian by a sultry female voice.

When he'd called Rudenko again, the NCO had answered the phone right away.

"We were not expecting you, my friend, but both the *kapitan* and I are very glad you are here. You, I suspect, will not be so happy after we talk."

"And talk we must, Pavel. The question is how can I get to you? There aren't any flights to Stavropol until tomorrow, and it's too far to drive." Stavropol was over seven hundred miles from Moscow.

"Stay there. I will arrange things."

Not fifteen minutes later, a heavily-tattooed young man who looked like he might be at home in a movie about the Russian mafia appeared. After introducing himself only as Drago, he led Jack through the airport to the cargo terminal. After Drago said a few whispered words to the airport security personnel, Jack was ushered outside, where a twin turboprop aircraft that Jack recognized as an An-32 stood waiting. An aircraft widely used in both military and civilian service, this one, bearing civilian markings, looked like it had been through World War Three.

Setting aside the fear that gripped him at the sight of the flying death trap, Jack reluctantly followed the young man up the rear cargo ramp and strapped himself in.

The trip south was a surprisingly smooth flight, but it ended with a white knuckle night landing in heavy rain, and Jack couldn't get off the plane fast enough.

Waiting for him was Rudenko, sitting behind the wheel of a *Tigr* four-wheeled tactical vehicle that was the Russian Army's equivalent of the Hummer. Two other soldiers sat in the rear, and all three men were heavily armed.

"It is good to see you, Jack." Rudenko extended a bandaged paw, and Jack hesitated. "I am fine. No worse than sunburn." He grabbed Jack's hand and shook it in a crushing grip.

"And you, Pavel." He winced as Rudenko let go his hand, then pressed something large and heavy into his palm. "What's this?"

"It is the pistol you sent me as a gift, the .50 caliber Desert Eagle. Strictly illegal, as you know, and even more illegal for a foreigner to possess. But necessary now, I fear."

Jack glanced at the two men in the back seat, who gave him respectful nods. He noticed that both had shotguns, and they quickly turned their attention back to the rain beyond the windows, their eyes scanning the darkness.

"They see and hear nothing of this, my friend. They were with us on Spitsbergen and know what we face."

Jack nodded, satisfied. The last thing he wanted was to land in hot water with the Russian authorities. It would be a bit difficult, even for Rudenko, to explain why Jack was carrying an illegal weapon on a Russian Army base.

Jack turned back to Rudenko. "How's *Kapitan* Mikhailov doing?"

"He is recovering rapidly." Rudenko put the *Tigr* into gear and headed toward the airport exit. "But he is in a great deal of trouble. Those things killed everyone else, all the men who accompanied us to that facility. He will likely face a military tribunal."

"A court-martial?"

Rudenko nodded, the instrument lights illuminating his grim expression. "He has led men into battle twice, and both times his unit was destroyed under uncertain circumstances."

"And no one believes what really happened?"

"I do not know for certain, but suspect not." He glanced at Jack. "Who could believe the things we have seen?"

Jack tensed as they reached the gate to the base that served as the headquarters for the 247th Airborne Regiment. The two guards approached the *Tigr* and peered inside. Rudenko nodded to the one who looked in on his side. The man returned the gesture, and together the two soldiers retreated back out of the rain into the guard post. A moment later the gate was opened, and Rudenko proceeded inside.

A few minutes later, he pulled into a spot at the military hospital.

"Come. Let us go see the good *kapitan*."

* * *

Nearly three hours later, well past midnight, Jack sat back, stunned. "My God, Sergei." Sitting in Mikhailov's room in the hospital, he not only felt as if he'd fallen down the rabbit hole, but had been accelerated to the speed of light into a horrible alternate universe as he listened to the Russian captain and Rudenko relate what had happened at the enigmatic facility near Elista.

"God had nothing to do with it, my friend." Sergei's eyes were clear, but he wore a haunted expression that Jack knew all too well.

"And there's no telling how many of those things may have been spawned?"

Mikhailov shook his head. "No. There is no way of knowing that. But if these larval forms you described consumed the car tires and other missing plastic and rubber parts, all the animals, the non-infected corn plots, and the people at the lab and those who came after, there surely must be dozens of them. Certainly the ones that we killed were not all there had been, and we know for certain that one capable of mimicking a human escaped."

"Sleptsev, I am sure of it. He was the only one who was alone long enough in the building with the corn to have been taken." Rudenko spat. "He was shaping into a good soldier."

"They were all good soldiers, Rudenko."

With a solemn nod, Rudenko handed around a small silver flask. Jack took a quick swig, holding back a cough as the fiery vodka blasted down his throat, before passing it to Mikhailov.

After clearing his throat, Jack said, "There's more that you need to know. Naomi's been researching the genetics of these things, and she's found differences between the original harvesters, like the ones we fought on Spitsbergen, and these new ones."

The two Russians looked at him expectantly.

"From what she understands, the original harvesters couldn't reproduce on their own, or they were sterile. That's one reason there were so few of them. But these new ones, the ones being spawned by the infected corn, apparently have the ability to reproduce asexually, meaning it would only take one of them, not two."

"How?" Mikhailov exchanged a horrified look with Rudenko.

"She's not sure exactly, but the genes that are involved appear to be similar to those of an amoeba."

"Like the microbes that cause dysentery?"

Jack nodded. "Right. She thinks they may reproduce by something like cellular fission, where one cell divides and becomes two, then four, then sixteen, and so on."

Rudenko gave him a blank look and turned to Mikhailov, who spoke to him in Russian for a moment with what Jack assumed was a brief explanation.

"*Chyort voz'mi*," Rudenko whispered. "How quickly? How fast?"

Jack shook his head. "She doesn't know yet. We might never know, unless we can set up some contained experiments where we can observe the things without them getting loose." Jack didn't like the idea, remembering how the last experiments had gone involving captured harvesters. Unfortunately, they might not have any other choice. "On the bright side, at least your people are still out there looking around the facility. They might get lucky and bag one or two of these things, which would validate your story and give us a specimen to study."

"They are not properly equipped. They do not have thermal imagers, nor do they have cats, of course. And while the Russian Army does not have a reputation for gentle interrogation techniques, the third field expedient, of trying to set suspected harvesters on fire, was not adopted, for obvious reasons. Nor are the men out there armed with proper weapons."

Rudenko hefted his KS-K shotgun. "Those *svolochi* definitely do not like the Dragon's Breath."

Jack nodded, impressed at what Rudenko had told him about the special shotgun shells. "Those rounds are something I already texted Naomi about. She'll pass the word to others. I have a feeling we're going to need a lot of those by the time all is said and done. But that brings us to the next question, the big one: what do we do now?"

The two Russians exchanged an unhappy look. "There is not much more we can do," Mikhailov said. "No one will listen to me, any more or less than they already have through the reports I have given, because I am considered incompetent, a madman, or both. No one will listen to Rudenko, because he is only a NCO and has an impressive list of past offenses, and he is guilty by association."

"So we do nothing?" Jack felt his hands begin to clench with frustration.

"I'm open to suggestions, my friend. You are faring better with this matter in America?"

Jack had no trouble discerning the sarcasm that crept into Mikhailov's voice. "No. Goddammit, no we're not. None of the things are loose there yet, as far as we know, but nobody's taking it seriously, either." He rubbed his eyes, then looked back at Mikhailov. "I'm sorry. I just feel like we're riding on an out of control train that's about to run off a cliff."

Outside the room, they heard the sound of boots coming down the hall, the guards snapping to attention.

Someone was coming.

CHAPTER FIFTEEN

"If you keep doing that to yourself, you're going to wind up as bald as I am."

Renee shot Carl a venomous look. "Hey, I'd still be better looking, Mr. G-Man." She rubbed her eyes before turning back to the computer monitors.

"And smarter, too." Carl pulled up a chair and sat down next to her. "But if you were smarter than me, you wouldn't be working yourself to death. Even I know when to take a break. Sometimes."

"I can't, Carl. I'm *this* close." She held up a hand, the index finger and thumb spread just a hair. "This goddamn close!"

Violating his self-imposed workplace standards of decorum, Carl gently put a hand on her shoulder and said in a quiet voice, "You'll figure it out. But as exhausted as you are right now, you could miss something as obvious as a dump truck in a swimming pool."

"That's what scares me. But we don't have time to screw around. Every minute counts."

"Yeah, I know." Carl gave her shoulder a gentle squeeze, then let go so she could try to focus on the image-matching algorithm. After several false starts in tying all the necessary programs together, it was running the way she wanted. The first few tries had resulted in so many false matches that the results were useless. Much of it was because the images she was using from the passport database were of terrible quality to begin with, and she'd muttered a long stream of curses at the makers of passport cameras and those who used them. After a lot of testing and tweaking, she'd gotten it to find a high percentage of correct matches while generating few false matches.

While the resulting process worked better than she'd initially expected, it wasn't perfect. Some potential matches were bound to be lost, although she'd still set the match threshold fairly low. But the biggest problem was that it was taking forever to run. She didn't have the computing resources available here that she'd had when she'd been with the Earth Defense Society.

On top of the mountain of frustration the image matching system had caused, the news she and Carl had received from Naomi and Jack had been chilling, to say the least. Naomi's revelation about the possibility that the harvesters might be able to reproduce on their own, no longer having to rely solely on the transgenic weapon of the New Horizons corn, was particularly frightening.

Worse, there were more reports cropping up in the news about events that fit Renee's search criteria for possible harvester-related incidents. The majority continued to be focused in Brazil, China, and India, but new reports had come in that morning from France and Italy, the leading corn producers in Europe.

"Whoever this asshole is, he's certainly gotten around. Check this out." She pulled up a French web site and hit the translate button. "This was posted just a few hours ago. It's sort of an alternate news site, and the post is about a mass disappearance in a little town south of Bordeaux, France."

Looking over her shoulder, Carl read a few bits of the text. "Over two hundred people disappeared...suspected alien abduction...police not available for comment..."

"It hasn't been picked up by any of the real news services. That's the way things have been with most of these reports, with the newsies just writing all this off as hoaxes or mass hysteria. Let's check this out." There was an image below the text summary that linked to a video. Renee clicked on it, and it began to play.

Carl watched as whoever was holding the camera moved slowly down a very quaint-looking cobblestone street. The sky was darkening, and the street lights were already flickering on. Had the scene been a still image, he could have pictured it on a postcard, a sleepy little French town where the only serious pursuit was drinking wine or coffee at a little sidewalk café.

But there was something wrong. He couldn't put his finger on it as he watched the video, but he could hear it in the voice of the woman who was narrating her exploration. He couldn't understand her words, but he could tell she was nervous. And scared. "Do you understand any of what she's saying?"

"Only a little. We'll have to get a French linguist to listen to it. But I think the gist of it so far is that she came here to visit someone, maybe an uncle. She was supposed to meet this person at the train station, but they never showed up. And whoever it is isn't answering the phone. So this gal's taking a hike from the train station to their apartment or whatever, and...oh, Jesus."

The woman narrating the video gasped and the image shook as she turned a corner and found a body on the ground. Sprawled amid overturned tables and chairs of a café like Carl had just pictured in his mind, the body belonged to a middle-aged man. Or so he thought, as the woman managed to steady the shot, focusing on the body. In the background, it was clear that the little café had been demolished, as if it had been the scene of a fight involving two rival biker gangs.

"Pause that!"

Renee clicked the pause button as Carl leaned closer to the screen. "Are you seeing the same thing I am?"

"If by that you mean that half of his torso is missing, yes." She put her fingers to her lips. "God, I feel like I'm going to puke."

"That's not a typical trauma wound, like from an explosion or even like the body was struck by something that sheared part of it away."

"It looks like he melted. Dissolved."

Renee's voice sounded very small in Carl's ears, and he put his hand back on her shoulder. While Carl hadn't seen it himself, the Norwegian officer, Terje Halvorsen, whom Jack and Naomi had met up with on Spitsbergen during the battle for the seed vault there, had reported seeing one of his men, dead, with a limb in similar condition. No one had an explanation then.

"Play it." Carl didn't need to point out to Renee something else he'd noticed about the body: while he wasn't any expert on uniforms, he would have bet a month's pay the dead man was wearing the uniform of a gendarme, a cop.

With an unsteady hand, Renee clicked the mouse button to continue the video.

The image stayed focused on the body for a moment more, and the woman somehow managed to get her voice under control. She was crying, but she wasn't hysterical. Even without knowing exactly what she was saying, Carl could tell she was determined to get to her destination. He felt as if he was watching one of those cheesy horror movies where the characters were holding a video camera. Only this was real.

"She hasn't seen anyone else so far," Renee whispered after the woman spoke a bit more. "Then she says, 'The town is dead.'"

The camera panned around, showing what looked like a small central square with an old stone church at one end. Aside from the woman with the camera, there was no one else.

The woman headed for the church, and Carl and Renee watched her hand move forward to push against the door, which was standing ajar. Breathing so fast now that she was nearly panting, the woman stepped inside. The video quickly adjusted to the dim lighting, but Carl suddenly wished it hadn't. Along with several pools of liquid, there were at least a dozen bodies. Some were draped across the pews, while others lay on the floor. Most of them were intact, while others had been partially consumed.

Unable to help herself, the woman bent over and vomited on the floor. The camera panned crazily across part of the floor, then the woman's stomach as the audio relayed the retching sounds. Then it shifted to show what was to her left.

Carl and Renee both gasped in recognition as they saw the dark, insectile form that grew with astonishing speed in the image as it rushed toward the woman.

Sensing something approaching, the woman looked up. Reflexively bringing up her hands to defend herself, the camera caught a final glimpse of the blurred image of a gleaming chitinous exoskeleton. There was a piercing scream from the woman, and the camera recorded its fall to the floor.

The video ended.

"Jesus Christ."

Carl looked at her. "You hadn't watched that yet?"

She shook her head. "No. I just read the translated text and cross-referenced it against the other French and international news services before you came by." She pulled up another web page and did a quick search, then scanned the result summaries. "Looks like the video's going viral on the web, but everybody thinks it's a gag horror film made by college students or something. I'll have to check with the other agencies to see if the French police have actually moved on this."

"Wait a minute. How did the video get to the web in the first place if she was killed?"

"There are apps and web services where you can stream live video, even from your phone. She was broadcasting live to this French alternate news site. Whoever was tuned in then saw the whole thing as it happened."

"And they think it's a joke?"

"That's the gist of the comments, according to the on-line translator. Thank God for that. My French sucks."

Carl sat there for a moment, staring at the black rectangle on the web page that was the end of the French woman's video, the recording of the last moment of her life.

"Don't stick your neck out too far on this, hon," Renee cautioned.

"I'm not. I know I've got to rein it in or the Director's going to have my guts. But I think I've got something legit on this one. I've had a team working with the French National Police on a kidnapping case, a French father and American mother, and the mother's accused the father of abducting their daughter to France, but nobody could find him." He pointed at the screen. "What's the name of this town again?"

Renee opened her mouth to tell him, but he grabbed a pad of sticky notes and handed it to her. "You know I can't pronounce anything that's not written on the sports page."

Rolling her eyes, Renee wrote down the name of the town, then handed him the note.

"The French are about to get a little tip on the whereabouts of our suspected kidnapper. Then we'll see what happens after that."

Popping his head above the cubicle walls, Carl took a quick look around the office before leaning down and giving Renee a quick kiss on the lips. "Keep up the good work, babe."

"Casanova," she sighed as she listened to the sounds of his footsteps quickly recede down the walkway, heading toward his office.

The warmth in her heart that she felt for Carl gave way to icy fear as she looked back at the screen and the video recorded by the unknown French woman.

Taking in a deep breath, she returned her attention to the image matching program on one of the other monitors, hoping against hope that it would finish soon.

* * *

"Just the person I wanted to talk to."

Naomi turned at the sound of Howard Morgan's voice. Just a moment before, the entire hallway behind her had been empty. The man was uncanny. She smiled. "Doing your magical appearing-out-of-thin-air act again, Howard?"

Morgan didn't return the smile. "A little birdie told me that you'd shifted your research focus to the Beta-Three payload, rather than the delivery system."

"Yes, I did temporarily. I helped the team get past the obstacles that had been holding up their progress on the delivery system, and Harmony has them hammering hard on the next stage of development."

"So you're telling me that your leadership on the project isn't needed any longer?"

She stopped and turned to face him, crossing her arms. "No, I'm telling you that your tech lead is doing a great job, and that when they've finished this part of engineering the delivery shells they're going to hit more obstacles, which I'll help them through. In the meantime, most of what they have to do is work that they're well-trained and well-equipped to perform, and I wanted to take a closer look at what to you represents an even greater windfall of genetic technology, but that to me represents a threat to our entire world." Morgan opened his mouth to speak, but she didn't let him. "And if this 'little birdie' happens to be my dear friend Dr. Kelso, he can go straight to hell. It's fine by me if he wants to poke his head in the door whenever he wants, but his refusal to even acknowledge my existence unless I get right in his face is unprofessional, to say the least."

By now, Naomi had worked up quite a head of steam. She was tired and worried to death, and the last thing she felt inclined to tolerate was someone tattling on her, especially if that someone had not a clue what she was doing or why.

Morgan didn't flinch. "Fair enough. I'll speak to Kelso and get him straightened out. But I also wanted to remind you who the boss is around here, Naomi. That would be me. I don't necessarily have an issue with you wanting to go off the reservation on your own for a while, but I do have an issue with not being informed about it." He stepped closer, his expression and voice softening. "Listen, you are, without doubt, the crown jewel of this company among the people in my employ. But even the crown jewel is bound by a few rules." He smiled. "Not many, perhaps, but a few. I try not to be a tyrant, but I like to know what my people are doing. From now on, it would make me a lot happier if you'd tell me about any changes, rather than Kelso or anyone else whispering in my ear."

He gestured for her to keep walking in the direction she had been before he appeared. "And another thing," he went on. "I want you to go home and get some sleep. I've also checked the vault and building access logs, and you've locked yourself up in this place for most of the last three days. I consider myself a workaholic, but you're too much. This isn't a residence."

She waved away his concern. "I nap on a cot in my office and take showers in the gym. I have several changes of clothes and can send them out to be cleaned." She shrugged. "I used to do the same thing sometimes when I was with New Horizons. While Jack's away, especially with everything that's going on, I need to be here."

"Naomi..."

She stopped and turned to face him again, this time reaching out and taking his arm. "I *need* to be here, Howard. I don't think you understand. One thing you don't know, because I didn't tell Kelso, and I don't think Harmony did, either, is that we think we identified a gene sequence in the harvester DNA contained in the

Beta-Three corn samples that may allow them to reproduce asexually. That's a game-changer, because the original harvesters couldn't reproduce. We don't know why, and probably never will. But the generation introduced with Beta-Three can. And my friends in the FBI think the possible incidents involving harvester infestations are growing both in number and severity." She looked at him with frightened eyes. "The genie is out of the bottle, Howard, and he's far more dangerous than any of us imagined. That's why my work on the harvester DNA from the Beta-Three samples is critical. If we don't understand them, we'll never have a chance of stopping them."

She started walking again. She'd been heading down the hall toward her office. She'd forgotten to feed the cats their dinner, and was dreading the mess that Alexander had probably made. When he was full, he just slept all day. When he wasn't, he could be a holy terror. Thankfully, she didn't have to worry about cleaning out their litter box: someone on the janitorial staff took care of it, but she'd never caught the person in the act so she could thank him or her.

"It's that bad?"

"It looks like it, yes. We know they're loose in India and Russia for certain, and I just got word from my FBI contacts that there's also been an outbreak in France, and probably Italy, as well."

"But why nothing here so far?"

"I don't know. Maybe whoever was peddling these seeds only sold to one buyer here, although that seems extremely unlikely, considering the number of companies that would kill for this technology." She looked at him. "I'm still waiting for you to fulfill your end of our bargain, Howard. I need the name of the seller."

"Remember, I only said that I'd consider it." Before Naomi could explode, he went on, "And I have. His name was Norman Kline."

"Was?"

Morgan nodded. "Kline was actually a middleman. He said the source was a New Horizons employee, but that was all he would give us. I had Karina Petrovsky, my head of security, keep tabs on him after our little exchange last year in hopes of discovering the source so we might be able to deal with him directly. New Horizons was defunct, of course, but he might have more samples or other information that we might have used. Unfortunately, Kline was killed in his home in Seattle during a robbery the day you started work here, and the name of the source went with him."

Naomi turned, intending to rush down the hall to her office to call Renee, but found Morgan's hand on her arm. "Remember, Naomi, that information didn't come from me, and Beta-Three doesn't exist. You may have friends in the FBI, but I've got friends, as well. I don't want you as my enemy. And you certainly don't want me as yours."

"I don't care about assigning blame, Howard. All I care about is finding out whatever we can about where the seeds went, and who has them besides us so we can try to stop this." She looked at his hand, still holding her arm. "Do you mind?"

Howard let her go, and she ran toward her office. The thought briefly passed through her mind that she always seemed to be running to her office, but she never got any farther from the nightmare that pursued her.

CHAPTER SIXTEEN

Jack, Mikhailov, and Rudenko exchanged helpless looks. Jack's presence on the base was a major breach in security that could easily send Rudenko, at least, to military prison, and potentially land Jack in prison as a spy. The Cold War was over, but that didn't mean the old suspicions weren't still harbored by East and West. His only cover had been the late hour of the visit, although he was sure Rudenko would have figured out some other way to smuggle him in had he arrived during daylight hours. But Jack would never pass for anything other than what he was: an American civilian on a tourist passport who had no legitimate reason or authority to be on a Russian military installation.

The door flew open.

Polkovnik Zaitsev, Mikhailov's regimental commander, stopped short, his mouth hanging open as he caught sight of Jack, who got to his feet. Zaitsev's face clouded over with what could only be anger, and he turned to Mikhailov and barked something in Russian. After a rapid-fire exchange that went on for what seemed like a long time, Zaitsev closed the door and turned to Jack. "So you are this Jack Dawson fellow who interfered with the Spitsbergen operation?"

Jack was surprised at Zaitsev's voice. He sounded like a Brit, with almost no trace of a Russian accent. "I like to think that we provided a bit of support to our Russian and Norwegian allies."

"From what you just told me, sir, we could use his help." Mikhailov's expression was grim. "He can be trusted, *polkovnik*."

Zaitsev glared at him for a moment, then turned to Jack. "I'm not in the habit of divulging our secrets to foreigners, least of all Americans, but I cannot in good conscience not take advantage of whatever information you might be able to provide." He moved to the other side of the tiny room and leaned back against the window sill. "There appears to have been another incident. Only this time it's a village, Ulan-Erg, which is a few kilometers from where the facility is located, and where many who worked at the facility lived. We don't have any details, only some hysterical reports from the local police that are quite similar to those we received about the facility that Mikhailov was sent in to investigate."

"Are we to deploy again, sir?" Mikhailov sat up, a spark in his eyes. Jack could understand his eagerness: while none of them wanted to face the horror again, Mikhailov wanted payback for his dead men.

"No. You, your troublemaking sidekick," he shot a glance at Rudenko, who was standing at attention, "and your American friend are staying right here. I've already spoken with the commander of the 247th Airborne Regiment here, and he's agreed to deploy a battalion for a cordon-and-search of Ulan-Erg under the guise of an unannounced night training exercise."

"Why mask it as an exercise?" Jack shook his head in confusion. "Your people, both the troops and the civilians, must know that something's happening. Even if you just label it as a terrorist attack, that'll help make it real. People have to be warned."

"Warned of what?" Zaitsev shrugged. "I am convinced that something is going on, but even if I could fully accept the idea of these harvester creatures, how does that help our people? What do I tell them, that they can be attacked without warning, that their neighbor or lover might be a monster? Perhaps we should order that every household should have at least one cat in residence, and toss them out of our planes with little parachutes."

While it wouldn't have been so great for the cats, Jack thought that wasn't a half-bad idea. But he let it go for now. Out of the box ideas would come later, if he and the others survived. "Fine, but please tell me that some of the troops going out will at least have thermal imagers."

Zaitsev grimaced. "They only have two. They are new, and the regiment here had them for evaluation purposes. But I'm not sure what to tell them to look for."

"They'll know when they see a harvester, colonel. Trust me, they'll know. And are the troops going out equipped with any of the special munitions that Mikhailov's men had?"

"No. They do not have that sort of thing here. As I understand it, those were another little specialty of Rudenko's."

The NCO made no outward sign that his name had been mentioned, but Jack noticed that he relaxed slightly at the colonel's complimentary tone. While Rudenko would no doubt still be in hot water for getting Jack onto the base, he probably wouldn't be tossed in prison.

Down below, they heard doors slamming open, followed by hundreds of pairs of boots slapping through the rain-soaked ground. Men shouted orders, and in the distance came the whine of helicopter engines spooling up.

Zaitsev pulled the curtains aside so he could glance out the window. "It's about time. Were it our regiment, we would have been boarding fifteen minutes ago."

As he turned back around to face the other three men, the door opened. None of them had heard the newcomer approach amidst the hubbub outside.

In the doorway, his drenched uniform dripping water on the floor, stood an officer, a major, if Jack recalled the Russian rank insignias correctly. In his hands he held an assault rifle, the muzzle pointed at Zaitsev's chest. Jack was sitting off to one side, out of the man's line of sight.

"Putin!" Zaitsev bellowed. "What is the meaning of this?"

In the hallway, out of view of his three companions, Jack caught sight of the sprawled forms of the two men who'd been on guard outside the room. They were the two who Rudenko had said had survived the battle on Spitsbergen. They were dead.

In Jack's eyes, the next few seconds seemed to unfold in an eerie, stroboscopic slow-motion sequence.

The muzzle flash from the rifle as Putin fired.

Zaitsev stumbling back, arms windmilling, a cone of blood spraying out behind him.

Putin turning, aiming the rifle toward Mikhailov, who was diving to the floor on the far side of his bed.

Rudenko, unable to fire his shotgun without hitting Jack, charging Putin. The heavy thud as the big man slammed into the Russian major, throwing off his aim as he fired at Mikhailov.

The big Desert Eagle in Jack's hands, the muzzle coming up slowly, so slowly, to track Putin as he grappled with Rudenko.

The NCO grunting in pain, then falling to the floor.

Putin, something that looked like a machete sticking out of his chest, slick with Rudenko's blood, again aiming his rifle toward Mikhailov.

The flash of the Desert Eagle firing, the heavy recoil hammering Jack's arms and shoulders.

The Putin-thing screeched as the bullet slammed into its body, which burst into flame as the incendiary filling in the slug exploded.

Time rushed forward again as the shrieking, burning harvester vaulted over Zaitsev's body and hurled itself out the window.

Jack rushed to the shattered window and caught sight of the thing three floors below. It had the good fortune to have landed in a deep puddle, which put out the flames of its burning malleable flesh. It had fallen amidst a group of the airborne troops double-timing out to the landing field, so while Jack held the thing in his sights, he didn't dare fire for fear of hitting one of the Russians.

Mikhailov appeared beside him, and he shouted something at the troops who were looking from what they took to be a fallen comrade to this lunatic wearing nothing but a hospital gown, yelling at them from the third floor.

The harvester decided the matter. Leaving gobbets of smoldering flesh behind, it raced away on all fours, a revolting hybrid of man and beast that shouldered aside any men in its way, knocking them to the ground like bowling pins.

Those who had been standing in shock, watching the spectacle, dove to the ground as Rudenko's shotgun roared and a massive jet of white hot particles flew from the muzzle. Either sufficiently confident in his aim that he wouldn't miss or simply willing to sacrifice any of his fellow soldiers who got in the way, he fired three times at the thing before it turned the corner. But the already short range of the Dragon's Breath shells was further shortened by the rain, and all he managed to accomplish was to elicit a stream of curses and shouts from the unsuspecting men below.

"*Tvoyu mat'!*" Rudenko slammed a bloody fist down on the windowsill in rage. He bellowed at the men below, pointing in the direction Putin had fled, and several men took off in pursuit. There was a deep cut in his arm, just below the elbow, where the harvester had wounded him. It was bleeding, drops splashing onto the windowsill as he angrily gestured for more men to follow after Putin, but the cut was clearly superficial.

The same could not be said for Zaitsev.

"Oh, shit," Jack hissed as he and Mikhailov knelt next to the fallen colonel, while Rudenko pounded out of the room, bellowing for help. Zaitsev's uniform jacket was wet with blood around the neat hole in the right side of his chest, and there was more crimson pooling under his body. The air was thick with the coppery scent of blood, with a faint trace of the nauseating scent of ammonia and burning hemp characteristic of the harvesters as they transitioned to their natural form.

Holstering his pistol, Jack pressed his hands to the wound in Zaitsev's chest, applying pressure to slow the bleeding. "Colonel? Can you hear me?"

Zaitsev's eyes blinked open. He nodded a fraction. "That was one of them?"

"Yes. And there could be more." Jack looked up at the sound of running feet. Two men and a woman wearing surgical scrubs ran into the room, with two more behind them, wheeling a gurney.

As one of them took over from Jack, pressing a pad of gauze against the wound, Jack began to stand up, but Zaitsev grabbed his arm, his grip surprisingly strong. "You must help those men," he whispered, a trickle of blood running from his lips. "You and Mikhailov. They will not know what to expect, will not understand."

Jack glanced up at Mikhailov, who returned a curt nod. "Yes, sir. I'll do what I can."

Four more men burst into the room, all wearing full tactical gear and holding weapons at the ready. One of them, wearing the same rank insignia as Zaitsev, glanced at Jack, then knelt next to Zaitsev, who whispered a few words to him.

Babbling something in Russian, the man who seemed to be in charge of the medical team pushed the new colonel, who Jack assumed must be the commander of the 247th Airborne Regiment, whose men were outside, out of the way. Then the medical team gently lifted Zaitsev onto the gurney before racing down the hall toward the elevators.

The colonel turned to Mikhailov and asked a few questions in Russian. Then he turned to Jack. The man was powerfully built, like a bodybuilder, and could probably have given Rudenko a good run for his money in a fight. He had close-cropped gray hair and blue eyes that seemed to take in everything, yet revealed nothing. "You are American?"

Jack nodded.

Looking at the Desert Eagle under Jack's left arm and his bloodied hands, the colonel asked, "You have combat experience?"

"Yes, sir."

The colonel glanced down the hall where the medical team had taken Zaitsev, then turned back to Jack. "He told me you are to come with us, if you wish. If he were anyone else, I would think him mad." He suddenly extended a hand to take Jack's, even though Jack's own hand was covered with Zaitsev's blood. The colonel's grasp was powerful. "You will come? As, ah, special advisor, we will say, *da?*"

Jack couldn't even imagine the diplomatic implications of what this man was asking, not to mention the risk to his own life. Jack knew that he'd been lucky so far, incredibly lucky. But eventually, that luck was going to run out. It was only a matter of time. Just in the last forty-eight hours, he'd been in two lethal confrontations, and was hurling himself into a third. He hadn't even had enough time for the shakes, the adrenaline crash, to catch up to him after the shootout with the Putin-thing. There was no time now to think, to ponder. He thought of Naomi, and cursed himself for a fool. He wouldn't even have time to let her know what he was doing, which he suspected was probably for the best. She would reach through the phone and kill him on the spot. The reasonable answer, the smart answer, was to stay here, to let the Russians handle this on their own. But he also knew that this wasn't a fight they were prepared for, and if he could do anything to help them, he would. He had to. "Yes, sir. I'll come with you. I'll need gear, though."

As if on cue, Rudenko appeared in the doorway with another soldier in tow, both laden with uniforms, equipment, and weapons.

"Hurry. We leave soon." The colonel spoke a few words to Mikhailov, then he and the three men who had come with him turned and left, their boots echoing down the hall until the sound was swallowed up by the growing roar of helicopter turbines.

"Shit, shit, shit." Jack quickly stripped out of his clothes and donned the uniform and equipment that Rudenko handed him, while the other soldier helped Mikhailov get dressed. "What, you're coming, too? You should be staying here!"

"Would you, after what just happened?" Mikhailov winced as he pulled on the uniform jacket, then the body armor. "I can walk, I can think, I can shoot. I will not stay behind."

Rudenko threw Jack a worried glance, but said nothing.

Jack cinched up the combat harness, heavy with ammunition and grenades. "Who's the colonel, by the way? The regimental commander here?"

"Yes," Mikhailov told him. "He is Valentin Kuybishev, *Polkovnik* Zaitsev's brother-in-law. Kuybishev is a heartless killer, with a fearsome reputation earned in Chechnya. But he is also very fond of Zaitsev, I have been told. That is why he agreed to Zaitsev's request to take you without any argument. With Zaitsev's blood on their hands, the harvesters have made this a personal vendetta for him. They will regret it."

"That's what I was thinking about Naomi," Jack told him as he finished donning his gear. He grabbed the helmet and shotgun that Rudenko held out for him and followed the others out the door. "When she finds out about this little stunt, she's going to kill me."

* * *

The Putin-thing loped through the dark and rain. It had easily escaped its pursuers, even the animals — dogs — the humans had set after it. It had shed the damaged flesh, and with it the pain caused by the human who had shot it. It had only gotten a brief glance at him, but knew it would recognize him again, as it would the others in the room, if such a time ever came to pass.

The man it had shot, Zaitsev, had not been its intended target, but was merely in the way. It had planned to kill Mikhailov in his bed, then track down Rudenko, to contain any knowledge of its own existence. It now realized that was a short-sighted strategy. Had it continued to mimic Putin, it could have put itself into a more advantageous position. While it was very young and with little survival experience, it was learning at an exponential rate, and now understood the concept and benefits of moving up the ranks, as the shadowy memories of the humans it had consumed called it.

As the thing came to a heavily wooded area, it looked up at the sound of helicopters flying low over the city, heading east. It waited until they were gone, wondering at their destination, before it continued on its way.

It was guided now as much by instinct as conscious thought. It had no wounds to heal, but would need to feed again to replace the malleable flesh it had lost.

There was that, but something more, as well. It stopped as it was overtaken with a peculiar sensation, and felt a sudden swelling in the malleable flesh that surrounded its thorax.

Focusing its visual receptors, its eyes, on its thorax, it watched as a lump the size of a human fist rose from the soft tissue. The base of the lump began to constrict until the lump detached and fell away, landing on the ground with a soft splash.

Curious, the thing probed the lump with one of its smaller appendages, the serrated tip poking into the newly formed mass of flesh. Outwardly, it appeared to be nothing more than malleable tissue.

But appearances, as it knew quite well, could be deceiving. A wave of searing pain shot up the appendage touching the lump of tissue. The thing shrieked and tried to jerk its appendage away, but the tissue clung on tenaciously. The pain became greater with every second as the lump, driven by its own genetic imperatives, feasted upon the appendage, greedily consuming it.

In desperation, the thing extended the blade from the pod in its thorax with which it had injured one of the humans. With a decisive slash, it amputated the appendage just above the lump. A spurt of ichor fluid pulsed from the mutilated limb.

Snarling at its cannibalistic offspring, the thing backed away and watched, brooding, as its "child" finished consuming the rest of the amputated appendage. The lump, larger now, paused, as if it were sniffing the air, then began to ooze toward its parent.

The thing backed away. Already, the bleeding from its wound had stopped, although the severed limb still throbbed with pain.

Its offspring continued to move in its direction, but the thing didn't wait for another close encounter. It turned and fled from the woods into the adjoining neighborhood. But it was not simply fleeing from its offspring. It had been overcome with a sense of ravenous hunger, and it needed to feed. And soon.

CHAPTER SEVENTEEN

Carl Richards was pacing in his office in the J. Edgar Hoover Building, from the window to the door, then back again. It was a luxury he afforded himself only when he was alone. It was an expression of anxiety, an old habit he'd picked up as a child, locked in his room for hours on end after being beaten by his alcoholic father.

He had conveyed his faked tip to the French National Police about the kidnapper they'd been searching for. He'd spoken for some time to his counterpart in Paris, who'd promised to send a team into the town right away. Richards couldn't, of course, tell him what they might really encounter, but didn't want them to be completely unprepared if they encountered harvesters. So he did the only thing he could: he told the French that the information the FBI had on the suspect indicated he was heavily armed and should be considered extremely dangerous. He was plagued with a sense of guilt, sending the French into what could easily turn into a slaughter, but he didn't see any alternative, other than to let the situation in the town fester.

Renee and her sidekick in the Directorate of Intelligence had found indicators of additional potential harvester infestations in France, and the situation was getting worse around the globe. While nothing had hit the mainstream news yet, the outbreaks appeared to be spreading to other parts of the countries that Renee had already pegged as hot zones. Oddly enough, the only major corn producing country where things were quiet was the United States, and Richards wasn't sure if that was a good sign, or if it was just the calm before the storm.

His cell phone, which he'd been holding in his hand while he paced, rang. He stopped in mid-stride, halfway to the window, and answered it. "Richards. Go."

"Sir, this is Special Agent Kayla Sweeney."

Sweeney was the leader of the team Richards had sent to investigate the home of the late Norman Kline, whom Naomi had fingered as a middleman for the person selling samples from The Bag. Richards knew that information had come as a huge relief for Renee, who wouldn't have to bang her head against the wall anymore on the image matching program. Richards had tried to pry out of Naomi who had been the source of the tip, but she had steadfastly refused, and he'd had to let it go. For now. The information had probably come from one of her Earth Defense Society cohorts, who were still working in a very loose coalition, he knew. But it didn't matter. It had been enough for Richards to get Sweeney a warrant to search Kline's condo and seize his banking and telephone records, along with any travel information they could dig up. It was highly unusual for an agent like Sweeney to be reporting directly to Richards, and not through a Special Agent in Charge, or SAC. But this particular investigation had to be both thorough and discreet, and Richards knew from having worked with her before that she was both. For this assignment, at least, she was to report the findings of her team directly to him.

"Make my day, Sweeney. What have you got?"

"To begin with, his real name isn't Norman Kline. It's Anatoli Klimov. He emigrated from Russia fifteen years ago and legally changed his name when he became a naturalized citizen. We ran a background on him, and it turns out he had some associations with Russian organized crime after he came here. Nothing big that we can find, and he doesn't have any priors either here or in Russia. But there are definitely some shady characters in his social network."

"I'm liking him as a bad guy so far. What else?"

Sweeney's deep Southern drawl went on. "He ran a boutique import-export business that specialized in biotechnology, special supplies and consumables that are used in a lot of different kinds of laboratory work. He had customers in all the countries in the background information you gave me, and others, as well."

"Was all of it legal?"

"From what we can tell so far, yes, sir, it looks legit. We haven't gotten through everything yet, but aside from his social connections to the Russian mafia, we haven't found any red flags. We ran him and his business through Commerce and State, and the results came back clean."

Richards frowned. He hadn't been under any delusions that there'd be a smoking gun marking Kline as the suspected purveyor of New Horizons seeds, but he hadn't expected him to be squeaky clean, either.

"How about travel?"

"That's the kicker, sir. Unless he's got a fake passport or two hidden away, the only travel he's done since coming to the States was a trip to Canada ten years ago and one to the Bahamas five years ago. Even here, as best we can tell, he didn't do much traveling. He was a homebody who conducted almost all his business over the phone and the web from his home office. We already pawed through his computer and came up blank. We're going over his bank records to see if anything stands out, or if there are any pointers to offshore accounts. Nothing stands out so far. If I had to label this guy based on what we've found so far, I'd have to say he was just a businessman who was making a decent living, or he really knew how to launder his money."

Carl started pacing again. "There has to be something. The information we have on this guy was very specific. Was he up to anything unusual right before he died?"

Sweeney was silent for a moment, then told him, "The only thing that I'd qualify as unusual was a phone call he received the day he died. It was the last call he got before the break-in when he was killed."

"Why does that stand out? Somebody had to have been the last to call the poor schmuck."

"It's because we think the caller was using a prepaid phone, with no associated user information, and that same phone called Kline a lot during the period you told us to focus on, from September through December of last year."

Carl stopped pacing, his heart suddenly hammering in his chest. "And?"

"That's just it, sir. This particular phone called Kline's cell number seventy-eight times between 9 September and 15 December, but not again until the day he was killed. I took the liberty of looking back a bit further, and found a series of calls from that phone to Kline starting exactly one month before the bomb went off in California. I couldn't find any other calls before that."

"Good God. I'm going to get you a warrant for a wiretap on that phone."

"There may not be a need to, sir." Sweeney sighed. "We got a warrant to access the calling records for that number, too, looking for any associations beyond the calls to Kline, but there was nothing, no other contacts. It was never used for anything but contacting Kline. It's probably in the landfill by now."

Stifling a curse, Carl asked, "What about follow-on calls or activity by Kline? Those calls must have been for a reason. The timing is too coincidental. Did he call anyone or do anything unusual after he got the calls from the throwaway?"

"From September through December, no. He was always on his phone, contacting clients all over the world, but that was his daily routine. So if our throwaway mystery caller had instructions for him, let's say to get in touch with potential buyers for whatever it was he had to sell, it would just blend in with his regular business calls." She paused. "The only exception was last year, in the weeks leading up to the bomb in California. Interspersed with calls with Mr. Throwaway, Kline made calls to two other unusual numbers. One was to another throwaway that doesn't have any associated user information. But the other number was in Los Angeles, which was unusual in itself, because Kline didn't make any other calls there in the previous year."

"Who was it?" Carl was gritting his teeth, willing her to somehow make a connection that would make sense.

"It was to a company called Morgan Pharmaceuticals. We don't know who he spoke to, because it was the company's public contact number and was probably routed internally to whomever he might have asked for. But it was a pretty short call, and not half an hour later he got the first call from the other number I mentioned, the second prepaid phone. There were a lot of calls between those two over the next week, then nothing until two days before the bomb blast in California, when there was one final call from Kline to the second prepaid."

"Setting up a delivery," Carl thought aloud, but his insides had suddenly gone cold. *Morgan Pharmaceuticals.* That was where Naomi was working, and she had tipped him to Kline as the provider. That meant that someone inside Morgan Pharmaceuticals had information linking Kline to The Bag, and Sweeney's analysis was pointing at Morgan as a potential buyer. And that meant someone at Morgan must have samples from The Bag, or at least knew where they might be. He couldn't believe Naomi was holding anything out on him, but she had been very cagey about where she'd gotten the information about Kline. She was trying to protect someone, but whom? And why? "Damn."

"Sir?"

"Nothing. Listen, Sweeney, that's some good work. Keep digging and let me know the instant you find anything else."

"Yes, sir."

Carl hit the end call button, then sat down in his chair to think. *Kline must have been the middleman,* he thought. *Mr. Throwaway was probably the guy with The Bag, and through Kline he must have made a sale to someone at Morgan Pharmaceuticals.* And the last call from Mr. Throwaway to Kline just before Kline was killed was a bit too coincidental for Carl's liking. It was probably to make sure Kline was home. "You were set up, buddy."

Something else was nagging at him, tickling his brain as he stared at the computer screen. All it showed right now was his email and calendar.

The calendar.

Leaning forward, he looked at the date when Kline was murdered. Like a bolt of lightning, he made the connection. It was the same day that Naomi started working for Morgan Pharmaceuticals.

"*Damn.*" He reached for the phone and buzzed his secretary. "Get me the Assistant Director in Charge of the Los Angeles Division on the line right away. And I want Renee Vintner and her sidekick from the Intelligence Directorate in front of my desk in ten minutes."

* * *

"I wish your people would learn to write things that actually make sense." President Daniel Miller glanced up at the Director of National Intelligence. While technically not a member of the cabinet, Miller insisted that the DNI be a regular attendee. In Miller's hand was a copy of the PDB, the President's Daily Brief, a highly classified document containing the latest and most urgent intelligence information that the DNI and his subordinates in the intelligence community thought the President should see. Miller propped his glasses on his nose, then read from the document:

Anomalous military activities have been observed over the last seventy-two hours in Russia, the People's Republic of China, India, and Brazil. Regular military and special forces units have made unscheduled deployments, and there are some reports of serious casualties inflicted by unspecified entities. The Chinese, in particular, have reportedly suffered the decimation of at least two divisions, and both the Chengdu and Guangzhou regions have been put on general alert.

The causes behind these activities, and whether they are somehow linked across the above mentioned nations, is unknown.

He let the document fall to his desk. "Where's the punch line? Are these countries going to war? Did they simultaneously decide to have civil wars? What? This sounds alarmist but doesn't really tell me anything. And what's this *unspecified entities* garbage?"

The DNI looked uncomfortable. "Mr. President, we aren't sure what's going on, yet. But the situation, particularly in China and Brazil, is quite serious. The Chinese have deployed five divisions into rural agrarian areas, and there's no question that those units are engaged in combat operations."

"And you're sure it's not an exercise?"

"Positive, sir. If you look at the first appendix in today's PDB, you'll see imagery that spells it out in rather vivid detail."

Miller picked up the document and thumbed through it to the appendices. There were several black and white overhead shots of a village or small town pockmarked with the circular craters of artillery impacts. Most of the buildings had sustained heavy damage. Vehicles marked in the graphic as tanks and infantry personnel carriers were in the town, along with dozens of little dots that Miller assumed must be soldiers. He had served in the Army many years before, and so had some appreciation for military tactics. He noticed that the troops in the village had formed a defensive perimeter, with their guns pointing out toward the surrounding fields, where more vehicles stood, blackened and smoking.

He looked up at the DNI. "These are the Chinese troops?"

"Yes, sir. The information we have so far indicates that the town had been overrun or taken over, it's not really clear by whom, and the Army was sent in to sort things out. They tried just marching into the town and got their clocks cleaned. Then they leveled it with artillery before going back in. Now it looks like they're trapped."

"Trapped? By whom? Has there been an armed uprising in China and we missed it?" The other members of the cabinet looked away. Miller's sarcasm could be quite acidic.

"Sir, if you look closely at the first image, in the fields."

Miller did so. "Besides the burning tanks, all I see are a bunch of, what, rocks maybe? What are all those things?"

"That, Mr. President, we don't know. They could be insurgents with some sort of special camouflage or body armor. But we know they move, and we think they're the ones that the Chinese are fighting." He paused. "By the way, the Chinese unit you're looking at now started out four days ago as a full infantry brigade with an attached armor platoon, around three thousand men. What you see there is all that's left."

Miller looked at the text sidebar on the image, then sat back, shocked. "There can't be more than two or three hundred men here."

"That's right, Mr. President. More are certainly hiding in the buildings or aren't easily distinguished in the rubble, but yes, as best we can tell, that brigade has pretty much been wiped out. And it's not the only one."

"So who the hell is responsible? The Chinese aren't blaming us, surely." Miller glanced at the Secretary of State, who shook her head.

"They haven't uttered a peep to us about it," she said. "They've deflected all our inquiries on the diplomatic circuit, telling us a lot of nothing."

"No, sir, whatever it is, it's an internal matter," the DNI went on. "But as the PDB indicate, China's not the only place where something odd is going on. We've seen unusual movements of Russian airborne units over the last week, including what appears to be a battalion-level exercise in southern Russia that kicked off last night. The situation in Brazil isn't clear, but something's definitely going on down there that involves regular army troops being deployed to the interior. And our military attaché in New Delhi got a whiff of some Indian special forces being sent off somewhere in central India a day or so ago, along with some credible information that the Indian Army's airborne brigade has been put on alert."

"Maybe in reaction to what's going on in China?" Miller's voice was hopeful. At least that would be a situation he could understand.

The DNI shook his head. "No, sir, I don't think so. Things are quiet along their mutual border. The ruckus in China is well to the east, away from India."

"Kyle, you look like you swallowed your kid's goldfish." Miller had noticed the change in expression on the face of his new FBI Director as soon as the DNI had mentioned India. "Do you have something to add?"

Harmon licked his lips. "Sir, I had a discussion the other day with Carl Richards, the former..."

"I know who he is."

Nodding, Harmon went on with obvious reluctance. "Richards believed, postulated, that there might have been a potential incident in India, and had some circumstantial evidence about a similar incident in Russia."

Miller cocked his head to one side, a look of growing incredulity on his face. "What sort of incident?"

Closing his eyes, Harmon spat out the word. "Harvesters."

For a moment, no one spoke. Harmon sat like a toad under a brace of spotlights as everyone in the cabinet, along with the President, stared at him.

The Vice President, Andrew Lynch, broke the silence. "You've got to be kidding me."

"No, sir, I'm not. I wish I was." Harmon turned back to Miller. "Richards said that Jack Dawson was in India and had found a village that had been infected, as he called it, and he had dug up some other information indicating that something similar had happened in Russia."

"And you didn't pursue this?" The DNI said the words, but the thought was clearly echoed in the expressions of the Secretaries of Defense and Homeland Security.

"Of course not!" Harmon's temper broke. "May I kindly remind everyone here," he glanced at President Miller, "that the whole topic of harvesters was shelved after the Curtis administration. SEAL came up with nothing after an entire year, and there wasn't any physical evidence to prove their existence. All of it was anecdotal or based on information that could easily have been faked. None of us believed it then, and I still don't. There's a rational explanation for what's going on. We don't have to haul the boogeyman out of the closet."

"You've made your point, Kyle." Miller glanced around the room. "Here's what I want." He picked up the PDB and waved it at the DNI. "First, I want to know what the devil is going on with this. And I don't want any eyewash because someone's afraid to use terminology that, up until now, wasn't considered politically correct." He shot an apologetic look at Harmon. "I want everything back on the table, no matter how unpalatable it might be, including the H-word. Harvesters. Whoever wrote — or edited — this PDB said that *unspecified entities* were behind what's going on. I want that *unspecified* replaced with something specific, and I want it pronto."

"Yes, Mr. President." The DNI looked and sounded relieved. "I'll have an update to you right away. I'd also recommend bringing in the CDC on this."

"Fine. Make it happen." Miller turned to Harmon. "Second. You're going to have to eat some crow and make peace with Richards. I'd eat it for you since I made the bed that we're all going to have to lay in, but that's not the way things work. Pump him for whatever information he has on this, then get it sent to the DNI, Defense, Homeland Security, and whomever else you think needs to know. If what Richards has is credible, figure out how to share it with the countries that are being hit with this outbreak without making us look like complete lunatics."

Miller paused, then looked at the Secretary for Homeland Security. "That brings me to the third thing: have there been any indications of this sort of thing going on here?"

"No, sir. We haven't come across any indications of anything like what's in that report. Not yet, at least."

"Good. Because I do *not* want to have whatever is going on in these places," Miller tapped on the PDB, "to happen here on our soil. I don't care who or what is behind it, we're not going to let it happen. The country was hit bad enough by the Sutter Buttes disaster, and by God I'm not going to let something like this take place on my watch." He looked every member of his cabinet in the eye. "I want this nailed down, and fast."

"What about Dawson?" Harmon asked.

"What about him?"

"From what I gathered from Richards, it sounded to me like he's in a position to gather a lot of information, but he's running loose as a free agent. I'm not so sure that's in our best interest."

Miller shrugged. "Then try to get him back on the payroll, and get some other eyes on the ground in these places. In the meantime, he's an asset. Use him. And if necessary, use him up."

CHAPTER EIGHTEEN

After Jack and the others had piled into the waiting Mi-17 transport helicopters, they took a short ride to the nearby Shpakovskoye Airport, which was a joint military-civilian facility. While Mikhailov had explained that there was normally only a small contingent of Air Force training units there, Jack saw that a line of An-12 four-engine turboprop transports was waiting on the tarmac, propellers spinning and ready for takeoff as soon as their human cargo was loaded.

"I thought we were going to make a helicopter insertion." Jack had to shout to be heard above the roar of both the helicopters and the engines of the big transports as he followed close behind Mikhailov in the line of men who ran to board the lead aircraft.

"We are airborne troops, Jack. We jump out of perfectly good airplanes, remember?"

"Ah, shit," Jack cursed.

"Do you want to stay behind?"

"Hell, no." He took a closer look at the men around him, who seemed to have more gear strapped to their bodies than he, Mikhailov, or Rudenko. "But we don't have any parachutes!"

"They are on the planes."

Jack was aghast. Preparing for an airborne jump wasn't something you just threw together at the last moment. Everything was checked, rechecked, and checked again before anyone ever set foot on the plane. "Oh, great."

As they ran up the rear cargo ramp, thankfully getting out of the frigid pouring rain, a senior NCO led them forward to a group of seats, each of which held a parachute. They struggled to get the rigs on over their soaked uniforms.

"The others had time to prepare properly at the base," Mikhailov explained as Rudenko helped him into the parachute harness. "We did not, obviously." Seeing the pained expression on Jack's face, he said, "You are jump qualified, are you not?"

"Yes, I am." Jack had gone to the Army Airborne School — Jump School, as it was more popularly known — at Fort Benning, Georgia, while he'd been an Army ROTC cadet. "I was gung-ho about jumping until my first time out of the plane. I absolutely hated it, and have every jump since."

"You are smart man, Jack." Rudenko slapped him on the back after finishing his check of Mikhailov's chute. "Much smarter than certain Russian Army captains I have known."

"But why are we jumping in? Why not just take a nice comfy helo ride to the target?"

Mikhailov shook his head. "Not enough lift capacity. The *polkovnik* wants the whole battalion on the ground as quickly as possible. We would have to make several lifts with the helicopters we have on hand. That would not allow us to concentrate our troops as quickly. We should be able to get everyone down in two drops with the planes." He smiled. "Look at it this way: at least you do not have to stand in the rain and wait like the other half of the battalion."

"It's a good thing. I forgot my umbrella."

Done with pulling on the parachute and having Rudenko check him over, Jack, shivering from the cold rain that had penetrated to his skin, sat clumsily on the seat beside Mikhailov. Most of the other men on the plane had taken their seats as well, and the loadmaster and officers were making sure everyone was accounted for. Looking out the yawning rear cargo door, Jack could see the An-12 in line behind them, and the navigation lights of that aircraft and those behind it, winking in the darkness. Over the steady drone of the engines he could hear another sound that he recognized as the rain beating down against the fuselage and wings. The plane stank of oil and jet fuel, of exhaust and the ozone smell of the storm outside.

The men around him were quiet, their faces calm but alert. Most of them had never seen combat, he surmised, but from their expressions and demeanor, an outsider would have thought this was nothing more for them than the routine exercise that the public was currently being led to believe it was.

Kuybishev and two other men strode up the ramp at the rear of the plane just as it began to rise with a high-pitched whine from the hydraulics. He moved past Jack to the cockpit, and a moment later the roar of the plane's turboprop engines rose in pitch and they began to move.

The plane turned onto the active runway and the pilot pushed the throttles all the way forward. Kuybishev came back and took his seat across from Mikhailov as the plane accelerated. He looked closely at Jack in the dim light of the cargo bay. "You do not like to jump? Mikhailov assured me you have done this before."

Jack offered him a grin that was more an exercise in gritting his teeth and pulling his lips back. "Is it that obvious, sir? I've done this plenty of times, and have never stopped hating it."

Kuybishev leaned over and slapped Jack's knee. "You are smart man." He and the others laughed.

Rather than being offended, Jack was relieved. Involving him in jokes, even at his expense, made him feel like he was part of the team. Kuybishev could have easily shut him out and ignored him.

They were quiet for a moment as the plane began to vibrate, shimmying slightly from side to side as the pilot fought the crosswind while the An-12 transitioned from earth to sky. The nose suddenly rose, and they felt the momentary pull of gravity in the pits of their stomachs as the plane left the ground. With a series of whines and thumps, the landing gear came up. Then the plane banked sharply to the left until it was headed east, toward Ulan-Erg. Their target.

"Concept of operation is simple," Kuybishev told them, speaking in heavily accented English for Jack's benefit as he unfolded a tactical map wrapped in a nylon case with a clear plastic face. One of the officers with him, probably the executive officer, Jack thought, held a flashlight to better illuminate the map. "There is road that runs east-west, three kilometers south of Ulan-Erg. We will drop most troops on this first lift just to the south of this road, *da?*" Everyone nodded. "We will sweep north through village, driving any enemies against river north of village. We will also drop one platoon north of river to secure road bridge, here." He pointed to where a paved road crossed the river to enter the town from the northeast. "Anyone," Kuybishev glanced up at Jack, "*anything* we flush from town is most likely to go this way. We will drop troops of second lift to either reinforce us, platoon holding bridge, or both, as needed."

"Where do you want me, sir?"

"You and Mikhailov stay with me. We will also keep men with thermal imagers to scan citizens of Ulan-Erg to make sure everyone is who and what they are supposed to be." He looked hard at Jack. "Now you tell me what we are fighting, and how we kill them."

Jack returned Kuybishev's stare, and decided to go for broke. "They're not human, colonel. We call them harvesters. They can take the shape of a man or woman and mimic them perfectly, not just in appearance, but in how they talk and act."

"Like Putin." Kuybishev spat the man's name.

"Yes, sir, like Putin. Normally they kill the people they mimic, so we can assume that Putin is dead."

"How do we kill them?"

"Fire is the best way. The outer part of their bodies are covered with flesh that can change shape, but it's highly flammable."

"That is why we burned the facility," Mikhailov interjected. "We learned this from Jack during the Spitsbergen operation. White phosphorous works quite well against them. Tracers also work, and the Dragon's Breath rounds from the shotguns do quite well, but only at close quarters."

Jack nodded. "Aside from fire, you just need to hammer them hard with the biggest guns you can. Their skeletons are as strong as reinforced carbon fiber. Your assault rifles can take them down, but you'll need to hit them repeatedly. These," he pulled out the .50 caliber Desert Eagle and handed it to Kuybishev, who turned it slowly in his big hands, studying it, "can take one out with a single shot. If you're lucky."

Kuybishev handed the pistol back, a look of envy on his face.

"And colonel, these things can move fast, a lot faster than a man. They're extremely strong, and they also have a stinger that can kill a man at a distance of more than ten feet. Three, maybe four meters."

After a moment of silence, Kuybishev said, "You expect me to believe this?"

"Every word is true, *polkovnik*," Rudenko told him. He had served under Kuybishev in Chechnya, when Kuybishev was a company commander, and they had come to know one another well. "*Kapitan* Mikhailov and I have seen these things with our own eyes. And you know what happened to *Polkovnik* Zaitsev." He shook his head. "No man could have jumped ten meters to the ground, then escape from airborne troops chasing him. Not possible."

"You are asking me to believe in aliens?"

"We don't know where they came from, colonel," Jack explained. "We killed all the original harvesters, which we believe were around for a very long time, maybe centuries. The ones we're facing now are a new generation. But trust me, they're just as deadly as the old ones. Maybe even more so."

Kuybishev grunted. "I will leave such details to men with imagination. I simply want to kill them. Perhaps we do not have best weapons, but we will leave none alive when we are through."

* * *

Forty minutes later, Jack was on his feet, his hand clinging to the static line that ran from his parachute and was clipped to a cable that ran the length of the An-12's cavernous cargo hold. He and the others had followed Kuybishev to the rear of the plane. The *polkovnik* always insisted on being the first out the door, and Jack found himself number six in the drop order on the starboard side, right behind Mikhailov and in front of Rudenko. Another line of men stood on the port side, ready to jump.

He felt his stomach fall away as the cargo ramp opened and the frigid air of the slipstream hit his face. He felt like puking, but wasn't about to give his Russian friends any last minute entertainment.

"You okay?"

Jack felt a reassuring hand on his shoulder and turned to see Rudenko peering at him.

"Yeah, I'll make it."

Rudenko grinned. "At least there are few trees here for us to land in!"

"Thank God for small mercies."

The jump indicator light on the side of the fuselage suddenly changed from amber to green. It was time.

The men ahead of Jack leaped out into the darkness. He kept pace with them, shuffling forward as his old training and experience overrode the more sensible part of his brain that was screaming in abject fear.

Ahead of him, Mikhailov leaped from the ramp, and with one final step, his breath coming in rapid heaves, Jack followed him, stepping into space. He felt a slight nudge against his back: Rudenko, making sure Jack didn't balk at the last second. Jack would have laughed had he not been so scared.

The moment of nauseating free-fall abruptly ended as the static line yanked the parachute open. After the chute deployed, slowing Jack's descent to a speed that was merely insane, rather than suicidal, he looked up to make sure the canopy had opened properly. He could barely make anything out in the dark and rain, but from what he could tell, all was in order. While night jumps were something all airborne troops trained for, Jack thought the Russians were complete loons for dropping in weather conditions like this.

"At least there aren't many trees to land in." He laughed as he repeated what Rudenko had told him, sure that if there was a single tree down there, with his luck he'd land right on top of it.

He didn't have much time to worry about such things. It was hard to judge distance under these conditions, but the ground, a vast stretch of deep black beneath him, was coming up fast. Off to his left, beyond a group of his fellow paratroopers, he saw a slightly less dark shape that ran in a straight line, parallel to the path the aircraft were flying. *That must be the road south of the village*, he thought. Looking a bit to the north, he could make out a few scattered lights that he thought must be Ulan-Erg.

The ground rushed up quickly enough during daylight drops. At night, to Jack it seemed like at one moment he was hundreds of feet in the air, and the next the ground was right *there*. He judged his landing more by the grunts and curses of the men who landed before him than by sight. His feet slammed into the wet ground and he fell to his side, absorbing the impact through his right calf, thigh and hip before rolling over onto his back.

Breathing a sigh of relief, he hit the quick disconnect on his harness and shucked it off as he got to his feet. Checking that his shotgun was ready for action, he trotted through the muck to where he heard Kuybishev shouting orders.

Mikhailov and Rudenko appeared out of the darkness beside him. As poor as the visibility was, Jack could see that Mikhailov was in pain.

"Did you twist something?"

"*Nyet*," Mikhailov told him through gritted teeth. "My ribs, from the battle at the facility. Perhaps I should have stayed in bed."

"Stupid bastard. You could've wound up with a punctured lung."

Mikhailov's teeth flashed in the darkness. "Thank you for your sympathy. You are a true friend."

"Come on, you lunatic. There's Kuybishev."

The three stood by as the colonel got the two companies of the battalion's first drop organized. Above, the An-12s droned away, turning back to the west to pick up the rest of the battalion for the second wave.

Quickly and efficiently, the Russians spread out according to Kuybishev's orders and moved north to the road that served as their first phase line. Jack was thankful that the Russian pilots managed to drop them right where they were supposed to. It was a short walk to the road.

After everyone had reached the edge of the pavement, Kuybishev whispered a brief order through the radio carried by one of the soldiers. As one, the men of the battalion started moving north toward Ulan-Erg.

It was three kilometers of slogging through wet muck before they reached the edge of the town. Jack's anxiety grew with every step, because he remembered all too well the horror that had greeted him in the village outside of Koratikal in India.

At least this time we've got some real firepower, he consoled himself. Even if they did run into harvesters here, he knew that a few companies of airborne troops would kick some serious ass. *There's nothing to be afraid of. We've got this.*

Despite his internal pep-talk, he was shivering. He tried to convince himself it was just the cold.

Kuybishev called a halt as they reached the southern edge of town, and the men dropped to their knees or lay prone in the mud. Pulling a set of binoculars from his combat webbing, he carefully scanned the nearest houses. Some still had lights on, others didn't.

Jack was listening carefully, but he didn't hear anything over the rain. No screams, human or otherwise, reached his ears.

Beside Kuybishev, the two soldiers with the thermal imaging sights mounted on their rifles swept their electronically enhanced vision over the nearest houses.

"*Nichevo*."

Jack turned to Mikhailov, who whispered, "They see nothing."

Kuybishev spoke again into his radio, then said, "*Vperyod*."

"Forward," Mikhailov translated for Jack's benefit as the men got back to their feet and marched onward. "He ordered the company commanders to halt as they reach each major east-west street to help us stay on line."

"So no one can flank us," Jack added. "How big is this place?"

"Not big. A hundred buildings, maybe more."

"A hundred buildings? We're gonna be here a while."

Kuybishev turned his head in their direction, and both men clamped their mouths shut.

As they reached the first line of houses, a squad surrounded each one, with three men at the front door. One knocked while the other two covered him.

No one answered at any of the houses.

As if on cue, there were multiple *cracks* as the first man in each entry team kicked in the door, and the other two ran inside, weapons at the ready.

After a few tense minutes, the radio operator murmured something to Kuybishev. Turning to Jack and Mikhailov, he said, "No one is in any of these houses."

"Any signs of a struggle?"

"*Da.*" Kuybishev said nothing more before he turned his attention back to the radio. All along the first street his men broke down doors and swept through the houses.

By the time they had made it halfway through the town, without having found a single person, alive or dead, or any sign of harvesters, Jack was deeply worried. "Something's not right," he told Mikhailov. Beside him, Rudenko grunted his agreement. "You can feel it, too, can't you?"

"I feel like I am being watched." Rudenko had taken to turning around periodically, staring into the darkness behind them.

"It is the darkness and rain, the disorientation," Mikhailov said, but his voice carried no conviction. "Although I cannot explain where the villagers have gone."

A shout of surprise came from off to their left. The soldiers around them stopped and knelt, training their weapons in all directions.

The shout was followed by a string of curses. Then a long cry of pain.

"Come!" Kuybishev dashed past them toward the sound, grabbing Jack's arm as he went.

"*Polkovnik!*" They were met by one of the officers. Even in the dark, Jack could tell the man was terrified. Without a word, he led them to where one of his men was writhing on the ground, screaming.

Breaking tactical discipline, Jack yanked his flashlight from the combat webbing, pointed it at the injured soldier and flicked it on.

"Oh, Christ."

The soldier's right foot was englobed in a mottled blue and yellow mass that Jack immediately recognized as what Naomi had thought a larval harvester might look like. The soldier reached for it, intending to tear it off.

"*No!*" Jack lunged forward, grabbing the man's hands. "Don't, or you'll lose your hands, too!"

Two other men joined him, restraining the thrashing soldier.

"What is this thing?" Kuybishev demanded. As tough as he was, as many horrors as he had endured and done unto others, Jack could hear the fear in his voice.

The thing pulsed and oozed its way up the man's calf, growing larger as they watched. His foot seemed to be shrinking, the toes and most of the heel clearly gone now.

"If you want to save him, we've got to amputate his leg! Now!" Jack wanted to vomit at the thought, but there was no other way that he could think of to save the man. The only alternative would be to burn the thing, but that would almost certainly kill the soldier, and it wouldn't save his leg.

"We will fly him to hospital," Kuybishev said, the strength returning to his voice.

"Colonel, there's no time! He'll be dead by the time he gets there, and this thing will kill the helicopter crew on the way!"

Kuybishev spoke to another soldier kneeling next to the stricken man who carried a large pouch along with his other gear. Jack immediately gathered that he was a medic, but he was shaking his head at whatever Kuybishev was saying.

"Jack, our medics do not have the tools to do this in the field." Mikhailov stared helplessly at the soldier as the thing oozed up his leg.

Without a word, Rudenko stepped forward. Leaning down, he drew the Desert Eagle from Jack's holster. The big NCO looked at Kuybishev, who nodded. "Hold him," Rudenko said as he took careful aim.

The soldier saw what was about to happen and began to struggle even more violently.

Rudenko squeezed the trigger, and the .50 caliber slug blasted through the soldier's leg not far below the knee joint, shattering bone and shredding the flesh. The soldier screamed even louder, then suddenly went quiet as he passed out.

Shoving the pistol into his web belt and then drawing his combat knife, Rudenko knelt down beside him. With a few powerful strokes of the razor sharp knife, the remaining flesh parted. Jack and the others dragged the man a few meters away, where the medic began treating a type of wound he was familiar with.

Jack, badly shaken, joined Rudenko and the others, who now stood in a circle around the amputated limb. They watched with grim fascination as the oozing mass quickly consumed the rest of it. In just a few moments, the flesh and bone had been dissolved, absorbed. Then the thing began to move toward Rudenko, who stood closest to it.

"I suggest you stand back." Rudenko raised his shotgun. The other men backed away, as well. Staring at the oozing thing, he said, "I believe term in English is *fuck you*."

He pulled the trigger, sending a fiery cascade of burning particles from the Dragon's Breath round into the larval harvester. The thing exploded, burning so furiously that everyone had to take several paces back.

As the harvester burned itself out, Kuybishev was in Jack's face. "You did not explain to me what that was."

"It was what we think is a larval form of the harvester, colonel. A baby. They can get bigger than that one. Much bigger. And the only thing that we know will kill them is fire."

"Perhaps smaller is worse," Mikhailov commented. "Big we might be able to see at night or in the rain. Ones like this."

"Will be like tiny land mines used in Afghanistan," Rudenko finished for him. "Only much more deadly."

"Come, we finish our sweep." Kuybishev was reaching for the radio when one of the men with a thermal imager tensed. He had been scanning the area while the unfortunate soldier was being taken care of. At the moment, his weapon was pointed in the direction from which they'd come, back toward the drop zone.

"*Polkovnik? Polkovnik!*" The soldier handed Kuybishev the rifle and pointed.

The colonel looked through the sight. "*Bozhe moi*." He thrust the rifle at Jack, then began bellowing orders to his men.

With a cold knot of dread congealing in his chest, Jack raised the weapon to his shoulder and looked through the scope. "Oh, God."

There were at least a dozen loping, deadly-looking shapes coming straight for them. Sweeping the scope from side to side, he saw more. A lot more.

Mikhailov was right beside him, "Jack, what is it?"

"It's a trap." He tossed the rifle to its owner before grabbing Mikhailov's web harness and pulling him after Kuybishev and the others. "Come on, *run!*"

CHAPTER NINETEEN

Renee felt as if she was going to explode, not from anger or even frustration, but from acute pressure. She'd left the young man in the Intelligence Division to keep track of the ever-growing pile of potential harvester incidents while she hammered away on the passport image correlation. After learning that Kline had just been a middleman and had probably never left the country, Carl had made finding The Bad Guy her number one priority. The Los Angeles Division had a team of agents standing by with a warrant to search the headquarters of Morgan Pharmaceuticals and seize any documents or materials related to The Bag, although that's not how it was phrased in the warrant. The only remaining piece that Carl wanted to have in place before the LA agents went in was a name. The name of whomever she'd been searching for before being sidetracked by Kline. Everything hinged on her now, and she couldn't fail.

She'd already sifted through the questionable results and discarded them. While there were valid matches, the same faces but different passports, none of them met the profile she was looking for. Some she'd passed to her new friend in Intelligence for follow-up as possible terrorists, smugglers, or other ne'er-do-wells, but the one she was hoping to find hadn't appeared yet. Carl had authorized the IT support section to give her whatever computer horsepower she wanted, and while that had helped, it was still taking time.

"Come on, come on!" She banged her fist against the desk, and coffee sloshed out of her cup.

At last, the scrolling list of computer processes stopped, replaced with this:

9 POSSIBLES FOUND

She quickly opened up the results file and sifted through them. Eight were clearly unrelated.

The ninth, however, was a good match. There were seven passports, with seven different photographs. The man, a middle-aged, heavy set caucasian, was clearly the same individual, despite the terrible quality of some of the photos. He had visited every country on her list, each one with a different passport. While he had seven different aliases, after cross-indexing them against various databases, one of them came up as a perfect fit for the profile she was looking for, and was probably his real passport.

Snatching up the phone, she rang Carl's direct number.

"Richards."

"I've got him, Carl. One of the matches came up as an employee of Morgan Pharmaceuticals."

"Name?"

"Dr. Adrian Kelso." She paused. "Shouldn't we let Naomi know?"

"No. We've got to keep this entirely aboveboard, for her sake and ours. I just pray that she didn't know anything about whatever deal was cut for The Bag or there's going to be hell to pay." He lowered his voice. "Thanks, babe."

"You owe me, hon. Now go catch this asshole. I'm going to go home and get some sleep."

* * *

Howard Morgan was enjoying the view from his penthouse office, sipping a cup of coffee and enjoying the morning sun when a chime sounded. From the tone, he knew that it was his head of security, Karina Petrovsky.

"Yes, Karina?" The system was voice activated, although if he wanted privacy, which he usually did if there was someone else in the office, he could use the phone handset on his desk.

"Sir, we have a problem. Look at the main entrance."

Morgan moved to where he could look through the glass walls to the parking lot, far below. A group of armed men and women had taken over the guard post, and a swarm of black SUVs was pouring in. "Who are they?"

"FBI, sir. They're sealing off the other entrances, as well."

In an unusual fit of anger, Morgan threw the mug to the floor. He had gone to such great lengths to fly under the radar of the authorities. This couldn't have happened at a worse time, just when they were making some real progress on the Beta-Three project.

That's when the image of Naomi's face flashed into his mind. It was too coincidental that the FBI was here so soon after he'd told her about Kline. "Damn. Karina, flush Vault One. And I want Naomi Perrault taken aside. Call me back when it's done."

"Yes, sir. Right away."

A soft beep signaled him that she'd ended the call. Morgan fumed as he watched more FBI agents enter the building. *His* building. "It's a setback," he reassured himself, "nothing more." He had invested too much in Beta-Three to have put all his eggs in one basket. The data was backed up, as were the samples.

He kicked one of the pieces of the shattered coffee mug across the floor.

Naomi, he thought, *you'll regret this.*

* * *

Naomi looked up as an alarm, a piercing wail, sounded in the vault, and a red light began to flash. Her first thought was that it was a fire drill, until she saw the stricken look on Harmony's face.

"Come on!" Harmony nearly leaped out of her chair and grabbed Naomi by the arm. "We've got to get out of here, now!" Turning to the others in the room, who appeared just as baffled as Naomi, she shouted, "Out! Now!"

Naomi yanked her arm away. She was sure she was just on the verge of identifying more genes associated with the reproduction cycle of the second generation harvesters, and she wasn't going to just walk away if it wasn't absolutely necessary. "What's going on?"

"They're flushing the vault, Naomi. We've got to get out of here, right now!"

"What does that mean?"

"It means that in less than five minutes, everything in here is going to be destroyed. It's an emergency protocol that only Mr. Morgan can initiate. We've got to go."

"And what if I don't?" Naomi stood there and crossed her arms in defiance.

"You'll die, Naomi." Harmony's face was pale with fright. "Only a few of us were briefed on this. There aren't any drills, and it's for real." The lock cycled open at the rear of the vault, and the others, shocked and surprised, headed toward it.

"But what about all this? We can't just leave it!"

"Yes we can! Now come on, let's go!" Harmony grabbed her hand and pulled her toward the door. After a quick head count, she hit the button to cycle the inner vault door closed. When it was closed and locked, she opened the outer door that led to the hallway. "Remember," she told the others, "what you were working on was classified. Discuss it with *no one*."

Naomi followed Harmony and the others down the hall toward the elevators just as Karina Petrovsky and two muscular men in suits stepped out.

"Naomi, a word, please?" The tone of the blond woman's voice made it clear that it wasn't a request. "Harmony, take the others upstairs. We'll make sure this floor is clear."

Naomi continued to follow Harmony, but one of the men with Karina stepped in front of her.

"Don't do anything to make an unpleasant scene." Karina was watching the elevator, waiting for the doors to close.

They don't want Harmony and the others to see what happens, Naomi thought. She wasn't going to give them a chance to do whatever it was they planned. As the elevator doors began to close, Naomi stamped her foot down on the man's instep, then bashed her right elbow into his jaw, sending him careening backward.

Before either Karina or her other strongman could catch her, Naomi dashed into the elevator just as the doors hissed shut.

* * *

On his way to work, Dr. Adrian Kelso had just turned the corner of the main street leading to Morgan Pharmaceuticals when he caught sight of a long string of black SUVs heading toward the building from the opposite direction. Instinctively, he slowed down, and watched as the vehicles pulled up in front of Morgan's headquarters. A group of armed men and women emerged from the lead SUV and surrounded the guards at the entry gate. Even at this distance, Kelso could see the letters *FBI* emblazoned on their dark jackets. A moment later, the gate was raised and the other SUVs charged into the parking lot.

A prickling sensation broke out along Kelso's spine, and he slammed his palm against the steering wheel in frustration. He didn't need his Ph.D. from MIT to know that he'd be a fool to drive into the middle of the small army of agents now flooding into the building.

"One more week," he ground out through clenched teeth as he passed by, moving with the flow of traffic that had slowed down to gawk at the spectacle. The plan he'd set into motion over a year ago might now be in jeopardy. He'd been so careful, and he was so close to his goal now. So close to not only leaving Howard Morgan behind, but crushing the sanctimonious bastard under his heel.

Kelso had been with Morgan since the beginning, and had been just as instrumental in building the Morgan Pharmaceuticals empire as its namesake. But Kelso had never been recognized as a partner, had never been granted his just due. He'd always been the sidekick, a glorified gofer. He'd been willing to put up with all that until Morgan had taken the research into genetic payload delivery systems that Kelso had spent years on and given it to Harmony. It had been Kelso's baby, the show-stealer that he knew would have vaulted him to the top of the scientific community, and would earn him the recognition from Morgan that he deserved.

But no. That had been taken away from him. Morgan had insisted that Kelso had to focus on the big picture, to have a hand in all of the company's many scientific endeavors, but he was little more than a member of Morgan's personal staff who parroted what Morgan said to those below, and parroted what they said back to Morgan. He had no power, no authority. As Morgan's senior scientist, Kelso had less impact on the company than Morgan's secretary. The papers that were written carried the names of Harmony and the others who'd been given his project. The accolades that should have been his went to them.

Just when he thought he would be consigned to the ash heap of history, however, a most curious thing happened. He received a phone call from a man who'd worked for him years before as a laboratory technician, before the man left Morgan Pharmaceuticals for greener pastures. As the man told Kelso, those greener pastures had been New Horizons, and the man had found himself assigned to a new, very hush-hush facility northwest of Lincoln, Nebraska. Upon hearing that news, Kelso's pulse had shot into the stratosphere, because he knew that New Horizons had been working on something much like his own delivery system idea. He didn't know the specifics, for that had been held so tight by New Horizons that even Karina Petrovsky hadn't been able to dig anything up. But Kelso had pieced together much of what they were doing based on the talent the company had hired. Part of his job for Morgan was helping Karina to assess their competition. She provided Kelso information, and he tried to read between the lines.

Kelso knew the man well enough to know that he was always looking for more ways to make money, legally or otherwise. He'd never been caught, so far as Kelso knew, but when he wasn't in the lab, he was finding new ways to try to get rich quick. He was cunning enough to stay clear of real trouble, but otherwise wasn't terribly bright.

His offer to Kelso was simple: he had access to the New Horizons blockbuster product, the *Revolutions* seed, and was giving Kelso first shot at it. At first, the man was demanding a million dollars for a bag of the seed. While Kelso would have gladly paid that if he'd had the money, he argued that the seed would eventually be available on the open market, and he could simply buy it at the local store or order it online. Getting his hands on it early wasn't worth a million dollar premium, and no one would pay any significant sum of money for it. If the man could get his hands on the documentation for the genetic engineering that had been done, that would be something else entirely, but the man didn't have the necessary access.

In the end, Kelso had agreed to pay five thousand dollars for the bag, making it clear that even that was an outrageous sum for something that was soon going to be available worldwide at government-subsidized prices.

Reluctantly, the man had agreed. A day before the *Revolutions* seed was to be sent out into the world, Kelso met the man late in the evening in the parking lot of a bar on the outskirts of Lincoln, Nebraska. He handed the man an envelope with fifty one hundred dollar bills, and the man dumped a brightly labeled hundred pound bag of corn seed into the back of Kelso's BMW. Then they went their separate ways.

Kelso took the bag with him to work the next day, but left it in the car, intending to have someone haul it in for him later. He turned on the television in his office so he could watch the announcement by President Curtis of the roll-out of the *Revolutions* seed. Like the rest of the world, he was stunned as the news broadcast showed the New Horizons plant being blown to bits. Feigning illness, he left work for home, and remained glued to the television and the internet for the rest of the day and most of that night. He learned that everyone at the New Horizons plant where his contact worked, including the man from whom he'd bought the seed, had been killed, and that the trucks carrying the seed had been hijacked.

Then President Curtis dropped a nuke over California.

Over the next few days, he managed to dig out a vital fact buried amidst the torrent of reporting on the Sutter Buttes disaster: the Earth Defense Society had destroyed the *Revolutions* seed carried in the trucks. Every kernel of it.

Two days after that, he learned that all the documentation on how the seed had been created, the blueprints, had been destroyed. The mastermind behind the *Revolutions* seed, Dr. Rachel Kempf, and the others on the original research team were dead.

The five thousand dollar bag of seed sitting in the trunk of his car had suddenly become unique, a priceless commodity.

The downside, of course, was that President Curtis had declared the *Revolutions* seed to be a weapon of mass destruction, a biological doomsday device, and that anyone having anything to do with it was likely to wind up labeled as a terrorist.

Kelso panicked. He got into his car and headed out of town, hoping to find a place where he could destroy the seed without drawing attention to himself. But as the miles unwound behind him as he raced westward out of LA, he began to calm down. One of his mentors at MIT had once told him, "In chaos, there is opportunity." Chaos was now abundant. So then, should be opportunity.

He was well aware how much Morgan Pharmaceuticals had already spent on research paralleling what New Horizons had done, and also had a good idea how much more Howard Morgan was willing to spend: he would have put his entire fortune on the line to unlock the secrets of the bag of seed in Kelso's trunk. The applications of what New Horizons had done were limitless, and so was the potential profit.

That's when the wheels in Kelso's mind began to turn faster. Profit. He had never been, by nature, a greedy man. Despite never having treated him with the respect that Kelso thought he deserved, Morgan had certainly rewarded him financially. But profit, the kind of profit the seeds in the trunk could bring from anyone interested in developing this technology, could also bring leverage. Power. Independence. What he could get for the seeds wouldn't make him as rich as Morgan, but it would provide enough for Kelso to step out of Morgan's shadow. He could determine his own destiny, and Morgan could find someone else to play the role of Tonto.

He stopped for lunch at a roadside diner, his eyes never wandering far from his car, and thought about what he could do. He had many contacts in corporations here and overseas who would be extremely interested in what he had to offer, but he couldn't expose his identity or he'd wind up on the FBI's most wanted list.

That's when he remembered Norman Kline, who had been a supplier for the lab Kelso had worked at years ago, before joining Morgan, and who had also been a supplier for Morgan Pharmaceuticals until Karina had discovered his unsavory Russian mafia connections and terminated his contract. The irony had not been lost on Kelso: Howard Morgan could be just as ruthless as anyone else, but he pretended to hold the moral high ground and never did anything outwardly unscrupulous. Any businesses that his company had dealings with had better have clean sheets or they were dropped. The same went for his employees, except when he ordered them to do otherwise.

Kelso was no spy or underworld kingpin, and it took a bit of research and thought to put his plan together. He contacted Kline using a disposable phone to set up a meeting, and Kline was the only one he called with it.

From there, Kline set things in motion. Kelso paid him twenty thousand dollars up front for his services, with the promise of more once Kelso began making sales.

That's where things got stuck. President Curtis pushed legislation through Congress that would have put Kelso behind bars for life if he were caught peddling the seeds. Kelso wanted the rewards, but the risk was simply too high.

He forced himself to be patient. It was an election year, and Curtis was scraping the gutter in the polls. Howard Morgan had also unwittingly been helping Kelso by pouring money into lobbying Congress to repeal the President's anti-biotechnology legislation.

Kelso had already planned to offer the seed to various American biotechnology companies, and was working on those arrangements with Kline when he had a flash of brilliant inspiration: why not sell the seed to Morgan himself?

He actually laughed out loud when the thought came to him. But why not? Morgan was just another potential buyer, and he would never turn away from this sort of opportunity, regardless of how illegal it might be. And with Kline as the front man, Morgan would have no idea that Kelso was behind it.

The irony was irresistible.

He had Kline contact Karina and arrange a meeting, and after that everything fell into place like a line of dominos, with Kelso pocketing twenty-five million dollars in an offshore account. He could have asked for more, but didn't want to be too greedy. And he vowed that he wouldn't spend a penny of the money until he was out from under Morgan's boot.

But the deal was perfect: Karina got the glory, Morgan got his Beta-Three samples, Kelso got the money, and everyone was happy.

For the next several months, Kline set up meetings with various other potential buyers in the United States, closing seven deals worth more than a hundred million dollars to Kelso. Kline was also rapidly becoming rich, and like Kelso, he was socking the money away until the time was right. He didn't want any of his almost-former friends in the Russian mafia to get wind of what he was doing, especially the deals in Russia and the other former Soviet republics, or they'd want in on the deal. Or just slit his throat.

By September, long before the polls would open in November, things were looking up for Kelso to begin the overseas part of the plan. It was clear that there was no way, short of a miracle, that Curtis would be elected. It was just as clear that the opposition favored a complete reversal of Curtis's stance on biotechnology.

Kelso again contacted Kline and had him set up meetings with contacts Kelso provided. They were people he knew by reputation, people who would be keenly interested in his "product," but who didn't know him personally, so he could keep his true identity hidden. In turn, Kline provided him with several fake passports and other supporting documents to help Kelso fly under the radar, figuratively speaking, of the authorities.

Over the next three months, he traveled to six countries, emboldened by the election of Daniel Miller to the Presidency and his proclamations that everything Curtis had done would be just as quickly undone. Kelso had taken some trips while on leave from work, but he didn't have enough time off to cover all of his time away, nor was he quite ready to part with Morgan. So he took a chance, risking Karina digging into his activities, and did some travel on company time and company money, but using fake documentation while away. It was dangerous, but he had to admit to himself that he began to enjoy the thrill.

Things were going perfectly until the fateful day when Naomi Perrault rose from the dead and Howard Morgan decided to hire her. Kelso knew she had been on the original research team for the *Revolutions* seed, working with Kempf. When Karina revealed that Perrault had been working for some recently cancelled government think-tank, it didn't take Kelso's IQ of 176 to figure out what

Perrault must have been focused on. She and her boyfriend Jack Dawson, also resurrected from administrative purgatory, knew too much and had too many connections. Once she got directly involved with the Beta-Three project, how long would it be before she started asking inconvenient questions?

By hiring Perrault, Morgan had put in place a bigger threat to Kelso's plans than Karina Petrovsky had ever been.

Kelso decided to stop the presses. He called Kline and told him that the deal was done, finished. But Kline didn't see it that way. Kelso was his cash cow, and he wasn't going to let him stop. Kline threatened to expose Kelso, both to Morgan and the authorities, if he didn't move forward on the remaining deals that Kline had lined up.

After letting him bluster for a while, Kelso agreed to back down. Once he ended the call, Kelso found the contact information for some of Kline's Russian mafia connections, whom Kline had periodically mentioned. Kline had said that he hated them, because they still had their hooks in him, even after all these years, and he did everything he could to get around them.

Through a set of anonymizer services on the web, Kelso tipped off a few of Kline's old friends that Kline had been doing black market business in Russia without cutting them in, citing several of the deals Kline had mentioned. Kelso didn't, of course, mention the deals in which he himself had been involved.

While Kelso was struck with a deep sense of guilt when he read the press article about Kline's death during a break-in at his home, he was also tremendously relieved. The Russians would have left nothing behind, no information about Kline's deals, because they didn't want anything traced back to them.

That little loose end had been neatly tied off.

Only two things had been left before Kelso planned to leave Morgan. There was one last trip to Brazil to meet with another buyer. It had already been arranged by Kline before he was killed, and Kelso had planned to fly out next week to Brasilia. It would have been his last official act as an employee of Morgan Pharmaceuticals. His last unofficial act would have been to smuggle out the thumb drives that contained all the information on the Beta-Three project.

Now, however, as he drove past the besieged Morgan Building, he realized that the drives, the data, were gone. It was infuriating, because the information would be worth even more than the New Horizons seed had been, especially with all the progress the Beta-Three team had made since Naomi had arrived. But there was nothing to be done about it. While he couldn't be positive they were after him, it didn't matter. He couldn't go back to the company. There was no way he was going to risk being taken by the FBI.

While he was shocked by this sudden turn of events, he was not unprepared. He drove to LAX and pulled the car into a spot in one of the long term parking lots. Reaching under his seat, he pulled out a small leather bag that he had velcroed in place there, out of sight. He had known there might come a time such as this, when he wouldn't be able to return to his home or the safe house where he kept his hoard of organic gold. He took out a fake passport, driver's license, credit cards, and ten thousand dollars in cash, then put his real documents into the bag and zipped it shut.

After locking the car, he slipped the bag under his suit coat to keep it out of sight. Once he reached the nearest shuttle stop, which was deserted, he walked past the trash can and surreptitiously dumped the bag.

Then he caught the next shuttle for the international terminal.

CHAPTER TWENTY

The night had dissolved into a maelstrom of screams and chaos as Jack and the others ran, following Kuybishev, who was still bellowing orders at his men. Gunfire had erupted all around them, the muzzle flashes illuminating the terrified faces of the soldiers.

Jack had no idea where they were going. He now had his arm wrapped around Mikhailov's waist, helping him along, while his free hand clutched the KS-K shotgun. Rudenko ran behind them, periodically turning around to watch their backs, his heavy footsteps splashing in the cold, muddy ground.

A man in front of them went down, clutching at his leg and screaming. Jack couldn't see him well in the dark, but knew what must have happened: he'd stepped on a larval harvester. As they ran, he saw five more men near them go down. Jack slowed down, instinctively wanting to help them.

"No!" Rudenko shoved him forward. "Too late for them!"

Jack didn't turn around at the boom of Rudenko's shotgun and the blinding flare of the Dragon's Breath. The screams of the men who were suddenly transformed into blazing pyres rang in Jack's ears, but he kept running.

Kuybishev stopped and made a series of hand signals while he spoke rapidly into his radio. The company commanders shouted orders to their men who were converging out of the darkness.

"Here, Jack," Mikhailov gasped. "We make our stand here. Defensive perimeter."

Looking around them, Jack could see that they were in an open field near the center of the town. While there was little light to aim by, it made for a good killing ground against opponents who had to close to short range. The only alternative would have been to hole up in some houses, but then the harvesters could have overwhelmed them piecemeal.

That made Jack wonder about the level of cooperation shared by the creatures. The old ones certainly worked well enough toward a common goal, although they typically operated as individuals. Then again, there had been so few of them that outside of very special circumstances, such as the attack on the seed vault on Spitsbergen or the final arrangements for shipping the New Horizons seed, gathering on any regular basis would probably have disrupted their many operations.

The ones here, however, had enough cognitive capability to set an ambush for a modern military force, and judging from the growing volume of fire from the airborne soldiers did not share the problem of scarcity.

While Kuybishev's men were terrified, they didn't break discipline. As they dashed into the expanding defensive circle, their officers and NCOs got them under control, prepared them to fight back.

The colonel shouted an order, which Mikhailov translated for Jack. "Lights!"

Hundreds of tactical lights, most of them attached to the men's weapons, flicked on, stabbing outward from the defensive circle like spokes on a wheel.

Men were still coming out of the dark, sometimes diving over the heads of their comrades, who opened fire on the sinister shapes that pursued them.

It was then that Jack had a terrible thought. Leaving Mikhailov and Rudenko, he ran the short distance to where Kuybishev stood, watching the progress of the battle.

"Colonel! We've got to make sure the men coming in are really human!"

Kuybishev looked at him as if he'd gone mad. "What else would they be?"

"Sir, remember! These things are perfect mimics. They can change their appearance to anything that's about the same physical size. Out there, in the dark, they could kill a man and replace him."

Without a moment's thought, Kuybishev unslung a rifle from his shoulder. It was one of the weapons fitted with a thermal imager. "Soldier who had this is dead. You use it. Find and kill any that get inside."

Jack wasn't sure he wanted the responsibility that Kuybishev was thrusting upon him. He reached out and took the rifle. There had been two such weapons. "Where's the other one?"

Kuybishev shook his head. "I do not know. Ten, maybe fifteen men killed by those small things on ground. That soldier was one. More will die. Go now."

Returning to where Rudenko was standing guard over Mikhailov, Jack told the big NCO, "I'm going to need you for this. Mikhailov, watch your ass, and keep an eye on the goddamn ground so none of those little bastards sneak up on you."

Rudenko paused, uncertain.

"Go, you fool!" Mikhailov pushed him away. "I will be fine."

"*Da, kapitan*."

As Jack and Rudenko moved off toward the perimeter, Jack cursed. "I wish I could put this sight on my shotgun. This rifle isn't going to be worth shit without tracers or Dragon's Breath."

"Let me see it."

Jack handed the rifle to Rudenko, who undid some quick releases on the scope, then attached it to Jack's shotgun before slinging the assault rifle on his back. "Joys of, what do you say, standards, yes?"

Pulling the shotgun in tight to his shoulder and peering through the sight, Jack told him, "Damn straight."

The world that greeted his eye was alien, unnerving. Everything was in shades of gray, with warmer objects and surfaces, like the faces and hands of the men, appearing almost white, while cooler surfaces appeared in differing shades of darker gray. The muzzle flashes were stark white spears of flame that stabbed out into the killing zone around them, accompanied by deafening staccato *cracks*. "I don't see any here."

The two men turned at a sudden scream from their left. Looking through the sight, Jack saw that one of the men nearby was clutching at his shoulder. Like most of the soldiers, he had taken a prone position in the mud so he could aim better, and one of the larval harvesters had attacked him.

Jack cursed as he compared the gray tone of the harvester with that of the ground. It was a near-perfect match. He wouldn't be able to pick them out of the clutter to shoot them.

Rudenko grabbed the man by his desperately kicking feet and pulled him back from the defensive line. He was thrashing uncontrollably, his hands already trapped in the harvester's pulsing flesh after he'd tried to tear it off.

The soldier managed to get one of his feet free from Rudenko's grasp and lashed out, knocking Rudenko to the ground. "Shoot him!"

For a moment, Jack stood rooted to the ground, paralyzed. He'd killed before, certainly, but he'd never killed a man in cold blood.

There's no hope for him, Jack told himself. In his mind it was a cold voice, a dead voice, and Jack wondered if someday someone might not say the same for him.

Raising the shotgun, he aimed at the darker, cooler mass of the harvester larva on his shoulder and pulled the trigger.

The thermal sight blanked out for a moment in the white glare of the Dragon's Breath, and the man's screams ended with sudden finality as the harvester spreading up his chest and neck exploded into flames.

Turning the sight away from the dead soldier, Jack scanned the others around him. "It looks like this area's clear. Wait." He saw something in the shape of a man, but whose "face" was distinctly cooler, darker in the thermal imager, than those around him. "Shit. Follow me."

Sprinting through the muck, Jack saw that his target was giving orders to the men around him, shouting with authority, and even taking shots with a rifle at the harvesters continuing to charge the defensive perimeter.

As he got closer, Jack could see the outline of the thing's skeleton beneath the malleable flesh. There was no question.

The only problem was that the thing was right in the middle of a group of soldiers. If Jack shot it now, it could easily kill other soldiers when it burst into flame.

"Rudenko! We've got to get him away from the others!"

The big man didn't hesitate. He simply charged him and grabbed the harvester by the arm, swung it around, and let it go, flinging it away from the men and putting it in Jack's line of fire.

The thing recovered its balance almost immediately, much faster than a man possibly could. The human-looking face glared at Rudenko, but before it could do anything more, Jack fired.

The Dragon's breath shell speared through its thorax and the harvester's malleable flesh exploded into flame. It did a dance of death, burning gobbets sailing away into the night.

The soldiers around the thing cried out in terror, turning their attention away from the other harvesters that were still coming on fast.

Rudenko bellowed at the soldiers, gesturing with his shotgun for them to turn away from the flaming harvester, harmless now, to watch for the enemies that could still kill them.

As if the sizzling pyre of the harvester was a signal, the firing around them died down, then stopped.

The silence was stunning.

"Did we kill them all?" It was Rudenko's question, but every surviving soldier was wondering the same thing.

"Don't count on it. They gave up too easily."

"Too easily?" Rudenko looked around them. At least a quarter of the men were down, either injured or killed. There were piles of bodies, soldiers who had fought and died at close quarters with harvesters that had made it to the perimeter. Most of the creatures were in their natural, insectoid form, their limbs and killing appendages exposed. A few were part man, part beast, as if they had come running at the humans in the process of changing form. The air was thick with the foul stench that the harvesters exuded in their natural state, and more than a few men were choking and gagging, the smell was so intense. "This must be all, Jack. There were not so many people living in the village to act as hosts for there to be many more."

Jack shook his head, remembering the poor monkey who was the very first victim of this new generation of harvesters. "Remember, these things don't need humans. They can use any organic material. Animals, plants, almost anything."

"*Da*. Even plastics and rubber." Rudenko wiped a bloodstained hand across his forehead. "I had forgotten."

"And we have no idea how quickly they reproduce, spawning the smaller larval forms. God knows how many of those little sons of bitches are oozing toward us right now."

Rudenko reflexively looked down at his feet, but he knew that one of the abominations could be right next to his foot and he probably wouldn't see it in these conditions. "*Chyort voz'mi*."

Jack finished scanning the men left in the defensive perimeter with the thermal imaging sight. He didn't see any others who looked like harvesters. "Come on," he said. "Let's go find Mikhailov."

* * *

They found the Russian captain where they'd left him, near the center of the defensive perimeter, not far from where Kuybishev was talking on the radio in quiet, urgent tones.

"That was exciting." Mikhailov patted Jack on the shoulder and nodded at Rudenko. "Glad to see you made it."

"You, too." Jack looked more closely at the Russian captain. "You seem a bit better than when we left you."

"Drugs, Jack, they do wonders. Our medic gave me something. My ribs still hurt, but it does not seem to matter as much."

Rudenko snorted. "Vodka is better medicine."

Jack nodded toward the regimental commander. "What's Kuybishev doing?"

"Trying to get air support. Unfortunately, he is having a difficult time persuading our superiors to bomb this place." Mikhailov glanced over at Kuybishev as the colonel gave the handset back to the radioman while hissing a stream of curses. "The memories of what happened in your California a year ago are still fresh, it seems."

Kuybishev stomped over, his feet splashing in the mud. Unable to help himself, Jack watched every step the colonel took. He'd become acutely aware of how dangerous the ground had become.

"We are ordered to withdraw." Kuybishev spat on the ground. "The fools are sending trucks for us."

"What about the rest of the battalion?" Jack had a sinking feeling. "When is the second drop supposed to arrive?"

"They are not coming. Second drop has been canceled. Army is sending 205th Motorized Rifle Brigade from Budyonnovsk to sanitize area."

"And what is to become of us, *polkovnik*?" Mikhailov asked, shocked. "They think we have failed, and so simply remove us?"

"No, they do not think we failed. We are being recalled as part of general alert of airborne troops and military operational commands. The Chinese have gone on full military alert." He shot a look at Jack. "I should not be saying this to outsiders, of course."

"I understand, colonel," Jack told him. "Your secrets are safe with me. But it's not the Chinese you should be worried about. One of my people informed me that she thought something like what is happening here was happening in China, too. There are also outbreaks in Brazil and India. Their military response is being triggered by the harvesters, just the same as yours."

Kuybishev's expression hardened. "I do not wish to believe you, but I cannot dismiss what I have seen with my own eyes. I requested air strike here, to kill any little horrors that might have survived, but command denied it. Now we count our dead and await transport."

Jack was about to point out that he didn't think the battle here was over when he heard something over the pattering of the rain. It was a mewling screech.

Soon the lone voice was joined by others, creating an unholy din somewhere beyond the nearest houses on the eastern flank.

"Colonel," Jack said quietly, "I suggest you reinforce that side. We're going to have company in a minute, and probably lots of it."

"What is that terrible sound?" Rudenko tightened the grip on his shotgun as, like every other man in the perimeter, he stared in the direction of the noise.

"Unless I'm badly mistaken, those are cats. They're the only animals that have an instinctive revulsion toward harvesters. We use them as living detectors, and I sure wish someone would figure out a way to bring them on operations like this." In that moment, he wished more than anything that he had his own cat, Alexander, here with him, but knew that the silly beast was a lot safer at home with Naomi. "One of them even saved my life a couple times."

One of the soldiers on the eastern side shouted something.

Mikhailov translated, his voice thick with dread. "Movement!"

Turning to the young captain, Kuybishev said, "Stay here. I am putting a platoon under your command as reserve."

"*Ponyatno.*"

Pointing at Jack, Kuybishev said, "You stay with him. Kill any that mimic my soldiers, and stay alive. You know these things, and information you bring back will be priceless." He looked at Rudenko. "You will protect him. At all costs."

Before Rudenko could respond, Kuybishev had spun around and was trotting away into the darkness in the direction from which the cries of the cats were growing steadily louder and more frenzied.

"I have never heard such a sound." Rudenko stood close by Jack while Mikhailov spoke to the men Kuybishev had pulled out of the line and sent to him, there in the center of the defensive ring.

As Jack had suggested, Kuybishev had pulled as many men as he dared from the other quadrants to reinforce the eastern sector, and made the perimeter even smaller in hopes of making it easier to defend.

"There's something about the harvesters that seems to override the cats' natural instincts," Jack explained quietly as he scanned the houses to the east. There was still nothing. "They'll band together, attack and fight."

"I wonder where the cats were before now?"

"There's no way of knowing." Jack saw small, light gray shapes dart around both sides of the nearest house. Like a school of fish, the cats seemed to move as one. They paused, just for a moment, and then made a beeline for the humans. A torrent of nightmarish shapes followed right behind them. "Shit, here they come! Tell Kuybishev they're coming!"

Mikhailov shouted something, but his words were lost in a fusillade of gunfire that again lit up the night. Jack was astonished to see that the cats, instead of shying away from the gunfire, bored straight on toward the Russians. He only saw two cats go down, caught by stray bullets. The rest passed through the Russian line and ran straight past Jack and the others. But before they reached the men on the other side of the perimeter, they suddenly spun about and gathered around him and the others in the center, mewling pitiably.

Turning his attention back to the fight, Jack watched through the thermal sight as several dark blobs arced outward from the Russian soldiers, grenades that exploded amongst the harvesters with spectacular results. Kuybishev had them use white phosphorus, and brightly burning fragments sailed outward from each grenade blast, many of them landing on harvesters and setting them ablaze.

He lowered the sight. It was nearly useless in the sudden glare of the flames.

"I do not understand." Mikhailov shouted to be heard over the gunfire. "Why do they come at us this way? Why did they not pretend to be humans and ambush us, as they did on Spitsbergen? Or try harder to infiltrate us, masquerading as our own men?"

Jack shook his head. He'd been wondering the same thing. "I don't know. We know so little about them to begin with, and this generation is genetically different from the old ones. They can obviously cooperate, but beyond that, only Naomi might be able to tell us."

A chorus of shouts erupted from behind them, to the west, followed by gunfire and screams.

Bringing up the shotgun, Jack took a look through the thermal sight and felt his heart leap into his throat. He should have paid closer attention to the cats' behavior. There was a reason they didn't keep heading west, away from the attacking harvesters. "*They're coming in behind us!*"

CHAPTER TWENTY-ONE

Naomi escaped from one form of captivity only to trade it for another. As the elevator opened on the ground floor, she and the others were greeted by a team of FBI agents.

One of them was a tall black woman with close-cropped hair sporting a few streaks of gray. While that suggested she was a bit older than the agents around her, she also had the build of an Olympic sprinter. "I'm Special Agent Angie Boisson of the Federal Bureau of Investigation. If you'll all please exit the elevator and move to your right," she gestured toward another group of agents who formed a cordon in the lobby, "I'd appreciate it."

Naomi let the others file past her as she pressed herself into the front corner of the elevator near the control panel. As the last person, Harmony, stepped out, Naomi jabbed the button for the floor where her office was located.

"Dr. Perrault?"

Naomi looked up in surprise to see Boisson, a bemused expression on her face, stepping into the elevator.

"You won't be able to go anywhere without this." Boisson held up an emergency key, which she stuck into the control panel. Giving it a turn, she asked, "Which floor were you planning to go to?"

"Three." Naomi had stepped back involuntarily, not sure what to make of Boisson's actions. "I need to get to my office. My cats are there. I won't leave them."

The FBI agent pressed the button for the third floor and the elevator doors slid shut on the pandemonium beyond. "Assistant Director Carl Richards sends his regards," Boisson said. "He wanted to thank you for the tip on Kline." She paused, her dark eyes locking with Naomi's. "He also wanted me to ask about what you've been holding out on him."

Naomi felt sick. She had been worried that this might happen. Her silence in exchange for Morgan telling her everything about the Beta-Three samples had been necessary, but had been a bargain with the devil, all the same. That, however, didn't mean she was going to spill her guts to an FBI agent she didn't know. "If I did know something, why should I tell you?"

"Because if you don't, you're probably going to wind up in prison for a very long time, and Assistant Director Richards indicated to me that he wasn't very fond of that idea." She turned the key and hit the stop button. "He wanted me to find you and have a little private chat before anyone else got hold of you."

"He could have just called me and asked."

Boisson shook her head. "No, he couldn't. This raid was based on your tip about Kline. But we also figured out on our own that someone here at Morgan Pharmaceuticals was involved in getting their hands on the biological weapon we believe Kline was selling. Richards is trying to keep this as above-board as he can, given the circumstances. By calling you about this, he would have been involving himself directly with a potential suspect in a case."

"And this little conversation doesn't amount to the same thing?" Naomi's voice was laced with skepticism, but she couldn't help but cling to the small hope Boisson might represent. Naomi didn't want to wind up in prison for many reasons, not least of all that she knew that her world could soon be under siege, and she was one of the few people who might be able to help stop it.

"Richards and I go back quite a ways. I was also one of the agents involved in the Sutter Buttes raid. He helped save my ass. I owe him."

Naomi put her hand to her mouth. "Oh, God, I'm so sorry." Fifty-three FBI agents had lost their lives in the raid the year before on the Earth Defense Society base, an old Cold War Titan-I missile complex, at Sutter Buttes, California. It was the most grievous loss the Bureau had ever suffered, and had come right on the heels of the destruction of the FBI Laboratory in Quantico, Virginia by the harvesters. Watching those men and women die among the mines that defended the base had been one of the most heart-wrenching, horrible things Naomi had ever witnessed.

Boisson shrugged. "I walked away when a lot of others didn't." She looked at her watch. "I'm going to give you three minutes. That's all I can spare before we're both sorely missed. If you come clean, I've got a cover story that I'll use to take you into protective custody. I can't guarantee it'll keep you out of the pen in the long term, but you'll at least have a chance." Her voice hardened. "If you want to keep up the 'I'm not telling' routine, you'll be walking out of this elevator in handcuffs."

Naomi closed her eyes. Once again, she had no choice.

Then she told Boisson what she knew about Howard Morgan and his Beta-Three project.

* * *

"How can I help you, Special Agent Boisson?"

Boisson turned to see Howard Morgan, a Cheshire Cat's grin on his face, striding toward her, with the woman Boisson recognized as his security chief right behind. They were flanked by a pair of her agents.

"You can start by telling me what the hell's behind this door." Naomi had told Boisson the critical facts about the Beta-Three research in the short time they'd had before Boisson had to turn her over to a trio of agents, who, after gathering up the two cats, whisked Naomi out of the building to a safe house. The most important thing Naomi had revealed was the existence of Lab One, and the rushed evacuation just after the FBI had arrived. Leading a team of agents to the basement, Boisson had found the lab, of course, but there was no way to get inside.

That was when she'd sent her people to find Morgan and drag him down here. She knew that she didn't have enough to pin anything on him, but he still had to comply with her search warrant.

Of course, compliance didn't necessarily mean she would get what she wanted.

"I'm so sorry," Morgan said, not sounding sorry at all, "but Lab One suffered a catastrophic breach this morning and had to be sanitized. I can get you through the outer door, here, but beyond that, I can't help you." He shook his head, pursing his lips. "For safety reasons you won't be able to get past the inner door. No one can, not even me, until the internal sensors judge it to be safe."

"We'll see about that," Boisson snapped. "Open it."

Morgan nodded at his security chief, who stepped forward and swiped her ID card over the outer door's control panel, then looked into the retina scanner.

The console beeped, a light turned green, and with a sharp hiss of air the outer door swung open.

Boisson led the way into the vestibule, and was confronted with the vault-like inner door. "Open it."

"I told you, Agent Boisson, that's impossible. Put your hand up against that door."

She did, and was surprised to find how warm the door was. It was almost painful to the touch.

"Lab One was designed for highly sensitive research that involved extremely hazardous substances. We had protocols in place to ensure that if anything happened, the lab could be contained and sterilized to ensure there wouldn't be any contamination."

"You lit a fire in there?"

Morgan laughed. "Oh, it was a fire, all right, although not a bonfire of paper and plastic like you're probably imagining. We based the fail-safe system on the incinerators used in the most advanced crematorium in the world." He put his palm against the door and quickly withdrew it, shaking his hand theatrically, as if it were on fire. "Along with the vault door, the entire lab, including the floor and ceiling, is lined with inch-thick steel and ten inches of reinforced concrete. All that will be left beyond that door is powdered ash, once it's cool enough to open, of course. That should be in two, maybe three days."

"A perfect system for destroying evidence."

Morgan's expression hardened. "Agent Boisson, you are welcome to come in here and dig through our files and do whatever else you feel compelled to do in this little witch hunt. But if you're going to imply or directly accuse me or any of my employees of wrongdoing, say it and say it loud so my legal team can hear it up on the sixth floor."

Boisson didn't blink. "Sorry, but I don't really feel like shouting, and some of my agents are already talking to your lawyers. But now that you mention employees and wrongdoing, where can I find the good Dr. Adrian Kelso? We've been looking for him everywhere and can't find him. I have a warrant for his arrest."

That, Boisson could clearly see, came as a shock to Morgan. While he recovered his composure in a heartbeat, she knew that had rocked his boat.

"On what charges?"

"Well, technically that's none of your business, but since you asked so nicely I'll give you a clue: we believe he's been peddling bio-weapons to other countries." She stepped closer. "I don't have anything on you right now, Mr. Morgan, but we'll see if Kelso wants to reveal any skeletons from your closet once we catch up with him. Of course, if you helped us track him down, that might look good when your turn comes up. Was Dr. Kelso supposed to show up today?"

"It's not my habit to keep daily track of my employees, Agent Boisson. I trust them to do their jobs, for which they're highly paid. If Dr. Kelso isn't in this morning, I'm sure he's engaged in work-related business or he's on sick leave. As my chief scientist, he has a lot of responsibilities, both here and at our other facilities, and the latitude to do as he sees fit."

"Harmony Bates said that she expected him today, if that makes a difference to you. It's sort of convenient that you have an accident at your lab and torch it and Kelso doesn't show up on the day that we decide to pay you a visit."

"If she says he was supposed to be in, then he was supposed to be in. He probably saw your army of thugs invading our building and just drove on home."

She shook her head. "He's not there, and his car's missing."

Rolling his eyes, Morgan said, "I'm sorry, but I can't help you there. You'll just have to do the job that I pay you to do with my tax money."

"So how about foreign travel? Does he travel often?"

"Of course he does. He's a leader in the field of genetics, and like other scientific illuminati, he attends seminars and other gatherings of great minds which, I might point out, are not routinely attended by FBI agents for obvious reasons."

Boisson ignored the insult. "What would you say if I told you that he's traveled to six different countries in the last year using fake passports?"

She suppressed a smile as she saw Morgan falter. His eyes widened in surprise.

"What?"

"That's right, Mr. Morgan. We may not go to all the gatherings of great minds, but we're still pretty good at figuring things out." She pulled a tightly folded sheaf of paper from her jacket and opened it up before showing it to him. Karina Petrovsky leaned over Morgan's shoulder to look, too. "Here are images of the passports he used and the dates and countries he traveled to while using them. And while we don't have any evidence yet, I'd wager my next month's pay that he was involved with another suspect, Norman Kline."

Morgan shook his head, and Petrovsky's expression suddenly clouded. "I don't know anything about that," Morgan said.

Lying sack of shit, Boisson thought, but didn't say aloud. *Fine, you can play that game. For now.* "I didn't expect that you would, Mr. Morgan. But how about Dr. Kelso. Any idea why he was traveling under false identities to all these countries? And was it with your permission and knowledge? Think very carefully before you answer, or do you want me to shout it out so your legal team can hear?"

After a moment more of looking over the papers, which Boisson then took back, Morgan shook his head. "No, I knew nothing of this. I knew he'd been taking quite a bit of leave over the last year for medical problems, but never gave it a second thought."

"And you, Ms. Petrovsky?"

"I had no idea. I'd have to check the personnel records, but I recognize some of the more recent dates as times that he was away. As Mr. Morgan said, Dr. Kelso had taken quite a bit of sick leave along with his normal travels."

"What do you think he was doing?" Morgan's tone carried a hint of anger, but Boisson suspected it wasn't directed at her.

"He was probably selling whatever *wasn't* in your lab here to as many people as he could. If I had to guess, I'd say that he was working with Kline." She put on a theatrical expression of thinking hard. "So if you bought anything from Kline, it probably originally came from Kelso." She smiled, a predatory display of teeth that would have looked at home on a shark. "That's just sheer speculation, of course. But it makes a good theory, don't you think?"

Morgan glared at her. "Is that all, Agent Boisson?"

"For now, Mr. Morgan. But I'd appreciate it if Ms. Petrovsky would facilitate our search of your personnel records for information on Kelso. And we'll also obviously keep digging for any information on whatever might have been in your torched lab. You'd better hope we don't find anything."

* * *

The FBI agents were pleasant enough, but Naomi didn't make the mistake of thinking they were her friends. Not now.

She wasn't sure where she was, because they had whisked her away from Morgan Pharmaceuticals in a van that didn't have any windows in the back. They'd driven for over an hour, taking a lot of turns. When the van stopped and they let her out, she found that the van was parked in the garage of a nice, if bland, three bedroom house. They wouldn't let her near the windows in the front, although she could move about as she wished through the rear part of the house. The windows of the bedrooms were masked by a six foot wall that went all the way around the back of the property.

The one redeeming feature was that she was free to wander into the back yard, where there was a covered porch and a pool. The brick wall and the lack of any buildings close by that were tall enough to see over into the yard made sure that any prying eyes couldn't see inside.

Of course, she couldn't see out, either.

She had Alexander and Koshka with her, and one of the four agents had been accommodating to their unexpected feline guests by going out to get a litter box and some food for them.

She had sat in complete silence during the ride here, wondering what was going to happen. She felt as if she'd betrayed Carl and the others. Making her deal with Morgan had been a necessary evil, but that didn't help lift the burden from her soul. She'd placed Carl in a terrible position, and fervently hoped that it wouldn't further damage his career.

And then there was Jack. She was worried to death about him. She had tried calling him all morning before the FBI raid, but all she'd gotten was a female voice speaking English with a Russian accent, telling her that the number was unavailable.

Now she didn't even have her phone. The FBI agents "protecting" her had confiscated it. They'd brought her laptop along from the office, but had made it clear that she wouldn't be allowed to use it. One of the agents was in one of the bedrooms, the door closed, and she suspected he was trying to hack into it to see what incriminating evidence it might contain.

She made it through a full thirty minutes from the time they'd arrived until she felt as if she were going to explode. She couldn't just sit here. She had to do something.

"Agent Garcia," she asked, "I need to call Jack Dawson."

The head of her protective detail, a stocky Hispanic man in his late twenties, shook his head. "I'm sorry, ma'am, but I can't let you make any calls at this time." The look on his face made it clear that he wasn't about to brook any argument.

"Fine, then. Could you make a call for me?" Garcia frowned, and Naomi sensed an opening. "Listen, it's to someone who works at the Bureau's headquarters in D.C., Renee Vintner. Maybe you've heard of her?"

Garcia shook his head, unimpressed.

"Look, could you just give her a call and ask her to track down Jack for me. He's my fiancé, and I'm worried sick about him. Renee can find him." She stared at Garcia, who's expression hadn't changed a bit. "Please?"

"Where does she work?"

"She's been reassigned to the Intelligence Directorate. Her phone number is..."

Garcia held up a hand and shook his head. Then he turned away, pulling his phone out of his jacket. He wandered into the kitchen, and she heard him speaking quietly for a few minutes.

He reappeared, a chastened look on his face. He handed the phone to Naomi.

"Yes? Renee?"

"Naomi?" Renee was nearly shouting into the phone. "Jesus Christ, woman, turn on the news!"

CHAPTER TWENTY-TWO

The open field at the center of the village of Ulan-Erg had become a killing ground as the harvesters swarmed over the Russian paratroopers. Jack forced down his guilt at falling for the harvesters' feint, using the cats to draw the humans' attention to the western side before they made their main attack from the opposite direction.

Mikhailov had no choice but to commit the battalion's tiny reserve of twenty men. With a roar that briefly rose above the sound of gunfire, shrieks and shouts, the troops of the reserve, guns blazing, crashed into the mass of harvesters on the eastern side of the perimeter.

Jack watched them through the thermal sight on the shotgun, feeling helpless and useless. He fired at a harvester that vaulted over the human line, and the night was again torn by a living bonfire as the thing burst into flame. Mikhailov pumped a round of Dragon's Breath into another nightmare shape, and its brethren leaped aside to avoid a similar fate. He, Jack, and Rudenko used their shotguns to good effect, picking off harvesters that broke through. In short order, the darkness had been peeled away by the light of the creatures' blazing pyres.

The harvesters changed tactics and began to snatch soldiers away from the line, dragging them away into the darkness. A few of the men screamed in terror, but most cursed and fought, blasting away at their opponents at point blank range with their rifles or stabbing at them with knives. Mikhailov shot a few of the snatching harvesters, but the things were so fast that they quickly escaped beyond the short range of the Dragon's Breath rounds. Some of the creatures that had dragged men away suddenly exploded, and Jack realized that the soldiers must have triggered grenades, killing their attackers along with themselves.

He heard Rudenko bellow, then felt himself flying through the air. Slamming into the cold mud, he rolled over onto his back just in time to see Rudenko blast a harvester at point blank range. The big NCO had knocked Jack aside just in time. The harvester's stinger landed inches from his face, and he rolled away as its flaming corpse collapsed beside him.

What shocked Jack was that this harvester had come from behind him, from the western side of the perimeter where Kuybishev was leading the battle.

The cats that had been swirling around them in a mixture of terror and rage converged on another harvester that had somehow vaulted past the defensive line. Jack had noticed that most of them were as big as Alexander, a Siberian cat who weighed just over twenty pounds, and some were bigger. He wasn't sure how many of them there were, but they swarmed over the creature in a snarling mass of fangs and claws. Jack doubted they could kill it, but there was no question the harvester was out of the fight for the moment as it collapsed to the ground under the weight of the feline assault.

"I change my mind about cats," Rudenko growled as he loaded a fresh magazine into his shotgun. "If we live through this, I will get one. Maybe ten."

Drawing his pistol, Rudenko stepped forward. Taking careful aim at the thing's thorax, he fired. The cats darted away from the boom and flash of the gun. The harvester convulsed once, then lay still, a hole as big around as Jack's thumb in its chest and a fist-sized exit wound out the back.

After a moment of blind panic, the cats seemed to again find their rage and attacked a group of harvesters that had pinned several soldiers to the ground.

Jack brought the thermal sight to his eye, but instantly wished he hadn't. It was clear they were losing. The Russians were fighting like madmen, but once the harvesters got in close, it was no contest. They were natural killing machines, just like sharks and killer whales were in their ocean domain. If Kuybishev's men had been armed with the right weapons, the story would have been very different. But there was no question in Jack's mind of the final outcome of this battle.

He swept his shotgun in an arc, taking in the carnage around him. As he looked to the northeast, he stopped: more figures were approaching, but they didn't look like harvesters. They looked like humans.

"Rudenko! There's a bridge northeast of town, isn't there?"

"*Da! Polkovnik* Kuybishev dropped a platoon there to hold it." He paused as he fired his shotgun again at a harvester loping toward them.

Jack was shocked to see the thing leap out of the way, anticipating the shot. Rudenko had to fire twice more before he hit the thing. It was so close by then that he and Jack had to back away to avoid being burned.

"Shit! They're learning fast!" He pointed toward the northeast. "I think the platoon from the bridge is coming. Look!"

He held up the shotgun and Rudenko took it, peering through the sight. "Da, I see." Rudenko dialed up the magnification and stared through the eyepiece.

He gave it back to Jack, and in the light of burning harvesters and muzzle flashes from the guns of the surviving Russian soldiers, Jack could see the horrified look on the big man's face.

Bringing the shotgun back up to his shoulder, Jack looked again through the sight at the approaching soldiers. He didn't see it before, because they were too far away, but now he could clearly make out their faces in the scope. While the shapes were right, their thermal profile wasn't.

The men running toward them weren't human.

* * *

Kuybishev fought alongside his men, leading by example. There was no finesse in this battle, no need for orders or thought. There was only killing and dying. He had little time for reflection as he blasted away at the nightmare creatures that savaged his men, but images of the battles he had fought in Chechnya came to him, triggered by the screams and gunfire, the smell of blood and gunpowder smoke. As horrific as those battles had been, he would have gladly traded his right arm to again be fighting the Chechens, rather than these things. The Chechens showed no mercy, but at least once they finished with you, you were dead. With these harvester creatures, who could take the shape of any man or woman, who knew what evil could be done in someone's name?

While few would have ever guessed it, Kuybishev was a deeply religious man, to the point of being superstitious, and the thought that something could steal his body made him wonder if it could also steal his soul. It would not be getting a bargain, by any means, for Kuybishev knew that there was no chance he would ever pass through the gates of Heaven, but it was all he had to offer. And the thought of his soul in the claws of one of these things frightened him far more than the prospect of a violent death.

Something whipped against his right arm. Dropping the rifle to dangle on its sling, he snatched at it with his right hand and brought up the knife he'd been holding in his left. With a savage slash, he cut the massive stinger from the tentacle-like umbilical that, somewhere in the madness around him, was tied to a harvester.

He heard the creature scream, and a glistening shadow turned toward him from where it had been tearing one of his soldiers to pieces. Grabbing up his rifle, he shoved the muzzle into its open jaws and pulled the trigger, blowing the back of its skull off.

Claws grabbed him around the neck, yanking him backward. Instead of resisting, he pushed as hard as he could with his legs, fighting for purchase in the cold muck. Throwing his attacker off balance, he twisted his body to the right, jamming the blade of the knife in his left hand into the harvester's thorax. He was sickened by the slimy feel of the soft malleable flesh as his hand sunk into it, but the tip of the blade bit deep into the creature.

With an ear-splitting squeal, the thing released him. But instead of trying to escape, he wrenched the knife free before forcing the creature, which was already off-balance, onto its back. Using the momentum of the fall and the weight of his body, he drove the knife up to the hilt in the thing's chest, using his left elbow to deflect the pod that held the creature's devilish arsenal.

The thing went still as he felt a gush of something warm over his hand. The smell was horrific, even worse than the already pungent reek of the creatures, and Kuybishev involuntarily retched.

Ignoring his heaving stomach, he scrabbled to his feet. Planting a foot on the dead thing's chest, he wrenched loose his knife.

"*Polkovnik!*"

Kuybishev looked at the soldier who'd called him, and was pointing off to the northeast.

"The platoon from the bridge is coming!"

"*Nakonets*," Kuybishev breathed. "Finally." When it had become clear that they were grossly outmatched here, he had called the platoon leader over the radio and ordered him to join the rest of the battalion. It had taken far longer than it should have for them to get here. *Perhaps they, too, ran into a bit of trouble*, he thought. No matter. It was something he would sort out later with the platoon leader, if he survived.

The platoon, approaching at a fast trot, spread out on a line, their rifles raised.

"Get down!" Kuybishev bellowed. He didn't want his men cut down by friendly fire. He cursed the platoon leader's stupidity. Then again, in this situation, there were precious few alternatives for them to fire on the harvesters without putting the men on this side of the line in harm's way. "Down!"

The men around Kuybishev knelt or dove down on the ground as best they could, although many decided to take the chance of being shot as they stood, grappling with the beasts.

The soldiers of the platoon opened fire, and the harvesters, taken by surprise, whirled to face this new threat. Several of them were cut down instantly, others were wounded and maimed. Some of Kuybishev's men died, hit by bullets from their comrades. It was tragic, but there were worse ways to die, as he knew all too well.

Firing on full automatic, Kuybishev knew that the platoon's ammunition would be depleted quickly. But if they didn't break the harvesters now, it wouldn't matter.

Around him, the men inside the perimeter kept firing, stabbing, punching, and biting their opponents as the harvesters were raked with bullets. Kuybishev was immensely proud of them.

The remaining harvesters suddenly broke and ran, fleeing into the darkness. Kuybishev got to his feet and turned to the east, where Mikhailov was still fully engaged. "On your feet!" He began to help up the men around him and shoved them toward the sound of the fighting behind them. "The fight's not over yet!"

The platoon leader, a young lieutenant, saluted him. It was technically forbidden in a combat environment, but under these surreal circumstances it seemed appropriate. "My apologies, *polkovnik*. We were detained."

"I can see that." Kuybishev offered a rare smile. "Better late than never, as the old saying goes."

"*Colonel, no!*"

As Kuybishev turned at the sound of the American's voice, a swarm of cats swept past him, brushing his legs, to attack several of the men of the bridge platoon.

Something stabbed him in the side, and he looked down to see the stinger of a harvester embedded in his flesh, the venom sack pumping obscenely. His torso was suddenly filled with a fiery pain.

Shocked, he followed the tentacle to which it was attached and saw that it led back to the young lieutenant, and disappeared into his chest.

Shotguns fired past Kuybishev, sending enormous jets of tiny blazing particles, like a terrible fireworks display, into the lieutenant and some of the other men of the platoon. But, as he now realized, they were not men. Not at all.

The lieutenant was instantly transformed into a living torch. Kuybishev fell to his knees as the thing tore away the stinger and began its dance of death, shedding burning chunks of its flesh and screeching as it died.

The surviving soldiers — things — of the platoon opened fire, and he heard Mikhailov shouting orders above more shotgun blasts that, he now understood, were fired by Jack and Rudenko. A white phosphorus grenade blossomed in the midst of the platoon, scattering the things as they tried to avoid being hit by the burning bits of phosphorus.

In the added light from the grenade, Kuybishev saw the shadows of the harvesters that had fled moments ago, now returning for the kill.

It was all a ruse, he thought in a mix of admiration and horror.

He grunted as he was struck by a bullet in the shoulder, and he felt another hit him in the side near where the stinger had stabbed him. There, he only sensed the force of the bullet's passage, for his nerves could not convey any greater sense of pain.

What looked and sounded more like a conventional firefight, with the exceptions of the snarling cats and brightly burning bodies of the harvesters, broke out around him as he collapsed to the wet ground.

Someone grabbed his combat harness and began to drag him back, away from the things that pretended to be soldiers. He looked up and saw Jack's face reflected in the nightmarish glare. The American had slung his shotgun over his shoulder and was pulling him with one hand while still blasting away at the enemy with his enormous handgun.

"Jack." Kuybishev reached up and grabbed Jack by the collar, pulling him closer so he might hear. "I called for helicopter to take you to safety."

"That's fine, colonel, as long as there's room for everyone." He took aim and fired twice with the big pistol at something Kuybishev couldn't see, then quickly changed magazines. "We're not leaving anyone behind!"

Releasing Jack's neck, Kuybishev grabbed his gun hand so he knew he would have the American's full attention. "If you do not live, all this will be for nothing. My men deserve better. Your word, Jack. I want your word."

Jack nodded. "You have my word, sir. But we're taking as many out of here as we can."

There will be precious few, Kuybishev thought bitterly as the agonizing pain of the venom swept ever further through his body.

* * *

Shivering with cold and fear, Jack stared into the darkness. Beside him, Kuybishev was still alive, although Jack knew the colonel was going to die. Only one test sample of harvester antivenin had ever been made, and Naomi had injected Jack with it after he'd been stung during the battle at the Earth Defense Society base the year before. Since then, making more had been impossible because there was no supply of harvester venom, which was essential to create the antivenin. Until more could be made, anyone who received so much as a scratch from a harvester's stinger was doomed to die.

For the moment, it was quiet, which Jack found unnerving. The harvesters had almost finished them off after the mimics of the bridge platoon had arrived, but the Dragon's Breath rounds and a desperate volley of white phosphorus grenades from Rudenko finally made them retreat. Some Russian soldiers had died or been horribly burned by the grenade fragments, but there had been no other choice.

The seventeen survivors, including himself, had gathered at the center of the field, huddled in a defensive circle behind a barrier of bodies they had piled up around them. Jack made the unpleasant discovery that the dead, especially the harvesters, drew the larval forms like flies to shit. The men tried to ignore the slight shifting of the bodies as they were consumed.

The only ones who had made it this far were men who could still fight. Those who'd been seriously injured had been left in the darkness. There hadn't been time or strength to find them and drag them in. The moans and screams of the injured and dying had stopped some time ago. Jack shuddered as he thought of those poor men, helpless and alone, and the things that must have come from the night to finish what they'd started.

Now, there was only silence.

Of the cats, there was no sign. Many of them, he knew, had been killed in the last convulsion of the firefight. The rest, their survival instincts apparently getting the upper hand, had fled into the darkness.

The rain had stopped, although the air still carried a frigid mist that could be felt, if not really seen. The mud inside their little fortress of the dead was ankle deep, and every square inch of Jack's skin, covered or exposed, was wet and cold.

He held a dead soldier's assault rifle, for that was all he had left. His shotgun and its priceless thermal sight were gone, torn from his hands and flung into the darkness by a harvester just before Mikhailov had killed it. Jack had fired all the ammo he'd had for his Desert Eagle, which he'd flung at a harvester that had been about to attack Rudenko. Even the rifle Jack held only had half a magazine of ammunition. A few of the men around him had more. Most had less. It took a lot of bullets to kill a harvester, and they'd killed more than their share that night.

Worst of all, they had lost all their radio gear, and if there had ever been any functioning cell phone coverage here, it was gone now. They were completely cut off from the outside world.

"Here, you drink this."

Jack took the battered metal flask that Rudenko handed him. Putting it to his lips, he tilted up the flask and felt a tiny trickle of vodka hit his tongue, then slide down his throat. He normally didn't drink the stuff, but he welcomed the sudden surge of warmth in his belly that momentarily drove away the penetrating cold.

"Thanks." He handed back the flask, then added, "I thought you already drank it all."

The older man chuckled. "I did. Then I spit back in flask."

Jack couldn't help himself. He laughed. "Cheap bastard."

They turned at the sound of feet squishing through the mud, and Mikhailov collapsed beside them. Rudenko offered him the flask.

Mikhailov waved it back. "Save your spit for Jack. He can't handle straight vodka, anyway."

Jack shook his head, smiling despite the miserable situation. "Here I am, at the very end, stuck with two Russian wise-asses."

"Things could be worse," Mikhailov said. "You could be stuck with two Russian dumb-asses."

In the distance, the silence was shattered as a cat hissed and screeched, then was quiet. The sound made the hair on the back of Jack's neck stand on end.

After a moment, he heard something else that made his pulse quicken, but for an entirely different reason. "A helicopter! It must be the one the colonel called for!"

Mikhailov pulled a flare from his combat harness. He waited until he could clearly see the helicopter's approaching navigation lights, then fired the flare. A small red ball of fire shot into the sky before lazily descending to the ground. As it fell, Jack could see things moving all around them, dark shadows creeping closer.

"Shit. They're coming."

Another cat yowled as the flare reached the ground where it sizzled on the wet earth before going out.

Mikhailov grunted. "I suspect our hosts don't wish us to leave before the party is over."

The helicopter adjusted its approach, and was now heading straight for their position.

The men raised a ragged cheer, but Mikhailov cut them off with some terse phrases in Russian. The sense of hope that had sprung up seemed to vanish into quiet despair.

Jack turned to his Russian friend. "What did you tell them?"

"He gave them my orders." Kuybishev's whisper was barely audible. Jack bent down, putting his ear to the man's lips. He was amazed the colonel could speak. By this time, anyone else would have been totally paralyzed, trapped in a body aflame with the deadly toxin. "Command refused enough aircraft to take us all out. Sent only one." He drew in a long, ragged breath. "You must be on it. Others will defend. And tell Rudenko...take care of me."

"Colonel?" Kuybishev only stared at Jack. His lips twitched, but that was all. Jack looked at Rudenko, who nodded gravely. "What did he mean, for you to take care of him?"

"Do not ask questions you do not want answered, Jack," Mikhailov told him softly.

"*Kapitan?*" One of the soldiers was pointing to the south, from where the second cat cry had come.

Everyone looked, and Jack cursed at what he saw.

Where a moment before had been sinister shadows moving in the pale red light of the flare, there now stood over a dozen "men," thirty or forty meters away, waving flashlights to get the helicopter's attention.

"The harvesters are closer to the helicopter." Mikhailov began.

"And it will see them first and land," Jack finished. "They won't have a clue that they're picking up the bad guys!"

The helicopter began to descend toward the impostors.

Mikhailov spoke quickly to Rudenko, who moved around the position, passing them on to the other men.

"What's the plan?" Jack reflexively checked the magazine in his weapon.

"Simple. We advance and attack. Under no circumstances can we let those things board the helicopter." He checked the two remaining grenades on his combat harness. "If we cannot keep them away from it, we'll destroy it." He stood up, and the other men followed suit. All of them had their bayonets fixed. "Stay behind us, Jack. And be careful of those larval forms beyond the barricade." Then, to the others, he quietly ordered, "*Vperyod!*"

The men quickly clambered over the wall of bodies, then leaped into the mud as far as they could.

Jack was about to go over when he caught sight of Rudenko, kneeling next to Kuybishev. There was a quick flash of steel and the unmistakable sound of the gurgling, gasping sound made by a severed windpipe. Then Rudenko gently lifted the colonel's body enough to carefully place something underneath. Getting to his feet, Rudenko saluted, then turned to Jack.

"Come. We go. I am to look out for you."

Both saddened and touched by what he'd seen, Jack clambered on top of the bodies and jumped out into the mud, with Rudenko right behind him.

Jack was amazed that all of them managed to make it out of their macabre fortress without being attacked by any larvae. He glanced back as he heard the pile of bodies shift, and understood why. The bodies on the outside had been reduced to an undulating mass of goo. He hurried to catch up with the others.

* * *

Mikhailov marched until the men were in a line on either side of him, then he broke into double time, moving as quickly as he could through the muck. His ribs sent searing pain through his chest with every step, but he fought to ignore it. He had few illusions that he would survive this last encounter. He would do everything he could to ensure that the helicopter took Jack away to safety, but he knew his American friend would be the only survivor. Had the soldiers with him been from his own company, men he could recognize in the darkness by their voices, even their movements and mannerisms, it might have been different.

But those with him were strangers, most with faces he'd never seen, except in this wretched darkness. Once they boarded the helicopter, especially after the confusion of the fight that was only a few seconds away, how could he know who was human and who was not? There would not be a thermal imager on-board the helicopter for him to use, and the Air Force was not in the habit of carrying cats. The third test for harvesters, fire, wasn't something that could be used indiscriminately, especially on an aircraft.

No. Despite the heroism all these men had shown, no one would board the helicopter but Jack. And if Jack was killed, Mikhailov would blow up the helicopter.

Halfway across the barren no-man's land, one of his men fell, screaming, as he stepped on a larval harvester, just as the helicopter touched down.

The creatures masquerading as men, about to board the helicopter, paused and looked their way.

It was time.

"*K boyu!*" Mikhailov bellowed what he knew would be his last command and charged, opening fire on the enemy.

* * *

Jack followed the line of screaming Russians as Mikhailov led them in a headlong dash across the remaining distance to the harvesters. They blasted away with their assault rifles, their only care not to hit the precious helicopter.

Behind him, Rudenko fired at something following them. While Jack couldn't see them, he knew that every last harvester must be converging on the surviving Russians.

The impostors began to return fire, and several soldiers went down under the barrage.

Then the two groups slammed together, right in front of the shocked eyes of the helicopter pilots.

Men and not-men from both groups tried to run toward the ramp at the rear of the helo, only to be cut down by men from one side or the other. Now that they were at arm's length, stabbing with their bayonets and slamming one another with rifle butts, there was no way to tell friend from foe. The only difference was that the harvesters were much harder to kill.

Jack moved to join the fray, but Rudenko grabbed him by the harness and hauled him toward the cargo ramp. Bullets sprayed around them, and Rudenko grunted as one took him in the left calf.

He turned and lobbed a grenade into the middle of the melee, and Jack watched, sickened, as bodies were sent flying when it exploded.

But the detonation served its purpose, blinding and temporarily shocking those who weren't killed outright.

"Get in!" Rudenko shoved Jack toward the ramp and the loadmaster, who stood there in a state of complete shock. Rudenko grabbed the loadmaster by the collar, nearly lifting his feet from the ramp, and shouted at him, their noses only centimeters apart. Then he propelled the man into the cargo bay, and he ran forward to the cockpit. "I told them to take off!"

"What about the others?"

The big NCO shook his head. "There will be no others! You kill anyone who approaches! Do you understand?"

His insides numb, Jack nodded.

With a final nod, Rudenko turned away and dove back into the savage battle, shooting indiscriminately.

Jack knelt there on the ramp, tears in his eyes as he watched the remaining Russians and the things that looked like them kill one another. Three got close to the ramp, and Jack did as Rudenko had told him. He killed them. Each of them went down with a short burst. But they were humans, not harvesters.

The whine of the engines grew and the rotors turned faster, and in a few seconds the helicopter, another Mi-17, began to lift off.

Bullets *spanged* off the metal around him, and a grenade exploded among the still-fighting men and creatures.

Out of the carnage staggered Rudenko, with someone slung over his shoulder. Jack tried to cover him, firing over his head at the men and not-men that began to charge toward the ramp.

Rudenko stumbled as he was hit, a spray of blood emerging from his chest as a bullet passed through.

He made it to the foot of the ramp as the Mi-17's wheels left the ground. Crying out with the effort, he unslung the body he'd been carrying. Jack grabbed the man — Mikhailov, he saw now — and dragged him up.

"*Do svedanya*, my friend," Rudenko called as he pulled two grenades from his combat harness. He wore a bloody smile on his face.

"No! Rudenko, *no!*"

The big man pulled the grenade pins with his teeth as the tip of a stinger burst from his chest. As if in slow motion, the smile still on his face, he fell away into the darkness as the helicopter lifted off.

Jack covered his eyes with his hands against the glare of the white-hot fragments of the white phosphorus grenades when they went off, turning the melee into an inferno as the harvesters, all of them packed in tight as they fought the remaining Russians, burst into flame.

The helicopter was far enough away by then to avoid the lethal fragments that arced through the air. But it was well within range of the RPG anti-tank rocket that someone, man or beast, fired from within the burning cauldron.

Jack dove to the deck to cover Mikhailov as the rocket sped past his head into the cargo compartment and exploded against the ceiling, blasting one of the helicopter's engines into flaming wreckage.

CHAPTER TWENTY-THREE

Still holding Garcia's phone to her ear, Naomi quickly crossed the living room and found the remote for the television. After some fumbling and a few curses, she had it turned on and tuned to her favorite twenty-four hour news network.

"Okay," she told Renee. "I've got it. Oh, my God."

On the television, in all its high definition glory, was an aerial view of Los Angeles looking north, with the mountains of the Angeles National Forest in the background. Smoke drifted up from half a dozen fires burning out of control across Altadena and Pasadena, spread out between NASA's Jet Propulsion Laboratory and Santa Anita Park.

Special Agent Garcia came up to stand beside her, his mouth open in shock. "Jesus. That's only a few miles from here."

"For our viewers just joining us," the male newscaster said, "what appears to be widespread rioting broke out in Los Angeles only half an hour ago. Police and firefighters are on the scene," the view cut to show a ladder truck spraying water on the upper floors of a blazing building, with firemen scrambling to get more hoses into action on the ground as dozens of people fled past, screaming, "but no one seems to know for certain who started the riots, or why. Let's cut to Michael Daley from one of our local affiliates, who's on the scene." The camera switched to a young black man who, despite his outward calm, was clearly afraid. He was standing next to a pizza restaurant on the corner of an outdoor shopping center. Two of the buildings behind him were on fire. "Michael, can you tell us what's going on there?"

"Jim, if I had to use a single phrase to describe things here, I'd have to say it's like a war zone." He reflexively ducked as the staccato bark of automatic gunfire sounded somewhere not far behind him. "That came from a SWAT team that we saw enter this commercial complex just a few minutes ago, responding to a call from the veterinary clinic here."

"The veterinary clinic?" Jim, the talking head in the newsroom, looked confused.

"Yes, that was the word we got from the police. Several firemen and two police officers who were sent to answer the call were reportedly attacked, but it wasn't clear by whom or what." He ducked again as several automatic weapons fired. Then came a series of screams and curses. "That's when they sent in the SWAT team."

He peered around the corner toward where the SWAT van was visible in the parking lot, and the camera zoomed in as a fusillade of firing erupted from the SWAT officers.

Naomi gasped as she saw the unmistakable shapes of harvesters in their natural form leap over nearby cars, hurling themselves at the policemen. There were only three of the things, but at close quarters against an opponent who didn't understand what they were up against, that was more than enough.

"Michael, can you tell us what we're seeing?" Jim's voice was incredulous. "That looks like something out of Hollywood! Are you sure this isn't a movie shoot?"

One of the officers screamed as a harvester's stinger speared him, right through his body armor. Then the harvester's cutting blade finished the job, neatly lopping off the man's head.

"Jim," the on-scene reporter gasped as the other members of the SWAT team were stabbed and dismembered, "our station checked on that with the film studios. This isn't a movie. These things are fuc..." He caught himself just in time. "Believe me, they're real."

The view lingered on the harvester that had decapitated the policeman. The thing ripped off the dead officer's helmet, then seemed to suck the head into its mouth.

The camera then panned to the gawkers who had been standing in the parking lot. Some applauded, no doubt thinking that what they were watching was a Hollywood production. Most, however, turned and fled for their cars.

The other two harvesters gave chase, while the third continued to feed. One of the two seemed to stumble, and Naomi saw an odd bulge in its thorax separate and fall away to the pavement. The camera panned to follow the creatures as they pursued the crowd, but the image of what had fallen to the ground was burned in her mind.

"*Amoeba dubia*," Naomi whispered, recalling her conversation with Harmony Bates in the lab.

"Amoeba what?"

"I'll tell you later. Renee, can you get the network to give us the footage of the report from Altadena that's playing right now? I need to look more closely at something."

"I'm on it. God, how did this happen?"

"I don't know," Naomi breathed, but in her gut she knew it must have something to do with Kelso. At Boisson's urging, Garcia had told her about the Bureau's suspicions about Kelso and his activities, and she had no doubts that somehow he had obtained samples from The Bag and done a double-deal to Morgan. Morgan's people had been far too careful for this disaster to have been their doing, for she knew that nothing could have escaped from Vault One. But Kelso couldn't have afforded the same extravagant safeguards, or he might've been careless. None of them, not even Morgan, had understood the true dangers of their precious Beta-Three samples. And all it would have taken, especially if the old harvesters had engineered in a reproductive method into the new generation, was a single kernel of that accursed corn to spawn Armageddon.

"Oh, no!" Michael, the on-scene reporter, turned a terrified face to the camera. In the background, several people were fleeing in his direction, and one of the creatures was right behind them. "We've got to get out of here!"

He bolted into the adjacent four-lane street, and the cameraman took off behind him. To his credit, the cameraman flipped the camera around, and the viewers were treated to a bouncing, jarring image of screaming people being pursued by *something*. The creature stabbed one person, then another, with a stinger from its thorax, and the victims dropped to the ground like rag dolls, screaming in agony.

The survivors passed by the cameraman, and an old joke, suddenly not so funny, came unbidden to Naomi's mind as she watched the harvester rapidly close the gap: you only had to be faster than the slowest person to avoid being eaten.

The shaking, twisting, vibrating camera view caught fleeting glimpses of the thing as it closed with the cameraman, whose terrified huffing and puffing was clearly audible to the stunned audience.

Something flashed across the screen, followed by a sound like a knife being plunged into a roast.

The cameraman screamed and fell, rolling on the pavement. The camera went flying, crashing to the ground a few feet away.

The picture dissolved into static for just a moment before the view cut back to Jim in the newsroom. He was shaken, his face pale as he spoke. "Ladies and gentlemen, our Los Angeles affiliate is having technical difficulties. We're going to cut for a commercial, and will be right back with the latest updates."

Naomi muted the television. "Renee, we need to find out where Kelso had The Bag. If we can do that, then we'll at least be able to figure out the epicenter for what's going on here, and how bad we can expect things to get."

"I'm already ahead of you. I've got the results of the search of his residence: it came up clean. But I was going through some of the financial records for his buddy Kline, who set up a limited liability company seven months ago. That was odd, because it's the only time he's ever done that, except for his own business." Naomi could hear some blazing fast typing in the background as Renee's fingers danced on the computer keys. "That LLC is listed as the owner of a single family home. Shit."

"What is it?"

"The address is just a few blocks from the intersection of Altadena Drive and Lake Avenue, and is right smack in the center of the hotspots on the map." She paused. "I just sent the address info to Garcia's phone."

Naomi shook her head. Something wasn't adding up. "How could a bunch of harvesters, which are still in their natural form for some reason, spread out like that without being seen until now?"

"Beats me. Maybe they were in the sewers or something?"

The thought sent a chill down Naomi's spine. The sewers would be a perfect place for harvester larvae to grow, with plenty of organic material to feed on, and completely concealed from human eyes until they matured and decided to see what was in the world above.

But this wasn't just one harvester. There had to be at least a few dozen to cause this much mayhem. "I don't understand why they're coming out into the open in their natural form like this. I would've expected them to blend in, mimic us."

Renee's voice was grim. "Maybe they don't think they have to. The old ones did because there were only a few and we would have killed them all. But maybe these aren't so worried about us."

"Maybe. I don't know, and that's what scares me."

Naomi stopped as her eyes caught the screen again. The view showed an entrance to a shopping mall near the mall's theater. Hundreds of fear-stricken people were trying to force their way out. Several had already fallen or been pushed to the ground by those behind, and the camera showed them being trampled. Others had clearly been crushed against the doors, for several arms, hanging limp, dangled through glass that had been shattered by the weight of the bodies pressing against it.

She turned to Garcia and pointed at the screen. "Where is this?"

"That looks like the Santa Anita mall. My God, what's going on?"

"Where is that in relation to Altadena?"

He pursed his lips, his eyes riveted to the horrifying scene on the television. "Maybe five or six miles as the crow flies. It's southeast of Altadena, on the other side of I-210."

Nodding, Naomi turned her attention back to Renee. "Are there any other signs of outbreaks here in the U.S.?"

"Not so far. Isn't this one enough?"

The carnage on the television suddenly intensified, and people who before had been panicked became frenzied. But they weren't simply intent on getting through the choked doors, they were simultaneously trying to escape from a young woman who was inside, stumbling toward the doors. The people nearest her went berserk, pushing, punching, kicking and biting those around them to get away from her.

Naomi didn't understand until the woman, who was hispanic and looked to be in her twenties, brushed against an older man who was battering away at his neighbors. He screamed and arched his back toward her as if he'd been electrocuted.

Then those around him, the people he'd been trying to push back so he could get away from the woman, reacted the same way to him as they had to her.

It was then, as the woman staggered out the doors, somehow dragging the man along behind her, that Naomi realized what was happening. The left half of her body was covered in what looked like a giant amoeba the color of a livid bruise. Her arm was mostly gone, and even as Naomi watched, the nightmarish thing oozed its way past her shoulder to her neck. The television was muted, but she didn't need the sound turned up to know the woman was shrieking in unimaginable pain.

Behind her, the man struggled, his own mouth open in screams of terror. The amoeba-like thing had brushed against him and stuck.

The two of them went down on the concrete just outside the entrance, and there they writhed, being eaten alive by what Naomi knew was a larval harvester.

The torrent of people escaping the theater and the mall streamed past them, doing all they could to keep their distance.

"Dr. Perrault," Garcia said softly, "what the hell is that?"

Ignoring him, Naomi asked Renee, "Are you seeing this?"

"The scene at the mall?" Renee's voice was hoarse, and Naomi could tell she was crying. "Jesus, Naomi. Those poor people!"

"Listen. Carl's got to lie, cheat, and steal to get the SEAL facility reopened. We're going to need the special containment chambers there, and soon."

There was a long pause at the other end of the line, before Renee said, "What for, Naomi?"

"We're going to have to learn everything we can about them if we're going to stop them. To do that we'll have to capture live harvesters." She stared at the horrible scene on the television as people continued to pour from the mall. "I've got to go. Call me back on this number if you find anything else."

"You got it."

Naomi handed the phone back to Garcia. "Call Boisson. Tell her to forget about Morgan Pharmaceuticals and to put a tactical team together. And tell her to make sure they're armed with the heaviest weapons she can get her hands on. Shotguns with slugs are best, unless you can load up your assault rifles with tracer or incendiary rounds. You can leave your pistols home unless they're . 44 magnums or bigger. Anything smaller is useless. And body armor. Make sure they've got that."

Garcia gaped at her. "I thought you were a geneticist, not a soldier of fortune."

"I've been both." She stared at him. "Are you going to call her, or not?"

He shrugged. "I'll call, ma'am, but I'm not sure she'll take kindly to you trying to tell her what to do." He was about to punch the quick dial for Boisson when the phone rang, startling them both. He raised his eyebrows. "It's her. Garcia here, ma'am." After listening a moment, he punched the button to put the call on speakerphone. "Dr. Perrault can hear you now, too."

"Good." It was clear that Boisson was far less than pleased. "There's been a change of plan, Garcia. We're on our way there and will pick up your detail and the good doctor in fifteen minutes. Dr. Perrault, I don't know where you get your pull from, but Assistant Director Richards and the head of our Los Angeles office ordered me to put myself and my team at your disposal. I don't like it, but I do what I'm told."

Garcia glanced at Naomi, his eyes wide. "Dr. Perrault told me just before you called that she wanted a tactical team with body armor and heavy weapons."

"We're loaded for bear. Do you need anything else, doctor?"

"Yes, actually," Naomi told her. "I need a couple of glass carboys, five or six gallon size, with metal caps."

"You need what?"

"Two carboys. They look like the big jugs on top of a water cooler. But they have to be glass, not plastic, and the lids absolutely have to be metal that can be tightly sealed without a rubber or plastic gasket. If there's a winemaking supply store somewhere close by, they'll have them."

"Done. Anything else?"

Naomi thought for a moment. "Bottles of lighter fluid, cans of hairspray, and disposable lighters. Get enough for everyone on the team."

"You're shitting me, right?"

"Not at all."

Boisson laughed. "Okay, this ought to be good. So where are we taking our cans of hairspray?"

Naomi looked at the television, which was showing yet more gruesome footage of the disaster at the mall.

Garcia followed her gaze. In a soft voice he said, "Oh, shit."

* * *

President Miller sat in the Oval Office, staring at the television footage coming out of Los Angeles. "My God, what in blazes is going on out there?"

"It's *them*, Mr. President." Carl Richards' voice carried an edge, but it wasn't because of any malice toward Miller or anyone else in the room. It was because he held himself responsible for what was happening. They should have found The Bag before any of this happened. The FBI and SEAL had both failed, and now the American people, and perhaps the entire world, were going to pay the price. He had originally thought he was being brought to this meeting as a scapegoat, but that hadn't been Harmon's intention. The President was serious about finding answers, and wanted them fast. "It's the harvesters."

Beside him, FBI Director Harmon frowned, but said nothing. Richards had shown him incontrovertible evidence in video footage and analysis by Renee Vintner that the "riots" in Los Angeles weren't riots at all, but an outbreak of an unspeakable biological horror, the same as was happening in Brazil, China, France, India, and Russia.

As they watched, the camera caught a dark, glossy insectile shape racing behind a group of screaming people. It stabbed a man with its stinger, then pounced on him as he fell to the pavement. Straddling his chest, it lowered its face to his, and in but a moment the man's head had disappeared completely into the thing's mandibles. Then it just sat there, immobile, as more screaming people ran by.

Another view showed a squad of National Guardsmen shooting at a pair of the things dashing toward them. One went down, shrieking and writhing. The other, clearly hit several times, kept coming. It leaped over the Hummer the Guardsmen were behind and savaged two of them before the other members of the squad killed it.

"How many of these things are out there in the city?"

The Secretary of Homeland Security shook his head. "Our best estimate thus far, Mr. President, is at least two hundred, and perhaps as many as a thousand."

"And those are only the ones you can see."

Everyone turned to stare at Richards. "Remember, these things can perfectly mimic human beings. Why these aren't, I don't know. But imagine what could happen if there were hundreds or thousands of these things disguised as people. Remember, Assistant Director Clement was murdered by one of these things last year and it replaced him without any of the rest of us — even people like me who'd worked with him for years — having the slightest clue that it wasn't him." He shook his head. "The only chance we may have of stopping these things is while they're in their natural form and we can see them for what they really are."

Miller grabbed the remote and angrily switched off the television. He couldn't bear to watch any more of the slaughter. "So what are we doing about it? We've got to protect those people!"

"The governor has activated the National Guard and is deploying them to contain the largest infestations," the Secretary of Defense explained. With a glance to the Secretary of Homeland Security, he said, "Mr. President, I'd like your permission to deploy some of the Marines from Camp Pendleton to backstop the Guard units and provide infrastructure security." He frowned. "I hate to suggest this, but we might also want to bring in some helicopter gunships."

"Not a chance in hell." Miller sat forward in his chair. "I'm not going to have one of the greatest cities in the world look like Mogadishu!"

"With all due respect, Mr. President," Richards told him, "that'll be exactly what's going to happen if we don't stop these things right now, and we need heavy firepower to do it." He pointed to the dark television. "You saw how many rounds from their rifles those National Guardsmen poured into the creatures that attacked them. Their weapons were designed to kill other human beings, not creatures with skeletons made out of carbon fiber. You can hammer away at them all day with an assault rifle and you *might* bring them down. But one round from a twenty or twenty-five millimeter cannon like the gunships have would do the job. And the harvesters can't get at the helicopters like they can the troops on the ground."

For a moment, Richards thought that Miller was going to charbroil him. Then the President's expression softened. "All right. All right, dammit. It doesn't help me to have experts if I don't listen to them." He glared at the Secretary of Defense. "But so help me, if those gunships shoot up the city, I'll be sending you out there in your underwear to fight these things. Clear?"

"Yes, Mr. President."

Miller turned back to Richards. "Anything else?"

Steeling himself for the President's response, Richards said, "We should close every airport in the area, sir, including LAX."

The President stared at him.

Vice President Lynch voiced what Miller was thinking. "Do you have any idea of the disruption, the panic, that would cause?"

"Sir, you've got to think of this as a biological threat," Richards went on, "like an outbreak of a deadly disease. Our strategy has to be focused on containment. The counter-terrorist security procedures we have in place simply aren't going to work against this threat. Emulating human form, these things will just walk right through. Imagine what could happen — what *will* happen — if they reach other major cities?" He shook his head fervently. "We've got to bottle them up in Los Angeles and wipe them out. Otherwise we may lose our only chance to stop them."

"Mr. President," Harmon said, much to Richards' surprise, "I agree. And I'd also suggest that we put up roadblocks around the city and screen anyone coming out. I'm sure we can come up with some procedures to verify that the refugees are human."

Richards nodded, glad that Harmon was backing him up for a change. He could see that his boss's eyes were haunted, and suddenly remembered that Harmon had family in LA.

"As much as I hate to," the Secretary for Homeland Security added softly, "I have to agree. Quarantine the affected areas and flood them with enough firepower to deal with these things as quickly as possible."

Miller wearily rubbed his eyes. "All right. God help me, but make it happen. What are the casualties so far?"

"Sir," the Homeland Security chief began, "we really don't have enough information to give you a good estimate, because we don't have anyone reporting those details yet. The police are fully engaged in trying to stay alive, and the local hospitals and other facilities are swamped."

"Just give me a number," Miller sighed. "I don't expect anything to the twelfth decimal point. Somewhere in the ballpark."

Before the Secretary of Homeland Security could dig himself in any deeper, Richards chimed in. He had asked Mozhdeh Kashani, the head of the Intelligence Division, to put something together for him. "Our estimates are at least five hundred dead and two thousand injured, and that's probably conservative."

Miller blinked in shock. "That many? But it's only been, what, a couple hours, if that, since this started?"

"Mr. President," Richards told him, "you have to understand that these things don't have any other goal than to wipe us out. That's what the original harvesters wanted, but they had to go about it in a subtle way over a long period of time because there were only a handful of them. If they were ever exposed for what they really were, they'd be killed. But the things in LA, along with the infestations in the other countries, apparently don't feel the need for subtlety. But the goal's still the same. They're butchering people as fast as they can." *And eating them*, he didn't add.

Miller thought for a moment before coming to a conclusion. "All right. Let's bring everything we can to bear on this." He looked at the Defense Secretary. "Keep me informed, but do whatever's necessary with our conventional forces to protect the people in Los Angeles and wipe these things out."

"Yes, sir."

Richards saw that everyone in the room had picked up on the President's specification of *conventional* forces. He remembered with painful clarity being on the wrong end of a nuclear weapon at Sutter Buttes the year before, and he fervently prayed that the same fate wouldn't befall Los Angeles or any other city.

Miller turned to Richards, which made him feel awkward. Harmon, his boss, was sitting right next to him. "Are there any signs of outbreaks anywhere else in the country?"

"No, sir. Not yet. But we've informed all of our field offices and legats overseas on what to look for, and we're coordinating with local law enforcement agencies and emergency responders across the country to get the word out." He grimaced. "A lot of people just don't want to believe the information, but we're telling them and we'll keep telling them until the crisis has passed."

Miller nodded appreciatively, and included Harmon in his gaze. "Thank you both." Then he turned to the Secretary of State. "Do we have anything from the other affected countries?"

She shook her head, clearly frustrated. "Not much, Mr. President. Everyone still seems to be in a state of denial. We've passed on the information provided by Director Harmon's people to the other governments, but aside from notes of bemused thanks, we haven't gotten much reaction or any deeper insight into their situations. All of them still seem to think that these outbreaks are terrorist or separatist attacks, despite mounting evidence to the contrary."

Miller frowned. "I can't say as I blame them. I still don't believe this myself. I keep expecting to wake up, that this will all have been a nightmare." Shaking his head, he told her, "Keep sending whatever information we can provide them, and let them know that the door is open for any dialogue or support we can give. And maybe have someone put together a briefing package for them using what we're getting out of Los Angeles. We've got to convince the other governments of how much of a threat this is, and give them any help we can on how to fight these things."

Turning to the Director of National Intelligence, Miller asked, "Has there been any significant change overseas?"

"Just more of the same, sir, and all of it bad. China's committed three additional divisions, and we've started getting indications that the cities of Chengdu and Chongqing in southern China may have harvester infestations." He glanced at the television, then back to Miller. "We weren't really sure what to make of the information we were getting until we saw the coverage of Los Angeles, but from the reporting we've seen thus far, the situation there is worse. A lot worse."

"Go on."

"As for Brazil, the southern part of the country is in complete disarray, with several areas completely cut off by the military. The government's instituted a blackout on all news out of the south, and we're working on getting some assets in place that can provide us some reliable information. But for now, I think it's safe to assume that they've got some serious problems on their hands.

"The same is true for India. Mass panic has set in among the rural areas east of Hyderabad in the south-central part of the country, and the Indians are deploying at least two infantry divisions, along with their independent airborne brigade, to help contain the outbreak there."

"And France?"

The DNI frowned. "That's the odd one of the bunch. There was clearly an outbreak in Bordeaux," he nodded to Richards, who'd tipped the intelligence community to the fact, "but either the French have contained it or they're remaining amazingly quiet."

Miller turned to Richards and Harmon. "Do you have anything?"

Harmon looked at Richards, who shook his head. "No, sir, nothing so far. We tipped the French National Police to suspicious activity in Bordeaux, but our legats haven't received any feedback on the operation, despite repeated requests."

"Damn French," Miller sighed.

"With all due respect, sir, at least with the investigation that we've been collaborating on, the French have been very helpful." Richards shook his head. "This makes me wonder if something else isn't going on. It's possible that the French government has already been penetrated by the harvesters."

"Fine," Miller said, raising his hands in supplication. "My apologies to our French Allies. So I guess we're saving the best for last: what about Russia?"

The DNI looked grim. "Not surprisingly, there's a lot of confusion in the Russian government. But what we do know for certain is that they put their conventional forces on full military alert a few hours ago, about the same time that one of their airborne units was wiped out in southern Russia."

President Miller looked again at Richards. "Wasn't that where your guy, Jack Dawson, was headed from India?"

"Yes, sir," Richards answered softly.

"Any word from him?"

"No, Mr. President. Not since yesterday."

Miller pursed his lips. "He wouldn't have been directly involved in any of their operations. I'm sure he's okay."

"Yes, sir, I'm sure he is."

In his gut, Richards wasn't quite so sure.

CHAPTER TWENTY-FOUR

The concussion from the RPG rocket exploding and the violent yaw that followed nearly sent Jack and Mikhailov tumbling out the still-open ramp of the helicopter. Jack scrabbled along the deck, trying to dig his bare fingers into the metal with one hand while he held onto Mikhailov's combat harness with the other. The Russian captain's legs were dangling over the side of the ramp. Jack cried out with the strain as he grabbed a nylon cargo strap, secured to the side of the fuselage and whipping about in the cabin.

Coughing from the smoke that poured from the destroyed starboard engine, Jack caught a glimpse of the pilots, struggling to keep the stricken Mi-17 in the air. Near the gaping hole that had been blasted in the right side of the craft, Jack saw that the crew chief was dead. There was nothing left of him above the waist.

The port engine was still running, but sounded like a garbage disposal that had been fed a handful of metal knives. A torrent of fluid poured from the top of the cabin from the ruptured hydraulic and fuel lines.

Jack was surprised, and not just a bit relieved, that they hadn't caught fire. Yet.

As he held Mikhailov, who had come to, but wasn't strong enough yet to hold on by himself, Jack tried to count off the seconds they stayed in the air. Every one of those precious increments of time would take them farther from Ulan-Erg and the dreadful horrors there.

In the dark, he had no idea where the pilots were headed. All he knew was that it was roughly fifty kilometers to the town of Elista, and over two hundred and fifty back to Stavropol. He'd settle for Elista, but doubted they'd get that far.

Then he happened to look down, behind them. The roiling flames of the burning harvesters had long since receded into the distance and the drizzling rain. Now he could see pairs of lights, moving in straight lines. Vehicles. Cars. Not many, but enough to make him realize that the pilots must be following the main road, A154 if he remembered correctly from the map Kuybishev had shown him, that had been the phase line for the attack on Ulan-Erg.

Nodding to himself, Jack gave a small whisper of thanks to the pilots. At least if they went down, someone would find them. But this close to Ulan-Erg and the mysterious facility, anyone in the cars below could be a harvester.

Jack had no words for how much he wished Alexander was with him now. He knew the cat would have been petrified, but at least he could have told Jack friend from foe.

Mikhailov, recovered somewhat from the ordeal, managed to claw his way alongside him to grab onto another cargo strap. "Rudenko?"

"He didn't make it," Jack told him. "I'm sorry, Sergei."

In the dim light of the cargo hold, Jack couldn't see Mikhailov's expression, but he did see Mikhailov lower his forehead to the floor. His lips moved in what Jack guessed was a quiet prayer for his friend.

They both looked up as something in the grinding machinery of the surviving engine gave way. Spinning chunks of sharp metal, accompanied by a gout of flame, raked the cargo area. Something else broke almost directly above them, somewhere in the base of the tail boom, and the helicopter went into a spin as it lost altitude.

"We lost the tail rotor! Hold on!" Jack looked out the back to see the horizon, blackness riding upon darkness, punctuated with a few lights along the road, whirling.

Before he looked away, he caught sight of something else: a town in flames.

Still spinning, the helicopter hit, its right main gear slamming into the ground. The nose rose into the air and the tail boom smashed into the ground, shattering the tail rotor.

Then he was falling through the open maw of the cargo ramp, straight into the whirling wreckage of the tail rotor.

Mikhailov tried to grab him, but only succeeded in losing his own grip.

Jack screamed and closed his eyes, but in the time it took him to fall, the helicopter continued to spin, and the lethal egg beater of the tail rotor was gone by the time he hit the ground. He landed hard on his side, knocking the wind out of him. His head slammed into the wet muck, and he lay there, dazed.

Beside him, only a few feet away, Mikhailov crumpled to the ground like a big rag doll.

Above them, the helicopter spun around three more times before it tipped over. The rotor blades, still driven by what was left of the port engine, tore themselves to pieces against the ground, sending fragments through the fuselage and for a hundred yards in every direction, and what was left of the tail rotor flew apart as the boom collapsed. The stubs of the rotor blades pushed the helicopter around in a full circle before there was nothing left but the rotor hub, still whirring around above the mud.

Getting to his feet, Jack staggered toward the wreckage, intending to help the pilots, when the fuel that had sprayed everywhere caught with a surprisingly soft *whump*. Raising his arms to cover his face, he moved toward the cargo ramp, which was the only part of the Mi-17 not wreathed in flame.

"No, Jack!" A hand fell on Jack's shoulder, pulling him back from the intense heat. "They are gone!"

Jack resisted for just a moment, then gave in. The front of the helicopter was covered in burning fuel. He only hoped the pilots had been killed or rendered unconscious in the crash.

Letting Mikhailov lead him away to a safe distance, they collapsed to their knees and watched the helicopter burn. Beyond the flames, what must be only a few kilometers to the east, they could see smoke billowing up from the town that Jack had caught sight of before the crash.

"Is that Elista?"

"*Da*," Mikhailov answered wearily. "That does not look so good, does it?"

"Sure as hell doesn't. But I wonder who set it on fire? Surely not the harvesters."

"Haven't you ever seen the movies with villagers chasing monsters with torches and pitchforks?" Mikhailov managed a humorless chuckle. "In chaos, Jack, there is always fire. Perhaps someone even discovered that it will kill the beasts."

"We can always hope. But that means we can't go there. What now?"

"We have to get back to Stavropol, or at least call the regimental headquarters and let them know what has happened." He narrowed his eyes as he saw a pair of cars pull up on the road, which was maybe fifty meters away. "But I am hesitant to get in a car here with a stranger."

"Yeah." Jack got a queasy sensation as he watched four people, two from each car, get out and stand there, staring into the flames. None of them spoke. Instinctively, he lowered himself into a prone position, and Mikhailov followed suit. "Do you still have your sidearm?"

"Yes, and two magazines. That, my knife, and my wits are my only remaining weapons."

"Two out of three isn't bad." Jack grinned as Mikhailov snorted.

"Here, take these." Mikhailov handed him the gun and spare magazines. "You can hold it and shoot. I cannot. Not now."

Jack took the weapon and shoved it in his empty holster, then put the magazines in a pouch. "So what's the plan?"

Mikhailov pondered for a moment as they watched the "people" near the cars. Apparently content that there were no survivors, and clearly not wanting to venture closer to the flaming wreckage, they returned to their cars and drove off, heading back toward Elista.

"The world has just become an extremely dangerous place, my friend," Mikhailov whispered.

"Yeah," Jack said, shaking off the chill that went deeper than the cold muck as he watched the cars leave. "That was pretty damn creepy. It's strange, though: I would have thought they would have acted more normal."

"Perhaps they have not yet learned?" Mikhailov mused. "Or perhaps they did not feel the need to, if all four of them were harvesters."

"Something else for Naomi to figure out, I guess."

Mikhailov shook his head. "What you observe and tell her will be just as important as anything she learns in the lab, and perhaps more. It is like with weapons: seeing how they perform at a test facility is one thing. How effective they are on the battlefield in the hands of a soldier is something else."

They were silent for a time, the only sound the crackling of the burning helicopter.

Then Jack asked, "How many harvesters do you think there were back at Ulan-Erg?"

"There must have been a few hundred, maybe more. Not including the ghastly little ones."

"That's about what I figured. And how many more do you think must be loose in Elista to cause that kind of panic?" He nodded toward the flames rising from the town.

"I cannot even guess. Where is this leading?"

"Naomi said that she believed they could reproduce, that they weren't limited to a host ingesting the engineered corn and transforming into a harvester. But if what she said is true, how fast do they reproduce? How long was it since that facility hereabouts was overrun?"

"Perhaps a week," Mikhailov said, uncertain, "maybe a few days more."

"And in that short time there are hundreds of the damn things."

"There is worse." Mikhailov turned to look at him. "There is still at least one in Stavropol, the one masquerading as Putin."

"Who's now probably spawned a lot more, plus any that might have come from here. Shit." Jack blew out his breath, forming a fog in the air that drifted upward until it vanished. "You still haven't answered my question about what we're going to do."

"When we came out on our mission to the facility where the harvesters here originated, I had some time to study maps of this area. Elista has a small airport that should be roughly five kilometers northwest of us. There should be little between here and there, a few scattered farm houses, perhaps, and several bridges that cross a small river, the same that ran north of Ulan-Erg."

"Do you know how to fly?"

Mikhailov winced. "I make no claim to being a pilot, but I spent several summers with one of my uncles, who owned a plane he used for spraying crops. It had two sets of controls. He let me fly with him many times, and let me take the controls when he thought it was safe to do so." He grinned. "That was not so often as I would have liked."

"Okay, let's assume you can get us off the ground without flying into the control tower. But why the airport? Why not try one of the other towns, or even here in Elista, and steal a car?"

"Because I want to be away from the ground, and leave here as fast as we can." Mikhailov's voice was shaking now. "I can cope with the adult harvesters. They are terrifying, but they are an enemy I can understand, after a fashion. It is the small ones, the amoebas. I do not want to die that way. I do not want to be eaten alive."

"But they can't get you in a car."

Mikhailov stared at him. "They are drawn to rubber and plastics, Jack. Cars attract them like honey. That is what we saw at the facility. And if you ran over one in the road, it would stick to the tires or the undercarriage, then eat its way in."

"Planes have lots of rubber and plastic parts, too, you know."

"Of course they do. But if we can escape in a plane, we are free for a while. And we may go as far as the plane can take us without fear of encountering other harvesters." He paused. "An aircraft radio would also allow us to contact any nearby military units, and hopefully get in touch with the regiment at Stavropol. My hope is that most of the larvae are in the town where there is an ample supply of food."

Jack took a deep breath. "Okay, fine, you convinced me. I don't have any better ideas." He looked at his watch. It wouldn't be long before it was daylight. They needed to get to the airport before dawn. "We'd better get a move on." He got to his feet, then helped up Mikhailov, who grunted in pain. "You should've stayed in the hospital, you know."

"No," Mikhailov gasped as they began to walk toward the road and the airport that lay somewhere beyond, "I should have been born a millionaire so I never would have had to do any of this in the first place."

* * *

Their trek to the airport was uneventful except for crossing the road and then, later, one of the bridges that spanned the small, meandering river halfway to their destination.

The A154 road was a challenge because of the cars that seemed to be perfectly spaced in distance and time to see anyone trying to cross. A road block had been set up outside of what looked like a truck stop just on the eastern side of town, and all the cars and the handful of trucks that had been heading west had been pulled off. A little less than a kilometer away, Jack and Mikhailov watched as policemen shepherded the unwitting passengers into the building. None of them came out again in the time the two men spent watching.

More time passed, and Jack knew that they were just going to have to take their chances. If they didn't move soon, they'd be caught in daylight when they reached the airport.

The two had crept up as close as they dared to the road. Waiting until the latest car sped past, Jack whispered, "Now!"

Grabbing Mikhailov by his harness, Jack hauled him to his feet and helped propel the gasping Russian across the road. He felt completely naked as they ran, their boots pounding across the fifteen meters of asphalt. The only blessing was that there weren't any streetlights this far away from town.

They had made it halfway across when a car pulled out of the truck stop and headed toward them.

"Hurry!"

Mikhailov ran, grunting with pain, and the two of them tumbled into a culvert on the north side of the road. Jack drew his Desert Eagle and crawled on his elbows, raising himself up just high enough that he could see the car.

It didn't slow, just kept on moving.

"Well, that was fun." He holstered the pistol and slid back down beside Mikhailov, who was still groaning. "Sergei, are you all right?"

"I have been better." He wiped his mouth with his left hand, while pinning his right arm against his. "*Chyort vozmi'*. I'm bleeding inside. I think one of my ribs has punctured a lung."

That certainly wasn't good news, but Jack wasn't surprised after the beatings Mikhailov had taken, first at the facility, and then earlier tonight. "Come on, then. All the more reason to get the hell out of this place so we can get you to a hospital."

From there, they made their way northwest past the rear of the truck stop and across open fields until they found a way over the river, which, after he saw it, Jack considered more of a creek. But with all the rain the creek was swollen and running fast. There was no way Mikhailov would be able to make it across through the water. The bridge they found was little more than earth packed over a big culvert pipe, with the water only a few feet below the road.

Standing in the middle of the earthen bridge was a dark figure in the shape of a man. He would have been invisible, except that Mikhailov had noticed his silhouette against the handful of lights that shone from around the buildings at the airport. Jack hoped that he and Mikhailov hadn't been silhouetted themselves against the burning town behind them, but there was nothing he could do about that.

"Stay here." Jack drew his pistol and stood up. If there was more than one of the things, he figured it would be better to draw them out with an obvious approach than to blunder into them while trying to sneak up on the thing guarding the bridge. He had to assume it was a harvester. Why else would anyone be standing out here on such an awful night?

Jack's eyes were constantly in motion, scanning around him using his peripheral vision, which was better suited to seeing at night. Everything was indistinct, shadows upon shadows, but he saw nothing that hinted at movement, which he took as a good sign. He was worried that the sound of the big gun firing would draw unwanted attention, but there was no way around it. There was no quiet way to kill a harvester.

The man-shaped silhouette remained still until he got within a few meters of it.

"Hey!" Jack called, trying to keep the fear out of his voice. "How's it going?"

The shadow didn't respond, but he noticed movement. The torso rippled, changed.

Jack brought up the Desert Eagle, aimed at the center of the dark, shifting mass, and fired. In the glare of the enormous muzzle flash that for an instant seemed to join him with his target, he could see what looked like an elderly man, except for the stinger-tipped tentacle uncoiling from his chest.

The half-inch diameter bullet smashed into the thing's thorax, knocking the creature backward, and Jack knew that he'd scored a direct hit. When bullets hit only the malleable flesh, they tended to pass right through. They did damage and hurt the harvester, but wouldn't kill it. Hitting their appendages and less well-protected parts of their skeleton could do severe damage, but again, the bullets tended to pass through and rarely would provide a first-round kill.

But the toughest parts of their skeleton could stop even a .50 caliber round from a Desert Eagle at close range. The downside for the harvester was that all the energy from the bullet was transferred directly to its body. So while the core skeletal structure remained more or less intact, the impact ripped the carbon fiber bones from the internal connective tissues and organs, causing massive internal damage.

Making a gurgling wail, the harvester tumbled off the bridge to land with a splash in the water and was rapidly carried downstream.

Blinking his eyes, trying to clear the afterimage of the muzzle flash, he ran back to Mikhailov, who was already moving toward him.

"Next time I will give you my knife," Mikhailov told him. "You were almost that close."

"I didn't want to miss." Jack wrapped his arm around his Russian friend's waist. "Come on, we're almost there."

Two and a half kilometers later, they were crouched behind what Jack took to be the only real hangar at the Elista airport. Across the street to the west was what he guessed might be a maintenance building, and beyond that, past some sort of park with trees, was the main administration building and the control tower. There were two tall masts with stadium-style lights in front of the tower building that illuminated the tarmac in that area, and poles bearing flood lamps about sixty-five meters apart illuminated the rest of the tarmac area.

Aside from that and a dozen or so other nondescript buildings, none of them very large, there wasn't much there.

"When you said the airport was small, you weren't kidding."

"Not everything in Russia is big, Jack." In the reflected light of one of the nearby lights, Mikhailov tried to grin, but it looked more to Jack like a grimace.

"How are you holding up?"

"Give me some vodka and I'll be fine."

"Smart ass." Jack saw that Mikhailov's chin was covered in blood. Mikhailov had been wiping his mouth with his sleeve, but it was easy enough to see that the bleeding was getting worse.

On his knees, Mikhailov leaned around the corner of the hangar. They were at the rear corner, farthest from the tower building, which was almost two hundred meters away.

"That will work."

Jack, standing in a crouch so he could see over Mikhailov's head, followed his gaze. He saw a trio of single-seat crop dusters lined up along the edge of the tarmac in front of the hangar. "Sorry, Sergei, I consider you a friend, but I'm not sitting in your lap."

"No, no! Not those little ones." He pointed past them at half a dozen large shapes that squatted on the tarmac beyond the single-seaters, about seventy meters away, right under one of the light poles. "Those!"

Jack looked closer. "Holy shit. Sergei, those are biplanes!"

"Is that what you call them? Biplanes. Yes, they are An-2 aircraft. My uncle had such a plane. He called it *Annushka*."

"Those have got to be older than my dead grandfather, Sergei. Are you seriously thinking of flying one of those crates out of here?"

Mikhailov glanced at him. "There might be other planes here that would hold both of us, but that is the only one I might stand any chance of flying. If I can remember how to start it. If any of them are fueled. And if I don't bleed to death before convincing you we have no other options." He nodded to the east. While it was still dark on the ground, the sky was beginning to lighten. Morning twilight was coming, and quickly.

"Right," Jack told him, accepting his fate. *Wonderful*, he thought. *I'm going to die in a bloody Russian biplane!* "Which one were you thinking of taking?"

"The third from the left. The entrance door is on the left side. The line of trees there will cover us from anyone who might be in the tower until we step out onto the tarmac."

Jack nodded agreement. "Let's do it, then."

With Mikhailov leading, they moved under the trees that led from the eastern side of the hangar toward the tarmac where the An-2s were lined up, tails facing them.

They were halfway to the planes when they heard a crash and a scream from the hangar.

Both men knelt down and froze, their attention riveted on the hangar behind them.

The scream came again, and Jack's insides turned to ice. It was a woman's voice, and she was clearly fighting for her life. A shot rang out, then another, and the hideous cry of a harvester tore through the darkness.

"Shit!" Jack turned to Mikhailov. "Get to the plane. I'm going to see if I can help her."

Mikhailov grabbed his arm. "Don't be a fool! Their struggle will probably draw more! We must go!"

Shaking the Russian's hand loose, Jack snarled, "I know, but I can't just walk away. Now, get to the fucking plane! I'll be there as soon as I can."

Leaving Mikhailov cursing behind him, Jack dashed along the trees, back toward the hangar.

He had almost reached the side of the big building when the personnel door there flew open. Reflexively raising his pistol, Jack tensed his finger on the trigger as a dark shape emerged.

It was a woman. With a gasp, she stopped short and raised a double-barrel shotgun, pointing it at his face.

Then there was something else coming through the door, something that was almost a man but wasn't.

"Down!" Jack hadn't even thought whether the woman might understand English. Even if she didn't, she got the message. She dove to the ground and flattened herself out.

Jack fired at the harvester coming out the door after her. It shrieked as a fist-sized chunk of flesh and skeleton exploded from its back as the bullet passed through, but the hit barely slowed it down.

The second shot, however, severed the thing's head from its thorax. The body fell into a twitching heap just behind the woman, who was scrambling to her feet to get away from it.

"*Spasibo*," she breathed, before kicking the thing with her booted feet.

"You understand English, I take it?"

"*Da*, some."

"Good." Jack took her arm and pulled her toward the plane. "Come on, follow me!"

There was no point in trying to hide behind the trees now: any other harvesters here would know there were humans loose. And it wouldn't take them long to figure out where to look.

Ahead, the engine of one of the ancient An-2's coughed into life, exhaust belching from under the cowling as the big four-bladed prop began to turn.

"That's our ride!" Jack shouted, pointing. The woman nodded as she ran, easily keeping pace with him.

Jack turned to look behind them, and his spirits fell as he saw a group of inhuman shadows bounding after them.

As he and the woman reached the plane, Jack gestured for her to get aboard. After she disappeared into the aircraft, he aimed at the nearest harvester and fired. The slug took off the appendage that would normally pass for a right arm, and the creature tumbled to the pavement. Jack fired at another and missed. He kept on firing until the magazine went dry, then he dropped the empty magazine and slammed in the last one he had. The creatures scattered, but clearly had no intention of giving up.

"Jack!" He heard Mikhailov screaming in his ear and felt an urgent tug on his shoulder. "Come on!"

With one last look at the harvesters, who were again charging after the plane, Jack turned and shoved Mikhailov back through the passenger door, then climbed up himself as the engine rose to a roar and the plane surged forward.

It suddenly struck Jack that Mikhailov wasn't at the controls. "Who's flying the goddamn plane?"

"That crazy woman you rescued. She is a real pilot!"

Something lunged at them through the door, even as the plane was gathering speed.

Jack fired. He missed, but the muzzle blast was enough of a distraction that the harvester lost its grip on the door frame and fell to the tarmac.

The An-2 sped across the badly patched apron toward the runway, bouncing and shuddering as it hit bad spots in the asphalt.

Leaning out the door, Jack saw three more of the things pursuing them. He fired twice at them, trying to drive them back, but they quickly dodged to the starboard side of the plane where he couldn't get a clear shot.

"Shit!" Jack yelped as the plane made a sharp turn to the left onto the runway. He would have fallen out had Mikhailov not grabbed hold of him.

The engine roared louder as their pilot shoved the throttle forward and they began to accelerate.

The turn onto the runway had left the harvesters momentarily exposed, and Jack fired again, hitting one of them in the head with a lucky shot. It collapsed to the runway in a tangled heap. He fired again at one of the others, missed.

The tail came off the ground, and a moment later the plane lifted into the air.

One of the harvesters leaped after them, sinking its claws into the bottom of the rudder.

The pilot shouted something in Russian, and the plane yawed violently to the right.

Jack didn't need a translation for what she'd said. Dropping prone to the floor, he shouted to Mikhailov over the sound of the slipstream and the engine, "Hold onto my legs!"

Then he wriggled on his belly until he was sticking out the door, Mikhailov pinning his legs with his own body.

The harvester was tearing strips out of the cloth covering of the rudder, and had managed to clamber up so it could reach the elevator. The plane's nose suddenly pitched down as the harvester yanked down on the elevator, and the pilot screamed as she fought the controls.

Jack had lost count of how many rounds he'd fired from Mikhailov's gun. The magazine held only seven rounds. He hung out the door, looking to the east as the sun burst over the horizon, putting the abomination hanging onto the tail of the aircraft into sharp silhouette. He took aim and fired.

The bullet missed the harvester and passed harmlessly through the rudder behind it.

Come on, Jack! He tried to calm himself. *Come on!*

He took aim and held his breath as the harvester again sent the plane nosing toward the ground, which was perilously close. He squeezed the trigger. The big gun fired, and the slide locked back: the magazine was empty.

The bullet grazed the back of one of the thing's claws. Had they been on the ground, the hit would have hardly injured the creature. Here, the pain was enough for it to reflexively loosen its grip, and even a harvester couldn't hang on with just one of its clawed appendages.

As the woman pulled the plane up into a steep climb with the earth mere meters below the main wheels, the harvester was wrenched free. Jack watched it tumble through the air until it splattered on the wet ground.

Holding onto his web belt, Mikhailov hauled Jack in. After tossing the Desert Eagle to the floor, Jack got to his knees and managed to close the door and dog it shut. Then he collapsed beside Mikhailov, leaning against the inside of the fuselage, which reeked of fertilizer, oil, and gasoline.

"I am thinking," Mikhailov shouted as a thin trickle of blood came from the corner of his mouth, which was parted in a pain-tinged smile, "that you need additional target practice."

Unable to help himself, Jack laughed. "Next time I'll let you do the honors, Sergei."

His smile evaporated when he stood up and looked out one of the round windows in the cabin.

Behind them, another plane was lifting off from the airport.

CHAPTER TWENTY-FIVE

"God, what a nightmare."

Garcia's murmured words effectively captured the unreal scenes that greeted the passengers of the three SUVs as they made their way toward Santa Anita. The I-210 freeway had been reduced to a standstill, and after forcing their way along the shoulder, in one case having to shove a car blocking their path out of the way, the small convoy managed to get off on the exit for Corson Street. From there, they began weaving their way through residential streets toward the mall.

Around them, people were in a panic. They were fleeing south out of Altadena, even as more outbreaks were reported in other parts of the metropolitan area from Burbank to La Habra. The roads were choked with cars, and the situation was made worse by thousands who were fleeing on foot, many of them having abandoned their cars on the jammed freeways.

Naomi cursed as Garcia took them over a curb and onto a sidewalk, then cut through someone's yard. He and Boisson were in the front seat of the lead vehicle. Naomi sat in the middle of the seat behind them, with a pet crate on either side, and two more agents sat behind her. Alexander was meowing constantly, while Koshka lay in a tense crouch, panting. Naomi hated to take them along, but they wouldn't be returning to the safe house, and where the team was headed, the cats just might be invaluable.

She was dressed in black tactical gear now, as were the FBI agents, and all of them were well-armed with a mix of shotguns and assault rifles. Boisson had been extremely reluctant to do so, but under orders from Carl Richards and her boss in Los Angeles, she'd offered Naomi her choice of weapons. Naomi had chosen a shotgun.

Like Naomi, each agent also had a can of hairspray and bottle of lighter fluid stuffed into pouches on their combat harness, and several of the agents had Tasers. All of them had exchanged looks as Boisson had handed out these new "weapons," but none of them had made any wisecracks. The fear that gripped the city had leached any trace of humor from all of them.

"Take a right up here, Garcia," Boisson said, her voice tense. They were on Hugo Reid Drive, coming up on Baldwin Avenue, which ran right past the mall.

"Shit!" Garcia slammed on the brakes as a car shot over the curb from Baldwin and careened in front of him, clipping the front left fender of the SUV.

Naomi held onto the crates, the cats crying out in fear at the impact. As the car flashed by, she caught sight of the driver. She couldn't tell if it was a man or a woman, because most of the poor soul's head was covered by a larval harvester.

There was a crash behind them as the car took down a telephone pole and then slammed through the white wrought iron fence of the house on the corner before disappearing into the back yard.

Ahead, Baldwin Avenue was a bumper to bumper traffic jam in both directions, with those fleeing north trapped by the parking lot that I-210 had become, and those heading south pinned by the traffic on Huntington Drive that bounded the southern end of the mall. Many of the cars were empty, the occupants having fled on foot.

"Park alongside the road here," Boisson told Garcia. "We'll have to go the rest of the way on foot."

The SUV bounced as Garcia took it over the curb and parked in the lush ivy ground cover that ran next to the sidewalk. The other SUVs followed suit.

Naomi had wondered why other cars hadn't been trying to head away from the mall on the street they were on. Then she saw that the street was marked one-way, and that the flow of traffic was enforced by a barrier that would puncture the tires of a vehicle going the wrong direction.

As the other agents got out, she opened the crates and released the cats. Both wore one-piece harnesses around their chests that had a clip for a leash between the shoulder blades. Jack had long been in the habit of taking Alexander for walks outside, and once they were together in San Antonio, Naomi had gradually gotten Koshka used to the idea. The memory of their "family walks" around the neighborhood brought a brief smile to her face that faded as Alexander looked up at her with big, frightened eyes.

"I know, boy," she whispered, clipping on his leash. She tried not to think of Jack, wondering where he was and what had happened to him. She now had her own set of worries to focus on. "I'm scared, too."

After leashing Alexander, Naomi repeated the process with Koshka. "It's going to be okay, baby. But I think we're going to need your help. Otherwise, I never would have brought you."

She stepped out of the SUV, and the two cats jumped after her. They circled around her feet, and Naomi had to sling her shotgun over her shoulder so she could keep the cats from tripping her with their leashes.

The agents, none of whom had ever seen a cat on a leash before, gawked and shook their heads.

"You're nuts, Perrault." Boisson was staring at her, a deep frown etched onto her face. "And if your stupid cats get any of my people killed, I'm going to kick your ass."

Naomi turned a cold gaze on the special agent. "These 'stupid cats' have saved a lot of lives, including mine. And by the end of the day, they might save yours, too. Let's get going."

"Whatever. Garcia, you've got point."

With Garcia in the lead, the group of sixteen FBI agents, Naomi, and the two cats set off toward the mall. Naomi, Boisson, and the two men carrying the big glass containers were in the center while the other men and women formed a protective ring around them. The cats slunk low to the ground, their tails down, beside Naomi, their eyes wide and their ears alternately pricking up, then laying back against their skulls. Neither of them were making a sound now.

"So let me get this straight," Boisson asked. "You don't want any of the big ones, just those nasty slimy things?"

Naomi nodded. "If we can capture one of the adults, that's a plus. But our priority has to be capturing at least one of the larval forms. We know a lot about the adults, but nothing about the larvae. And we'll learn about the adults as the captured larvae mature."

Boisson didn't bother to mask her distaste. "Well, that makes things simpler, at least. God, what's that noise?"

Off to their left came a horrible sound, screams, but not from any human throat.

"I think it's the horses," Garcia called over his shoulder.

"Horses?" Naomi was confused.

"Yeah. There's a horse track right over there," Boisson nodded in the direction of the cries of equine terror and the hammering of the horses trying to batter their way out of their stalls. "Santa Anita Park, just north of the mall here. Thank God there isn't a race today, or there'd be thousands more people here. God, those poor animals."

Garcia turned to look at Boisson. "Which way?"

"Straight across the parking lot to the nearest set of doors."

The parking lot was roughly half full. Most of the cars had been abandoned, and the rest were desperately trying to get out the mall exits, but had nowhere to go because the adjoining streets were already blocked. People fled past them, nearly all heading south along Baldwin Avenue. None of the people were fleeing north, for no one wanted to come any closer to the unholy cries coming from the stables.

"Look at that!" One of the FBI men was pointing at a dark form loping across the parking lot, chasing after some of the refugees from the mall. He and several others raised their rifles.

"Hold your fire!" Boisson's command cut through the air like steel.

"But..." The agent stared at her, mouth agape.

"Hold your fire, Perkins." She spoke directly to him, but her words were meant for the others, too. "We've got a job to do, first. We can't afford to get tied up out here." To Naomi, her eyes following the thing as it leaped upon a running woman and shoved its stinger in her back, she whispered, "They're real. Sweet Jesus, they're real!"

Beside Naomi, the cats had come alive. Alexander, his ears laid back flat against his big head, stared at the harvester and hissed, exposing his half-inch long fangs. Koshka, who hardly ever vocalized, growled deep, sounding like a large dog, as she, too, watched the creature.

Triggered by some unknown imperative, they both lunged in the harvester's direction.

"Shit," Boisson breathed, unable to credit what her eyes were telling her. "I've never seen cats act like that!"

"You won't, except around harvesters," Naomi said tightly as she pulled the cats along, their claws scratching on the pavement.

They continued across the lot toward one of the big box department stores on the corner. Naomi hoped and prayed that they'd be able to find what they were looking for without going too deep into the mall. There were plenty of victims near the theater, but that was on the other side, and she suspected that by now most of them would be too big to get into one of the glass carboys.

The glass doors at the entrance were shattered, and four bodies, including a young boy, lay in bloody heaps after being trampled to death.

Garcia glanced over his shoulder at Boisson, and she gave him the hand signal to proceed.

Assault rifle tucked tight into his shoulder, his boots crunched on the glass as he led the other agents inside.

The interior of the store was a shambles. Worse, parts of it had been cast into darkness.

"What happened to the lights?" One of the female agents asked.

"The larval forms love rubber and plastic," Naomi answered. "One of them might have gotten into the power cables or breaker boxes and shorted something out."

"Christ."

As they passed by the jewelry display, Naomi caught sight of something. "Wait a minute."

"Halt," Boisson called to the others. The agents stood or knelt, facing outward, weapons at the ready.

Naomi went to a display that had necklaces for girls made of bright plastic beads. She grabbed all of them. "Bring me the carboys."

The two agents carrying the big glass jugs set them down. Naomi unscrewed the caps, then dropped the necklaces through the narrow mouths of the carboys before screwing the lids back on.

"Bait, right?" Boisson asked.

"Right. Plastic and rubber has a lot of carbon. We can't handle the things or allow them to touch us. I'm hoping the plastic will entice them to just crawl right in."

"Nice. A great new use for plastic baubles. Okay, let's go." Boisson motioned for Garcia to start forward again.

"Boisson," Naomi said, looking up at the ceiling. A lot of tiles were missing, their remains scattered around the floor.

Boisson's eyes followed where Naomi was looking. The other agents noticed, and looked up, too. "Do you think...?"

Naomi nodded. "Yes. Some crawled along the pipes and wiring up there, then dropped down through the ceiling."

"Great." Drawing a deep breath, she called to Garcia, "Move it. But make sure you guys watch the ceiling, too."

There were muttered oaths from the men and women around her as they began moving forward again, each of them casting fearful glances at the ceiling with every step.

They passed seven more bodies before they reached the entrance to the mall itself. Four of them had been crushed in the panic, and a fifth was an elderly woman who had probably died of a heart attack, a rictus of terror still frozen on her face.

As for the remaining two, they had been decapitated.

Naomi knelt next to the first one to examine it. "Hold them, will you?" She handed the leashes for the cats to Boisson. Naomi knew it was safe at the moment, because the cats were back to merely being terrified.

The body was that of a man, Naomi guessed in his mid thirties. She examined the wound, which looked like something had taken a nearly perfectly semicircular bite out of the top of his torso. But it wasn't a bite, nor was the wound made by any weapon: the edges were soft, as if the flesh had been dissolved. Of the head, there was no sign. There was a large pool of blood on the floor, although not nearly as much as she would have expected. The victim's heart must have stopped beating before the wound had been completed.

The other body, of what looked like a teen girl, was the same.

"So they just eat heads?"

Naomi looked up at Boisson, who was studying the girl's body with professional interest. "We don't know anything about their feeding patterns. We captured some of the adults when I was in the Earth Defense Society, but they had refused to eat anything while in captivity. But this?" She shook her head. "Why would they bother to eat the heads over any other part of the body, unless..."

"Unless what?"

Naomi's mind raced. *That must be how they do it*, she thought. They can mimic a body's appearance perfectly, but what about the mind? How did they acquire the victim's mannerisms, how they talked, the things the victim knew that made him or her unique, and in no time at all? There had been a great deal of speculation in the EDS about how the harvesters managed the behavioral side of their mimicry, but they'd never had any hard data from which they could form conclusions.

She feared that she was looking at the answer. Somehow, the things must be able to absorb at least part of the information stored in the victim's brain. And as they learned more, they could adapt ever faster to new circumstances and environments.

"Naomi?"

"Nothing." She took the leashes back from Boisson and stood up. "Let's keep going."

With a scowl, Boisson signaled Garcia, and the team moved into the mall.

* * *

Garcia had to work hard at controlling his breathing. He'd done a hitch with the Marines and had seen some action in Afghanistan before joining the Bureau, but this was something else entirely. He still couldn't believe the things he'd seen, both on the television before coming here and then the thing out in the parking lot. He wanted to believe it was nothing more than a huge hoax, that they had been co-opted into some sort of new reality show, and that maybe Boisson was the only one in on the deal.

But he'd worked with her long enough to know that she was scared, too. Most people who didn't know her wouldn't be able to tell, but he could. And he'd never seen anything scare that woman.

Keep it cool, he told himself. He scanned ahead of them, swiveling his torso as he aimed the shotgun. The mall here was empty, although he could still hear screams echoing through the corridors. The devastation wasn't quite so evident as it had been in the store they'd come through, although there were still plenty of signs of panic. Several of the small kiosks in the center of the mall had been upended, their contents spilled over the shiny tile floor, and the displays in the storefronts were in disarray. In one of them, a large glass pane had shattered outward, with some of the shards coated in blood. Garcia imagined that someone must have leaped through it in an effort to escape *them*.

He gulped involuntarily as he thought again of what he'd seen in the parking lot. It was something out of a horror movie, but wasn't nearly as terrible as the larval forms, as Dr. Perrault called them. The oozing things that he'd seen on the television, and the focus of their mission here, were an abomination.

As they passed a shoe store, the cats started hissing and growling again. That, too, was something Garcia found to be terribly unnatural, but at least the cats were on their side.

One of the displays in the store fell over, spilling colorful shoes to the floor, and everyone on the team pointed their weapon in that direction.

"Let's take a look," Perrault called softly as she reined in the cats. The big black and white one, bigger than any cat Garcia had ever seen, was straining at the leash like a dog, his razor sharp canines gleaming.

Boisson gave him the hand signal to move toward the store.

"Watch where you step," Perrault called. "And watch the ceiling."

Right, Garcia thought. He already felt as if he were turning into a chameleon, with eyes swiveling independently in their sockets to look up and down at the same time.

He stepped quickly around one of the black pillars that flanked the entrance to the store, his finger tensing on the trigger.

And there, at the base of the toppled over display, was one of the things.

"There's one in here, doctor!" His voice was hoarse, as if he'd been shouting all morning.

* * *

"Here, hold them." Naomi handed the leashes to Boisson again. The FBI agent reached for them, but wasn't prepared for how hard the cats were pulling, trying to get to the harvester, and nearly lost her grip.

"Jesus!" Alexander almost pulled Boisson off-balance before she got control of him.

Naomi shot her a look, but refrained from saying anything. Instead, she gestured for one of the men carrying the glass carboys to come with her.

The two of them moved into the store where Garcia stood, his gun trained on the oozing mass on the floor.

"Good, Garcia," Naomi told him, patting him on the shoulder as she stepped past him toward the creature. Turning to the wide-eyed agent carrying the glass jug, she said, "Here, give me that."

The man gladly handed it to her, then brought up his shotgun. Naomi wondered how he'd react when he discovered that he'd have to continue carrying the carboy, this time with the harvester inside.

The harvester was the size of a small watermelon, and had wrapped itself around one of the shoes that had been on the display rack. The plastic of the shoe was quickly giving way under the acidic assault of the creature, and even now the harvester was extending pseudopods toward the other shoes that had fallen around it.

Using the muzzle of her rifle, she moved those shoes away. She set the carboy down for a moment to remove the metal cap, then gently tipped it over on its side and pressed the open end right up against the larva's bruised-looking, glistening flesh.

The thing didn't hesitate. As if it smelled a gourmet dinner, it began to flow through the narrow mouth of the carboy.

Her plan worked perfectly, right up to the point where the harvester tried to pull in the partially digested shoe. The remains of the shoe were still far too large to fit through the neck of the carboy, but the creature had no problem elongating itself to reach the plastic bait.

"Dammit." She didn't want the thing to eat the beads and then ooze right back out again. "Knife! Does anyone have a combat knife?"

The agent who'd been carrying the carboy did. Without a word, he unsheathed it and handed it to her.

Taking a deep breath, she drew the knife in a smooth motion across the mouth of the carboy. The larva didn't even flinch as it was cut in two. The part still consuming the shoe fell to the floor with a wet plop, while the other half pulled itself all the way into the carboy where it was greedily consuming the plastic necklaces.

Pulling the carboy back from the part of the larva that had fallen back to the floor, Naomi double checked that the cap had nothing in it but metal, then screwed it onto the neck of the carboy as tight as she could.

Picking up the container, she shivered as she watched the thing oozing and squirming against the side of the carboy, with only the thickness of the glass between it and her hand.

Turning to the agent, she handed him the big jug and its horrid contents. "Hold it upright, and tell me if it looks like it's trying to force its way out the top. And don't drop it."

"Yeah, right." The man gulped and took the glass container

"And I wouldn't use this again." She tossed his knife on the ground. She didn't want to take the chance that any small bits of larvae were clinging to it.

The agent tried to hold the carboy out, away from his body, but Naomi knew that he'd only drop it. Naomi pressed it toward him. "You're perfectly safe as long as it stays in the carboy. It can't get through the glass." A sudden vision of the equipment in the lab at the Earth Defense Society base after the first harvester larva had done its work flashed through her mind. The only three things that had survived its touch were concrete, metal, and glass.

"Is that it?" Boisson looked at the thing, which had gravitated toward the side where the agent held the carboy against his chest, as if it knew that just beyond the glass lay another tasty morsel.

The cats continued to hiss and growl, although now they were behind Boisson, trying to flee.

"Not quite." Naomi turned back to the remaining half of the larva, which was still gorging itself on the shoes. "I'm going to need another one." She would have taken this one, the second half of the pair that she'd created, but by now it had drawn in half a dozen shoes and was rapidly growing. Trying to play the same game she had the first time would be a bit trickier, and she didn't want to take the risk.

Taking out the bottle of lighter fluid, she sprayed some on the creature and then made a small trail of fluid away from it. Kneeling down, she flicked her lighter and stepped back.

The fluid ignited with a soft *whump*. As soon as the flame reached the larva, the thing erupted.

"Christ!" The agent with the carboy stumbled back, almost dropping it. The others took an involuntary step backward as the harvester burned like jellied gasoline.

"Fire is our best weapon," Naomi explained as she watched the thing die. "But we can't use it indiscriminately, for obvious reasons."

"Let's go," Boisson said, handing the straining cats back to Naomi, "before the fire extinguishers in here come on. I don't like getting my hair wet."

* * *

Thank God I don't have to carry one of those things, Garcia thought as they continued deeper into the mall. He exchanged looks with Cardon, who was stuck with carrying the doctor's specimen, and could see that the man was frightened out of his wits.

Garcia didn't blame him one bit. He tried to imagine what it must be like having that little monster glommed onto the side of the glass right against his chest, whatever brain it had, if any, trying to figure out how to get through it to the meat on the other side.

"Garcia!"

He looked up at Boisson.

"Pay attention or you'll be carrying the damn thing!"

"Yes, ma'am," he said, feeling ashamed. *Steady, man*, he told himself. Focus on the mission. Just get the job done so we can get the hell out of here and go home.

Something wriggling on the floor caught his eye. "There's another one!" The larva was making a beeline for another body that lay bloodied and broken on the floor.

Garcia couldn't help himself. He went over to the body and dragged it away before the harvester could reach it.

"Good job, Garcia." Perrault flashed him a quick smile as she passed by, again handing the cats, which had again gone berserk, to Boisson. The other agent with a carboy handed it to her, and she knelt down and poked the neck of the jug into the harvester. Just as before, it instantly began to flow into the glass container, hungry for the plastic beads.

Garcia felt a sense of relief, knowing that once Perrault sealed the lid on the second little monster, they could get out of this tomb. The screams from elsewhere in the mall had stopped, and the place was far too quiet.

The cats were growling and hissing, carrying on like mad. Boisson was having trouble holding onto them, especially the big black and white one, Alexander. Garcia had learned very quickly, even in the short time they'd been in the safe house, that the cat was a big, purring cream puff. But the nice big kitty was gone. What Garcia was looking at now was an enraged predator.

Then he noticed where the cats were looking. They weren't looking at the creature Perrault had coaxed into the glass prison. Their attention was focused on something above her.

Garcia looked up at the second floor walkway just in time to see one of the larvae ooze through the railing. But this one wasn't small, like the one Perrault was capturing. It was the size of a fifty-five gallon drum. "*Up there!*"

His shout startled the agent helping Perrault, and he stumbled backward, firing his shotgun at the thing now hanging down toward the doctor like warm putty.

The others opened fire, too, but it had no effect on the creature. The bullets distorted the flesh where they impacted, but otherwise caused no damage at all.

Perrault stared upward, mouth open, her arms wrapped around the horror in the carboy as one of its larger brethren loomed over her.

The rest of the thing squeezed through the railing, and it fell.

Garcia took no time reflecting on the value of his own life as he charged. The two steps that separated him and Perrault was such a short distance, but seemed to take a lifetime. Wrapping his arms around her, he knocked her off her feet, his momentum carrying her out of danger. The huge larval form landed behind them with a loud splat, and was instantly wreathed in flames as the other agents doused it with lighter fluid or used their lighters and cans of hairspray as homemade flamethrowers.

As he and Perrault hit the floor, the bottom of the carboy between them struck the tile and shattered. Garcia's eyes locked with Perrault's, and for the first time he noticed that one of her eyes was brown, the other blue. They were open wide with terror.

"I've got this," Garcia gasped. He rolled away from her, clutching the harvester larva to his chest. His hands, lacerated from the shattered glass, quickly sank into the sickly, mottled flesh.

The last thing he saw before the pain blotted out the world was Dr. Perrault kneeling beside him, tears streaming down her face.

CHAPTER TWENTY-SIX

"I think we've got company." Jack watched the plane, another An-2, as it cleared the end of the runway and climbed into the sky. "They must have found themselves a pilot."

Mikhailov got to his feet and looked out the window, following Jack's gaze. "What could they be thinking? They cannot shoot us down."

"They can ram us if they get close enough."

The plane behind them began to turn, then leveled out on a northeasterly heading.

"*Slava Bogu*," Mikhailov breathed.

"I'm not so sure this is good news."

Mikhailov turned to him. "Why do you say that?"

"What's the range of a plane like this?"

Pondering a moment, Mikhailov said, "I believe a bit over eight hundred kilometers, if I remember correctly."

"Then that's how far the infection here might be able to spread if that plane goes the whole distance before it lands."

"Oh."

The two of them watched the other plane in silence until it disappeared, swallowed by the rising sun.

Jack glanced at Mikhailov in the bright light streaming through the window. His friend looked ashen, and he was holding both arms protectively to his chest. While he couldn't hear his breathing over the muted drone of the engine, he could tell that Mikhailov was wheezing. "How are you feeling, Sergei?"

"I feel like I should have taken your advice and stayed in bed." There was an angry shout from the cockpit. "Perhaps we should become better acquainted with our pilot."

"I meant to ask you about her. It's a good thing she wasn't lying to you about being able to fly this crate."

"Had I been at the controls when that thing was hanging on the tail," Mikhailov said, "we would never have made it." He offered a haggard, tired grin. "That is why I joined the Army and not the Air Force."

"And then went airborne. The worst of both worlds." Jack wrapped his arm around Mikhailov's waist and helped him toward the cockpit. "Come on."

Making their way to the forward end of the empty cargo compartment, which Jack thought resembled the unadorned framed interior of most of the military cargo aircraft he'd ever been on, Jack helped Mikhailov step up through the cockpit doorway to collapse into the copilot's seat. Jack stepped up and stood between him and the woman flying the plane.

She looked up at him for a moment. "I thank you. You saved my life."

"You're welcome." He smiled. "My name's Jack Dawson, by the way."

"I am Khatuna Beridze."

Jack glanced at Mikhailov. It didn't sound like a Russian name to him.

As if reading his mind, Mikhailov mouthed *Georgian*.

"And I am *Kapitan* Sergei Mikhailov of the Russian Army."

Khatuna nodded, then looked more closely at Mikhailov. "You are hurt. Badly, I think."

"*Da*. Punctured lung. I think it is getting worse." He shrugged.

Jack thought that, if anything, Mikhailov was even more pale than he had been before. "We've got to get you to a hospital, Sergei."

"No," he said, reaching for the headset that hung next to the copilot's seat. "First we must warn of what happened at Ulan-Erg and Elista." He leaned forward, grimacing at the pain, and tuned the radio.

* * *

Breathing was agony. Speaking was worse. Every movement seemed to jam the spear of broken rib deeper into his lung. But he had come too far now, and too much depended on them. On him.

Waving Jack away, appreciating the concern his friend showed, and also knowing that there was nothing Jack could do for him, Mikhailov tuned the radio to the international military aircraft emergency guard frequency.

His earphones crackled into life, and he sat back in shock. There should have been silence, for this channel was only used if there was a military aircraft in trouble. Instead, the frequency was alive with distress calls and controllers giving hurried instructions.

In the pilot's seat, Khatuna turned to look at him, an expression of surprise on her face, as well.

Behind him, he heard Jack ask, "What?" He couldn't hear because he had no headphones.

Khatuna pulled off her headset and handed it to Jack. He put it on, his puzzled expression turning grim. Mikhailov knew that Jack wouldn't understand what was being said, but the simple fact that anyone was communicating on that channel was evidence enough of trouble.

"I guess we're not the only ones up the creek," Jack said, handing the headset back to Khatuna. The radio had two receivers, and while Mikhailov continued to listen to the military guard frequency, she tuned to the civilian emergency channel.

"So it would seem," Mikhailov said. He and Khatuna listened for a few moments, and he repeated to Jack the names that he could identify. "Stavropol. Budyonnovsk. Mozdok. Salsk. These are military air bases in this area that are talking. Some I cannot hear directly, for they are still too far away at our altitude. But I can hear the aircraft. Those fields are diverting aircraft away or calling for assistance."

"It is same on civilian emergency channel," Khatuna added. "I count at least three, maybe five airports reporting emergencies."

"But how could there be so many in the time since they broke out of the facility?" Mikhailov wondered.

Jack thought for a moment before answering. "Naomi had no idea what their reproductive rate is, but it's got to be ridiculously high. I mean, there were hundreds of the damn things just at Ulan-Erg, and who knows how many more at Elista. Then there are more at these other places. Most of the ones we saw were in their natural form, but they're a lot more dangerous when they copy us, and there's no way to tell how many of them are walking around as impostors."

Like Mikhailov, Khatuna had slid aside one of the ear pieces of her headset so she could hear Jack while still listening in to the civilian emergency channel. She looked from Jack to Mikhailov with frightened eyes. "They came for us last night," she told them. "Some people disappeared over last few days and never came back. Others changed. One of them was my father. He was gone for most of yesterday after he went to machine shop to get some parts, a trip that should have been an hour." She shook her head. "When he came back to work at airport, he was different. No one else noticed, but I did. He spoke like my father, acted like him, but there was something wrong."

"It must take a while for the harvesters to be able to mimic us perfectly," Jack said. "Or perhaps they can never really fool someone who knows the victim as well as you knew your father. I'm sorry."

She nodded. "Last night, fighting began in the town, in Elista, just before we were to go to sleep." Khatuna blinked her eyes rapidly, trying to clear them. "Creature that looked like my father killed my mother. We were all sitting there together, and when we heard screams from other houses, it killed her. My two brothers fought with it. They begged me to run." She took a deep, shuddering breath. "I left them. Left them to die. Creature tried to find me, kept looking for me, and others came to help it. I spent all night trying to reach airport." She looked at Mikhailov. "It found me there."

"It must have known you would go there to escape," Mikhailov said.

"And it would make sense that they would try to kill anyone who knew how to fly and replace them so they could spread the infection," Jack added.

"*Da.* That is when I met you, at hangar." Khatuna reached out and took Jack's hand, giving it a fierce squeeze. "Thing chasing me, thing that you killed, was creature that killed my family. Thank you."

They were all quiet for a moment, and Khatuna turned away, busying herself with leveling off the plane. They'd reached three thousand meters. The plane wasn't equipped with oxygen, so they couldn't go much higher. Besides, biplanes weren't designed for high altitude cruising.

"I will try to get through to someone at Stavropol," Mikhailov told them. "Perhaps they will know where we can land." He keyed the microphone and said in Russian, "This is *Kapitan* Sergei Mikhailov, calling Stavropol with an in-flight emergency, come in."

He had to repeat the call three more times before he was able to make a clear transmission through the frantic chatter. He was surprised when the man at Stavropol airfield seemed to recognize him.

"Mikhailov, *da*. Please stand by."

A few anxious moments passed, then a new speaker came on. He, too, had difficulty in getting through the other transmissions on that frequency, but at last there was a brief pause where he could speak.

"Mikhailov, this is *Mayor* Kurmansky of the 247th Regiment. Where is *Polkovnik* Kuybishev?"

"Dead." He glanced at Jack, who was watching him closely, no doubt wishing he could understand Russian. "The entire unit was destroyed. The only survivors are myself, the American Jack Dawson, and a civilian. Ulan-Erg was completely overrun by..." He paused, not sure how to characterize the harvesters to Kurmansky, not knowing if the man had seen any of the things with his own eyes. "...the enemy, as was Elista. We are returning to Stavropol in a civilian An-2."

"Negative," Kurmansky told him. Mikhailov could hear what sounded like automatic weapons fire in the background. "The airfield here is not secure, and the regimental garrison is under attack. By order of *Polkovnik* Zaitsev, you are to proceed with the American to Moscow by any means possible and report to Airborne Forces Headquarters."

Kurmansky's transmission broke up, overridden by other emergency calls. Mikhailov tried to get him back, but to no avail.

With an exhausted sigh that sent another spear of pain through his chest, he slipped off the headphones and let them fall into his lap. "We are ordered to Moscow," he told Jack, even as Khatuna banked the big biplane smoothly to the right, bringing them onto a northwesterly course.

"Will this thing have enough fuel?"

They both looked at Khatuna, who shook her head. "*Nyet*. We will need to land somewhere." She nodded toward a map case next to the copilot's seat where Mikhailov was sitting.

He leaned forward and tried to reach it, but fell back, gasping and holding his side. He bit his lip to keep from crying out. He was worried that he might not make it to Moscow, for it would take them hours to get there.

"Here, let me." Jack reached past him and opened the case, extracting several charts. He quickly sorted through them and pulled out a large-scale one that covered western Russia. He spread it out on Mikhailov's lap.

After a moment of gauging the distances involved, Mikhailov said, "Lipetsk. There is both a civilian airport and a large air base there, and it should just be in range." He had checked the fuel level during his very hurried preflight, before Khatuna had taken over, and had been enormously relieved to see that the An-2's tanks had been full. It was one of the few times that fortune had favored him recently.

"How long?" Jack looked at him with grave concern, and Mikhailov knew what he was thinking.

"Four hours, perhaps a little longer."

Khatuna shot him a glance, then shook her head, muttering under her breath.

"Can't we land somewhere closer and take a faster military plane?"

Mikhailov considered. "Excluding the bases that are already experiencing emergencies, we might. But consider: by the time we land, explain our situation to the Air Force, which probably does not have any idea what is really happening, and then try to explain why we have on board an American in Russian military uniform who was involved in combat on Russian soil." He shook his head, resisting the urge to laugh at the absurdity of it all. They would be caught in red tape, as he knew Jack would say, for hours, if not days. "When we are close to Lipetsk I will see if I can get them to contact someone in VDV, the Airborne Forces, who knows of our situation. If yes, then we will land at the air base and take advantage of the Air Force's hospitality. If not, we will land at the civilian airport to refuel."

"Right," Jack said. "Regardless of where we land, and assuming you don't die on us in the meantime, I want your word that you're going to get your ass into the nearest hospital."

"I'm not exactly going to win any wrestling matches with you." Mikhailov grinned, even as he fought to suppress another coughing fit. He could feel the blood gurgling in his lung with every breath now. "But the only place I will go into a hospital is in Moscow, after we report to VDV Headquarters." His grin faded. "We cannot afford to waste the time I will have to spend in a hospital. We have to get to our headquarters so we can tell them what is happening. Perhaps someone will even believe us."

"And what if you bleed to death on the way, you moron?"

"Then Khatuna will be in charge."

She scowled at him. "*Durak*!"

Mikhailov smiled. "*Da*."

Then he began coughing up blood.

* * *

It was a long four hours as the plane droned northward. Khatuna periodically spoke over the radio, but otherwise she remained quiet, intent on flying the plane. The only times she took a break was when she excused herself to go to the bathroom in the back, just as the men did. There was a metal bucket for the purpose, and to keep the plane from reeking even worse, they made an unspoken agreement to dump each deposit out the door over the empty landscape below.

Beside her, Mikhailov was hanging on, but he was terribly pale. Jack was really worried about him, but there was little he could do except scold his Russian friend into trying to rest.

Below them, the vast enormity of Russia crept by, the land a patchwork quilt of farms, more and more of them covered in snow as they proceeded north, that stretched to the horizon in every direction.

Having taken the headphones from Mikhailov, who was drifting in and out of consciousness, Jack listened to the military guard channel. There was less activity the farther north they went, but it was clear even to him, unable to understand the language, but differentiating the speakers, that havoc was spreading across southern Russia. And as the harvesters found more ways to disperse, piloting or riding as passengers in aircraft or on trains, driving cars, or even moving on foot, they would spread their unique form of cancer ever wider through Russia, then beyond that massive country's borders.

He knew that the same must be happening in India, and wondered how Kiran was faring. Perhaps they got lucky and destroyed the harvesters before they'd spread beyond the Koratikal area.

He wondered what was happening elsewhere in the world, but especially back home. All he could hope was that Naomi was safe, still at work in her lab at Morgan Pharmaceuticals. He knew that she, of all people, held the key to solving this disaster, because this wasn't a war they would win through force of arms alone. The harvesters must be able to breed like flies, and the only advantage that the humans had at the moment were that most of the things seemed content, or were forced for some reason as yet unknown, to stay in their natural form. Once they got smart and really focused on mimicking humans, there would be no stopping them with sheer firepower. The fate of the Russian paratroopers the previous night proved that: while they weren't properly prepared or equipped, they were well-armed and well-trained, and were still wiped out to the last man. They killed at least their own number of harvesters, but that hadn't mattered in the end.

No. Weapons alone wouldn't do it. What they needed was a miracle, and he pinned his hopes on the genius of Naomi and others like her. He just wished that he could call her right now, just to hear her voice, to know that she was all right. But he had to wait until they landed, and hoped that the cell service would work this time.

"What are you thinking?"

He broke from his reverie to find Khatuna looking up at him, and he could tell from her expression that she was afraid of what he might say. "Just missing my fiancée," he said with a wan smile. "It's been a long trip."

She looked at him more closely, and he could only imagine what a mess he must appear in her eyes. His uniform was covered in a grisly mixture of mud and blood, both human and harvester, and was ripped and punctured in several places. He must look like a war movie extra done up by a Hollywood makeup artist. And he reeked of stale sweat, body odor, the unique stink of gunpowder, and blood. The oil, fuel, and fertilizer smells of the old biplane were pleasant by comparison.

Unable to help himself, he laughed.

"What is funny?"

"I'm such a stinking mess. Almost as bad as him." He nodded to Mikhailov, who was sleeping.

She wrinkled her nose, and the trace of a smile touched her lips. "You do smell bad. Worse than zoo." Then she asked, "Can you stop them? Those things?"

Jack's humor evaporated. He could see the pleading in her eyes, wanting him to tell her some good news, along with a fierce hatred of the things that had taken her family. "I don't know, Khatuna. They're intelligent, tough, and very deadly. We went into Ulan-Erg last night with two companies of airborne troops, and Sergei and I are the only survivors. And you know all too well what happened in Elista." She nodded gravely. "But they *can* be killed. They're not invincible. Our biggest problem is just going to be getting people to believe that they exist, then teach them what they need to know to fight them."

"They will soon believe," she said. "They will have no choice."

"Yeah. There aren't any alternatives."

They were silent after that, until some time later Khatuna said, "We are coming near Lipetsk. I must get clearance to land."

She changed frequencies on the radio, then keyed her microphone and spoke. After a moment, she spoke again, anger plainly evident in her voice.

Jack didn't like the sound of that. "What's wrong?"

"They are refusing permission to land to any aircraft from Caucasus region!" She spat what Jack suspected was a particularly potent curse before talking again on the radio. "I told them we have injured military officer. They still refuse."

Jack's earphones suddenly came to life. It had been almost an hour since he'd heard any emergency calls over the military guard channel. A new voice now came on, very loud and strong. Jack didn't understand the words, but he heard "Lipetsk" and could tell that the person on the other end of the line wasn't very happy.

"Khatuna, take a listen to this."

She switched over to the guard channel and listened. The controller at Lipetsk spoke again, and Khatuna snapped her head around to Jack. "We are ordered to turn back, or they will shoot us down!"

Jack felt something tug on his arm, and glanced down. Mikhailov was awake.

Pulling off the headphones, Jack told him, "It looks like they're starting to quarantine aircraft coming from the south. Lipetsk won't let us land, and are threatening to shoot us down if we approach any closer."

Mikhailov took the headset and put it on. In rapid, angry Russian, he spoke to the Lipetsk controller. With a grimace of disgust, he tore the headset off. "I told them I was a VDV officer and was on urgent orders to report to Moscow."

"They didn't buy it, I assume."

"No, and the Air Force refused to put me through to VDV Headquarters. The quarantine orders were just issued by the government: all aircraft from anywhere south of the Don and Volga Rivers are to be turned back, no exceptions. Even military aircraft. If they refuse, they are to be shot down. We are lucky they took this long to decide this, or we would not have made it this far. They are allowing no landings now, not even for passenger jets. All aircraft must return to airfields south of the quarantine line." He leaned his head back and closed his eyes. "Everything south of Rostov, Volgograd, and Astrakhan has been declared a quarantine zone."

"Shit," Jack said, trying to absorb the enormity of what the Russians had just done. And it wouldn't be good news for the countries on the borders of the quarantine zone, he thought. They would soon be flooded with people trying to get out. It was a situation that would get ugly, fast. "It probably won't matter in the long run, but at least they've recognized that there's a threat and are trying to do something. I'll give them that much."

"And what are we to do?" Khatuna asked. "We are nearly out of fuel. We cannot go that far."

"Turn south, as the controller orders," Mikhailov told her. "Then descend — slowly." He grinned. "I have an idea."

CHAPTER TWENTY-SEVEN

"Garcia!" Perrault took a big shard of glass from the shattered carboy and tried to pry the harvester larva from the agent's chest.

"Get back!" A pair of hands roughly pulled Naomi away from the screaming, writhing man who had saved her life. It was Boisson. She had handed the cats off to one of the other agents before dashing over beside Garcia. "We can't risk you, doctor. My boss made that explicitly clear. What do you think is going to happen if that thing gets on your hands?"

"Damn it," Naomi said through gritted teeth, wiping the tears away. She'd hardly known Garcia, but had taken an immediate liking to him. Now, watching him being eaten alive by this *thing*. "God dammit!" She tossed the glass shard away.

"Is there anything we can do for him?" Boisson's face was a grim mask.

Already, the harvester had absorbed most of Garcia's hands and was working its way up his forearms. It was also spreading over his chest, greedily consuming the nylon of the combat vest, and Garcia's screams grew louder as the thing worked through the body armor to attack the flesh beneath.

"No," Naomi said. "If it were just a hand or a foot, we could try a field amputation, but this?" She shook her head.

"Yeah." Boisson gestured for one of the other agents. "Get on the horn and call for an emergency helo evac. Tell them to extract us from the race track parking lot east of the mall. There are too many cars abandoned in the west mall parking lot for a safe landing. Take the others and get the good doctor and her menagerie moving. I'll be along in a minute."

The agent nodded in small jerks, his eyes fixed on Garcia.

"Move it, damn you!"

"Yes, ma'am!" That snapped him out of it. "Doctor, if you'll come with me, please?"

Naomi shook off his arm. "What are you going to do, Boisson?"

The older woman turned to look at her with dead eyes. "What's necessary. Now get your ass moving. Go!"

Taking back the cats, Naomi did as she was told, and the other agents again formed a protective ring around her as they headed through the mall toward the east parking lot and the theater.

* * *

Boisson knelt down next to Garcia, whose face was contorted in unimaginable agony, his throat a conduit for unending screams. That told her just how much pain he was in, because while he'd never been a macho asshole, he'd always been tough. He'd been a good agent, and a good human being.

"I'm sorry," she said softly as she drew her Glock 23. While Naomi had said that standard caliber handguns would be useless against harvesters, Boisson hadn't found anything more powerful in the brief time she'd had to put a team together, and she felt naked without it. It might not harm a harvester, but it would do for the unpleasant duty she now had to perform.

Garcia's eyes registered recognition, and she thought she saw a glimmer of pleading behind the madness brought on by the ever-growing pain.

Making sure to keep away from the undulating horror on top of him, she put the gun to his temple, and he closed his eyes. "Forgive me," she said softly.

Then she pulled the trigger.

* * *

Naomi whirled around at the single gunshot that echoed from behind her. She tried to stop, but the two agents on either side of her gently took hold of her arms and propelled her forward.

"Ma'am, keep moving, please," one of them said with a wooden voice.

Numbing her feelings, she did as he said. She'd seen plenty of people die before, but not like that. Never like that.

"Hurry up!" Boisson's voice called from behind them as she ran to catch up. "Let's get the hell out of here." She paused next to the agent carrying the remaining carboy and its lethal cargo. "Just be careful with that damn thing."

"You got that right." He held the heavy glass jar close to his chest, trying to ignore what squirmed hungrily inside.

They passed several other larvae of varying sizes. The cats gave warning against all of them, and the team burned them all with quick blasts from their makeshift flamethrowers.

One, however, caught Naomi's attention.

"No, not that one!"

"We can't afford to stop," Boisson told her.

"No, I've got to see this." Without another word, she thrust the leashes for the hissing cats into the hands of one of the agents and moved closer to the larval harvester. The other agents moved to keep her covered.

The thing was roughly the size of the glass carboy, and, unlike the other larvae they'd seen, lay motionless on the floor.

What had caught Naomi's attention was the ring of liquid quickly spreading around the creature. Dark and foul-smelling, it oozed from all over the creature's body and ran down in rivulets to pool on the floor.

Boisson stood close beside her. "God, what's it doing?"

"It's shedding the excess water and other compounds that it doesn't need for further growth," Naomi explained. Even as she watched, the thing seemed to shrink slightly, and the ugly yellow and blue colors became more vibrant. If she'd had any suitable containers, she would have taken some samples.

As they watched, a diamond engagement ring emerged from the thing's side and plopped into the growing pool of excreta.

"Jesus," Boisson whispered.

"He's got nothing to do with this." Naomi continued to stare at the thing until the flow of fluid and bits and pieces of metal ceased. The larva sat there for a moment. Then, as if it had reawakened, it began to flow toward them. Quickly.

"We've got to go, doctor." Boisson took Naomi's arm and pulled her away. Then one of the other agents torched the oozing mass.

Naomi took back the cats and pulled them along. Reaching some unknowable threshold, they lost interest in the larva behind them and cowered close to Naomi, slinking low to the ground.

At the mall's east entrance, there were more bodies, those who'd been crushed in the panic to escape the mall, and more larvae feeding on them. Boisson had the team stop just long enough to set fire to the horrid things before she led them back outside, heading toward the race track parking lot.

The area immediately around the mall was ominously quiet, but pandemonium was clearly audible from the neighborhoods and businesses surrounding it. Screams, car horns, emergency sirens, and gunfire could be heard from every direction, and the horrible cries of the horses in their stalls still went on.

Looking around, Naomi could see that smoke from more fires was evident along the skyline, and several cars on Huntington Drive were burning.

"Keep it tight!" Boisson ordered. "Let's move!"

The team made its way through the eastern parking lot, which was over half full of cars. There were also some people milling about aimlessly, no doubt in shock.

They had almost reached the edge of the lot when the cats, panting furiously from the unaccustomed exertion and fear, suddenly laid their ears back and began to hiss and growl at a cluster of five people who were just ahead.

"Stop!" Naomi called, and the agents came to an instant halt.

"Help me," one of the two women cried. "Help me find my baby! Those things took her. I can't find my baby!"

The others began to beg for help. As they moved closer, one of the men raised his arms toward them. "Save us!"

"Come no closer!" Boisson ordered. "Stay where you are or we'll open fire!"

"My baby!" The woman was hysterical, tears streaming down her face. She came toward them, leading the others. All of them were crying for help, for salvation.

The cats were going crazy. Alexander was pulling so hard on his leash that the pads on his feet were bleeding on the pavement, and it was hard for Naomi to hold him back. He suddenly backed up, relieving the tension on the leash, and then lunged forward. The nylon burned Naomi's hand, and the cats slipped free.

In a flash, both cats were tearing toward the people, who were now coming toward the team at a run.

"Alexander, Koshka, no!" Naomi tried to chase after them, but one of the agents, a big man whose name she didn't know, wrapped his arms around her and held her back. "Let me go, goddamn you!"

"*Open fire!*"

The words had barely escaped Boisson's lips when fifteen shotguns and assault rifles fired. The woman in the lead, the one who'd lost her baby, went down like a rag doll, collapsing to the ground in a bloody heap.

"Oh, God," Naomi cried, realizing then that the woman had been exactly what she'd claimed to be. Human. One of the men, perhaps her husband, was gunned down next to her.

The other three, however, kept coming, wading into the hail of fire while giving off unearthly screeches. One collapsed to the pavement as both legs were blown off, and it continued to scrabble toward the agents.

Leaping onto its back, Alexander and Koshka attacked the wounded harvester with unbridled fury. Not wanting to hit the cats, which had saved their lives several times already, the agents concentrated their fire on the remaining two harvesters, bringing them down a handful of paces from the lead agent.

The others gathered around the remaining harvester, which was still being savaged by the cats. One of the agents bravely stepped forward into easy range of the stinger whipping to and fro to deliver a shotgun blast to the thing's head.

Rushing forward before the cats could regain their senses from the blind rage that possessed them around harvesters, Naomi snatched up their leashes and pulled them off the thing as it twitched in death.

"Remind me to never get on the bad side of your cats," Boisson said with awed admiration. "I have a feeling that as soon as word gets out that cats are perfect harvester detectors, they're going to become more valuable than gold."

"I just pray it won't come to that," Naomi said as she took a moment to pet the cats, but nothing she could do would calm them. Koshka was still growling, and Alexander snapped at her.

The agent who'd been carrying the larva specimen picked up his burden again. He'd set it down when Boisson had given the order to fire so he could add his weapon to the mix. Now he was back to being a pack mule. "I hope the choppers get here soon."

They set out again, moving as quickly as they could, crossing the hedge-filled median that separated the mall and race track parking lots.

The latter was completely empty, and Boisson brought them to a halt halfway across. Keying her microphone, she called to ask what was holding up the helicopter.

Naomi watched the agent's expression darken.

"This is a priority mission, damn it!" Boisson snarled. She listened for a moment more, then said, "Understood. Out." She turned angry eyes on Naomi. "The helo's been delayed for at least half an hour."

"Why?"

"They didn't say, other than to inform me that all available aircraft are on 'higher priority missions.' I personally can't think of anything that's a higher priority. Shit."

Naomi looked around them. While the vast, empty parking lot gave them a clear view and field of fire in every direction, it also made her feel terribly small.

On a whim, she asked Boisson, "Have you tried your cell phone?"

"No, I haven't." Boisson took it out and tried to make a call. "Just a busy signal. The network is probably saturated." She shoved the phone back into her pocket. "Damn it! I feel like we're sitting ducks out here."

They waited. There wasn't anything else they could do.

After a while, Naomi was able to calm down Alexander and Koshka. They relaxed slightly, but remained uptight: the larval harvester in the jar was still too close, setting off their internal alarms. "You poor baby," she murmured as she checked Alexander's paws. He was limping badly now from the torn skin on the pads of his rear feet.

"There's a helo," one of the agents said, pointing.

A pair of helicopters were flying in formation, with two more pairs flying behind, all from the southeast.

"Those are Marine Cobras," Boisson said. "Must be out of Pendleton."

The first pair of helicopters broke away and began slowly circling maybe two kilometers away, while the others continued to the northwest toward Pasadena.

"I wonder what they're doing?"

The 20-millimeter gatling guns in the noses of the Cobras thrummed. What looked like solid streams of shells briefly connected the attack helicopters with the ground as smoke streamed behind them and falling shell casings glittered in the sunlight.

The two gunships continued to circle, periodically spitting brief gouts of fire at the ground.

"It'd be nice to have them watching our asses," one of the other agents said.

"Yeah." Boisson called the mission controller again. She cursed when she ended the call. "More delays." She looked at Naomi. "At least another half hour. We may have to think about hoofing it back to the SUVs and joining the great unwashed sitting in traffic."

Naomi thought for a moment. "Is there a way they could patch me through from the radio to FBI Headquarters?"

"You going to try Assistant Director Richards?"

"No. Somebody who's got a lot more pull: his girlfriend."

* * *

Renee had suddenly found herself the head of a team in the FBI's Intelligence Division. On paper she was a "senior consultant," because as a contractor she couldn't actually be in charge of FBI employees. But in reality, everyone was looking to her for answers and leadership. It was a very uncomfortable position and one that she didn't care for, but with the world flying to pieces, it was a burden she decided that she'd have to bear.

The worst part was that she'd had to spend more and more time in meetings trying to explain things to other people at Homeland Security, Department of Defense, and the various agencies of the Intelligence Community, rather than actually doing analytic work. It was frustrating to be away from her beloved computer, and trying to be a good "people person" with some of the idiots she had to deal with was increasingly difficult.

This meeting was a good example. It was her third today, and had already gone on for an hour, on top of the drive she'd had to make here to the Central Intelligence Agency in Langley, Virginia. This was an inter-agency analytic working group, and there were nearly forty people packed into a conference room that might have comfortably held twenty-five. Most of the meeting had involved half a dozen analysts from different agencies presenting briefings on what they thought was happening, much of it based on outdated information (Renee now considered anything more than a few hours old as outdated), with Renee correcting them. Gently, of course. Respectfully, of course. And all the while grinding her teeth with frustration, wondering about what was happening *now* back at her desk in the Hoover Building.

One of the phones on the wall rang. There were two: one was an outside line, the other was a secure phone for classified discussions. The one ringing was the secure phone.

One of the CIA analysts reached over her shoulder and answered it, while Renee tried to focus her attention on a point one of the imagery analysts was making about what was happening in southern China.

"Renee," the woman said, puzzled. "It's for you."

"Me? Oh, joy." Renee got up and side-stepped through the close-packed chairs. She was seated near the front of the room, and the phone, of course, was near the back where the door was. "Sorry."

She took the phone from the young woman with a nod of thanks. "Renee Vintner."

"Ms. Vintner, this is the FBI watch center. We have an incoming emergency call for you. Stand by."

"Okay." Renee held her breath, wondering what this could be about.

"Renee, it's Naomi."

Renee could barely recognize Naomi's voice, it was so distorted. "Naomi? Where the hell are you? Are you okay?"

The other analysts in the room suddenly fell quiet. All of them knew by now who Naomi and Jack were, and they listened intently to Renee's part of the conversation, wishing they could hear Naomi's, as well.

"No, I'm not. We're trapped in LA at the Santa Anita mall. We captured a harvester larva that we need to get to SEAL for analysis, but the FBI can't send in any helicopters to get us out. Even headquarters isn't sure what's going on, but I think most of the helos are probably trying to evacuate civilians in the hardest-hit areas. Getting out by car or on foot isn't an option." Her transmission broke up for a moment. "The harvesters must have a phenomenal reproductive rate. They're all over the place, and it's only a matter of time before we're overrun. We need a ride. Fast."

Renee could tell that Naomi was scared, and she had every right to be. "Okay, how can I get in touch with you?"

"The watch center at headquarters can patch through to us on the radio. That's what they're doing now. It's that or carrier pigeon. The cell network here is down and none of us have satellite phones."

"Got it. Hang in there, hon. Help's on the way."

"Hurry, Renee. We don't have much time."

The line went dead.

Turning back to the analysts in the room, Renee said, "Does anybody in this joint have an internet terminal I can borrow?"

CHAPTER TWENTY-EIGHT

After turning around and heading south, away from Lipetsk, Khatuna did as Mikhailov instructed, gradually descending until they were literally at treetop level. Jack had noted with growing dismay that they were actually flying below the trees in most places. He knew he should be strapped into one of the seats in the cargo compartment, but morbid fascination kept him in the cockpit, his hands locked in a death grip on the back of the pilot's and copilot's seats.

"Jesus Christ!" He yelped as the plane zoomed over a line of trees, the tops centimeters from the landing gear, only to drop back down on the other side, Khatuna pulling the nose up at the very last second before the plane could smash itself against the ground.

But instead of facing more frozen fields, they were now flying above a small meandering river maybe a hundred meters wide, with trees lining both sides.

"Good," Mikhailov said. "This should shield us from their radar."

Jack gave him a sour look. "I have a hard time believing that this is going to be that easy."

"I never said it would be easy. Possible, perhaps, but not easy." He looked up at Jack. "Have you ever heard of Mathias Rust?"

"No, can't say that I have," Jack told him.

Khatuna glanced at Mikhailov, curious.

"He was a West German who flew a small civilian plane from Finland through our air defenses to land in Moscow on a bridge just outside of Red Square, back in the late nineteen eighties. The air defense forces could have shot him down several times, but they also lost track of him, and he was not trying to avoid them. Confusion and hesitation were his allies, but there were also clearly major gaps in radar coverage. Much of that was fixed afterward, but I suspect much was not."

"And you think that's going to get us through to Moscow?"

"If Khatuna can keep us from hitting the ground, I think perhaps, yes."

Khatuna snorted. "I fly like this for my work every day."

"I think you're nuts," Jack said. "We should just land and try to find someone who can get us to Moscow."

"I will trust no one but VDV command with you, Jack," Mikhailov told him. "Several of our senior officers know all of what happened on Spitsbergen. Most of them did not believe it, but they know, and they will believe it now. They also know your situation, and I think will take proper care of you. Do you even have your passport and visa with you?"

Jack felt his gut tighten. "Shit! No, I don't. I left them in my civilian clothes back at Stavropol." He frowned. "I didn't expect we wouldn't be returning there."

Mikhailov nodded. "And you were on the base without proper written authorization. So. An American in VDV uniform, covered in mud, blood, and other unspeakable things, who has engaged in combat on Russian soil, appears before uninformed authorities without papers. And did I forget to mention he has just come from south of the quarantine line? What do you think will be their reaction?"

"The gulag, I suppose."

"Not quite so dramatic, but at best you will be lost in a giant knot of bureaucracy that could take weeks to unravel. At worst you will be arrested and deported back to the south, along with Khatuna and myself."

"I am not going back," Khatuna spat as she pulled the plane into a sharp bank to the right. Jack's eyes bulged as he watched out Mikhailov's window and saw the right wingtip nearly brush the white surface of the frozen river before she leveled out again. "Not ever."

"So it's the Mathias Rust plan, then," Jack said, holding tight as Khatuna made a sharp turn to the left this time.

"Yes, but first we need fuel." He looked at the map for a moment, then turned to Khatuna. "Zadonsk is just ahead. The M-4 highway runs just south of it. There!"

As Khatuna brought the An-2 out of another left turn, far more gentle this time, there was a highway bridge just ahead, maybe a kilometer away, spanning the river. She brought the old biplane up, and Jack breathed a sigh of relief as they climbed away from the disturbingly close ground below.

All three of them looked around for anything that looked like a gas stop as Khatuna flew over the bridge, then turned west to parallel the highway.

"There!" She pointed to a pair of nearly identical structures on each side of the divided highway, about half a kilometer west of the river. A couple of trucks and cars were stopped there, and Jack could make out what looked like fueling islands.

"I hate to ask," Jack said, "but are they going to have the right kind of gas for this thing?"

Khatuna shook her head as she circled over the truck stops, then headed back the way they had come, toward the river. "Not the best kind, which is one hundred octane. But they will have premium, you call it? That will do. You need to strap in now, Jack."

"Oh, shit." Jack stepped down from the cockpit and strapped himself into the nearest seat just before Khatuna banked the plane hard to the left, nearly standing it on its wingtip. That's when he realized that she was going to land the old crate on the highway.

As the plane leveled out, he got the queasy sensation in his stomach that was familiar to all air travelers as the plane slowed, the nose coming up slightly even as the An-2 dropped more quickly toward the ground. The engine noise fell off to a quiet thrum except for a few times when Khatuna nudged the throttle to adjust the rate of descent.

With a brief squeak of rubber on asphalt, the main wheels kissed the highway, and Khatuna eased the tail down until the plane was fully on the ground. Jack had expected her to slam the plane down in an imitation of a carrier landing, but was glad to be disappointed.

They taxied for a couple minutes before Khatuna swung the tail around and killed the engine.

"Jack," Mikhailov called. "Do you still have your pistol?"

"Yes, but it's empty." Jack unstrapped and stood up, stepping aside as Khatuna climbed down from the cockpit.

"Take it along, just for show. Keep it in your holster, but make sure everyone outside can see it." Mikhailov grimaced as he clutched his chest. "You will have to pretend to be nasty VDV officer requisitioning this plane and fuel to fly it. Khatuna will do the talking. Just look like you will shoot anyone who argues with her."

"Jesus, Sergei."

Khatuna passed by him and opened a door at the tail of the cargo compartment. Leaning inside, she dug around for a moment, then stood up with a heavy coil of thick rubber hose. "Here." She handed it to him, and he was hit with the smell of gasoline. "Hoses from pumps cannot reach. We must use this. Many planes like this have hoses for refueling in, how do you call it, remote places."

Then she swung open the passenger door and hopped nimbly to the ground in front of a dozen curious onlookers.

Jack jumped down, nearly losing his balance when he landed. *Doing a face plant right now wouldn't be so great*, he thought as he recovered. He sucked in his breath. It was cold, a lot colder than it had been down south.

Khatuna was speaking in rapid-fire Russian, and two men, whom Jack took to be workers at the station, were exchanging disbelieving looks. Then they began arguing with her.

Jack stepped up next to Khatuna, shifting the heavy hose to expose the Desert Eagle under his left arm. Unable to help themselves, the two men who'd been arguing with her gawked at him. He saw their eyes take in the blood stains, gore, and mud, the rips and tears in the fabric. Then they looked at his face, and he didn't have to work hard to put on an expression that gave them pause. He'd been through a lot in the last few days, and the last thing he was going to deal with now was crap from this motley crew.

After a moment, the two returned their attention to Khatuna and mumbled something. With a curt nod, she turned and took one end of the hose from Jack, while one of the two men took the rest of it. While Khatuna connected her end to the plane, the man took his end to where the fuel tank fill caps were. Dropping the hose, he opened one of the caps, unscrewed something inside, then dropped in the hose.

Khatuna climbed inside the plane, and Jack heard a hum from inside the aircraft. The hose twitched as fuel began to flow into the An-2's dry tanks.

His role in their little play concluded, Jack stepped close to the cockpit, making sure to keep clear of the still-hot engine.

Khatuna slid the side window back and leaned out.

"I'm going to try to call home," he told her.

She nodded, then turned away. Jack could hear Mikhailov saying something. "Sergei says do not talk too long. And keep watch for *politsiya*."

"Yeah, good idea." Jack stepped under the plane to the side opposite the people who continued to point and jabber about the plane. Pulling out his phone, he breathed a sigh of relief to see that, although the battery was low, it was still working. He dialed Naomi's number.

"We're sorry," a recorded female voice told him after a few rings. "That number is currently unavailable."

"Shit." He tried again, but got the same recording. Then he dialed Renee's number.

After two rings he heard her voice. "I'm sorry, hon, but you're going to have to leave a message. I'll ring you back as soon as I can. Leave a message at the beep."

"Dammit," he hissed. He hit the end call button. He didn't want to waste the little bit of battery power he had left leaving a message.

That left only one choice. He dialed the number for Richards' cell phone.

He answered on the first ring. "Dawson! Where the blazes are you?"

"I'm in Russia with Mikhailov, trying to make our way to Moscow. Listen, we've got to make this quick. My phone's about ready to die."

"Understood. Status?"

"Things are going to hell fast here, Carl. Last night I jumped into a village in southern Russia with half a battalion of Russian paratroopers. They were all wiped out in the fight. And it wasn't just that village: the harvesters have spread like wildfire through the Caucasus region, causing hell all over the place, especially at military facilities, and the government's declared a quarantine line along the Don and Volga rivers. They're turning back planes, even threatening to shoot them down."

"You jumped in with Russian paratroopers? You're insane, Dawson." Jack could imagine Richards shaking his bald head in disbelief. "But thanks for the tip on the quarantine. We hadn't heard that from our intel people, yet."

"When you do, believe it. And if things are moving this fast here, India's going to be just as bad, maybe worse." India was a lot more densely populated than Russia. *More food for the harvesters,* he thought darkly.

"That's not the worst," Richards told him. "LA's been hit, Dawson. It's a war zone out there, and we're doing everything we can to keep those damn things from spreading."

Jack felt as if someone had just punched him in the gut. "Naomi?"

Richards was silent for a moment. "She's in the field. We're trying to get her out."

Leaning back against the cold metal skin of the plane, Jack said, "Christ, Carl. What the devil was she doing?"

"Her job, Dawson. Just like you and the rest of us. There aren't any sideliners in this one, not anymore." He paused. "Listen, if it's any consolation, she's with a team led by one of our best. You remember Boisson, don't you?"

"Angie Boisson? Yeah, she was on the Bronsky case, wasn't she?" Jack recalled the tough African-American woman who'd been in the shootout that was the finale of the multi-state killing spree by the murderous Bronsky brothers. When the FBI had sprung the trap that Jack had helped lay, Boisson had taken two rounds to the chest. Her body armor had stopped the slugs, but Jack knew that getting hit like that was an extremely painful experience that you didn't just shrug off. But Boisson did. Ignoring the pain, she got back to her feet, grabbed up her weapon, and continued blazing away at the bad guys, and was credited with the killing shot for one of the two murderers.

"Yeah, the same. She'll get Naomi out of there. You just need to stay focused on getting yourself home. Don't let the Russians screw with you."

"That's the trick," Jack told him. "I don't have my passport or visa, and we're escapees from the quarantine zone. Mikhailov's trying to get us to his superiors." He glanced up at the An-2 looming over him. "And let's just say that we're taking an unconventional mode of transportation."

"I'm not even going to ask. I'll tell the embassy people about you losing your passport. Dumb-ass."

"Tell me about it." He glanced at his phone. "I'm about out of juice. I'll call you back when I can."

"Take care of yourself," Richards told him. "And don't worry about Naomi. We'll get her out of there."

"Right." Jack hung up, not feeling at all reassured. He knew that whatever Naomi was doing must have been necessary, and he told himself not to worry himself sick over her. *She's a big girl and can take care of herself.* And he knew that it was true. That thought helped, at least a little.

He looked up as Mikhailov slid open his window and poked his head out. "Jack, get in here. We've got trouble."

* * *

"What is it?" Jack was again standing in the cockpit behind Mikhailov and Khatuna.

Mikhailov had his cell phone to his ear and held up his hand for Jack to be quiet as he listened. His eyes met Jack's, and he shook his head slowly.

"*Da*," Mikhailov said. Then he spoke some more in Russian. He listened again, then hung up and put the phone back inside his tunic.

Khatuna looked frightened.

"Now what?"

"That was my division commander in Pskov. You are now a wanted man, Jack. The FSB, what I think you translate as Federal Security Service, which is actually a new name for the old KGB, thinks you brought the infection here."

"*What?*"

"Do not shoot the messenger, please. They have issued orders to all police and military forces that you are to be arrested. And if you resist, you are to be shot." He winced. Talking was becoming more and more of an effort. "Apparently some in the FSB do not believe the American government's revisionist history, resurrecting you as a 'good guy' from your earlier status as a murderer and terrorist last year."

"And the fact that the outbreak at the facility where you were first ambushed happened before I arrived here obviously eluded them," Jack said bitterly.

"They are paranoid, faced with a disaster they cannot begin to comprehend," Mikhailov told him. "Blaming disasters on a scapegoat is a very old game, my friend."

"How did they even know Jack is involved?" Khatuna asked.

"Colonel Zaitsev informed VDV Headquarters that Jack was with us, and that he was a valuable source of information that must be protected. The FSB has ears everywhere, even in the VDV." He frowned. "I suspect my division commander will be arrested for helping us."

"Why did he?" Jack was curious. "Why didn't he follow orders? They could've just waited for us to appear and then clapped me in irons."

"I think because he realizes that you can help us, and that if the FSB gets you, it will not be a good thing for our country."

Jack sucked a breath of air in through his teeth. "What do we do now? We can't just waltz into Moscow to VDV Headquarters, and there's no way I'd be able to get to the American Embassy or a consulate anywhere; they'll be covered by FSB surveillance. And this crate won't get us out of Russian territory."

"This plane could get to Ukraine or Belarus," Khatuna told him defensively. Jack realized that she really loved the old Antonov.

"That will not help," Mikhailov said. "If they have not already, they will soon close their borders, and they still have deep ties to FSB. They may not turn you over, but they will probably hold you for interrogation. Perhaps for a long time." He shook his head. "None of the former Soviet Republics will be safe. We need to get you to a NATO country."

"What about the Baltic states? Aren't Estonia, Latvia, and Lithuania in NATO now?"

Mikhailov snorted. "Yes, but we could only reach either Estonia or Latvia; we would have to cross over Belarus to reach Lithuania. True, they are NATO members, but do you really wish to trust yourself against the FSB backed by Russian military forces in either of those countries, where they have maybe ten thousand men, combined, in their active defense forces? And Finland is not a NATO country. They have no love for us, but you would likely be swallowed for some time there, too. Quarantined, if nothing else."

Jack scowled at him. "Well, Sergei, you're not leaving us with a lot of choices. We can't go east, because that's just more of Russia until we get to China, which is probably also in the shitter by now. We can't go south. We can't go west. With the Baltic countries and Finland out of the running, the only country that's left is..." Jack paused as the light bulb went off in his head.

"*Da.*" Mikhailov nodded, his blood-streaked lips curling up in a smile. "Norway."

CHAPTER TWENTY-NINE

"I don't like this."

Naomi looked up from her study of the larval harvester in the carboy to see Boisson staring at the racetrack and stables to the north of the mall. The horrid cries of the animals there had finally stopped. Now, from that direction, there was only silence that was in marked contrast to the sounds of panic and chaos coming from the other points of the compass.

The worst was from the hospital complex just east of the racetrack parking lot where the team had been huddling for the last half hour. There had been a steady stream of ambulances coming in, trying to push their way through a crowd of hundreds of people, all trying to get into the emergency room.

But about fifteen minutes ago, there had been a sudden flurry of shots fired, and since then there had been nothing but panicked screams, even as more ambulances arrived.

Naomi could only guess, but she had no doubt that at least some of the people who'd been taken there had been attacked by larval harvesters. She shivered as she watched the oozing thing in the big glass jar, imagining what a nightmare the hospital's emergency room must be now. Beyond that, there were probably casualties now among the hospital's staff, doctors and nurses who had been attacked by the creeping horrors as they'd fought to save their dying patients.

"I doubt we'll have to worry about any threats from the hospital," she said, turning her attention away from the larva and getting back to her feet. "The harvesters will congregate there as long as there's a food supply."

"I don't mean that." Boisson pointed to the stables. Several harvesters had appeared, running headlong away from the stables. "That."

Everyone tensed, watching the creatures as they bolted across the huge parking lot. A couple were heading in their general direction, but the others weren't. They were heading in random directions, anywhere that took them away from the stables.

"It looks like they're trying to get away from something."

Naomi forgot whatever else she'd planned to say as a flood of harvesters, dozens of them, came out of the stable area across the parking lot. She watched in fascination as one of them stumbled, then fell to writhe on the ground. She tapped Boisson on the arm. "Can I borrow your binoculars?"

Boisson reached into a pouch and pulled out her Pioneer binoculars and handed them to Naomi.

Putting them up to her eyes, Naomi stared in rapt fascination at the downed harvester. It took her a moment to understand what she was seeing. In their natural form, the harvesters tended to gather their malleable flesh around the torso, which in part gave rise to their quasi-cockroach appearance. This one had that, but had more wrapped around one of its arms, and that arm was clearly quite a bit shorter than the other one. "My God! It's being attacked by one of the larval forms!"

"Cannibals? Now there's a pleasant surprise."

Naomi wasn't sure if she should be surprised or not. This was their first insight into how the larval forms and the adults interacted. It looked like a little bit of good news for a change.

"There goes another." Boisson pointed to another creature that tumbled to the pavement, maybe twenty yards from where the first had gone down. "Oh, Jesus!"

They saw what the adult harvesters, of which there must have been hundreds now, were fleeing from across the expanse of the parking lot.

Naomi swiveled the binoculars to the left, toward where the stables were, and gasped. There was a line of larvae advancing across the parking lot. Unlike the specimen they'd captured, or even the one that had dropped from the upper floor of the mall when Garcia had pushed her out of the way, these were huge. They were, literally, each as big as a horse. Some were larger.

As she watched, she saw that some still hadn't fully digested their most recent victims. A horse's leg rose up, as if begging for help, from the mass of one of the biggest larvae as it rolled across the parking lot. It slowly disappeared, sinking into the bruised-looking mass of tissue.

"Naomi."

Naomi couldn't speak. She was both fascinated and repelled by what she was seeing.

"Naomi!"

"What?" Naomi lowered her binoculars and looked at the team's leader.

"I think we'd better get going," Boisson told her in a tight voice. "Maybe you didn't notice, but we have an awful lot of company heading our way."

Looking back to the north, seeing the entire view rather than just the narrow perspective provided by the binoculars, a chill ran through Naomi as she saw just how many harvesters were fleeing right toward them.

Boisson called out to the men and women on the team. "Make a line in front of us with the lighter fluid, but don't light it yet! Carson," she said to the agent holding the larva, "set that damn thing down about twenty meters behind us, then get on the firing line. Doctor, you stick with me."

Then she keyed her radio. Naomi noted that it took her several tries to reach the LA ops center this time.

"This is Boisson. Yes, we're still at the fucking mall. I know you can't send evac yet, but there's a pair of Marine Cobras working over some positions one or two kilometers to the south of our position. I want at least one of them up here to cover us." She listened for a moment, and Naomi could see her face go rigid with anger. "Get me the SAC. Now."

To Naomi, she rasped, "Those stupid fools are going to get us killed. Not only do they not have any choppers available to pick us up, but the LA FBI building was attacked by rioters and the mobile command post doesn't have any communications with the local military commands. Christ, what a fuckup. Hang on." She listened a moment. "Yes, sir, this is Boisson. No, there's been no evac. We were told that no choppers are available for at least another half hour. We've got an army of these monsters coming right for us, and there's a pair of Marine Cobras just to our south."

By Naomi's guess, the closest harvesters were maybe a hundred and fifty meters away. She turned around to look at the helicopters, which were still circling. *So close*, she thought.

Boisson nodded at whatever the SAC on the other end of the radio was saying, but her expression told Naomi that it wasn't good news. "Yes, sir. Understood." Keying off the mic, she looked at Naomi. "He's going to do what he can, but I think the only way we're going to get out of this is on our own."

Taking a quick look at the approaching harvesters, she reached into her combat vest and pulled out a flare. "Get ready! Try to knock some down close to us. We'll set fire to them and maybe that'll help keep the others away."

Naomi knelt down, gathering the cats close to her. They seemed to be overwhelmed by terror now, knowing that so many harvesters were close. She tied their leashes to her web belt so she could have her hands free for the shotgun. Boisson had positioned her behind the defensive line of FBI agents, but that hardly meant she was safe. And ten or so meters behind her sat the glass carboy with its precious, horrible contents.

"Steady." Boisson held her assault rifle in one hand and a lighter in the other. She stepped forward and knelt down to the pitiful stream of lighter fluid that was all that separated her team from the oncoming horde of apparitions. "Steady."

When the closest of the creatures was a mere ten meters away, she ignited the lighter fluid and jumped back. "Fire!"

As her team opened fire, she turned and slammed her fist against the base of the flare, launching it in the direction of the Cobras orbiting to the south. Naomi saw her mouth something, maybe a silent prayer that the Marines would see the dazzling red ball that soared toward them. A red flare. *Send help.*

"Back up!" At Boisson's order, the agents began to slowly move back, away from the sputtering line of burning lighter fluid.

Harvesters went down under the barrage of fire, and just as Boisson had hoped, several of them skittered or stumbled forward into the burning lighter fluid and exploded into flames. Other harvesters, unable to stop in time, tried to leap over. Some made it, only to be blasted to pieces by the concentrated fire from the FBI agents. Others didn't, and they joined their brethren in flames.

In no time at all, the pitiful line of lighter fluid had been transformed into a conflagration, with flames reaching a dozen or more meters into the sky. The agents had to move back, away from the blistering heat.

"Spray more fluid on our flanks!" The harvesters were now streaming around them. Most were keeping well away from the flames, but Boisson wasn't taking any chances.

"I'm out!" One of the agents tossed away his empty can of lighter fluid and raised his rifle toward a harvester passing close by. He didn't see the one that skittered perilously close to the fire. It stabbed him in the neck, just above his armor, with its stinger in passing, just before two of the other agents blasted the creature in the torso, knocking it down.

Naomi held her fire, mainly because of the cats. They howled in fear at the roar of the guns, the crackling heat of the creatures now burning on three sides of them, and the sense of harvesters all around them. Alexander panicked, but instead of bolting away, he clawed his way up her leg. She cried out in pain, but let him go. She wasn't about to try to pull him off in the middle of a firefight, not that she'd be able to, anyway. There was nothing else she could do.

He climbed up her back, where his claws found purchase on her web gear, but couldn't sink through her body armor. With his front claws lodged in the web gear over one shoulder, his muzzle was right next to her ear, and his pitiful cries joined the maelstrom of noise around them.

Koshka, not about to be left alone, followed her feline companion, lodging herself on Naomi's back next to Alexander.

Making a decision, Naomi undid their leashes from her belt. If she went down, at least the cats would have a chance at survival on their own. She wouldn't doom them to die because they couldn't escape the anchor of their dead mistress.

Three harvesters leaped over the flames on one side. Four agents went down under them in a ferocious melee of whipping tails, slashing claws, and automatic weapons fire.

Naomi stepped forward with her shotgun and blasted one of the harvesters in the head while two of the agents pinned it down. One of the other creatures leaped to its feet and ran off after decapitating another agent. Naomi dropped it with two rounds from her weapon. The third harvester twitched and died after another agent stuck the muzzle of her shotgun in its gut and pulled the trigger.

Grabbing the woman under the arm, Naomi pulled her to her feet as the other two agents scrabbled away from the still-twitching harvester.

"Thanks," the woman gasped.

As bright and hot as the harvester bodies burned, they didn't burn long. Already their protective wall of fire was guttering, dying out.

Naomi froze as she saw one of the enormous larvae pass by. The smaller ones couldn't move very quickly, but the relative speed of which the things were capable seemed to increase with size. Naomi could easily escape one, but she'd have to move at a brisk trot to do so.

Boisson stood beside her, watching the thing glide past. "Holy shit."

They both heard a sound, a loud, deep hum. The giant larva rippled, then exploded. Burning chunks of it were sent skyward in all directions as the main body caught fire.

Naomi looked up to see one of the Marine Corps SuperCobras coming up fast from the south. The sound she'd heard was the gunship's twenty millimeter triple-barrel gatling cannon. It fired again, blasting another larva that she couldn't see.

That's when she remembered the bits of the first creature now arcing down all around them. "*Don't let any of it touch you!*" She shouted out the warning again, pointing up at the bits of what looked like flaming bacon grease.

Boisson and most of the other agents looked up, horrified expressions on their faces as the gunship continued to fire at targets all around them.

Naomi screamed again, trying to warn the agent that had carried the carboy. He looked up in time to catch a fist-sized piece of the giant larva square on the face below his helmet. Dropping his weapon, he put his hands to his face and fell to his knees, writhing.

Then she was flying through the air, landing hard on her chest. Her chin and the end of her nose banged into the asphalt. The brim of her helmet saved the rest of her face from the impact.

Dazed, she rolled over on her side to look back. A piece of the giant larva, as large as Alexander, had landed right where she'd been standing. It was on fire, but was rolling around, as if still looking for more prey.

On the far side of it stood Boisson. She'd pushed Naomi clear.

"That's the second time one of those bastards has tried to fall on me," Naomi said to Alexander through his non-stop cries. "I think I'm a bit sick of them doing that."

Boisson helped her back to her feet, weighed down by over thirty pounds of terrified felines in addition to her combat gear.

Now both of the Marine gunships that had been to the south were circling over them, firing non-stop. One of them hovered for a moment, and with a *whoosh* fired several rockets back toward the stables. Then it fired more. The southeastern end of the stables disappeared in the resulting explosions as the rockets hit, sending a shower of wood and metal into the air.

"I'm out!" One of the agents nearby tossed his rifle to the ground. While they had come armed with heavy weapons, they hadn't planned to take along enough ammunition for a full-up firefight.

Naomi handed the man her shotgun, then took the ammunition out of her pouches and stuffed the shells into his.

She backed up next to Boisson, feeling utterly naked without anything more powerful than the Glock 23 that she pulled from the holster strapped to her thigh.

One of the Cobras fired again. Then it came down low and hovered where they could see the pilot and the gunner. The gunner pointed to the nose where the cannon was, then ran his finger across his throat.

"Looks like we're not the only ones running dry," Boisson shouted.

"No," Naomi breathed as the helicopter pulled up and turned away. The other Cobra turned to join up with it. "Oh, no."

"Come on," Boisson said. "We've got to move."

While most of the adult harvesters had moved past, the bulk of the larvae, large and small, were coming right for them, converging. The clinical part of Naomi's mind wondered how they could possibly sense anything, as they seemed to be made up of nothing more than a variant of the harvester's malleable flesh. But they clearly could. The larva in the jar, which miraculously still stood, undisturbed, had proved that. Even now, it was plastered against the side of the carboy that faced her and the others, trying to get at them.

"Great. Adults ahead of us, larvae behind."

"Yeah, and the big ones are fast." Boisson gestured for one of the surviving agents who had run out of ammo to pick up the carboy. Grimacing, the man knelt down and cradled the thing to his chest, then followed Naomi and Boisson as they began trotting south across the parking lot toward Huntington Drive.

They quickly discovered that while the harvesters had learned to fear their own children, the humans were still nothing more than food. Two of the things attacked, killing another agent before they were brought down.

Now, the only thing the FBI agents had were their pistols.

Boisson cursed. "We should've brought more hair spray."

More of the harvesters slowed, then turned to watch the humans. There was a ring of the creatures now, hemming in the team as the larvae continued to approach from behind.

"Shit," Boisson breathed. "We're trapped."

She was right, Naomi knew. They were caught in a vice. "Dammit," she whispered. She reached up and scratched Alexander behind the ears, wishing she could do the same for Koshka, who continued to cling to her back. She raised the muzzle of her pistol, pointing it over her shoulder, just under the big cat's chin. There was no way the cats could escape, and she wouldn't let them suffer.

Beside her, Boisson nodded.

Naomi's finger was just applying pressure to the trigger, squeezing it gently as Alexander rubbed his muzzle against her neck when she heard the sound of an approaching helicopter.

Easing her finger off the trigger, she looked to the west and saw a bright blue Bell 412, larger than the Marine gunships, zoom over the mall. It was flying so low that there couldn't have been more than a few inches between the tops of the air conditioning units and the aircraft's skids. It flew over the parking lot where they'd been, then suddenly banked to the right, heading right toward them, coming in low over the larvae converging on what was left of the team. The doors on both sides slid open, and a man in combat gear and wearing a flight helmet, supported by a safety harness, stepped out onto the skid on the starboard side. In his hands was a machine gun.

"Let's go!" Boisson pushed Naomi toward the helicopter as the skids brushed the pavement. Glancing over her shoulder, Naomi saw that the harvesters had decided that it was time to play again. As one, they were rushing the helicopter.

The door gunner opened fire, sending a solid stream of tracers just inches over the heads of the agents and Naomi as they ran toward the helicopter.

Boisson shoved Naomi in first, then the agent carrying the carboy gingerly handed it up before climbing in after it.

Naomi turned to help the other agents in, noticing how accurate the fire from the door gunner was. It seemed like every round the man fired hit one of the harvesters. Like inflammable marionettes, they danced in a costume of flames before they collapsed to the pavement.

As the last agent was hauled aboard, the helicopter lifted away. The man on the machine gun continued to fire until the harvesters were out of range.

Someone thrust a headset into Naomi's hands, and she pulled it on while two of the other agents tried to pry the cats off her back.

"Jesus Christ, girl!" The voice was familiar, and belonged to someone she'd known well, although she hadn't spoken to him in almost a year. "Why is it that every time I haul your ass around the sky, something's either blowing up or somebody's shooting at us?"

"Al?" She nearly burst into tears, she was so relieved. "Al Ferris?"

"Who else do you think would be stupid enough to land in the middle of a bunch of monsters?"

Pushing herself out of her seat, she leaned forward against the pilot's seat and wrapped her arms around the older man, hugging him tight. "Oh, God, Al."

"Take it easy, kid." Ferris, a retired and highly decorated veteran of Combat Search and Rescue, had been the main pilot for the Earth Defense Society. Even though Naomi had been his boss, he'd always been like a gruff but loving uncle. "It's damn good to see you. But I'm getting too old for this shit."

"How did you know to come for us?"

"Renee called me," he explained as he pointed the helicopter to the east. The nose dipped as it picked up speed. "She told me that if I didn't pick you up, she'd never make me any more of those meatballs of hers. Couldn't have that." He jabbed a thumb back toward the man who was still manning the door gun. "Hathcock got hired as a security weenie, 'cause he's too dumb to fly."

Naomi turned to look at the door gunner. He raised his visor and gave her a thumbs up and a smile. It was Craig Hathcock, one of the hired guns that had been with the EDS and a world-class sniper. "Good to have you back, Naomi."

"Thanks for the cover, Craig," she told him. "You saved our asses."

"All in a day's work." He smiled again, then turned his attention back to the ground below. They were flying at well over a thousand feet now and still climbing, so the harvesters were no direct threat, but his job was protecting the helicopter, so he kept his eyes and the muzzle of the machine gun pointed outside the ship.

Naomi was still confused. "But where did you come from?"

"Unlike you, kid, I had to find a real job after the EDS got burned. This rich guy heard about what a hotshot pilot I was and offered to hire me as his personal aerial chauffeur. Who knows, you might even know him." He nodded toward the copilot's seat.

Both Naomi and Boisson looked at the copilot, who happened to be wearing a very expensive suit. Turning toward them, he raised the dark visor on his helmet to fully expose his face.

It was Howard Morgan.

CHAPTER THIRTY

"Norway?" Khatuna stared at both men as if they had lost their minds. "*Duraki!* Idiots! That must be two thousand kilometers from here. We cannot reach so far."

Jack looked back into the cavernous space in the back of the plane. "How much cargo can this thing carry?"

"A little more than two thousand kilograms."

"And how much fuel?"

"Twelve hundred liters." Khatuna narrowed her eyes. "What are you thinking, Jack?"

"I think I saw some fuel drums behind the station here. What if we get them in here and fill them up with fuel. We should be able to extend our range."

"Not enough." Khatuna shook her head. "We could not carry enough safely to reach Norway. We would still be perhaps three hundred kilometers short. And I doubt we will be so lucky to make another refueling stop like this."

"Then we carry what we need to get where we want to go, Khatuna." Mikhailov coughed, then wiped the blood from his lips. "We have gone well beyond what is merely safe, I think. But we need to act quickly. The authorities will come soon. That will not be good."

"We must get you to hospital." Khatuna put a hand to his chin and lifted his head to get a better look at his face. "Your bleeding is worse."

"I am fine." He closed his hand over hers, gently, then pushed it away. "Now go. Hurry."

Jack led her out of the plane, Khatuna muttering what he knew must be venomous curses. Without a word he pushed through the ring of onlookers and headed toward the rear of the station. Sure enough, there was a stack of fuel drums.

"Each holds two hundred liters." Khatuna rapped her knuckles on one, then another. They were empty. "We will need at least eight, Jack. Nine if we are to have any reserve at all. But that will put us over maximum load of plane."

"What does that mean?" Jack began to roll the first drum toward the plane. The two men who ran the station had come over to see what they were doing, and Jack pointed at them, then at the fuel drums. One of them opened his mouth to protest, and was met by the muzzle of the Desert Eagle, about three inches from his nose. Jack stared at him for a moment, then twitched the gun in the direction of the fuel drums. The men, dark expressions on their faces, moved past him and grabbed a drum each, and Jack shoved the gun back in its holster.

"It means we will probably crash on takeoff, or soon after."

"Then I guess you'll just have to be an ace and fly very carefully." He glanced over his shoulder at her. "You don't have to come with us, Khatuna. But Sergei and I have to do this. We have no choice."

"And who will fly plane? Sergei? He can barely raise his arms!" She cursed again. "Get drums inside, as far forward as you can, and tie them down."

"How many?"

"Ten. If we are going to die, let us die with maybe enough fuel to get there. But you have forgotten one thing."

"What's that?" Jack set the barrel on its side and began rolling it toward the plane.

"We have no way to get fuel from barrels without landing."

"I've got an idea about that."

She shook her head, sending her hair flying in a golden halo around her head. "*Durak*."

* * *

It didn't take long to get the fuel drums aboard, and after raising the flimsy metal seats in the cargo area to make room, Jack lashed them down with the rope he took from the storage compartment in the tail. The drums were packed in tight, with no walkway to reach the cockpit.

Khatuna had to crawl over them to come aft. "Main tanks are full. Now we fill these. Come."

Outside, she disconnected the fuel line from the plane and handed it to Jack. "Put this in first drum. When it is almost full, tell me. We will shut off pump, then move to next drum." She glared at him. "Do not spill fuel in plane."

"Got it."

While Jack hauled his end of the hose into the plane, Khatuna pulled the other end from the underground fuel tank and dragged it over to the premium fuel pump. In Russian, she ordered the two men who now followed her like hyenas, "Turn on the pump."

"And who will pay?" They were very angry now. "Do you know how many rubles this is costing us?"

"You will be reimbursed by the VDV, and given extra as a reward for your cooperation," she said smoothly. "*Kapitan* Mikhailov is keeping careful records of what we are using." Her voice softened slightly. "He is an honorable man on an urgent mission. You will not be cheated."

Mollified somewhat, the two men shrugged. One went back to the office and started the pump while the other continued to keep an eye on her.

She removed the pump handle and laid it on the ground, end to end with the fuel hose. Taking a roll of duct tape that she'd found in a tool box in the plane's rear compartment, she carefully spliced the two together, winding the tape back and forth across the join.

When she was finished, the artificial joint between the pump handle and the hose was solid enough, although she knew it wouldn't be long before it started leaking. Looking up, she saw Jack standing in the door of the plane. He gave her the thumbs up.

She squeezed the pump handle and locked it open. The hose to the plane twitched, and fuel began to flow.

* * *

In the cockpit, Mikhailov stared at his phone, dithering over the next action he knew he had to take. Most of what he had done thus far could have been excused in a military tribunal. At most, he would suffer a reduction in rank, or perhaps dismissal from the service.

But what he was about to do now, especially with his country at war, albeit not in a conventional sense, could very well be considered treason. Assuming he survived, of course.

Like Jack's phone, his was almost out of power, and they had no chargers. He had considered sending Jack and Khatuna into the station to see if there might be one that was compatible, but he could see from his vantage point that the crowd around them was becoming less curious and more apprehensive.

He pushed the call button.

"Hallo?"

"*Kaptein* Halvorsen?"

"*Ja*. Mikhailov, is that you?"

Mikhailov imagined Halvorsen's expression, trying to match it with the shock he heard in his Norwegian counterpart's voice. Terje Halvorsen was a company commander in the Norwegian Army's *Hans Majestet Kongens Garde* (His Majesty the King's Guard) Battalion. The two men had met during the during the battle for the Svalbard seed vault on Spitsbergen the previous year. "Yes, Terje. It is me," Mikhailov said in English. While he could speak some Norwegian, both men were more fluent in English.

"What in the devil is going on there?" He lowered his voice. "You are lucky you called when you did. We have been placed on alert and are getting ready to deploy. An hour later, and I would not have had my phone."

"Terje, I do not have much time to explain." Mikhailov paused, gathering his thoughts. It was becoming more and more difficult to think clearly. "I have Jack Dawson with me. The harvesters, they are back, Terje. And not just a few. There must be thousands, perhaps tens of thousands, in southern Russia and elsewhere. India for certain, and from what Jack heard, probably China, too."

His phone began beeping a low battery warning.

"But why are you calling me?"

"The FSB, our security service, has posted orders to arrest Jack on suspicion that he caused the outbreak here." Halvorsen made a rude sound on the other end of the line. "*Da*. He came to help us, and they want to blame him. He has vital knowledge of these things, as you know, and learned much while here and in India. I am trying to get him out."

"You are trying to come here? Sergei, the border has been closed and all air traffic between Norway and Russia has been suspended."

"That is where you come in, my friend. We will be coming by air and will need clearance."

"I cannot guarantee anything, but I will try. What is your call sign and where will you try to cross?"

"I am not sure where, but our call sign is..."

The phone gave one final beep, then went silent. Mikhailov looked and saw that the display was dark.

Closing his eyes, he stuffed the phone in its pocket and leaned his head back, exhausted.

"It will have to be enough."

* * *

In a cubicle deep inside a three story complex on a side street known as Bol'shoy Kisel'nyy in Moscow, a young woman wearing high-end stereo headphones sat at her computer. She was a linguist of the *Sluzhba spetsial'noy svyazi i informatsii*, the Special Communications and Information Service, or *Spetsvyaz*, of the Russian Federal Protective Service.

Spetsvyaz, the roof of which was festooned with a variety of antenna domes and arrays, was Russia's Signals Intelligence, or SIGINT, organization, the Russian equivalent of the American National Security Agency. The woman and her coworkers were responsible for intercepting, decoding, and translating signals intelligence from communications intercepts, and forwarding that information on to other government agencies and the military for information or, as necessary, action.

She had been pulled from her normal portfolio that morning and put on a special team providing direct support to the FSB in hunting down the American, Jack Dawson, who was involved in the biological disaster rapidly unfolding in southern Russia. She was one of her department's best English linguists, and her selection for this particular job had come as no surprise.

Unfortunately, her queue so far had contained nothing of interest, and she was not alone in her frustration. The team had nothing to go on with Dawson other than his name, photograph, and some background biographical information. The FSB had yet to obtain any more detailed information from his service in the military or FBI, and there was nothing at all for the year that Dawson had gone missing after his reported death.

That left them with no information they could use to find him. The two phone numbers, old ones from when he'd worked for the FBI, they'd fished out from internet searches hadn't turned up any results.

As she finished going through the last intercept, a new one popped to the top of her queue on the computer screen. It was associated with Sergei Mikhailov, now known to be in company with the American. While they had nothing yet that would help find Dawson, they had plenty on Mikhailov. She only wished they would have started searching for him earlier than this morning, when the team was formed.

Hitting a particular key, she ordered the computer to play back the audio, and her skin prickled with excitement as she listened:

"Hallo?"
"*Kaptein* Halvorsen?"
"*Ja*. Mikhailov, is that you?"
"Yes, Terje. It is me."

After she listened through the entire intercept, she stood up and walked quickly to her supervisor's desk. "Norway," she said, breathless. "They are flying to Norway!"

* * *

Jack was growing increasingly impatient. It was taking forever to fill the barrels in the plane. He knew that filling up ten two-hundred liter barrels, more than five hundred and thirty gallons, was going to take a while, but they were running out of time. He knew their landing here must have been reported by someone, probably the two disgruntled station owners, and was surprised that no police or other authorities had arrived yet. He suspected the only thing that had saved them thus far was that Zadonsk was big enough that the story of their arrival hadn't spread to everyone in town yet, but small enough to not have many police out and about.

When the eighth barrel was almost full, he leaned out the doorway and signaled Khatuna to stop the flow.

Waiting for her to give him the thumbs up that she'd released the trigger on the pump handle, he quickly pulled the hose out of that barrel and shoved it into number nine. Then he leaned out and gave her the thumbs up to start again.

He noticed that there was a pool of gas on the concrete near the pump that was growing larger every minute. The tape holding the hose to the nozzle was deteriorating quickly. Khatuna kept moving it so she didn't have to stand in the fuel, but Jack worried about her being so close to it. Many of the people still watching them smoked, and all it would take was a hot ember to light everything off. He could see the fuel on the ground going up, then spreading to the fuel pump and, worse, to the plane.

"Come on, dammit."

Khatuna checked the pump handle, then jogged up to him so she could talk to him without anyone else hearing. She couldn't exactly call out to him in English. That would give just a bit too much away. "How are we to refuel in the air? You said you had idea. Now might be good time."

"Don't worry. The main thing we need to do is get this hose connected back up to the onboard pump like it was when you filled the main tanks."

She looked at him, hands on hips, a frown on her face. "And then?"

"Then I'm going to smash out one of the windows so we can bring the other end of the hose in here and stick it in the barrels."

Shaking her head, she stomped away, cursing under her breath.

"Jack!"

He looked up at Mikhailov's shout. "What is it?"

"We will have company shortly."

Scrambling over the barrels, Jack joined him in the cockpit.

"There." Mikhailov pointed to the east, across the river.

Jack caught sight of a white car and a flashing blue light, then another. They were hard to make out through the trees that lined this side of the river bank near the bridge that carried the M4 highway they'd landed on.

"They are coming from Zadonsk," Mikhailov told them. "They will be here in a few moments."

"Shit."

Jack scrambled back over the barrels and leaned out the door. "Khatuna! We've got to go!"

The people around the plane looked at him in shock, as if he were a three-headed alien. Only then did Jack realize that he'd shouted in English.

Khatuna stopped the pump, then used a pocket knife to slash the remaining tape holding the end of the hose to the pump nozzle. Dragging it back to the plane, fuel spilling out the end, she began to attach it to the external fuel pump.

"I'll do that! Get in the cockpit!" He pulled the end of the hose out of the barrel and tossed it to the ground. The ninth barrel was maybe two-thirds full. The tenth was empty.

It'll have to do, he told himself.

As he jumped down to help Khatuna into the cargo hold, the plane's big four-bladed propeller started turning with a high-pitched whine. Mikhailov was starting the engine, which suddenly coughed into life.

Ignoring the momentary blast of smoke from the exhausts, Jack grabbed one end of the hose and quickly secured it to the external fuel pump's inlet. Grabbing the other end, he clambered onto the plane's lower wing. He twirled one hand in the air and shouted to Khatuna. "Let's go!"

She disappeared inside, and the plane began to taxi back out onto the highway.

While holding onto one of the cross braces supporting the wings, he pulled out his combat knife and used the butt end to smash through one of the round porthole-style windows. Then he pried and chipped away any sharp bits that might have damaged the hose before shoving it inside, taking up as much slack as he could.

Khatuna gunned the engine, and he fell onto the wing, almost losing his grip on the cross brace.

The sudden gust of the prop wash startled some of the people who were gawking, and Jack shouted a warning that was lost in the roar of the engine. He watched as one of the two men who ran the station raised his hand to his face to ward off the dust and dirt kicked up by the propeller, and the cigarette he'd been smoking twirled away to land in the pool of gasoline.

The fuel ignited, and in the blink of an eye the entire island area of the station was engulfed in flames. Fortunately, all the onlookers had been far enough away not to be caught in the maelstrom.

Looking back down the highway toward the bridge, he saw four police cars speeding toward them.

Khatuna obviously saw them, too. Instead of turning that way, which would otherwise have been best for their takeoff run, she swung the plane out onto the highway in the opposite direction, heading west.

Jack immediately saw that there was one minor problem. There was an overpass maybe three hundred meters away. "Shit, shit, shit," he breathed as he held on for dear life to the cross braces. There was no way he could get back into the plane until she stopped. If she stopped. The plane accelerated down the highway toward the overpass. He knew she couldn't hear him, but he couldn't help shouting. "Khatuna, don't even try it!"

Behind them, there was a tremendous explosion as the fuel pumps at the station went up. The police cars screeched to a halt on the far side of the conflagration as burning gasoline and debris were strewn across the highway, which, fortunately, was empty of traffic.

The plane was still heading toward the overpass, beyond which the highway disappeared to the right in a gentle curve. He couldn't imagine what Khatuna was thinking.

She surprised him: the plane suddenly veered to the right, taking the exit from the highway onto the road that passed over the M4. When she reached the end of the ramp, she slowed, then turned the plane onto the road, pointing back toward the overpass, and stopped.

Jack slid to the ground and then leaped into the still-open passenger door.

He dogged the door shut, and Khatuna pushed the throttle forward. The old biplane shook and rattled as the one thousand horsepower Shvetsov radial engine roared. Khatuna held the brakes until the engine's power peaked, then let them go.

The plane began to move, but much slower than Jack had expected. The sight of the fuel drums in the cargo compartment made him understand why. He suddenly hoped they'd be able to get off the ground at all.

As he moved forward toward the cockpit, climbing over the barrels, he glanced out one of the starboard windows. The police cars had crossed over to the other side of the highway and were coming toward them, the few oncoming cars dodging out of the way.

But instead of turning onto the ramp Khatuna had taken, they took the one on the other side of the highway. He could see that it would put them on this road up ahead, on the far side of the overpass the plane was about to cross. They'd be right in the plane's takeoff path.

"They're trying to cut us off!"

"I know!" Khatuna's shout was barely audible against the roar of the engine as the An-2 gradually gained speed up the incline that led to the overpass.

"Are we going to have enough room?"

"I don't know! Shut up and let me fly!"

He held onto the backs of their seats as the plane crested the overpass, then started down the other side, now gaining speed more quickly.

The first of the police cars emerged from behind the line of trees that separated the road from the highway exit. It turned and accelerated fast, right toward them.

Khatuna cursed, but there was nothing she could do.

The plane's tail came up, but Khatuna held the control yoke forward to keep the plane on the ground, trying to build up airspeed.

The other police cars emerged. Two of them parked and blocked the road, while another chased after the first toward them.

"Come on," Jack growled, urging the old plane into the sky. "Come on!"

At the last second, Khatuna hauled back on the wheel, and the overloaded biplane staggered into the sky, the big propeller and main landing gear missing the top of the first police car by a hand's breadth.

Jack saw the police standing by the two blockading cars draw their weapons, and the spark of muzzle flashes were accompanied by several pings as bullets hit the plane.

But what drew his attention was the trees just beyond them. There was a junction where this road narrowed, and on either side was a thick stand of trees that would swat the plane from the sky.

"Khatuna!"

"I know!"

The trees grew larger and larger as the ancient plane clawed for altitude.

"Pull up!"

"I cannot, or we will stall and crash!"

Jack held his breath as the treetops came straight for the windscreen.

Khatuna pulled back ever so slightly on the wheel, easing the nose up. There was a loud boom and the plane shuddered as one of the landing gear whacked into a treetop. Her lips pulled back in a grimace of desperation, Khatuna eased the wheel to the right, turning over a vast open field.

"After having a full bladder and then nearly crashing into the trees, I think I just wet myself."

Jack turned to Mikhailov and chuckled. When he saw that Mikhailov wasn't joking, he couldn't help himself. He burst out laughing.

Khatuna, turning to look, also began to laugh.

"I am glad I could provide you some entertainment," Mikhailov said, a sheepish grin on his face. "So much for the honor of the Russian airborne troops."

"I can't believe we made it." Jack felt a huge surge of relief. He looked out the window at the flames blazing from the wrecked fuel stop. "I hope nobody got hurt."

Mikhailov grunted. "I think you should worry more about how long it will be before we are shot down." He glanced to the north. Lipetsk Air Base was only fifty kilometers away. "I hope the Air Force has forgotten about Mathias Rust."

CHAPTER THIRTY-ONE

As the helicopter headed east across the city, Angie Boisson said, "No offense, Mr. Morgan, but by all rights you should be in jail."

Morgan turned around in his seat. "No offense taken, Agent Boisson." He smiled. "By all rights, you should be dead."

"So what's going on?" Naomi asked. "Why are you here?"

"Let's just say that I was in a unique position to offer my services to the United States Government at a time when they had precious few alternatives. Not only to help rescue you, but to get the research effort against these creatures jump started."

"But you destroyed everything in Lab One! And who knows how long it will take to get the archived data we had from the EDS and SEAL. That's assuming they reopen the SEAL facility."

Morgan shook his head, still smiling. "My dear, we have backups for everything. Nothing was lost in Lab One except whatever was physically there. All of your data is still safe, believe me. I invested far too much to toss it all away, even under threat of Agent Boisson's wrath."

Next to Naomi, Boisson rolled her eyes.

"And SEAL won't be reopened. I've already spoken to the powers that be about that. We'll be using one of our facilities that's at least as well suited for the job and isn't in the middle of a heavily populated area."

Naomi frowned. She wasn't happy about being under Morgan's control again, even indirectly, but that had been a major issue with the location of the SEAL facility when it had first been established: if something ever did go wrong, the people of San Antonio would be at risk. But for a variety of reasons, some good and some bad, that's where they'd put it. Now it was nothing more than an empty shell, and apparently would remain that way.

"Where is this place you're taking us to?"

"You'll find out."

Naomi looked out the still-open door as the helicopter headed east. A heavy pall of smoke lay over the Los Angeles basin from dozens of fires across the metropolitan area. Nearly every street was backed up as people tried to flee the city. "Where are we going now?"

"San Bernardino Airport," Ferris answered. "We'll fly out a corporate jet with the rest of your research team." He shook his head. "All the other airports from San Bernardino west to Oxnard have been closed. Even LAX. And once we fly out, San Bernardino will be closed, too."

"They've ordered a quarantine?"

Ferris nodded. "Yeah. All flights in or out of the LA area are cancelled. Planes already in the air are being diverted to Air Force bases by friendly neighborhood F-16s. It's the same sort of thing with maritime traffic with the Navy and Coast Guard sealing the ports, and all the roads have been closed."

"It's a good try, but it'll never stop them from getting out."

"You know that and I know that, but what else can they do? Nuke the entire valley?"

Naomi didn't say anything, but the cold analytical part of her mind answered that question with astonishing rapidity. The rest of her mind shied away from the unspoken reply.

"Naomi," Morgan said, "there's one thing that I don't understand. You said these things originated with the Beta-Three corn, that anything eating either the seed or the resulting crops would be transformed."

"Yes. It's basically a transgenic weapon that rewrites the host's DNA with that of the harvesters."

"You also said that you thought this new generation could reproduce."

Naomi nodded. "Yes. That's what we thought based on Harmony's comparison of some regions of harvester DNA with *Amoeba dubia*, and I think I saw one of the adult harvesters actually give birth to a larval form on the news video at the mall. Where are you going with this, Howard?"

"Only the obvious: how the hell could there be so many of them?"

"That all depends on their reproductive rate and when the first host — or hosts — was exposed to the infected corn." She frowned. "And we won't have any idea when that might have happened without going to the safe house where Kelso stashed The Bag. That's where it all must have started."

"Kid, I am not turning this bird around," Ferris said. "Pretty please or not."

"I wouldn't ask you to, Al." Naomi hated to admit it to herself, but she was scared. She shivered as she remembered the sight of the enormous larvae coming at them. They were abominable, far worse than the adult forms.

"That was somebody else's job."

Everyone turned to look at Boisson. "We sent a second team to check out the safe house. They reported their arrival, but nothing after that."

"How many?" Naomi had to know. "How many agents were on the team?"

"Eight. They went in with tactical gear, but without the homemade flamethrower stuff we had. They never came out, and that entire area's been overrun."

"I'm sure this won't mean much to you, coming from me, but I'm sorry, Agent Boisson." Morgan had turned to look out the windscreen, surveying the unfolding disaster that was destroying the Los Angeles area. "You and your people demonstrated extraordinary courage in what you did."

Boisson nodded, as if to herself, but said nothing.

Now that Naomi had a chance to think beyond her immediate survival, her thoughts turned to Jack. "Al, did Renee say anything about Jack?"

"No, but that doesn't mean anything. Listen, that guy can take care of himself. He's got more lives than a litter of cats."

And how many has he used up? Naomi wondered, praying that Jack was all right.

Ferris went on. "And I'm sure Renee's had her hands full while I was doing the whole knight in shining armor bit. With Mr.

Morgan's help, of course." Al turned around and grinned at her. "He bought this bird just for you, you know. None of the corporate copters were big enough. Three million bucks! I like this job. Except for the parts where we get shot at or things are trying to eat us."

Naomi turned to stare at Morgan, who continued to look out the windscreen at the city, below. "You just walked up to somebody and bought this?"

"I've got a pretty impressive limit on my company card," he said dryly. "Think of it as a small contribution toward my penance for my misdeeds."

At that, Boisson laughed. "Okay, Morgan. You may be a corporate crook, but you're a crook with style. I'll give you that much."

"Why thank you, Agent Boisson."

Alexander, who'd been cowering with Koshka under Naomi's seat after one of the other agents pried them from her back, climbed into her lap. Koshka remained coiled at her feet, occasionally glancing up at her human companion.

The big Siberian cat curled up and submitted to her stroking his fur, but his intensely green eyes never left the glass carboy and its lethal prisoner.

* * *

At San Bernardino, Ferris landed on the grass near the end of runway six-zero. Morgan and the others got out as Ferris shut down the Bell 412 and hurried after them.

"You're just leaving it here?" Naomi pointed to the helicopter.

"That's what the boss said," Ferris told her. "I guess we'll come back and get it later." He frowned. "Or not."

"Three million dollars is a lot to pay for a one-way fare."

Morgan dropped back to walk beside her. "I suspect, Naomi, that it's only a small tithe of the price we may all have to pay before this is over."

Ahead of them, already waiting at the end of the runway with engines running, was a white Boeing 727 passenger jet, a boarding ladder truck pulled up beside it.

Boisson shook her head. "Did you buy that, too, Morgan?"

"No, I just leased that one for this flight. The owner gave me a good deal. Otherwise, the plane would be stuck here. We were the plane's ticket out of the quarantine zone."

Ferris led them past the whining engines to where the boarding ladder was pulled up to the port side entry door, just aft of the cockpit. A man wearing the uniform of a copilot waited for him. They shook hands, and the copilot disappeared back into the cockpit while Ferris remained by the door.

"Get your butts in your seats and strap in. No safety briefing today, folks. Oh, and no shopping magazines, either." He grinned. "Those cost extra. Sorry."

"Smart ass." Naomi shook her head as she passed by, leading the two cats on their leashes.

"Holy shit," Boisson breathed. "I've got to get me one of these."

The interior of the plane was lavish, to say the least. This was no cattle car: the plane could probably hold fifty people in oversized cream colored leather chairs. There were also love seats, along with conference tables and audio/video equipment. The bulkheads and doors that in a regular aircraft would be made of plastic and metal were all done in polished wood.

Naomi saw Harmony Bates and the other members of the Lab One team, already strapped in toward the rear of the plane. They waved and called their greetings, but real conversation would have to wait. Ferris wanted to get the plane off the ground.

Naomi collapsed into the seat next to Morgan and strapped herself in, the cats settling at her feet. She noticed that both kept their eyes on the carboy containing the harvester, which was held by one of the agents on the opposite side of the plane. "Thank you, Howard. I thought we weren't going to make it."

"No thanks are necessary, Naomi." He turned to her. "I'll confess that I wasn't exactly happy with you when the FBI came down on us." He stopped. "My God, that was just this morning, wasn't it?"

"Yes. It seems like forever."

Morgan grunted. "No, I wasn't happy with you at all. But I understand now that what you did was the right thing. And believe it or not, I want to do the right thing, too. I still want my legacy,

Naomi. And despite the terrible tragedy that's unfolding around us, this is a God-given opportunity for me to help create that legacy."

"What about Kelso?" Boisson sat across from them.

"I hope he burns."

Both women were taken aback at the intensity of Morgan's words.

"He's been with me for years. Beyond the not inconsiderable amount of money I paid him to do his job, I trusted him. He was in on everything the company did. Then he betrayed us all. He betrayed me." He looked at Naomi. "And that's something that I very rarely forgive."

They looked up as Ferris shut the forward door and dogged it shut. "Okay, boys and girls, the ladder's clear. We're taking off immediately."

He disappeared into the cockpit and closed the door behind him.

As the engines spooled up, Morgan looked at Boisson as he continued. "Off the record, Agent Boisson, let me just say that I'll use every resource available to me to find Dr. Kelso. When I do, I'll deliver him to your doorstep."

"What, you're not going to take off his head?"

Morgan laughed. "No, that's not my style. I'll do what I need to in order to protect my interests, but I'm not a violent man." He glanced out the window as the 727's three engines began to roar and the plane accelerated down the runway. "I'll be content to let the FBI have its due. But I wouldn't shed a tear if Adrian Kelso went straight to Hell."

* * *

Kelso had been nursing a drink in the first class lounge when he noticed people gravitating toward the television at the far end. He hated television, particularly the news. His preferred method of whiling away the handful of hours he had to wait until his flight to Brasilia was to read. He preferred mysteries and thrillers, but would bend toward the occasional horror novel if one took his fancy.

Today's fare was the latest thriller in a series he'd greatly enjoyed, and from which he'd taken several ideas that had helped him build his fortune with Beta-Three. Despite the setbacks he'd suffered earlier that morning at not being able to retrieve the data, he wasn't unhappy. He already had millions of dollars tucked away, more than enough to start a new life on a sunny beach somewhere in South America. His only true regret was not being able to drive his vengeful spear all the way through Morgan Pharmaceuticals.

Another couple, whom he'd thought were absurdly young to be well-off enough to be in the first class lounge, got up to go watch the television, and those already watching it were murmuring in what he could tell was shock.

Annoyed with himself, he dumped his e-reader into the traveler bag he'd bought when he got to the terminal, picked it up, and went to join the others watching the television.

He leaned over to an older gentleman who'd been watching for some time now. "What's happening?"

"There are riots all over the city! And there are these things running about. Look, there goes one!" He pointed at a dark, clearly inhuman shape that pounced upon a young man who was at the trailing end of a crowd of people running across a parking lot. "They thought at first that it was a Hollywood production, but these things are now all over Altadena and Pasadena. It's incredible."

Kelso's gut turned to ice at the mention of Altadena. That was where his safe house was, the repository for the Beta-Three, the New Horizons corn.

Could it be? He wondered silently as he watched the carnage unfold on the television. He had been extremely careful with the corn after he'd learned about how truly dangerous it could be. *After* he'd learned. But what about before, when he'd first gotten it? He had tossed the bag in the trunk of his car after he'd obtained it from the now-dead New Horizons employee, then stored it in his home, which was only three miles from the safe house that he'd eventually acquired.

No. He'd put the corn into containers before taking them to the safe house, then he'd burned the bag. Nothing could have spilled at his house when he'd filled the containers. He'd been very careful. And at the safe house, the containers were kept in locked freezers, except when he was putting together a package for a buyer.

Kelso thought back, trying to remember if anything had ever gone awry. His heart sank as he recalled with vivid clarity the package he'd prepared for his French buyer. He had been in a rush that day, because he had been delayed at one of Morgan's board meetings and was going to be late for his flight. Not only was he late, but he was angry, Morgan having taken him to task again for the Beta-Three team's failure to make more progress. And this, after Morgan had removed him as the team lead!

Still overcome with fury, Kelso had washed his hands as he always did, but hadn't taken the time to dry them properly. With his hands still damp, he couldn't get the rubber gloves and mitts on that he normally used.

"Fuck it!" He remembered cursing as he reached into the freezer and took one of the sample containers in his bare, still damp hands. The freezer was an industrial model that kept the temperature at minus 180 degrees fahrenheit.

He hadn't realized the severity of his mistake until he'd pulled out the metal sample container. Holding it with one hand, he opened the lid with the other, only to discover that the skin of both hands was now stuck to the frozen metal.

Feeling foolish, embarrassment mingling with rage, he remembered trying to pull his fingers away from the lid, and how much pain that had instantly caused.

It was then, he knew. It was in that one moment of sheer stupidity that some of the corn had spilled out onto the floor. Not much, but he knew now that even a single kernel would have been too much.

After managing to separate his skin from the container under cold water from the kitchen faucet, he swept up the kernels from the floor. But he'd been in a rush. He hadn't checked under the freezer or any of the other nooks and crannies where small things can hide. He'd only been concerned with people discovering his treasure.

If what Naomi had told the Beta-Three team about the New Horizons corn was true, and he had no reason to doubt it, any creature could act as a host organism to the transgenic weapon of the harvesters. He'd seen mouse droppings in the safe house, but hadn't cared about them. He wasn't living there, after all, and they could hardly get into the freezers. But they could get under the freezers, or along the baseboards. And even had it not been a mouse, even if an industrious ant, which he'd also found in the house on occasion, had taken an interest in one of the kernels and hauled it back to the nest, the effect would be the same. Once consumed, the host organism's DNA would be reshaped. Even so tiny a thing as an ant could be transformed into a monster.

Or a race of monsters. Naomi and Harmony thought the harvesters could now reproduce. As he watched the television, Kelso knew that they had been right.

The scene shifted to the Santa Anita mall, and the people around him who were watching recoiled in horror at the footage from the news helicopters covering the massacre.

Rooted to the floor, the drink still in his hand, forgotten, he watched in a daze as the battle raged across the Los Angeles metropolitan area. The police, trying to defend civilians but ill-equipped to face the harvesters, had largely been wiped out. The same was true for the firemen and other rescue workers who had gone into the burning areas of the city, never to return. People had taken loved ones, stricken with malignant, terrible growths on their bodies, to hospitals, unwittingly turning those places of hoped-for refuge into abattoirs.

He wasn't sure how much time had passed before the coverage shifted back to the Santa Anita mall, where a team of black-clad FBI agents was making a futile stand against a tidal wave of the monsters coming out of the racetrack stables. His companions in the lounge goggled in disbelief at the nightmarish things that oozed across the parking lot toward the doomed agents, whose escape was cut off by the adult harvesters. But they also cheered the agents on as they set fire to the things that came closest to them, forming a burning moat that warded off the other creatures. The view briefly shifted to a pair of Marine helicopter gunships that began pouring fire into the monsters, and his fellows cheered some more.

But then, all too soon, the helicopters left. Out of ammunition, the voice of the newscaster speculated. The camera zoomed in on the team, who had lost several of its members in the battle, and was now surrounded by an army of nightmares. The people with Kelso were silent, knowing that the FBI agents were doomed.

The image steadied on one of the team, and Kelso blinked.

"What are those things?" One of the others stepped closer to the screen and pointed at a dark, furry lump on the agent's shoulder, and another, whitish lump on the agent's back.

"They're cats." Kelso heard his voice, but didn't realize that he'd actually spoken. He knew in that moment who the "agent" was. It was Naomi Perrault and her two cats, clinging to her.

That's when the nausea hit him. While he had been angry, furious, when Morgan hired Perrault, and had been desperate enough to conspire to have Kline killed, he had never in his wildest imagination thought that something like this would happen. According to the news, hundreds, and possibly thousands of people were believed to have been killed already, just in the hours since the first reports of these creatures had surfaced.

He had only wanted to be rich, and to put Howard Morgan in his place. Kline had hardly been an innocent, and Kelso refused to shed any tears for him, or feel guilty for his role in Kline's demise.

But the others, all those innocent people, their blood was on his hands. And Naomi, while he had seethed with professional jealousy when she had been hired, was now about to be another victim. He didn't hate her, only what she represented in his own twisted relationship with Howard Morgan.

She didn't deserve to die.

"I'm sorry," he whispered.

"Excuse me?" The older gentleman beside him turned and looked at him curiously. "You don't look so well, my friend. Are you all right?"

Kelso ignored him as the scene on the television changed and he listened to the newscaster as she reported that all the airports in the Los Angeles area, including LAX, were being shut down, and that the entire area was being quarantined.

He was trapped here in the hell that he himself had created.

"No," Kelso said in a weak voice amidst the shocked exclamations of the other passengers in the lounge. "No, I don't think I am."

CHAPTER THIRTY-TWO

"The air activity over Russia, particularly in the southern part of the country, is unprecedented, sir."

U.S. Air Force General Matt Selig, Commander, U.S. Air Forces in Europe (USAFE), nodded for the colonel to continue. This wasn't the regularly scheduled daily intelligence briefing, but an ad-hoc presentation that Selig had ordered after things had suddenly gone crazy around the world. While he was peripherally interested in all of it, he was specifically interested in what was happening with the Russians. Even though the Cold War had been over for years, their air force was still the greatest potential threat his airmen might have to face.

The front wall of the conference room was a rear-projection display that showed a map of the southern half of Russia, with icons indicating the location of their air force bases, coded to indicate which type of aircraft were normally based there.

"Let's have it," Selig ordered.

"General, intelligence that's been corroborated by DIA, CIA, and NSA indicates that the Russians have established a quarantine line along the Don and Volga rivers." A red line appeared on the map, following the trace of the rivers between the Sea of Azov and the Caspian Sea. "They've backed it up with very aggressive enforcement by no fewer than six fighter squadrons that have orders to turn away any aircraft flying out of the Caucasus region or, if they refuse, shoot them down." He hit a button on the podium, and a swarm of aircraft icons appeared along the quarantine line, extending along the adjoining border with Ukraine in the west, Kazakhstan to the east, and over the coasts of the Black and Caspian Seas. He hit the button again, and more aircraft icons appeared. "As you can see in this view, Belarus, Ukraine, and Kazakhstan have put up barrier patrols along their borders with Russia, and are refusing any aircraft passage across the border. The Finns have their F-18s up, and the Norwegians have F-16s on orbit opposite the Kola Peninsula." By now, the colonel wore a distinctly unhappy expression. "In fact," he went on as the borders between Russia and all of its neighbors, including China, turned red on the screen, "every neighboring country has closed their borders with Russia. They're effectively isolated."

Selig grimaced. "Just what we need, to make the Russians feel like they're cut off. They're paranoid as it is."

Major General Sean Cranston, the USAFE Vice Commander, frowned. "What's the status of their nuclear forces?"

"So far, sir, we haven't seen any changes in readiness, and there haven't been any incidents reported at any of their strategic sites."

"Keep a close eye on that. The last thing we need is for any nukes to get loose in this mess."

"Yes, sir."

"What about the military aircraft in the south?" Selig asked, getting things focused back on the air situation. "They've got a lot of assets in the Caucasus Military District."

"Yes, sir, they do. We haven't received corroboration on this yet, but it looks like all their fighter and bomber aircraft in the Caucasus have been ordered to fly to six of the nearest airfields in the Volga-Ural Military District." The airfields blinked on the map.

"Just their fighters and bombers?" Selig frowned. "What about the transports and helicopters?"

"They're destroying them on the ground, sir."

The response from both Selig and Cranston was simultaneous. "*What?*"

"That's correct, sir. Imagery has confirmed that transport and rotary wing aircraft are being destroyed, and not just at the air bases or other military installations where intelligence has reported ongoing combat against..." The colonel ran out of words. They'd received an update from the Pentagon on what was happening in Los Angeles, and had been told that the same "biological agent" was at work in Russia, China, India, and elsewhere. But none of them could truly believe what they'd read in the report.

"Regardless," he went on, "it looks like they're destroying everything beyond fighters and bomber aircraft."

"The crews can't be happy," Selig said. "How are they supposed to get out?"

"They're not, sir," the colonel told him. "We've already received some reports of transports trying to leave that have been shot down, and FSB teams have been tasked with securing the airfields that haven't already been compromised."

"In God's name, why?" Cranston was shocked. "Not only are they torching billions of rubles in assets, but they're condemning invaluable aircrews! That's insane!"

"We're trying to get more details, sir, but right now our assessment is they don't want to risk any possible contagion from those aircraft. For the aircraft that are being sent out, it looks like the crews are going to be quarantined and the aircraft sterilized. CIA reported that the FSB has sent special detachments to those six receiving airfields, along with Army decontamination units."

"FSB?" Selig asked. "Not military police or GRU?" GRU, or *Glavnoye Razvedyvatel'noye Upravleniye*, the Main Intelligence Directorate of the General Staff of the Armed Forces of the Russian Federation, was the rough Russian equivalent of the U.S. Defense Intelligence Agency, or DIA.

"No, sir, CIA was firm that they're FSB, operating under direct orders from the prime minister. As for the aircraft, they're being escorted by fighters outside the quarantine zone. Once they get to the receiving bases, from what we've seen so far they're just packing the aircraft in as tight as they can."

He pressed the button to move to the next graphic, which showed a satellite image of one of the air bases. "This is Sennoy Air Base, taken forty-five minutes ago. As you can see, it's not a large facility, and only has a single runway. It typically hosts a small number of transport aircraft and helicopters. But here," he pointed with a laser pointer at the eastern end of the apron, where fourteen aircraft were haphazardly clustered, "you can see a squadron of Su-27 Flankers that just arrived, along with what we believe are decontamination vehicles." Eight military-style trucks with large liquid storage tanks were parked in a ring around the aircraft.

Selig shook his head. "They pushed those planes off into the grass?"

"Yes, sir. And here," he moved the pointer to a spot about a hundred meters north of the main apron, "you can see portable shelters. We believe this is where they're processing the flight crews, presumably to make sure they're not, um, infected."

Cranston pursed his lips. "I also see, what, a company of infantry combat vehicles around the shelters?"

"Correct, sir. And there are two tank platoons over here." The pointer moved another hundred meters beyond the temporary shelters to where six brooding shapes sat, their barrels pointing in the direction of the shelters. "The other five quarantine airfields have similar heavy security for the new arrivals."

"Okay," Selig said, trying to force himself to fast forward into the surreal nightmare that reality had suddenly become, "what else."

"In the European theater, the ground forces are on alert, but the only movements have been internal, mainly deploying units along the quarantine line."

The colonel pressed another button, and a larger scale map appeared, showing all of western Russia and Europe as far as Germany.

Selig scowled at the clusters of red icons in the Black Sea, in the Gulf of Finland off Saint Petersburg, and in the Barents Sea outside of Severomorsk, where the Northern Fleet had its headquarters. "It looks like everything they have that can float has put to sea."

"In a nutshell, general, that's exactly what's happened, but we believe for different reasons. We have information indicating that the Northern Fleet units put to sea as part of the general Russian military alert. But in the Black Sea, we believe the ships that have deployed, mostly out of Sevastopol and Odessa, are Russian ships forced to leave by the Ukrainians." After the breakup of the Soviet Union, Ukraine wound up with the main Soviet Black Sea Fleet ports. After a great deal of political wrangling between the two new nations, Russia and Ukraine agreed to partition the fleet, with

Russia leasing port facilities for their vessels from the Ukrainians. But Ukraine had never been terribly happy with the situation.

"Oh, shit," Cranston said. "The Ukrainians got their wish: an excuse to kick the Russian Fleet out of the Crimea."

"Yes, sir," the colonel agreed. "Of course, that leaves the Russians with a problem. While the Russian ships so far have been steaming toward their own coast, the Russians don't have port facilities available for all those ships in their own territory. At some point soon, we're probably looking at a large-scale deployment of surface and submarine combatants into the Mediterranean. And that's assuming that the Russians and Ukrainians don't start a shooting war over this."

Cranston shook his head. "Vice Admiral Lafferty in Sixth Fleet must be going ballistic."

"To say the least. Whatever this contagion is could blow up into World War Three." Selig turned to his senior staff officers, all of whom were sitting around the table. "Make sure we're tied in tight with Lafferty's people. If things get out of hand, I want contingency plans in place so we can cover Sixth Fleet. The same goes for our NATO partners up north in case the Northern Fleet goes looking for trouble." He considered his next words for a moment. "We haven't received orders yet to do so, but I want the command pushed up to maximum combat readiness. Quietly." He looked at his operations officer. "I want as much AWACS coverage as we can get, looking as deep as possible into Russian airspace without getting under their skin. Get a basic weapons load on our fighters and strike aircraft, but otherwise keep things low key. Keep the training tempo as it is; if we increase our training activity now, it's going to worry them, and if we do a stand down, it'll be worse. So far this is an internal problem for them. If it becomes something more, I want to be ready, but I don't want our contingency preparations to inadvertently push them over the edge." To the personnel officer, he said, "I'm not going to recall folks from leave yet, but as of now I'm curtailing everything but emergency leave. Our folks are going to have their hands full."

Heads nodded and a murmur of "Yes, sir" went around the room.

Selig nodded for the colonel to continue.

"Sir, the last thing I have on the European theater is about a group of eight MiG-29 Fulcrums out of Lipetsk in the Moscow Military District." The map changed again, zooming in on western Russia, with Moscow in the middle of the view. Lipetsk Air Base, more than two hundred kilometers south of Moscow, was highlighted. "One of the analysts in the 707th ISR Group somehow pulled this out of the clutter of all the other military aircraft movements that are taking place." The 707th ISR, or Intelligence, Surveillance, and Reconnaissance Group, was headquartered at the National Security Agency at Fort George G. Meade in Maryland. One of the group's many jobs was to serve as the lead for the Global Air Analysis SIGINT mission, providing analysis and reporting on high-interest aerial activity. What was happening in Russia now definitely fell into that category.

The display showed a series of undulating tracks that began just south of Lipetsk. The aircraft the tracks represented were making long east-west sweeps, with the westerly legs taking them right up to the border with Ukraine, then Belarus, and then east as far as the Volga River, with the aircraft gradually moving north.

"What's really interesting is this." The colonel pointed to two aircraft icons that were different from those representing the fighters. "It looks like they've dedicated two Il-78M tankers out of Dyagilevo to keep these Fulcrums in the air. Just as a side note, those are the only tankers not supporting the barrier operation in the south."

Selig, along with everyone else in the room, stared at the image, perplexed. The fighters doing sweeps like that was odd enough. That the Russians had dedicated two of their precious tankers to them was the real kicker. "What the devil are they up to?"

The colonel glanced at the map behind him, then turned back to Selig. "We think they're looking for something."

* * *

"Do you think they're looking for us?" Jack stared out the windscreen, helping Khatuna and Mikhailov watch for other planes. They'd seen quite a few, far above their own tree-skimming altitude.

"Probably, but stop worrying," Mikhailov advised. "The first we will know if they have found us is a warning over the radio, if they choose to give one. Otherwise, it will be cannon shells or a missile. Then, pfft!" He looked outside at the endless white expanse, his expression turning serious. "The FSB will likely determine that it was we who stole the petrol in Zadonsk, and from that they will know the type of aircraft we are flying, and some fool at the petrol station probably took down the plane's number. But they cannot know our destination, at least not for certain."

"Sure they can. Where are we going to go with this thing loaded with fuel drums? Siberia?"

"Maybe we should. They would never think to look for us there."

"Do you have wife?" Khatuna suddenly asked, looking at Mikhailov.

"No, I do not."

"If you did, she would hit you."

"I think that means she is interested in the job," Mikhailov said to Jack, with a wink to Khatuna.

Exasperated, she rolled her eyes and focused her attention on keeping the badly overloaded biplane in the air.

Mikhailov looked again at the map, on which he'd penciled in their course. From Zadonsk, he'd had Khatuna fly northwest for an hour, which took them nearly two hundred kilometers to Oryol. The next leg, the one they were on now, took them north-northwest for more than seven hundred kilometers, and was probably the most dangerous part of their long journey. Moscow, two hundred kilometers off their starboard wing now, was ringed with Air Force bases, with more spread throughout the rest of the military district around them. "I think we will be able to avoid most of the fighter bases," Mikhailov said as his finger traced their course. He had marked the bases he knew about, and had Khatuna take the plane lower, sometimes down to less than thirty meters, when they came within fifty kilometers of any of them. It was terribly dangerous, because the plane, which normally was almost impossible to send into a stall, was so heavy that it seemed to want to fall from the sky with only the slightest provocation.

But they had no choice.

Mikhailov craned his neck to the left, looking out Khatuna's side. Vyazma Air Base was close, only twenty kilometers away. If he remembered correctly, only rotary wing aircraft were stationed there. Of course, helicopters could carry weapons, and a Mi-24 attack helicopter could easily catch the laboring An-2.

"So if we make it past Moscow, then what?"

Looking back at the map, Mikhailov pointed. "Once we reach Lake Ilmen, here," his finger rested on a large lake almost two hundred kilometers south of Saint Petersburg, "we turn north to fly over Lake Ladoga, which will still probably be mostly frozen over, and keep going until we reach Norway."

"Nice. All we need now is in-flight service."

Khatuna huffed. One of the things they hadn't found in the plane had been food, nor was there anything to drink other than a half-empty ("Or half-full," as Mikhailov happily pointed out) bottle of vodka behind the copilot's seat. If they were lucky and made it to Norway, they'd be in the air at least ten hours. It was going to be a hungry and thirsty flight. Jack mentally kicked himself for not thinking of raiding the truck stop for whatever munchies they might have had.

"Look at it this way," Mikhailov said, glancing down at his lap and the fading stain there from when he'd wet himself, "without food and water, we will not have to worry so much about the lack of a toilet."

Khatuna fixed him with a hard gaze that she couldn't hold. Her scowl dissolved into a grin.

Mikhailov told Jack, making sure Khatuna could hear, "I think she likes me." He chuckled at her scandalized expression.

Then he began to cough up blood. Lots of it.

"What has happened?" Khatuna stared at Mikhailov, and Jack could tell what she was thinking.

"No, he's not infected! He has a shattered rib that punctured his lung, and it's finally collapsed." From the amount of blood Mikhailov was coughing up, he clearly had other internal injuries.

That didn't surprise Jack at all, considering the shape Mikhailov had been in before the harvester had tried to kill him in the hospital in Stavropol, and everything that had happened since. "Damn it!"

"What can we do?"

The large veins in Mikhailov's neck were standing out, and his skin was starting to turn blue as he desperately gasped for air.

Jack had seen this once before, in Afghanistan after one of his soldiers had taken a bullet to the chest. He'd been there when the medic had treated the young man by sticking a needle into his chest to relieve the built-up pressure in the chest cavity, allowing the lung to reinflate. Jack couldn't remember the details, but he remembered that much.

"Is there a first aid kit in here?"

"*Da*, there is one here, next to me." Keeping one hand on the control yoke, she leaned over and pulled out the kit, handing it to Jack.

He pulled it open and cursed. There were bandaids, gauze, tape, and a few other odds and ends that were of absolutely no use to him. "Shit! I need a needle, a big needle. Or maybe a pen." He checked his own pockets, but came up empty. He hadn't had any need for pens, or time to grab any, before they'd jumped into Ulan-Erg.

"Here!" Khatuna snatched up a cheap ballpoint pen in a pocket beside her. It was the same kind as the one Mikhailov had used to draw their course on the map, but that one had gone clattering to the floor when he began to thrash around.

Jack grabbed it and shoved it in a pocket for the moment. "Hang on, buddy," he said to Mikhailov. "Sorry, but I'm going to have to pull you out of here."

Unbuckling Mikhailov's harness, Jack awkwardly hauled him out of the copilot's seat. Mikhailov's eyes bulged and he gasped in agony, more blood streaming from the corner of his mouth.

As gently as he could, Jack laid him on top of the nearest barrels in the cargo hold. He ripped open Mikhailov's tunic, then slit his shirt open with his knife to expose the Russian's battered chest. The lower left side was badly bruised, and Jack assumed that's where the lung had been punctured.

Jack couldn't remember exactly where the medic had inserted the needle back in Afghanistan, but seemed to recall it was in the upper part of the chest. Taking the pen, he placed the tip between two of Mikhailov's upper ribs on the left side. "Sorry, Sergei, but this is going to hurt like hell."

Then Jack shoved the pen into Mikhailov's chest.

Mikhailov opened his mouth to scream, but no sound came out. He clenched his hands at his sides and banged his feet against the top of one of the drums.

Had the pen been a needle, Jack remembered that he would have left it in. But the pen wouldn't let any air into the chest cavity, which was the whole point.

Gritting his teeth, he pulled it back out again.

Mikhailov moved his right hand over the wound, covering it. Jack tried to get him to move it away, but Mikhailov shook his head as he inhaled. Miraculously, he was able to take a partial breath. As he exhaled, he lifted his hand from the wound, then covered it again when he took his next breath. He was able to breathe more deeply, and as Jack watched, Mikhailov's color began to return to normal.

Jack leaned back against the bulkhead to the cockpit, relief flooding through him.

"Rudenko taught me about this," Mikhailov said as Jack wiped the blood from his friend's mouth.

"The old bastard probably operated on himself." Jack smiled, thinking of what a character Rudenko had been. It seemed like a lifetime since his death.

"Thank you, my friend."

Jack nodded, but didn't smile. "You're still bleeding inside, you know."

"About that, there is nothing we can do. I will settle for being able to breathe again."

"What is happening?" Khatuna's shout caught them both by surprise.

"He's okay," Jack told her. "He's going to be okay."

"You might have wasted your time," she called back. "I think the Air Force has found us."

CHAPTER THIRTY-THREE

When Morgan revealed the destination of the Boeing 727, Hathcock, the sniper, was less than enthused.

"Grand Island, Nebraska?" He turned to Naomi, a grimace on his face. "You've got to be kidding me."

"Is there something about the good state of Nebraska that you don't like, Mr. Hathcock?" Morgan favored the sniper with a quizzical look over steepled fingers as he sat at the main conference table with Naomi, Hathcock, Boisson, and Harmony.

"It's where this whole story began," Naomi told him. "This new generation of harvesters was born in the research labs at Lincoln Research University, which was really nothing more than a New Horizons front operation to lure in geneticists like me. Before the Sutter Buttes incident when the Earth Defense Society was branded a terrorist organization, we recruited an FBI agent, Sheldon Crane, to help us get into the lab to find out exactly what the harvesters were up to. He found what we needed, the first samples of what you know as the Beta-Three corn, but it cost him his life." She looked up at Morgan. "They vivisected him, cut him apart, looking for the corn, while he was still alive."

"Then there was our little op at the New Horizons production plant." Hathcock took a sip of coffee. "That was here, too."

"So that really was you." Morgan raised his eyebrows. "You don't believe in half measures, do you. Harvesters weren't the only living beings you killed."

"We had no choice." Hathcock's voice, like his eyes, turned hard. "As it was, one of the damned things nearly got away." He could still picture the harvester in the sights of his rifle, running on all fours to safety before he blew it to flaming bits.

Morgan held up his hands in mock surrender. Naomi could see that the gesture made Hathcock angry, and she shook her head slightly. *Now's not the time.*

Hathcock got the message and clamped his mouth shut.

"Why Grand Island?" Naomi cocked her head. "And why in the world would anyone give a name like that to a town in Nebraska?"

"I'll take the second question first: I don't know, but I wish it really was a grand island. Then it might be a bit more balmy than it must be now, this early in the year. As for the second question, I have to confess that the choice of location was a bit of industrial brinkmanship. I wanted to position our company to start a new division that could compete with New Horizons. To do that, I needed our people to learn what our competitors had learned, to put them in a similar environment. We could have put the division in Lincoln, but that would have been a little too obvious with the research university there." He nodded toward Naomi. "Yes, like you, we knew that was basically a research center for New Horizons. We couldn't match that, but we did have a few sources of information there that helped things along."

"More spying?" Boisson sat back, arms folded across her chest.

Morgan shrugged. "Call it what you will, Agent Boisson, but it boils down to competition. And not that it'll make any difference to you, but we knew that New Horizons had their share of sources in my company. Fair's fair."

"Well, the location aside, we're going to need some special equipment from the SEAL lab," Naomi said, "and I'm not sure you fully understand just how tough it's going to be to create a containment chamber for that thing." She nodded toward the bottled harvester, which was being closely observed by the two cats.

"It looks like a big glass jug and a metal cap is working just fine." Morgan smiled, but his quip failed to lighten Naomi's mood. He sighed. "The equipment you want from SEAL is already on its way, courtesy of your friend Renee in Washington. As for the containment chambers, we have several large ones, originally intended for controlled crop plantings, that actually should work well. My people are modifying them as we speak to completely seal them and eliminate anything that's not from the mineral kingdom, as it were. When they're done, which should be before we land, we'll be ready to handle our little friend there." He glanced toward the carboy and the squirming larva.

"Just make sure the chambers can handle our tiny tot when he grows up," Boisson told him. "The adults are like threshing machines."

Morgan nodded. "We're reinforcing one of the smaller chambers with steel, and are also adding a sensor pod with a taser-like device. Renee sent my people the schematics from the containment lab at the SEAL facility to work from."

Boisson cocked her head. "Your people must be working awfully fast."

"For what I'm paying them, they'd better be."

* * *

Their arrival at the Central Nebraska Regional Airport was uneventful, and after Ferris shut down the aircraft and opened the door, everyone filed down the mobile stairway into the cold Nebraska air.

"I hope there's a stash of coats close by or we're going to freeze," someone muttered.

While the operational areas of the airport and the roads were clear, there was a dusting of snow everywhere else.

"Don't worry," Morgan said, loud enough so everyone could hear. "You'll have everything you need where we're going."

Waiting for them was a group of big SUVs with four Nebraska Army National Guard Hummers, two at the lead and two bringing up the rear of the convoy. The barrels of the big .50 caliber machine guns protruded over the gun shields on the top of each vehicle, the muzzles pointed in alternating directions, with a soldier manning each one.

"Talk about loaded for bear," Boisson said quietly to Naomi.

Naomi nodded, noting that the machine guns weren't locked in their travel positions. The soldiers had their hands on the triggers, and their eyes weren't watching her and the others as they disembarked, but were scanning the approaches to the plane.

"A special request I made to the governor," Morgan said, noticing where Naomi was looking, "backed up by Agent Boisson's superiors. A prudent measure for troubled times."

Boisson frowned. "A more prudent measure would have been a platoon of M1 tanks."

"Unfortunately, even I don't have that much pull, Agent Boisson. Now, if you'll just get in, we can be on our way."

Naomi was about to get into the SUV with the agent carrying the harvester, but Boisson guided her to the lead vehicle, where Morgan was waiting.

"No way are you riding with that thing," Boisson said. "If there was an accident, you wouldn't stand a chance. Then I'd be dead, too, because Richards said he'd kill me if I let anything happen to you."

Trying to conceal her relief, Naomi followed Morgan into the lead vehicle. Boisson, Hathcock, and Harmony got in behind her.

Morgan called to the driver. "Let's go."

The driver spoke into his headset, and a few seconds later the convoy was moving.

"Hathcock, can I borrow your phone?"

"Sure." He pulled his phone out and handed it to her.

Naomi dialed Jack's number again. She'd dialed it several times on the flight out of San Bernardino, but the only thing she'd gotten was an out of service message.

"He's still not answering?" Boisson asked.

"No. God, I hope he's all right." She handed the phone back to Hathcock. "And you left my phone back in LA, didn't you?"

"Yeah, sorry about that. I put it in one of the evidence boxes with the other stuff from your office. I meant to bring it to you at the safe house, but when I got orders to get the tac team together..." She shrugged. "As soon as we get this sorted out, I'll get you a new one. Whatever color you want."

Despite her worries about Jack, Naomi had to smile. "Purple, I think."

"Done."

Morgan's phone chimed. "Yes?" He listened for a moment, looking at Naomi. "You're sure it's secure?" The other person said something more, and Morgan winced. "Here," he said, handing the phone to Naomi. "It's your friend Renee."

Surprised, Naomi took the phone. "Renee? What's going on?"

"You'll find out soon enough, hon. But tell that bonehead billionaire that I know my stuff."

"What are you talking about?"

"Our pet adult harvester. We've got one."

Naomi caught her breath. She would have loved to capture one in Los Angeles, but just getting one of the larval forms had nearly done them all in. "That's wonderful! When will it be at Morgan's facility in Nebraska?"

"It's already here. *We're* here. We got in a couple hours ago, and they dragged the harvester in here maybe half an hour ago. Christ, I can't remember the last time I slept, and I've got coffee in my veins and pouring out my bladder."

"Renee, stop babbling!" Naomi rolled her eyes heavenward. "Who's 'we,' and where did the harvester come from? If it was snatched in LA, we should've known about it."

"Carl and I are here. Well, he'll be here tonight. He sent me out early with some of the former EDS and SEAL folks to make sure these guys have a clue about what they're doing. I have to admit, though, that Morgan runs a tight ship. This place isn't as cool as our old base was, but I think it'll do."

"What about the *harvester?*"

"Yeah, the harvester. That was a fast-moving lucky break for us. The goddamn thing was on a plane out of Los Angeles that left earlier this morning, before flights out of there were cancelled, and it got off in Kansas City. It was mimicking a woman and had her boarding pass, ID, and everything else. It even ordered drinks on the plane. Talk about chutzpah."

"How did they catch it?"

"They didn't. The stupid thing walked out of the terminal and stepped right in front of one of the shuttle buses. I guess traffic etiquette wasn't part of whatever it learned from its victim. The legs were crushed and it sustained some other injuries, and the airport security team had the good sense to wrap it up in nylon straps while it was still stunned. They called the FBI and Carl found out about it, of course, so he had them fly it up here. We've got it in one of the adult containment cells now, and it's mad as hell. The gal it's mimicking had a really impressive vocabulary. May God rest her soul."

"You know what this means, don't you?"

There was a long pause at the other end of the line. "Yeah. They're already out. That's why Carl's going to be late getting out here: there's another big wheels meeting at the White House. The FBI and Homeland Security are going nuts trying to track down all the flights that left before the airports were closed to see where the next outbreaks might be." She paused again. "Counting all the passenger planes, cargo jets, and small planes, there were a lot, both here in the U.S. and overseas."

"Are they trying to get the overseas flights turned around?"

"The U.S. planes, yes, but we don't have any jurisdiction over the foreign airlines. The State Department's working on that, trying to at least warn the countries where those planes are heading so security is ready. Well, as ready as they can be for these nightmares."

In Naomi's mind, she saw a deadly spider's web expanding away from Los Angeles and spreading across the world. There wouldn't, of course, be a harvester on every plane; the chances of that were astronomical. But if even a fraction of them had harvesters aboard, many of those planes would have already reached their destinations by now, and the harvesters would have escaped. Chance had favored her new team with the mishap suffered by the harvester in Kansas City, but they couldn't count on that happening very often.

"Jesus," she breathed.

"Yeah, I know." Lowering her voice, Renee said, "I'm shaking, Naomi, and it's not just from the coffee or lack of sleep. I've never been this scared, even back at Sutter Buttes when one of those bastards almost got me when my fat ass was caught in the door to the lab."

"Listen to me. I'm not going to tell you that everything's going to be okay. You and I both know that it's not, at least not for some time. But all of us have to be strong, Renee. Everyone's counting on us, now. Shaking hands are okay. Being afraid is okay. Peeing out coffee is okay. But you're not allowed to fall apart on me, all right? Especially with Jack away." She almost said *gone*, but that sounded too final, too terrifying. She quickly blinked away her tears. She wasn't about to cry in front of Boisson and Morgan. "Have you heard anything from him?"

"No, hon, I haven't, but Carl did. Jack called him from Russia when he couldn't get hold of either of us. Jack's with Mikhailov and they're okay." She paused. "When you get here, I'll tell you the rest of what he told me."

That didn't sound good, Naomi thought, and she bit back the urge to demand that Renee tell her now. "Okay. I'll talk to you then." After hanging up, she looked up at Morgan. "How long until we get there?"

Morgan nodded out the window at an expanse of stark white snow, in the midst of which was a gleaming silver and glass two-story structure. "We're almost there."

* * *

As the convoy approached the building, the vehicles passed through a checkpoint manned by Nebraska Army National Guard troops, backed up by a pair of armed Hummers. Naomi could see more soldiers at work, unloading materials from large CONEX storage boxes, and there were camouflage-painted bulldozers and ditch digging machines pushing snow and dirt around.

"They're putting up a perimeter fence," Morgan explained, and Naomi could tell from the tone of his voice that he wasn't happy about it. "Actually, they're putting up two fences, one inside the other, both topped with barbed wire." He pointed at a small structure some soldiers were building in between the fences. "Normally, they'd be using German Shepherds to patrol between the fences. Here, they'll be using Maine Coon and Siberian cats that can stand up to the cold, and all the soldiers will be armed with incendiary ammunition and Tasers."

"So the fences are to keep the harvesters in," Naomi said.

"So they say." Morgan shrugged. "And maybe us, too."

The SUVs pulled up in front of the doors and stopped, and the team got out. Led by Morgan, they headed inside, where they were met by Renee.

"It's good to see you, hon." Renee threw her arms around Naomi, giving her a fierce hug, which Naomi returned.

"We brought you another inmate," Naomi told her as they pulled away. She nodded at the larval harvester in the glass carboy.

"Oh, great, another one!"

Naomi's eyes widened as they began to follow Morgan through the outer vestibule, which had another set of thick coded access doors that hissed open with the help of hydraulics. "What?"

"The harvester we picked up in Kansas City spawned one of those little horrors right after you hung up. A bulge formed in its thorax and then — plop! — the thing fell away and splatted on the floor, just like that one in LA in that video footage we saw."

"Have this one put into a containment chamber. I want to see the adult and its offspring."

* * *

Morgan's facility had four levels, two above ground and two below. The smaller containment chambers intended for the larval forms, which in many ways were deadlier than the adults, were on the lowest level. The elevators opened onto a central corridor that ran the length of the sub-basement, which was nearly two hundred feet long. Thick doors were spaced every thirty feet or so, and could isolate the various sections like watertight doors in a ship. The doors along the corridors were labeled, with about a third of them containing laboratories geared toward different specialties, and the rest split between storage and the containment chambers.

The chambers varied in size, ranging from what could accommodate a large dog to one that could comfortably hold a horse. They passed by a dozen men and women wearing hard hats who were putting the final touches on them.

"These chambers were intended for test animals, of course," Morgan said as one of the technicians led them to a room that contained several of the smaller chambers. They followed the lab-coated woman through a door with a wheel that would have looked at home in a submarine. "They've been modified for our latest guests to eliminate anything that they might be able to attack. The chambers here are metal, but aren't reinforced. However, this room," he pointed above them, "has been reinforced with metal and ceramic, and there aren't any penetrations through the metal except for the main door. All the sensors in here are wireless, and the main door has an expanding metal seal. So even if any of our little friends get out of their chambers, they can't get out of this room." He grinned, but the expression was totally devoid of humor. "And if they get unruly or the door is somehow breached, this little baby," he pointed to a device on the ceiling that had two stainless steel tanks and several nozzles, "will burn them into ashes."

"But you don't want to be in here when that happens," the lab technician warned.

"Right," Naomi said absently as she watched the technician take the carboy from the agent, who surrendered it with obvious relief.

The woman opened one of the dog crate-sized containment chambers, which had a top-loading door. Then she removed the metal cap on the big glass jar and upended it over the opening to the chamber.

Naomi had to admire the woman's nerve, for she didn't show the least bit of fear in handling the carboy and its occupant.

As if sensing the opening, the harvester larva quickly oozed toward the neck of the bottle and dropped into the chamber below.

The technician set the carboy right side up in another chamber, then closed and locked the door. Then she opened the adjacent chamber and set the carboy inside, then sealed it. "Until we're sure the organism can't propagate on a microscopic level, all containers will be quarantined."

Naomi nodded, impressed. She had made the assumption that the creature was contiguous unless it was physically separated, as she'd done with the larva that had killed Garcia at the mall. But assumptions with anything dealing with harvesters could be deadly. She vowed to not make that sort of mistake again.

"Now let's take a look at mama monster and her squirming bundle of joy," Renee said.

* * *

The adult harvester containment cells were on the main basement level, which was laid out in similar fashion to the sub-basement, but was slightly larger. Over half of the level was devoted to labs and equipment storage, while the rest was taken up with containment cells.

"Some of the cells we set up are much like those you had at SEAL," Morgan told her as they passed through a thick armored door in the main hallway that passed into the containment area. "They've got thick polycarbonate walls, reinforced doors, and sensor pods in the ceiling, and are airtight. Those, of course, wouldn't work for the larvae, so we had two metal cells installed. They're like the ones downstairs, except larger and reinforced. But we've only got two."

"That should be enough," Naomi told him as they entered a room that had monitors taking up space on every wall and a series of computer consoles on a large U-shaped table that ran around the walls except the one holding the door. Some showed various status displays, but most showed views of the containment chambers. Seven technicians in white lab coats had their attention focused on the screens.

"This is our main monitoring station," Morgan said. "We have at least two cameras looking into every chamber, along with what few instruments we can insert without compromising containment integrity." He turned to Naomi. "That's going to limit much of the data you'll be able to get from the larvae."

"We don't have much choice," she replied, but her attention was riveted on the screens that showed the chamber with the adult harvester. It was an abomination, its upper half still in the form of the woman it had mimicked, while its lower half looked like a crushed cockroach. The thing was pulling itself along the floor with its arms, periodically glancing behind it. "What's it doing?"

"It seems to be trying to avoid the larva it just spawned," one of the technicians said. "As soon as the larva separated, the adult moved away from it, and the larva is clearly pursuing the adult."

"Has the adult said anything?"

The technician shook his head. "Only an endless string of curses. We've tried asking it questions, but it's completely ignored us. The only thing it's concerned about is the larva."

"Here's the police report," Renee pointed to a screen. "I thought you might find it interesting."

Unwillingly taking her eyes away from the strange pursuit in the chamber, Naomi skimmed over the report from the airport security force at Kansas City.

Then she stopped. "Oh, my God." She reread one of the lines of the report:

Officer Baginsky reported that suspect appeared to drop a small object soon after the suspect was struck by the shuttle bus. Baginsky saw the object roll under the bus, but was unable to find it again after suspect was restrained.

She leaned back, looking up at Renee. "If this is right, it reproduced around the time that it was hit by the bus."

"What?" Renee leaned over Naomi's shoulder and read the report again. "Oh, shit! I missed that. How could I have missed that?"

"Forget it. What's important is that if this is right, it's spawned two offspring in as many hours."

"How many?" Morgan was staring at Naomi.

"Two offspring in roughly two hours." Turning back to Renee, she said, "Get me a propagation model. And contact the airline. See if the cabin crew remembers this woman. It's a long shot, but I'd like to know if they saw her going to the bathroom, and I'd like someone to look at the sewage tank on that plane. Carefully." The things could feed on both the sewage in the tank and the tank itself if it wasn't made of metal. The people on that plane were probably very lucky indeed. "Does anyone have an idea of how long it takes to fly from LAX to Kansas City?"

"Yeah," Ferris said. He'd been silent since they'd arrived, but now wore a haunted look on his face. "I used to fly that run. Most of the flights have a stopover and the trip takes around eight hours." He frowned. "So you think this thing was heading back to the bathroom every hour or so to dump one of its babies into the toilet?"

"I know we're making some big assumptions right now, but yes, that's right."

He shook his head. "Then unless the little bastards ate through the tank wall and are crawling around inside the plane, they've already been pumped into the main sewage system at the airport."

"Into the main sewers," Boisson said. "Jesus." She looked at Naomi. "You were thinking that's how the ones in LA could have multiplied without being noticed, right?"

Naomi nodded. "It's the only thing that makes sense."

"Holy sh..." Ferris suddenly looked pained. "Ah, jeez. I can't even say it."

Renee, who'd been madly typing at one of the computer consoles, suddenly leaned back, her mouth dropping open in shock.

"What is it?" Naomi asked.

"It's the population projection," Renee said in a hoarse voice. "I'm really tired, and I hope this is all messed up, but I already did it three times."

Everyone leaned over her shoulder to take a look.

"I think," Morgan said slowly as he took in the horrifying numbers that Renee had come up with, "that I need to call Richards. The President is going to want to see this right away."

CHAPTER THIRTY-FOUR

"There is a fighter sending out a warning to us," Khatuna said nervously as Jack helped Mikhailov back into the copilot's seat.

"You have not answered, have you?"

She turned to the Russian captain, scowling. "Of course not! You think me an idiot?"

"Never," he said as he slipped on his headphones and switched over to the civilian guard channel that Khatuna had been monitoring.

"What are they saying?" Jack scanned the sky around them, looking for any other aircraft. For probably the first time since they'd left Zadonsk, there were none.

"They are ordering us to Andreapol. If we do not comply, they will shoot us down." He frowned, then looked at Khatuna. "Did you hear that?"

With wide eyes, she nodded.

"What?" Jack was frustrated that he didn't have headphones, and couldn't understand what was being said even if he did.

"Another aircraft answered!" Mikhailov looked out his window, trying to see beyond the bare trees that reached for them as Khatuna guided the old biplane north. "The fighter is after someone else!" He listened a moment more. "Whoever they are pursuing is refusing to turn. The fighter warned them again."

"*Bozhe moi!* Look!" Khatuna pointed out her side to the left.

Jack leaned down so he could see where she was pointing. Off in the distance, barely visible, he saw a thin white streak arrow down from high in the sky. Just when he was sure it was going to hit the ground, a tiny orange and black fireball appeared.

Khatuna ripped her headphones off, and Jack heard the voice of the pilot of the plane that had been attacked, screaming.

The fireball gave birth to a fuzzy trail of smoke that plummeted earthward. The scream suddenly ended.

* * *

The old Antonov droned north for what seemed like forever. As each barrel ran dry, Jack shifted the fuel hose to a full one. Then he went through the onerous task of opening the cargo door and kicking out the empty barrel. The first few times he'd done that, he'd felt an odd sense of wrongness, like he was dumping a huge pile of trash along an interstate at home. You just didn't toss fuel drums out of airplanes. But here he was, doing just that.

After the third or fourth, he stopped caring. He and the others were thirsty and hungry. He just wanted the flight to be over. He wanted to be in Norway and find out what the hell was happening with Naomi.

By the time they reached Lake Ilmen and Khatuna turned the plane due north, they had heard intercepts of two other aircraft. One had quickly given in and diverted to the airbase the fighter had ordered them to. The other had refused. Fortunately, it had been too far away for Mikhailov and Khatuna to hear the pilot of the doomed plane when the missile hit.

Jack had tried to convince himself that maybe it had been a harvester. It was a convenient thought that he clung to.

The damnable thing was that the Russians pursuing them weren't the enemy. He couldn't hate or despise them. They were simply afraid and were leaping to conclusions, looking for someone to blame for the horror that had befallen them.

He just wished he could have spoken to Naomi, both to know that she was all right, and to find out if what he knew was really as important as Mikhailov believed. Mikhailov, perhaps even Khatuna, might be willing to sacrifice their lives to get Jack out of Russia. Jack just wished he knew if such a sacrifice would be worth it, or if they were going through all this for nothing. What if the FSB had just wanted to question him, and would then have been happy to turn him over to the American Embassy? But both Mikhailov and Khatuna had dismissed the idea. If the FSB got their hands on him, he wouldn't be seeing daylight for quite some time. And every minute he spent in custody was another minute the harvesters could solidify their hold on the world.

No. What they were doing was necessary. The risks they were taking were worth it. They had to be.

Below them, the endless expanse of northern Russia swept by, uncomfortably close. It seemed to Jack that as they burned off the heavy barrels of fuel, Khatuna flew lower and lower. Three times he'd heard the thump of frozen tree limbs hitting either the landing gear or the lower wings, but he said nothing. He was terrified of crashing, but he knew that her skill at low-level flying was the only thing that had kept them all alive.

Khatuna pointed ahead. "Lake Ladoga."

Looking out, Jack watched as the plane left land behind and flew over a vast sheet of ice that stretched ahead of them and to both sides as far as he could see.

"A man named Alexander Nevsky fought a famous battle here against the Teutonic Knights in the thirteenth century," Mikhailov said. "The Battle of the Ice."

Jack glanced at him. "Who won?"

With a smile, Mikhailov said, "Nevsky and the Russians, of course. The Teutonic Knights were wearing heavy armor. They fell through the ice and drowned."

"That's not very reassuring."

The An-2 droned northward across the lake for a full hour before reaching the other side, and Jack was relieved when they were again over land. Frozen and inhospitable as it might be, he would rather take his chances in the forests of northern Russia than the icebound wasteland of Lake Ladoga.

Khatuna turned to him. "Jack, check fuel."

"Right." Stepping into the cargo area, Jack rapped the side of the single remaining fuel barrel with his knuckles, trying to determine how much was left. It was nearly empty.

He undid the strap holding the barrel in place, then leaned it over partway so the fuel would gather in the bottom corner. He guided the hose to the auxiliary pump into the remaining bit of fuel, waiting for it to run dry.

He called up to Khatuna. "That's it!"

In the cockpit, Khatuna turned off the pump. Now all the plane had left was the fuel in its main tanks. While it was technically a full load, they still had more than eight hundred kilometers to go.

Jack pulled out the hose, then wheeled the barrel aft. Bracing himself against the bitter cold, he opened the door, then kicked the barrel out. He watched to make sure it cleared the tail before he slammed the door shut.

"Christ, it's cold out there," he muttered as he made his way forward again.

As they continued on, the earth below seemed to be made of nothing more than snow-covered forests and irregularly shaped lakes covered in ice. Had this been the first time he had ever set eyes on the world, he would never have known that humans existed.

"That does not look so good," Mikhailov said.

Ahead of them, dark gray clouds began to fill the horizon.

* * *

Starshiy praporshchik Pavel Ignatiev stared thoughtfully at his radar console. He was the senior operator on-board a Beriev A-50M "Mainstay" airborne warning and control system (AWACS) aircraft orbiting over the Kola Peninsula in northern Russia near the border with Norway and Finland. He was tasked with finding an aircraft bearing a fugitive who was attempting to reach Norway. For the last four hours, he and his fellow crewmen had been watching for any aircraft that matched the profile of the plane they were looking for, an antiquated An-2.

He knew that four planes had been intercepted to the south of their patrol area by MiG-29s that had been assigned to the hunt, but the powers that be had not been content to let the matter go. The MiGs, after having finished their search grid to the north, had been allowed to return to base. Now only the Mainstays like his and their assigned fighters maintained the vigil against the renegade aircraft.

The frustrating thing was that this sector had been entirely quiet. The hours had crept by as they watched their screens for any unauthorized aircraft, but there had been nothing. While the southern part of his country had fallen into chaos, literally overnight, and the Air Force was called to action, he and his fellows in the north could do nothing but bore holes through the frigid skies.

The only excitement, such as it was, was the barrier patrols put up by the Finns and the Norwegians on their respective sides of the border. They would pose no real threat to the Russian Air Force if battle were joined, but it would have been something to focus on to help pass the time. Unfortunately, that task was assigned to another group of controllers on the plane, leaving him and the two other controllers of his section to look for phantom planes.

His only entertainment had been a possible contact that had first appeared roughly one hundred and sixty kilometers south of the Mainstay's patrol station. He had initially filtered it out as most likely being a fast-moving automobile or a bogus return. But he saw a similar return over an hour later, fifty kilometers northwest of the Mainstay's position.

With a frown, he assigned the initial contact a target number, then associated the second contact with it, forming a track on his display. Looking at the plot, his frown deepened. If it was indeed an aircraft (although he could not imagine how low the pilot must be flying to avoid being classified as an aircraft by the Mainstay's radar), it was heading on a northerly course that would take it straight to Norway near Melkefoss. Looking at the estimated airspeed, he saw that it was just shy of one hundred knots. Checking his aircraft guide, a shiver of excitement ran up his spine as he saw that it closely matched the economical cruise speed of an An-2, precisely the type of aircraft they were hunting.

* * *

"God, I think we might actually pull this off" Jack was looking over Mikhailov's shoulder as the Russian captain held open the map, trying to figure out their location.

"I think," Mikhailov said uncertainly, glancing out his window to the right, "that is Lake Alla-Akkayarvi." It was a long, narrow patch of ice, maybe two kilometers wide, that stretched off to the northeast. But it was very difficult to make out: the longer night of late winter was coming, the sky was filled with low, leaden clouds, and snow had begun to fall. "If so, then we are within fifty kilometers of the Norwegian border."

Khatuna said nothing. Jack worried about her, although there was really nothing he could do. Her eyes flicked across the instruments, to the outside, then back again, never still for more than a few seconds. He knew she must have been exhausted from so many hours of low-level flying and the constant fear of attack by Russian fighters. And now the weather was turning sour.

"We will have to fly higher," she told them. "There are no large mountains here, but with snow, we will hit trees before I can pull up."

Both men nodded. They knew that it would increase their chances of being detected, but the game would be over if they slammed into a tree or one of the low hills.

"Just do the best you can," Jack told her with a gentle squeeze on her shoulder. "You're doing great so far."

"Thank you." She stiffened. "Sergei! Switch to my frequency!"

Grimacing as he leaned forward to reach the radio console, Mikhailov switched over to the civilian guard channel and listened.

In Russian, a male voice said, "Unidentified aircraft proceeding on bearing three four nine, position six-nine zero-five North, three-zero two-four East, altitude five zero meters, this is a Russian Air Force controller. You are ordered to identify yourself immediately or you will be fired upon. Over."

Mikhailov did a quick translation for Jack.

"Dammit!" Jack cursed.

"He is repeating," Mikhailov said in a tight voice. "I do not think he will ask again."

* * *

Polkovnik Dmitri Andropov, the Mainstay's mission commander, looked at the track of their quarry on Ignatiev's scope.

"Give them a warning shot and order them to Kilpyavr Air Base," the *polkovnik* said. "If they do not comply, shoot them down."

"Yes, sir." Ignatiev switched from the intercom to the control frequency for the aircraft assigned to him, two MiG-29s. "*Tigr* flight, you are cleared to fire a warning shot past the target's nose."

"*Tigr* lead, understood."

* * *

Jack cringed as a stream of cannon shells blazed past the canopy, followed by a pair of fighters that thundered by, insanely close. They quickly disappeared into the slate gray clouds like great white sharks sinking into dark water.

"Jack!" Mikhailov had to shout over the An-2's straining engine. Khatuna had pushed the throttle forward to keep the old biplane from falling out of the sky as it flew through the slipstreams of the two fighters. "They say they will shoot us down if we do not land at a nearby air base."

Mikhailov's face bore an agonized look, but it was not of physical pain. It was the anguish of failure.

They had reached the end of the line, only spitting distance from their objective. But there wasn't any point in fighting the inevitable. Jack had thought earlier that it would be worth any sacrifice to get out of Russia, but now that the time had come, he couldn't bear to sacrifice his friends. Had it only been himself, it might have been different. He knew that, if he asked, Sergei would gladly go on and perish in the fireball of the missile that one of the fighters must even now have locked on this antiquated plane. Perhaps even Khatuna would.

But he wouldn't ask them to. "Do as they say," he said. "Getting ourselves killed isn't going to help anyone."

Mikhailov nodded wearily, then spoke to the Air Force controller, informing him that they were turning toward Kilpyavr. "Khatuna," he said, "bring us around to the east. Khatuna?"

She was staring straight ahead, a slack expression on her face. "I will not go back."

The voice was hers, but something in how she said the words sent a chill down Jack's spine.

"We must turn about, or they will fire!" Mikhailov tried to turn the copilot's wheel, but Khatuna's grip was like iron and the controls didn't budge.

Twisting in her seat, she turned toward Mikhailov. Jack let out a shout of horrified surprise when a stinger burst from her chest and shot across the cockpit to stab Mikhailov in the stomach.

The Russian screamed, but it was as much in pain as it was in rage. His combat knife was suddenly in his hand, and with a savage slash he severed the stinger from the undulating tentacle connecting it to the Khatuna-thing. She/It, in turn, screamed, the shrill call of a wounded harvester.

Jack drew his own knife and drove it up to the hilt into the thing's neck.

With an ear-shattering shriek, it elongated one of its arms, then slammed a fist against his head, then again. Reeling from the blows, Jack lost his grip on the knife and fell against the bulkhead at the rear of the cockpit.

Mikhailov, the stinger still embedded in his gut, managed to release his harness and hurled himself at the creature, driving his knife into its head again and again.

With a hiss, the harvester slammed Mikhailov backward against the instrument panel, one of its clawed appendages latched around his throat. In his struggles, he shoved the throttle to the idle position, and the plane shuddered as it lost airspeed.

Getting back to his feet, Jack yanked his knife from the thing's neck and jammed it in again, twisting it savagely.

It released its grip on Mikhailov, then slammed him back against the bulkhead with an elbow that hit him like inch-thick steel rebar.

Jack sank to his knees, stunned.

"Get out, Jack!"

He looked up at Mikhailov, who was still wrestling with the creature. The Russian was bleeding in a dozen places from where the harvester's claws had savaged him, but he refused to give in. It tried to drive a claw into his chest, but he managed to deflect it with one hand while pinning the thing's other claw against its chest with his knife.

Beyond the two struggling figures, Jack could see snow-covered trees through the windscreen.

Mikhailov screamed as the thing wrestled its claws free, then shoved one of them into his chest, deep into his rib cage.

There was nothing else Jack could do. He ran back toward the rear of the plane. As the thing in the pilot's seat flung Mikhailov's body aside and regained control, Jack swung the door open to the bitterly cold air outside.

"Jesus," he whispered as he watched the ground flash by, maybe fifty feet below. Even shuddering in the air on the verge of a stall, moving just fast enough to stay airborne above the trees, the An-2 seemed to be moving as fast as a rocket sled.

He caught a glare out of the corner of his eye, and saw something streaking out of the darkness toward him.

A moment later, the warhead of the R-73 air-to-air missile launched by one of the MiG-29s detonated, blotting the old biplane from the sky in a fiery cloud of smoke and debris.

CHAPTER THIRTY-FIVE

Naomi stared at the monitors, watching the crippled harvester drag itself around the containment cell. It was obviously keeping its distance from the larva that mindlessly pursued its parent, which the larva viewed as nothing more than food.

Morgan had made his call to Richards, who had been stunned into momentary silence by the numbers Renee had come up with. Her projections had been checked by an analyst at FBI Headquarters and a team at the Center for Disease Control in Atlanta. All of them had come up with similar numbers. All of them had been scared out of their wits.

Richards had bumped the information up the line, and now they were waiting for a secure video teleconference call with the President. Morgan had wanted Naomi to come up and wait in the conference room, but she had preferred to stay in the monitoring room, focusing her thoughts and her hate on the harvester. Alexander and Koshka were with her. Koshka was in her lap, purring, while Alexander lay in a Sphinx position, his attention riveted on the thing in the monitor. She knew that normally he didn't watch television, even when she turned on a nature program with birds or small rodents that fascinated Koshka. But here, the big cat somehow sensed that the thing on the screen, while not right there with them, was real. Every now and then a low growl escaped from his throat.

She knew that, as a scientist, it was wrong to hate the harvester and the others of its kind. Scientists were supposed to be objective, to make dispassionate observations of their subjects. These creatures weren't inherently evil, nor did they bear any particular ill will toward humankind for what it was, any more than the average person despised a steer. The steer, however, did not realize its lot in life. Naomi and the others who now understood the full scope of the harvester threat, however, did. And she hated them for what they were, what they were now doing to her world.

Renee hadn't helped lift her mood with what she'd told Naomi about what was happening in Russia. There had still been no word from Jack, and intelligence information that Naomi normally wouldn't have been privy to indicated that the Russians were trying to find him because they believed he was the source of the harvester outbreak there. Naomi only hoped that Mikhailov and Rudenko could keep him safe.

The rest of the world where the other harvester outbreaks had occurred were mirror images of what was happening in Russia and, in a smaller microcosm, Los Angeles. Very little news was coming out of China after the government had severed most of the connections to the internet and telephone communications, but it was clear from what the Intelligence Community was reporting that southern China was a massive battleground, far worse than in Russia because China's outbreak had occurred earlier. Martial law had been declared in several states in India, where a massive military mobilization was taking place. In South America, Brazil was quickly falling into anarchy, and French Army troops were fighting for their lives in southwestern France from the Bay of Biscay to the Mediterranean.

In the United States, unconfirmed reports of harvesters had already come in from Seattle, Dallas, Las Vegas, Minneapolis, and New York City, and people across the country were starting to panic.

Giving in to a sudden impulse, she reached out and activated the Taser in the instrument cluster at the top of the containment cell. It automatically tracked the adult harvester, and with a single press of her finger on the control it fired.

The weapon coughed as it spat its electrodes into the harvester's flesh before hitting the creature with thousands of volts.

The harvester spasmed and went rigid. The features of the woman that it mimicked melted away to reveal its natural form.

The larva reached its prize, and Naomi leaned forward, aroused by morbid curiosity as the amoebic creature flowed onto one of the adult harvester's shattered legs.

Sooner than should have been possible, the adult harvester began to gain control of its body. It twitched, then began to thrash, and a high keening issued from its throat as the larva moved farther up its leg.

Naomi watched as the limb began to disappear, dissolved and consumed by the larva. "The consumption rate is so fast," she whispered, double checking that the system recorder was capturing the scene.

The harvester was in a frenzy now. Unable to shake the larva from its leg, it swung out its cutting appendage and began to hack away at the damaged limb. But the wave-edged blade must have touched the larva, for a tiny part of it stretched away from the oozing mass and clung to the blade.

Pitching and twisting, the harvester did everything it could to dislodge its cannibal offspring, all to no avail. Its legs, then the rest of its body, disappeared under the cover of the mottled blue and yellow of its child.

In just under five minutes, the adult was gone. The larva, much larger now, paused a moment to excrete a small pool of dark liquid, then moved around the chamber, searching for more prey.

Out of curiosity, she hit it with the Taser. The weapon had no effect. The electrodes disappeared into the mottled flesh and arced, but that was all. The thing continued to move about the enclosure, mindlessly searching for more food.

"Where's the harvester?"

She looked up to see Renee staring, horror-struck, at the screen.

"Right where it belongs," Naomi told her softly. "In Hell."

"Come on kid." Renee put her hand on Naomi's shoulder. "It's time."

* * *

"I've been told the numbers, doctor, but frankly I'd rather hear them from you. Maybe your words will make more sense to me."

President Miller looked as if he had aged a decade in the days since she had last seen him on television. In the high definition video teleconferencing display, he looked haggard. She couldn't imagine the stress he was under, and little of what she had to tell him would bring any relief.

At the table beside him in the White House Situation Room were the vice president and several cabinet members, along with Carl Richards, who sat at the president's right hand. All of them wore uniformly grim expressions.

"I'll do my best, Mr. President."

Miller nodded. "Then let's get started, doctor, if you please."

"Sir," she began, "based on what is, as yet, a very small amount of directly-observed data, we've put together a rough projection of harvester population growth. While we need to refine our model with more detailed information, I think it's close enough to give you an idea of the magnitude of the problem we face."

Pressing a button on the computer beside her, she brought up a slide that showed an image of a harvester, and that would be projected on the president's display. "The harvesters appear to be asexual, meaning that any harvester is capable of producing offspring by itself, without the need to mate. From what we learned in the confrontation with the first of these new generation creatures at Sutter Buttes, they also mature extremely quickly, and can transition from larva to adult in roughly twenty-four hours, perhaps less."

"Christ," someone muttered off-screen in the Situation Room.

"We don't know yet for sure, but we're assuming the worst at this point, that they're able to reproduce as soon as they achieve their adult form. From what is admittedly still very sketchy data, it looks like they may be able to reproduce as often as once every hour."

The vice president leaned forward. "That's from your analysis of the creature from Kansas City?"

"Yes, sir," Naomi said. "That and some other circumstantial data that one of our people," she glanced at Renee, "put together. Again, it needs to be refined, but we believe it's close."

"All right, doctor," the president said quietly, "I accept your assumptions. Now tell me exactly what it all means."

"What it means, Mr. President, is that in just twenty-four hours, a single harvester could lead to a population of more than three hundred."

On the screen, the chilling image of the harvester was replaced by an even more frightening chart that showed time along the horizontal axis and the number of harvesters along the vertical axis. For one day, the number of harvesters leaped from one to just over three hundred.

"In a week, the population that began with that single harvester would be more than fourteen thousand," Naomi continued. "And in a month, there would be nearly two hundred and sixty thousand." She paused, letting the numbers sink in. "This fits with what we saw in Los Angeles. We don't have any way of knowing exactly when the index case, the first harvester, was created there. But my theory is that it was roughly a month ago, and that the first host was probably a mouse or rat that made its way to the sewer system where there would be an ample supply of organic material for them to live on. But with that sort of population growth..."

"They'd eventually have to move above ground," Miller finished for her.

"Yes, sir. And I believe that's why we saw such a sudden, overwhelming invasion of the city." Turning back to the chart, she hit the forward button again, and the population leaped upward, going nearly vertical up the chart. "In a year," she went on grimly, "the population would be more than thirty-eight million harvesters."

"And all of that stemming from a single individual?" Miller looked like he was about to be sick.

"Yes, Mr. President." She took a breath and pushed on. *He has to know the whole truth.* "But we're not dealing with a single founding individual. We have *six* known initial clusters: Brazil, China, France, India, Russia, and Los Angeles, here in the U.S. We know for certain that India and Russia didn't stem from single individuals: Jack Dawson reported that an entire village in India was exposed to infected corn, and the members of a research facility in Russia were similarly exposed. Each of those individuals would be an index case for an entire harvester population as I just described. As for Brazil, China, and France, we don't have enough data to determine whether their infestations stemmed from a single individual or mass exposure."

At the mention of Jack's name, Carl looked up. He said nothing, but his expression was a mixture of sadness and pain that spoke volumes, and Naomi felt a worm of fear burrow its way into her stomach.

"So what are we talking about for longer term numbers? Doctor?"

She took a breath, trying to compose herself and set aside her instinctive fear. "Sir, the thirty day global estimate starting with the six initial hot zones is one point five million individuals. Minimum. In roughly five and a half years, the harvester population will exceed the current human population of the planet." She paused. "If they breed unchecked, we're looking at an extinction level event, and not just for humanity. The harvester larvae could eventually scour the planet clean of every form of life larger than a microbe."

Everyone sat back, stunned. Several of them, including Miller, had already heard the numbers, but it had been impossible for them to grasp their sheer enormity and the terrifying implications.

"I must point out, however, that these figures are extremely conservative, and assume only a single initial harvester in each of those six countries. We know there were more, so the pace of their population growth is likely to be much higher."

One of the others at the table in the Situation Room asked, "What about environmental impact?"

"Who gives a crap about the environment when we have people being killed?" The vice president shook his head in angry bewilderment.

"It's actually a good question, sir," Naomi said. "The harvester larvae eat nearly everything that isn't based on something from the mineral kingdom, and can consume huge quantities of food before they molt into the adult form." She suppressed a shudder as she remembered the enormous monstrosities they had seen coming from the race track at Santa Anita. "And since the ground zero for each infestation, with the exception of Los Angeles, is in the middle of the world's largest grain producing regions, harvester larvae could devastate critical segments of our food supply, in addition to attacking people in those areas directly."

The president's fists clenched on the table. "So on top of everything else, we could be looking at an imminent famine?"

"Between destruction of crops and attacks by harvesters on people working in agriculture, yes, sir, I'm afraid so."

"What about water?" The same person, a gray-haired woman with sharp blue eyes, asked. "Can these things thrive in freshwater lakes and streams, or in the oceans?"

The vice president frowned. "Again, who cares?"

Naomi suppressed her irritation at him, and was heartened that the woman refused to be cowed. The President seemed content to let the conversation run its course.

"I'm asking, because even if we can somehow beat these things on land, if they can infest our fresh water supplies we won't have to wait until the food runs out. And if they can destroy the native ocean life, our long term prospects for survival are nil."

The vice president shut his mouth.

"I'm sorry, ma'am, but we just don't know," Naomi told her. "Based on testing we did when I was in the Earth Defense Society, the adult harvesters can survive in both fresh and salt water, but like us they require oxygen to breathe. As for the larvae, we'll have to do tests. At this point we know terribly little about them, other than they eat nearly anything and are cannibalistic."

"Cannibalistic?" Miller cocked his head.

"Yes, sir. The larvae are just as dangerous to the parents as they are to us. We've conclusively proven that."

"How do we kill them?" That from the Chairman of the Joint Chiefs of Staff.

"We're preparing a detailed package on that, general, and will be sending it out as soon as this meeting is over. But to summarize, you have to think of the adults and the larvae as two separate enemies that have different vulnerabilities. Both are highly susceptible to any type of open flame, although electric arcs, like from a Taser, don't seem to harm them. Even something as small as a cigarette lighter will turn them into a torch. Incendiary rounds are also highly effective. High explosive, based on what we saw in Los Angeles, fragments them and creates more larvae."

The vice president, whose fingers hadn't been still since the teleconference began, looked aghast. "You mean to tell me that if you chop or blow one of these things up, it just makes more?"

"That is correct, sir." She frowned. "So far, fire seems to be the only real weakness of the larval form. They simply absorb bullets or other projectiles, and we haven't had time to run tests on any other ways — poison, for example — to kill them. That will, of course, be one of our top priorities."

After taking a sip of water, she went on. "Other than fire or incendiary bullets, the adult harvesters can be killed with conventional weapons, but standard infantry rifles and handguns aren't powerful enough."

The Chairman of the Joint Chiefs nodded. "I saw the footage of the National Guard troops in Los Angeles. We're already looking at fielding larger caliber weapons with tracer and incendiary ammunition."

"Their only other real weakness is one that we know of from one of the harvesters at Sutter Buttes before the base was destroyed, and that's ionizing radiation."

"What," the president asked, "as in a nuclear bomb?"

"Yes, sir. Again, we haven't tested this directly, but the last surviving harvester at the base could have escaped, but didn't because it feared the radiation effects of the weapon that had been used on the base."

"We're back to neutron bombs," the Chairman of the Joint Chiefs said quietly as he leaned back in his chair. Neutron bombs, also known as enhanced radiation weapons, were a product of the Cold War. Their primary lethal effect was radiation, rather than blast or heat.

"Speaking of nuclear weapons, general," Naomi said, "you need to put in place new safeguards for the nuclear arsenal, and make sure the other nuclear powers know what to do. What we're seeing in Los Angeles and elsewhere, the larvae and harvesters swarming in their natural form, isn't the greatest threat. What we have most to fear is this." She hit the forward button, and an image came up of a young woman in her twenties who would have been attractive had her face not been twisted into an angry snarl. "This is a photo of the harvester we captured in Kansas City. Everything about her outward appearance, right down to her fingerprints and retinal patterns, and her behavior match the woman the creature killed and chose to mimic. There are likely dozens, perhaps hundreds or even more, of these doppelgängers now loose in our population. They could be anyone, anywhere, and even their closest friends and relatives couldn't tell the difference."

"We're already working on that one, doctor," the president said. "Assistant Director Richards here has been working hand in hand with the Departments of Defense and Homeland Security, but I'd appreciate it if you'd take a look at our protocols and make sure we didn't miss anything." He managed a grin. "I've always been a dog person, but when I came down here for this meeting I was greeted by half a dozen cats and a brace of Secret Service people wearing thermal imagers."

Naomi smiled. She didn't really care much for Miller, but the man was proving to be more capable and flexible than she initially would have given him credit for. "That's all I have for now, sir."

The grin faded from the President's face. "I owe you an apology, doctor. Well, I owe it to you and Jack Dawson, both." His face clouded. "I just wish I could tell him, too."

"Sir?" Naomi could sense it coming, the way some animals knew that an earthquake was about to happen before it struck.

"Naomi, I'm sorry that I waited until the end to bring this up, but was compelled to do so by the extremity of the peril that faces us. I had to have your objective input. I can only beg you to forgive me for that." He pursed his lips, then said, "I was told just before this meeting by the Director for National Intelligence," he nodded his head at one of the men sitting at the table, "that a plane was shot down by the Russian Air Force near the Norwegian border. We confirmed that a Russian Army officer, Sergei Mikhailov," he glanced at the DNI, who nodded, "was aboard, and Assistant Director Richards indicated to me that it would be almost certain that Jack would be with him. I've got the State Department working hard to confirm what happened with the Russians, and to bring his body home when it's recovered. I'm terribly sorry, Naomi. You have my deepest condolences."

"Yes, Mr. President," she said, her tongue a numb lump in her mouth. "Thank you."

Miller looked around the table. "And now I think we all have a great deal of work to do."

The screen went blank. The teleconference was over.

EPILOGUE

Adrian Kelso fled down the basement corridor, somewhere under the international terminal at Los Angeles International Airport. Above, in the main concourse area, a battle raged between the hopelessly outmatched airport police and the harvesters that had reached the airport. Kelso had tried to escape, but the roads in and around the airport were clogged with cars, many of them empty now. The only other way out was on foot, and Kelso was too old and out of shape to have made it far, and he knew that anyone fleeing through the army of approaching harvesters would be doomed.

The others in the passenger lounge had tried to persuade him to come with them on their run to safety. He had told them they were insane, had tried to warn them that it was a hopeless endeavor, but they didn't listen. Watching from the concourse windows, he followed their progress across the parking lot as they joined hundreds, thousands, of others fleeing from the airport's terminals. He even rooted for them, hoping that someone might be able to be saved from the nightmare that he had created.

His words of encouragement died on his lips as his almost-friends were torn apart by a fresh onslaught of the nightmarish creatures.

"No! No!" Kelso hammered his fists against the glass and his eyes misted with tears as he watched them die.

As he turned away, a huge orange and yellow fireball erupted on the other side of the terminal, and the windows on that side blew in. Kelso fell to the floor as glass shards rained all around him. He was deafened by the blast, and the concourse was filled with smoke that carried the smell of burning jet fuel and plastic.

Staggering to his feet, he made his way to that side of the building and looked out. Two airliners had collided on the taxiway.

He guessed that the pilots of one or the other, perhaps both, had decided to ignore the airport closure order and tried to get their planes into the air. Or, worse, they had been piloted by harvesters. They had crashed into one another while trying to reach the main runway.

"It wouldn't have mattered, you know." His whisper was intended for the ghosts of the men and women whose bodies were now wreathed in flames, the fire burning so hot that it was melting the aluminum skin of the planes. He looked up as a pair of Air Force fighters thundered overhead. Even had the planes managed to take off, they would not have made it far.

It was then that Kelso heard the screech of harvesters as they entered the building, followed by a volley of shots from the airport police. Some had deserted their posts, but most had stayed. He gave credit to their courage as he himself fled.

With his lungs heaving with every breath, his heart hammering in his chest, Kelso ran as best he could, but there was nowhere to go. Every entrance to the concourse was now the scene of a firefight. He was trapped.

Then he found a nearby door marked "Authorized Personnel Only" that had been left ajar. Without hesitation, he pushed through it into a stairwell that led down into a basement service corridor.

Kelso had no idea where he was, but that didn't matter. What did matter was finding a place to hide. He passed a set of bathrooms, but kept going, thinking that too obvious.

Then he came to a janitorial closet. Twisting the handle, he found that it was unlocked. He stepped inside and closed the door just as a blood-curdling screech echoed down the corridor from the stairwell he had just taken. He locked the door.

Not daring to turn on the light, Kelso inched his way back, deeper into the closet, using his shaking hands to guide him. He bumped into something, and there was a clatter on the floor. He stopped where he was and did his best to breathe quietly. His hands found what he suspected was a mop handle, and he drew it toward him. It was a pitiful weapon, but it was something to hold. From that, he drew some small comfort.

He waited.

In the corridor beyond came another screech. Then he saw shadows dancing in the light that seeped in under the door. He had no idea if there was only one of the abominations or more out there. He gripped his mop tighter.

A long, tearing-scratching sound came from the door, and Kelso nearly screamed in fright. The handle moved. Then stopped.

With a loud bang, the thing outside wrenched the handle from the door. Kelso bit his lower lip so hard that he drew blood, flooding his mouth with the coppery taste, but he remained silent.

Outside, there was a strange grunting sound. Then the shadows under the door danced again, and he heard the harvester retreat down the corridor.

It was gone.

Kelso stood there, shivering with the release of adrenaline as tears coursed down his face.

He didn't notice the small shadow that momentarily blocked some of the light from under the door.

It wasn't until he felt a searing, burning sensation in his left foot that he realized anything was wrong. He reflexively reached for his foot, trying to get whatever it was away from him. His fingers pressed into something soft and cool, like gelatin. Then his fingers, too, began to burn.

With a scream, he pulled his hands away. His entire foot was on fire now, and he'd lost all sensation in his toes.

Blundering toward the door, he tried to open it, but the handle came off in his burning hands, the other side having been ripped away by the harvester. He was trapped.

Brushing his hands along the wall, he found the light switch and flipped it on. The fingers of both hands were covered in what he instantly recognized as larval harvester tissue, with the main body of the horrid thing consuming his foot.

That was the last rational thought Adrian Kelso had before he collapsed to the floor, screaming in agony.

* * *

"I am not leaving!" Vijay Chidambaram struggled, but Kiran pushed him back down onto the gurney. Vijay's cat was in its crate, sitting on top of his legs. Kiran watched it carefully: it had already warned them of two harvesters among the people swarming around Begumpet Airport in the northern part of Hyderabad. Kiran had initially been ordered to get Vijay out through Rajiv Gandhi International Airport, farther to the south, but the Army couldn't hold it against the combined onslaught of harvesters and panicked civilians. Kiran, Vijay, and the soldiers guarding them watched with tears in their eyes as Indian Air Force Mirage 2000 and Jaguar strike aircraft bombed the airliners and smaller aircraft that remained intact to keep them out of the hands of the enemy. Huge pillars of fire and smoke rose into the night sky as Kiran ordered his men to turn north.

It had been a long, terror-filled trek back through the city to Begumpet Airport, which was being held by two battalions of the 50th Para Brigade. Kiran's company of elite Black Cat special operations soldiers had been whittled in half during the fierce fighting of the last few days, and by the time they fought their way through to Begumpet, fewer than a dozen were left. He had been ordered to get Vijay, who was still recovering from his auto accident, out of the city. His commander had made it crystal clear that Kiran was to keep Vijay alive at any cost. As the only Indian who had any real knowledge of the harvesters, Vijay was considered a priceless national asset against the sudden holocaust sweeping through the southern part of the country and, as it happened, much of the rest of the world. His commander confided that he believed the plan was to send Vijay overseas to the United States, where he would rejoin his former comrades from the Earth Defense Society and hopefully find a way to stop these creatures.

And that is what had Vijay so upset: he didn't want to leave his homeland.

"Yes, you are leaving!" Kiran told his cousin over the angry and terrified shouts of the crowd as the Army truck slowly bulled its way forward. His men stood along the side rails of the cargo bed, their weapons pointing into the river of people through which they passed. None of them wanted to shoot, but they would if they had to. They had done so several times already on this accursed night, and not all the targets struck by their bullets had been human.

"Over half my men died tonight, protecting you. What you have in your head, not this," Kiran brandished his rifle, "is the only thing that can defeat the enemy. If the Government tells you to go to America, you will. If they tell you to go to Hell, if that is the best place to put your knowledge to use, then that is where I will take you and that bloody cat of yours." He took Vijay's hand in his and squeezed it tight.

After another hour, they reached the first barricade the paras had set up on Begumpet Airport Road. The commanding officer, a grim-faced captain, passed them through the barbed wire and past the machine gun emplacements. High-output lights on poles and powered by small generators illuminated the crowd, which roared in anger as the barricade was closed.

As the truck rumbled down the empty road toward the airfield, there was a sudden volley of gunfire behind them, and people began to scream.

"Can't they take anyone else?" Vijay was propped up on his elbows, looking back toward the barricade. "Are we going to leave all these people here?"

"We can't take the risk. If we let some through, everyone will want through. It would start a stampede."

Behind them, there was a sudden roar of voices over the gunfire.

"I think we just did."

In the stark illumination of the lights over the barricade, they saw a wave of people surge forward, hurling themselves into the barbed wire and the bullets fired by the soldiers, who were still screaming at the civilians to stop. Like a living organism, the entire crowd of tens of thousands of people shifted against the defensive line, which suddenly snapped.

In the blink of an eye, the road behind the truck was filled with people chasing after them toward the airport.

"Bloody hell!" Kiran turned and yelled to the driver. "Hurry!"

As the truck accelerated, Kiran left Vijay's side so he could guide the driver. They passed by the trees of the airport's park, but instead of heading toward the passenger terminal, the truck took the road that led to the left side of the complex, where they came to another barricade and stopped.

A lieutenant who wore the turban of a Sikh stepped forward. "Captain Chidambaram?"

Kiran leaned over the side of the truck to speak to him. "Yes, I'm Chidambaram. Pass us through, then get the devil out of here! The main perimeter's collapsed and there's a mob coming right behind us. Save yourselves if you can!"

"Go on, sir! We'll try to buy you some time!"

The young man stepped back and gave Kiran a sharp salute. Silently damning the man for a fool, Kiran couldn't help but admire his courage. He snapped a salute in return as the truck rumbled forward. "*Jai hind!*"

The truck drove past the terminal complex and onto the tarmac, where a single Air Force Il-76 transport waited, its four jet engines already running. A cordon of paras stood around the plane, weapons at the ready.

Beyond the plane, the perimeter the para battalions had been holding along the northern part of the airport gave way, and thousands of people began pouring over the wall, running across the open fields toward the runway.

Kiran and his senior surviving NCO exchanged a look. "Allah help us all," the older man said.

The driver brought the truck to a screeching halt near the rear of the plane and the cargo ramp, which was already lowered. Another young officer rushed up to Kiran as he and his men carefully lowered Vijay's gurney to the tarmac.

"Sir! I'm Lieutenant Kapoor, sir. I'm to place myself and my men under your command."

With those words, Kiran felt as if the weight of the entire world had fallen on his shoulders. He looked into the lieutenant's eyes, and saw that the younger man knew what must come.

As if reading his mind, Kapoor said, "I'll take my men and keep the runway clear, sir, if that's all right."

With a heavy heart, Kiran said, "Carry on, lieutenant."

With a quick nod, Kapoor was off, ordering his men to the north edge of the runway. Like the other soldiers who had been guarding the airport, they would be left behind to suffer the less than gentle ministrations of the terrified mob and the harvesters.

"I'm sorry, Kiran." Vijay gripped his cousin's arm.

There was another round of automatic weapons fire near the terminal, and a few moments later the crowd that had pursued them down airport road flooded out of the side entrance onto the tarmac.

Kiran leaned down over Vijay. "Stay well, cousin." Then, to one of his junior NCOs, Kiran said, "Get him aboard."

"Kiran? You are to come with me!" Vijay reached for his young cousin, but Kiran stepped away, shaking his head. "Your commander ordered it! I heard him!"

Shaking his head, Kiran said, "There are times when even proper orders must be disobeyed."

"Very true, sir." The senior NCO chopped his young commander in the back of the neck. As Kiran's body crumpled, the NCO caught him, holding Kiran under the arms. "You lot, get the captain and the doctor aboard the plane. The rest of you, with me!"

"Thank you." Vijay's words didn't reach the man who'd saved his cousin's life at the cost of his own. All through this horrible night, the NCO had stood guard over Vijay, yet he had never even learned his name.

A pair of men pushed his gurney up the ramp and into the plane, while another pair carried Kiran's unconscious body aboard.

To the north, gunfire erupted as Lieutenant Kapoor's men fought to keep the runway clear. A heartbeat later, the NCO and the remainder of Kiran's Black Cats opened fire on the crowd approaching from the terminal building. Most of those they were shooting weren't the enemy, only helpless and terrified civilians. Vijay knew then that the NCO's sacrifice had not only saved Kiran's life, but his honor, as well.

With a roar of its engines, the Il-76 began to move across the tarmac, accelerating onto the taxiway. Vijay was facing the rear of the plane as the cargo ramp began to close. The mob barely paused before sweeping away the rest of Kiran's soldiers and turning to pursue the plane. Some of the people were quick, fast enough to come within a few meters of the still closing ramp, which was guarded by the last survivors of Kiran's company.

Vijay's cat hissed in its crate, and he stared out the maw of the cargo door, a band of fear clutching at his heart. While it was difficult to tell in the lights that illuminated the tarmac behind them, he swore that he saw the face of his dead cousin Surya, just before the cargo ramp closed.

* * *

At Morgan's facility in Nebraska, the former members of the Earth Defense Society and SEAL were rapidly being reunited by direct order of President Miller. More soldiers and equipment from the Army Corps of Engineers had come, and were quickly turning the lab into a self-sufficient fortress, far more formidable than had initially been intended. By the time they were done, it would be a small self-sufficient city. The soldiers of the Nebraska National Guard were to be relieved by a full company of Marines from the 1st Marine Division being flown out of Camp Pendleton.

Carl Richards barely noticed the activity on the ground below as his helicopter settled in to land next to the main building. The landing pad was nothing more than snow over barren earth now, but by this time tomorrow there would be a full-blown helipad here, including a service bay and fuel depot.

As the Blackhawk settled to the ground, Richards followed the crew chief out the cargo door and ran, bent low, toward where Morgan and Renee waited for him in the bitter cold. The sun had long since set, but there were enough high-output floodlights around the perimeter to make it seem like daytime.

"Mr. Richards." Morgan extended a gloved hand and Richards shook it. "Welcome to SEAL-2."

"That's what you're calling this now?"

"We had to call it something," he said as Richards gave Renee a quick hug, "and that seemed as good as anything else, especially since the original SEAL facility is being reopened for data backup and research that doesn't involve viable harvester tissue."

Richards followed Morgan and Renee toward the building. Behind them, the Blackhawk's crew shut the bird down and a team of soldiers rushed to refuel it. Richards wouldn't be here long. "How's Naomi doing?"

"How the hell do you think?" She gave Richards an angry look. "The girl just had her heart ripped out and you have to ask a question like that?"

"Right now I'm not asking as her friend," he said, curbing the sharp retort that instinctively came to his lips. He'd prided himself for years on being the Bureau's number one asshole, but he knew he couldn't afford that prima donna luxury now, and certainly not with Renee. Her tongue could be just as sharp as his, and she never took any crap from him. That was one of the many reasons he loved her. "I'm asking because the President wants to know if she's able to do the job that needs to be done, or if we need to replace her."

Renee cursed under her breath. "Jesus, Carl."

The outer doors swished open to the weather vestibule, then they passed through another set of doors to the lobby area, which was manned by six heavily armed National Guardsmen and as many Siberian and Maine Coon cats. The soldiers did an identity check on all three of them, even though Morgan and Renee had just passed through here minutes before on their way to greet Richards. Then they were paraded by the cats, who seemed terribly bored by the entire affair.

That was always a good sign.

"You know how I feel about Naomi," Richards said after he bent down to give one of the cats a quick scratch behind an ear. "I'd give or do anything for her, especially now that Jack's gone. But too much is riding on this. On her. We need to know if she can hold up under the strain."

"And if she can't," Renee snapped, "who can we replace her with? Nobody knows this shit like she does!"

Richards turned to her. "Don't you think I know that? Right now, she's probably the single most important human being on the planet. And the president needs to know that she can function." He hated talking about, and treating, Naomi like a particularly important cog in a heartless machine, but that's what they'd all have to become if humanity was to stand a chance of survival. Before he left Washington, Richards had seen the revised projections of harvester population growth and estimated current human casualties. Both sets of numbers had been staggering.

"Right this way." Morgan led them down to the first basement level where most of the labs were. After Morgan passed them through the security door, he pointed out Naomi.

She sat in the far corner at a desk loaded with lab equipment, surrounded by four large computer monitors. Even at this distance, Richards could see data flashing and scrolling by on the screens as she stared at them. He caught a glimpse of something white and fluffy hanging off the side of her chair, twitching periodically: the tail of Koshka, sitting in her lap. Sprawled across the desk, taking up every inch that wasn't devoted to lab equipment, was a huge tuxedo-colored cat. Alexander.

Catching sight of Richards, the big cat sat up and yawned, then hopped off the desk and trotted through the lab toward him.

Richards felt a momentary twinge of guilt as he knelt down to stroke Alexander's head: he'd forgotten to bring him and Koshka any treats like he used to when he came to visit Jack and Naomi in San Antonio. Alexander nuzzled and licked his hand. "Sorry, big guy. Maybe next time."

Seeing Alexander hammered home the reality of Jack's death. Richards was suddenly struck by a deep sense of loss, even more acute than what he'd felt at the bedside of his former director when she passed away in the hospital a year ago, the victim of a particularly brutal murder by a harvester. Jack had been a good guy, and the closest thing Richards had ever had to a real friend. He'd also been a patriot and someone who did the right thing, who did his duty, no matter the cost, and that was something that Richards could identify with. He couldn't even imagine what Naomi was going through.

"I'm sorry, Alexander," he whispered hoarsely as he picked the cat up in his arms and carried him to where Naomi was working.

She didn't look up until he called her name, and it seemed like it took her a moment to recognize him.

She's still in shock, he thought as he set Alexander back down on her desk.

"Carl, what are you doing here?" She set Koshka down and stood up, facing him.

"Naomi, I'm so sorry." He stepped forward, intending to embrace her, but she held her hands up, gently but firmly pushing his arms away.

"No, Carl. No. Thanks for your concern, but I'm fine. Just fine."

Richards looked at her. Her expression was perfectly neutral, revealing nothing. Her eyes were clear but unreadable. He may as well have been looking at an emotionless robot in the guise of a beautiful woman.

"Was there something you wanted me to show you?"

"In a little while. I just wanted to come down and see you first. I've got some things to talk to Morgan about, then maybe you can give me an update."

She gave a small nod. "Just let me know when." Then she sat back down at her desk and resumed her work.

Giving Alexander one last pat on the head, Richards made his way back to the door where Morgan and Renee had stood waiting.

"Is this how she's been since she got the news about Jack?"

Renee nodded. "She's been like a goddamn robot. She won't sleep except for quick naps. She's eating, but not enough. And she doesn't say diddly to anybody unless it's about the lab work or testing on the harvester specimens." She paused, sparing an agonized glance at Naomi. "She hasn't had time to grieve, Carl. She never cried or cussed or anything after the president told her about Jack. She just got up and walked out of the conference room, went straight to the lab and went to work. She won't do anything else."

That's exactly what we need, Richards thought grimly. *A heartless, tireless robot genius that's hell-bent on finding a way to defeat these damn things.*

With a final glance at Naomi, he followed Morgan and Renee out of the lab.

* * *

He was trapped in a nightmare. Horrible shadows danced and screams echoed in his mind. There was a bright light and fire, burning heat. Then he was falling, forever falling into the endless, bitter cold that was slowly choking the life from his body.

Jack's eyes flickered open as his chest heaved. It was dark, pitch black, and his eyes felt as if someone was rubbing sand into them. His senses told him that his body was in an odd position, neither standing nor laying down, and that his extremities were pinned. But that was for later. Of more immediate concern to his muddled mind was the sensation of having something cold and wet lodged in his windpipe. He couldn't breathe.

Snow. He remembered now. He had jumped into snow. And it was choking him to death.

As he coughed, trying to clear his airway of the snow that he'd accidentally inhaled when he hit, he twisted his body, drawing his elbows in close to his chest. Then he gradually forced his hands toward his face and began to punch the snow away to clear a breathing space around his mouth and nose.

Gagging and wheezing, he cleared his lungs, gratefully sucking in fresh air from the pocket he'd created.

He knew he couldn't be too deep, or there wouldn't be so much air. Using his already numbed hands to explore, he found a loosely packed channel of snow that he suspected had been left by his body when he plowed into the snow bank.

That was when the realization struck him that he had somehow survived the fall from the stricken An-2. When he'd seen the fiery trail of the approaching missile, he'd jumped. He had heard stories about Russian paratroops in the nineteen-thirties leaping from the wings of transport planes into deep snow drifts without using parachutes, but had written them off as urban legends. Maybe they were, or maybe they weren't. Regardless, he'd been lucky enough to somehow survive the blast of the missile and the fall. For that, he gave silent thanks.

He wasn't sure how long it took him to kick, claw, and dig his way to the surface, but he was gasping with the effort as he flopped out into the open air.

It wasn't snowing as hard now, and some distance away he could just make out a pillar of smoke rising from behind a stand of trees, marking where the An-2 must have crashed.

The Russians would come looking for the wreckage, he knew. Part of him wanted to just go to the wreck and wait for them to arrive. Even if they arrested him, at least he wouldn't freeze to death, and the State Department might be able to free him.

He was about to start off toward the wreck when a sound carrying through the curtain of snow stopped him. It came again, and his gut turned over in fear. It was the sound of a woman crying out for help. The words, faint but clear now, were in Russian, but there was no mistaking the voice.

It was the Khatuna-thing. It had somehow survived the explosion and the crash. When the Russians came, unless they knew what to look for, they would be caught completely by surprise. Or, worse, the thing would simply allow itself to be taken back to civilization.

There was nothing Jack could do, either to warn the Russians or prevent them from taking the harvester back with them. He couldn't kill it before they arrived: even if it were injured, he had no weapons but his bare, frozen hands. And if it knew that Jack was alive, it would hunt him down and kill him.

No, going to the crash site and waiting for rescue wasn't an option.

He looked around, trying to get his bearings. But in the dark and snow, without a compass, he had no idea which way was north. The only thing he could figure was that the plane had been flying on a northerly heading when it went down. In theory, the line between his position and the crash site should point northward. It sounded good, but he knew that even if it were true, the theory would be useless as soon as he hit the first tree line. From there on, he wouldn't have any reference points to keep him on course.

"Well, there's not much for it," he said to himself as he started off toward a set of trees, sinking calf deep into the snow. His intended path would take him well away from the harvester, but hopefully would still be "North."

With every step he took, the cold wormed its way deeper into his bones. The uniform and boots he wore weren't intended for arctic use, and he had nothing to cover his head or his hands. On top of that, he was hungry and dehydrated. He was tempted to eat some snow to ease his thirst, but it would cost him body heat that he couldn't afford to lose.

"Not good, Jack," he muttered. "Not good at all."

Time passed as he staggered forward. He left the wreck and the menace of the harvester behind as he passed through the first stand of trees, his original goal, and then another. And another. More trees and stretches of snow blended into an endless wasteland of torment as he lost all sensation in his feet, then his hands. His face and ears went numb, and his eyes felt as if someone was driving pins into them.

He had almost made it across another clearing when his legs collapsed beneath him and he pitched forward into the snow. He lay there for a minute, maybe more, his lungs heaving, his body completely exhausted.

"Come on, you bastard," he rasped through frozen lips. "Get up. Get the hell up!"

He made it onto his hands and knees, then tried to get to his feet. But his legs were too exhausted to move, glued solid to the snow.

With a weary sigh, he sat back and stared at the shadows of the tree line ahead. It seemed so close, but his body had nothing left to give.

"Shit." He closed his eyes, wishing that he was home in bed, with Naomi's warm body wrapped around him.

He opened his eyes again, and noticed that some of the trees seemed to be moving. *No, that's not right*, he corrected. Something in *front* of the trees was moving. Stealthy, almost invisible shadows.

Shadows in the shapes of men.

"Who are you?" Jack's call was weak, and for a moment he wasn't sure the shadows had heard him.

"Dawson? Jack Dawson?"

The largest of the shadows moved closer. As it did, the others, perhaps a dozen in all, seemed to melt away and disappear.

A man wearing an arctic camouflage uniform and holding a white assault rifle shuffled forward on cross country skis. Stepping out of them, he knelt in the snow in front of Jack. "Dawson?"

"Yeah," Jack croaked, confused. "That's me. Who the hell are you? You're not Russian."

The man pulled up his goggles and peeled back the white balaclava that covered his face under the hood of his parka, revealing a wide, toothy grin that glowed in the darkness. "No, I assure you we're not Russians, and they would not be happy to know we are here. I'm *Kaptein* Frode Stoltenberg of the *Forsvarets Spesialkommando*, Norwegian Special Forces." He made a signal with his hand, and two men materialized beside him. One of them, the team's medic, opened a large satchel of medical supplies and began to wrap Jack's hands, while another pulled over a rescue sled next to Jack before unrolling a thick white sleeping bag onto it. "Your Russian friend Mikhailov telephoned a mutual acquaintance, Terje Halvorsen, who raised a bit of a ruckus about your escape. With the rest of the world going to hell, our government also decided to leave sanity behind and sent us across the border to find you." His grin widened. "I've always wanted to take a piss on Russian soil. And imagine my surprise when we discovered your tracks on our way to the crash site. You've been walking in circles, my friend. We just made some coffee and waited for you to come back around."

"Glad I could make your job easier." Jack tried to smile, but his face was a numb plaster mask. The medic daubed something on his face and ears.

Another soldier appeared and spoke to Stoltenberg in Norwegian while pointing off into the distance.

The big captain nodded. "It is time for us to go. The Russians probably won't search this far from the crash site, but there is no point in pushing our luck with their helicopters flying about." He took the balaclava the medic handed to him and gently pulled it over Jack's head. "You've done enough. Just lay back, relax, and enjoy the ride."

With the help of the medic and the soldier who had been pulling the sled, Jack gratefully crawled into the sleeping bag, which Stoltenberg zipped up. After patting Jack on the shoulder, he quietly gave a command in Norwegian, and the team began the trek to safety.

Laying on his back, listening to the rhythmic swish of the team's skis through the snow, Jack imagined he could see menacing shapes in the dark clouds above him. He closed his eyes, shutting out the phantoms before falling into a deep, dreamless sleep.

DON'T MISS THE EXPLOSIVE CONCLUSION OF THE HARVEST TRILOGY: *REAPING THE HARVEST*

The final book of the Harvest trilogy, *Reaping The Harvest*, is slated for release in the Summer of 2013. For details, visit AuthorMichaelHicks.com!

DISCOVER OTHER BOOKS BY MICHAEL R. HICKS

In Her Name: The Last War Trilogy
First Contact
Legend Of The Sword
Dead Soul

In Her Name: Redemption Trilogy
Empire
Confederation
Final Battle

In Her Name: The First Empress Trilogy
From Chaos Born
Forged In Flame
Mistress Of The Ages

***In Her Name* Trilogy Collections**
In Her Name: Redemption
In Her Name: The Last War

Harvest Trilogy
Season Of The Harvest
Bitter Harvest
Reaping The Harvest

Visit AuthorMichaelHicks.com for the latest updates!

ABOUT THE AUTHOR

Born in 1963, Michael Hicks grew up in the age of the Apollo program and spent his youth glued to the television watching the original Star Trek series and other science fiction movies, which continues to be a source of entertainment and inspiration. Having spent the majority of his life as a voracious reader, he has been heavily influenced by writers ranging from Robert Heinlein to Jerry Pournelle and Larry Niven, and David Weber to S.M. Stirling. Living in Florida with his beautiful wife, two wonderful stepsons and two mischievous Siberian cats, he's now living his dream of writing novels full-time.